CRAIG HOLDEN

THE LAST SANCTUARY

MACMILLAN

First published 1996 by Delacorte Press,
Bantam Doubleday Dell Publishing Group, Inc.
1540 Broadway New York, New York 10036, USA

This edition published 1996 by Macmillan

an imprint of Macmillan Publishers Ltd
25 Eccleston Place, London SW1W 9NF
and Basingstoke

Associated companies throughout the world

ISBN 0 333 66937 1

1 3 5 7 9 8 6 4 2

A CIP catalogue record for this book is available from the British Library

Printed by Mackays of Chatham PLC, Chatham, Kent

For my parents,
Frederick and Carolyn Holden

Believe the couple who have finished their picnic
and make wet love in the grass, the wise tiny creatures
cheering them on. Believe in milestones, the day
you left home forever and the cold open way
a world wouldn't let you come in. Believe you
and I are that couple. Believe you and I sing tiny
and wise and could if we had to eat stone and go on.

Richard Hugo
from "Glen Uig"

It's the end of the world as we know it
And I feel fine.

R.E.M.

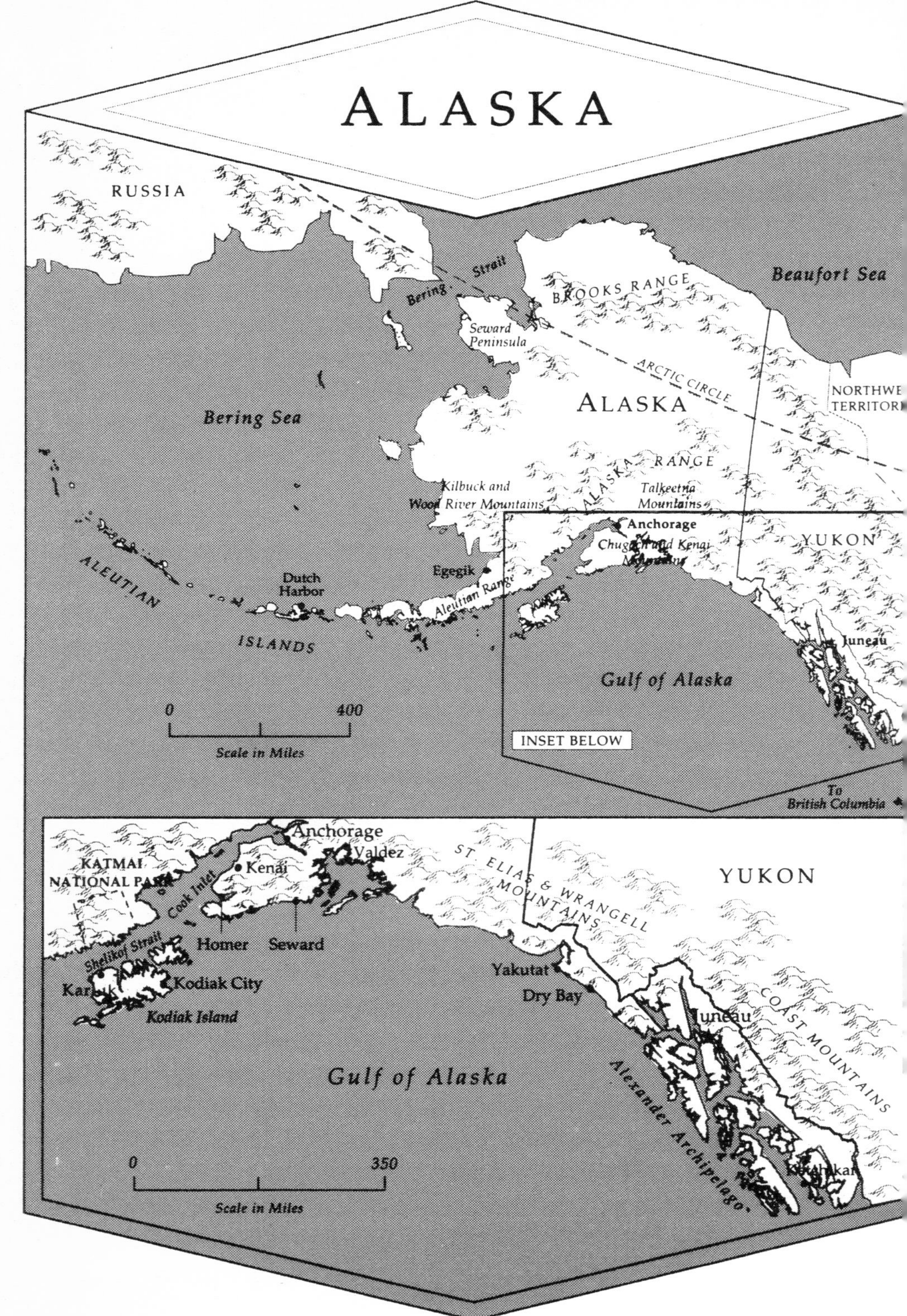
ALASKA
RUSSIA
Bering Strait
BROOKS RANGE
Beaufort Sea
Seward Peninsula
ARCTIC CIRCLE
ALASKA
Bering Sea
ALASKA RANGE
Kilbuck and Wood River Mountains
Talkeetna Mountains
Anchorage
YUKON
Egegik
Dutch Harbor
Aleutian Range
ALEUTIAN ISLANDS
Juneau
Gulf of Alaska
0
400
Scale in Miles
INSET BELOW
To British Columbia
Anchorage
Valdez
KATMAI NATIONAL PARK
Kenai
Cook Inlet
ST. ELIAS & WRANGELL MOUNTAINS
YUKON
Homer
Seward
Shelikof Strait
Kodiak City
Kodiak Island
Yakutat
Dry Bay
Juneau
COAST MOUNTAINS
Gulf of Alaska
Alexander Archipelago
0
350
Scale in Miles

THE
LAST SANCTUARY

North of West

1

In his gut Joe Curtis knew when he first heard the sound, a certain arrhythmic thrum deep in his Pontiac's engine, a nauseating whack of hot metal on metal, that he had a big problem. He knew cars well, and so he knew this. But for the same reason, and others (he was both optimistic and, in some measure, desperate), he let himself believe it was a thing he could fix if he needed, that in any case he could nurse the thirteen-year-old J2000—an '82 showing 125,000 miles—to the west coast, his destination, and deal with the problem there. And as if his faith were enough, the thrumming stopped then, after a minute or two.

He was on I-94 a hundred miles west of Fargo, North Dakota, halfway between there and Bismarck. He had three hundred dollars in his pocket, and was hoping the car, a beater he'd bought for four hundred and fifty dollars and refurbished economically but very nicely, including even new paint, could be sold on the coast for maybe fifteen hundred, at least a thousand—more than enough to fly himself and his brother, Terry, back home to Detroit. Even if he couldn't sell it, the two of them together could make the drive back in a few days.

This was the fourth time Terry Curtis had tried to leave home, and the fourth time his younger brother had come after him. But on this run, Terry had gone a long, long way, clear to Seattle, 2400 odd miles, in the belief, perhaps, that with that much distance he had to stay away, that whatever happened, he couldn't call for help, because even if he did, no one could come.

Near a town called New Salem, fifty miles past Bismarck, the thrumming came back, louder, angrier this time. *Whack, whack, whack,* so strong it vibrated the steering wheel. Joe pulled over and stopped to listen. He felt sick in his stomach at the thought of what this might be, here in the true middle of nowhere, as far from home as he was from Terry, over a thousand miles either way. He needed this car to get him there, and either the car or the money from it to get them both back. So he'd have to have someone take a look. He accelerated gingerly, not pushing it above forty, and rode on the berm with his hazard lights flashing.

The farthest Terry had gone before was Nashville, eighteen months ago, where, he'd said, he was going to break into the country music business. Then he just went broke, got evicted from his weekly-rate motel room, and lived on the street for two weeks with a scabby woman named Edie until he was arrested for vagrancy and held in jail while the cops rifled his wallet and called his family. Joe drove the nearly six hundred miles in one long shot, bailed his brother and signed an agreement to sacrifice that money as a fine, and made Terry drive all the way home the same night, straight through. In all, the trip hadn't taken much over twenty-four hours, and prodigal Terry was back in his rent-free room in the attic of their parents' home, where he'd lived, except for these failed trips, for most of the twenty-seven years of his life.

Joe had seen Terry tell people himself, with a kind of simpering smirk that was supposed to be cocky but came across more as pathetic, that he was a fuck-up of the highest order. No one had ever disagreed.

Just past the sign saying NEW SALEM, NEXT RIGHT, as Joe pulled onto the exit ramp and slowed to thirty miles an hour, he heard a gunshot crack, felt a shudder run through the car's frame and then the power beneath him just quit. In the rearview mirror, during the silent coast down the ramp, he watched a long slick of oil and grease and gas spreading out on the hot, white pavement behind him, as the car bled quickly to death.

He kicked at the Dakota dirt and watched the grease-bellied mechanic chew an unlit cigar. "I was going to sell the damn thing," Joe said. "Cleaned it all up, ran new wires, put in a stereo, rebuilt the carb, tuned it. Even replaced a body panel and a rocker arm. Shit, man, you know?" What killed him was that he had another car sitting at home in front of his apartment building, an '86 Ford Taurus.

The mechanic nodded. "Done a good job, looks like. You want it fixed?" Eight hundred the man had estimated.

"Can't afford it," Joe said. "Not worth it anyway. I'd've taken a grand for the car."

"Grand," the mechanic said, and smiled a little.

Joe took off his sunglasses now, looked around at the small, closed-up town and the open prairie beyond and shook his head. When he looked back at the mechanic he could see the reaction in the man's eyes to his own eyes, which were so pale as to surprise people. They were a shade of gray, but not slate or gray-blue. Their color approached silver, the color of polished metal, almost. And they had that kind of shine, of new steel, say.

"I'll tell you," the mechanic said. "You get west to Billings, 94 merges back into 90, lot of trucks run west there, coast-bound. I was you, a young guy out for a trip, know what I'd do?" He waited, then said, "I'd dump this puppy for what I could get and hitch it the rest of the way. Go out and get yourself a ride. Hell, you could luck into a rig that'd take you all the way in one shot. Single guy, strong built like you, you ain't in any danger. And that way you save your cash."

"And what could I sell this for?"

"Give you hundred and fifty for it right now, as is."

"One fifty?" Joe laughed again. He turned and looked up the access road he was on to the on-ramp a half mile away. He thought about thumbing. He'd thumbed before, short hops when he was in basic at Fort Benning, Georgia. In the South it wasn't an easy thing to do, either, but he'd done it. He'd liked the sensation, strange people, some weird, some interesting, some closed-mouthed, some generous with talk and, sometimes, even with their wallets, stopping to buy a soldier lunch or a beer. He wore no uniform now. And the road-side prairie in August would be scorched. But these weren't really considerations.

He thought of other options: spending his money to get back home, then starting the drive again with the Taurus or maybe scrounging around and borrowing enough cash somewhere to buy round-trip air tickets. Or he could call the old man from here and beg for some kind of help. But he hated the thought of going back, and worse would be asking the old man for anything. So he decided.

To the mechanic he said, "Make it two fifty." They agreed on two hundred.

When he finally came off the plains and rode into the foothills of the Rockies near Bozeman, Montana, Joe was hungry. It had turned out to be a bad series of rides across that endless, dusty expanse. Short hops, people with sour attitudes, no generosity other than a perfunctory "Get in," drive in silence fifty miles or so, then "This is it" or "Get out now." And always in the wrong place to grab a bite. It had taken thirty hours and a cold night spent shivering alongside the road just to cross the rest of North Dakota and half of Montana, with only a couple fast dinners and some stale rolls he carried for emergency in his bag. He'd have died of thirst, too, if he hadn't laid down by a run-off under an overpass near Billings and drank from that. He had no way of knowing what kind of poison was in that water, and had thought about it inside him, eating away, but he'd had no choice.

Outside Bozeman that night, he sprang for a thirty dollar room. The next morning, now two days since his car had died, he waited an hour on the berm of the northbound on-ramp, and when he looked out ahead at the rest of Montana, which he knew was still something like three hundred miles to the border, and the low mountain foothills rolling and fading into haze off in the far, far unimaginably distant west, a kind of panic found him: he had such a strong premonition of failure, of knowledge that he'd made a mistake, that he wouldn't be able to raise the cash to get Terry home, it was physical; his stomach turned and his knees went weak and he felt dizzy. The bright red sores which he'd carried on his ankles since he came back from the war burned, too. Sweat wetted his forehead and the air seemed to grow thicker. So he sat and picked at some stones in the dirt.

It turned out, though, to be only a few more minutes before an old Chevy Nova, jacked up with wide tires on the rear and badly painted with gray primer, slowed and stopped up the on-ramp. So maybe the mountains would be luckier. Joe slung his bag over his shoulder and ran.

"Hey, thanks—" he said into the passenger window. A woman looked out at him. She wore an over-sized white T-shirt with a pink bandanna around her throat. He thought at first she was young, until he looked in her eyes, which were heavy with mascara and bordered at the outside edges by the beginnings of age lines that grew more pronounced when she squinted. They were sharply pretty, green and slanted slightly upward. She smiled. She was about thirty, he guessed.

"You hitching? Didn't have your thumb out."

"Got tired," he said. "Yeah. West. Seattle."

She looked over at the driver, a skinny guy dressed only in cut-off shorts and sunglasses, who leaned across and looked up at Joe, too. "We're goin' there," he said in a throaty, Vaseline voice. "Eventually."

"I got to get there soon," Joe said. "But I'll ride as far as you'll take me."

The driver looked him over for a few more weird seconds, then said, "I'm Rick. Get on in."

Joe opened the back door and sat on the edge of the seat, his feet still on the ground. Rick adjusted the rearview mirror so he could watch Joe without turning around.

The woman said, "My name's Kari, so it rhymes with Atari."

"I'm Joe."

"Joe," she said. "A regular old Joe."

Joe nodded. He took off his dark sunglasses. He could see Rick watching him in the mirror. Kari turned sideways and leaned back against the door, so she could see him, too.

"Wild eyes," she said.

"You gonna close the door?" said Rick.

Joe hesitated another moment, deciding. They were off somehow, these two, the pale, edgy guy and a woman who acted tough but didn't look that way. Her teeth were flawless for one thing, Joe had noticed. He was conscious of teeth, having himself a slightly snaggled right front incisor that was twisted and jutted out a little, pressing on his lip. He'd learned a long time ago not to smile with his lips open. Most people never knew about the tooth. The folks hadn't ever been able to afford to get it fixed, and it had always bothered him.

Her skin was perfect, too, and her hair, wavy, hanging past her shoulders, was a most amazing color of dark red. It almost had a black cast to it, a color you could look into for days. He'd never seen hair quite like this.

He tossed his canvas shoulder bag onto the back seat and closed the door.

The two didn't talk much, which suited Joe. He preferred riding in silence, watching as the land outside the window grew from foothills to mountains, until before long they were crawling up the long steep grade toward the continental divide, on the other side of which all water flowed west, to the Pacific.

As they began the descent toward the valley floor that held Butte, there appeared out in the distance an anvil-headed thunder cloud that was probably still a hundred miles away but which they could see clearly in all its glory, rising up thousands of feet from the high plain. A part of Joe felt less angry at having to make this trip. He liked to travel. He had always loved cars, always worked on them, and it felt as if he'd always been riding somewhere, although that was not true. He was only twenty-five, two years younger than Terry, but had his own apartment and a job, and could even, if he chose, drink at the local VFW hall because he was one, a veteran of a foreign war. Sometimes, though, he wondered if he was missing life, if driving like this cross country was the kind of thing he should be doing instead of fighting every day just to pay the bills, which up to two months ago had meant punching in at the Monarch Cabinet Shop every morning at eight, until somebody waved the cutback wand and started laying guys off. They hadn't let Joe go completely, because they knew how good he was, but he was also low on the pole, so it had meant a slash to only twenty hours a week, loss of benefits, all that crap. That had wiped out most of whatever cash he'd been able to build up. Still, he made a little side money doing freelance car repairs, and buying beaters and fixing them up to sell for some profit, enough anyway to keep getting by.

So a part of him thrilled at this chance to be able to skip out for a week or two, begging some vacation time he hadn't quite earned yet, to pull his last cash out of the bank and to just tool. But the greater part of him sustained the anger, at losing the vacation time, maybe five, maybe ten days, depending, at losing what little extra money he had, at being forced—even though it was a thing he could enjoy doing—to make this trip because Terry, again, again, again, couldn't make it work, couldn't keep himself picked up off the ground.

The first time with Terry, almost seven years ago, Joe had only been eighteen, hadn't served in the army yet, hadn't seen anything of the world, or gotten in his own trouble, which he was destined to do later that year. One of Terry's roommates called from Indianapolis, where Terry had been for four months, and said someone better come down, Terry was going nuts, trashing the place, cutting himself up, just wacked out.

The old man, as the boys called their father, the man who had adopted them, swore in the gruff, muscle-headed way he always had and said he'd be goddamned if he was lifting a finger to help that drug-addict bastard. The old lady just shook her head and fretted. "He's got to grow up sometime," she said. "You can't run after 'em."

Joe talked the old man into letting him borrow his car, promising he'd cover the gas himself. The old man finally gave in. Terry was a mess when Joe got there, strung out on coke and hung over, chain smoking with hands that shook so badly he could barely light one butt from the other. Joe offered to send some money to the roommates for the damage but they shook their heads and said, "Man, just get him the fuck outta here." So they drove north, and along the way took a motel room where Joe stood Terry in the shower and held him there for an hour, until the water had gone cold and Terry was shivering and blue-lipped. Joe lay with him in the bed then, Terry under the blankets, Joe on top with his clothes still on, and wrapped an arm and a leg over Terry and held him like that until the shivering stopped, until Terry fell asleep. He slept for twelve straight hours.

Well before nightfall the old Nova got the three of them through Missoula, the high pass in western Montana leading toward Wallace in its narrow Idaho valley, and through that to where it opened out a little in the western panhandle alongside Coeur d'Alene Lake, just short of the Washington border. A good day's run.

That evening, in the motel room, Joe sat on the floor next to the bed looking at the TV. Rick had hesitated at first when Kari suggested Joe could sleep on the floor, but then she whispered something to him and he mumbled back and said all right. Now, Rick was out, Kari was taking a shower, and Joe was wondering what he was going to do when he finally got to Seattle. Even with a seven day advance, he knew, two plane tickets would cost five hundred bucks, just about what he had on him right now. But by the time he got there, there was no telling what he'd have left, and they'd still have to survive for those seven days, or come up with even more cash for the tickets. He couldn't count on Terry to contribute anything, cash, a car, even a good idea. It would be up to Joe to figure how, in some strange city, to get what they'd need.

He'd never applied for a credit card because he didn't want the debt, although guys at work told him anyone could qualify, and realized now he'd been stupid. He was going to have that ad slogan tattooed on his chest when he got back— "Don't leave home without it." Again, he thought, he could try getting the old man to cut loose some cash, wire it out, swear to God he'd pay it back quick. But he knew he couldn't do it.

In the air-conditioned coolness he'd begun to feel bursts of pain in his head that grew rapidly in intensity until now they were so sharp and powerful, in his forehead and along a line above his right ear, that he could only close his eyes and grip the edge of the table and wait, trying to remain conscious. Sweat poured from his face and his jaws ached from clenching. It lasted only five minutes, though, then began to fade, and before long was low-level enough that aspirin would take care of it. Next, his vision began to blur so that he could not make out details on the TV in front of him, but this too passed in a matter of minutes.

The episode did not surprise him. Roughly twice a week for four years he'd had similar ones, since the war in the middle eastern desert. The bright sores that formed a neat ring around his ankles, which sometimes opened and bled, were another souvenir of that campaign, all symptoms of the vague malady people were calling the Desert Storm Syndrome. But Joe had vet buddies back in Mo-town and other places who had it a lot worse than headaches and blurred vision and a few sores on the ankles. A whole lot worse. Some of those boys were dead, and others crippled for life, or getting there—malignancies, immune-system crashes, huge never-healing sores, spontaneous bleeds from various openings—all manner of bizarre symptoms cropped up.

The shower stopped. Then the bathroom door opened six inches or so but only steam came out, not Kari. Joe heard squeaking as she wiped the mirror. He realized that from where he was sitting he could see into the bathroom on an angle, could see the sink and the mirror. And as the mirror cleared a little he could see a slightly blurred image of her, but only from the shoulders up. Quietly he raised himself from the floor to the bed so he could see all of her reflection, fuzzy but he could tell what was what. He got dizzy with the sight of her body. She was not tall, maybe five four, and had seemed shapeless and flaccid under her baggy clothing—the T-shirt and old khakis—but now he could see she had real hips and breasts, full and rounded, and some tone as well. Jesus. He had such a hard-on he thought it would break off.

She opened the door a little wider. He watched as she towelled, scrubbing her head, running the towel down over her tight belly, then twisting to get the back of each leg. The mirror cleared more. Her pubic hair looked lighter than the hair on her head. She ran her fingers through it a couple of times, fluffing it, and Joe felt himself go lightheaded.

Then he heard the door open. He flicked his eyes to the TV screen and acted as if he were engrossed in this fascinating dog food commercial he'd seen several hundred times.

"Joe, Joe, bo bo, banana banna fo fo," Rick said. He sat down on the bed, not even glancing at Kari in the bathroom, slapped Joe's foot and said, "We gotta talk."

Joe nodded.

"You know how to talk, right?"

"What do you mean?" Joe said.

"You don't do it much," Rick said. "Since this morning, I bet you haven't said twenty words."

Joe shrugged.

"You upset about something?"

Joe nodded.

"Having some problems?"

"Yes," said Joe.

"All right," said Rick. "Don't worry, my man. You're with the Rick and Kari show, now. We're groovin' and movin' and always improvin'. We'll be in rain town by tomorrow night. And you need some money." Just like that, he laid it right out there.

"What?" Joe said. He sat up a little straighter on the bed.

"Cash. Green, my friend. You use some?"

"Shit, yeah. I mean, you don't know."

"Oh, I know, Joe. I fucking know what it feels like, buddy."

"Why? I mean, why ask me?"

"Got a way for you make a little."

"How much?"

"How much you need?"

Without any hesitation, Joe said it: "Five hundred bucks."

And without any hesitation, Rick answered, "No problem. We make this thing work, you'll get it."

Now his antennae went up: "What thing, Rick? What are we talking about here."

Rick smiled. He knew antennae. He had a whole high tech radar system built into his head. "You been busted."

Joe looked at him, at the narrow, dark-lashed eyes, almost pretty eyes for a man, the hard, thin mouth, the skinny, veiny neck. He nodded.

"I knew," Rick said. "I could tell. Do any time?"

"Not really. Probation and a fine. It was a long time ago."

Rick smiled and shook his head. Joe saw no need to elaborate. If this guy was thinking of pulling some crazy—

Rick said, "What I'm talking about, there's no danger. Nothing to get busted for. I'm not a stupid man. It's a simple thing—I'm over here doing business, in Montana, in Idaho. You know. And there's this guy here I know, see. I need to have a talk with him. He owes me some money. And when I talk to him, I'd really like to have someone standing behind me. Someone that looks like you. Kind of built, you know. Someone who someone would have to think twice about before fucking with."

"I can't be getting in any fights."

"My whole point," said Rick. "This thing either sets up to happen without a scene, or I walk away. I mean I already lost the shit. It's gone, you know. Not worth going down for now. And I'll make you this deal—even if it doesn't work and I don't get back what he owes me, I'll still slide you a hundred, for your time."

"No crimes."

"Well," Rick said. "It's like this. The guy ain't gonna give me what he owes me. I know that. So I'm gonna take it. The thing is, what this guy owes me for, see, even if I rip him off cold, he can't do nothing. No cops. You know the kind of deal."

"What is it?" Joe said. Drugs, he thought. Hot property, maybe. Could be anything.

Kari stepped out of the bathroom with a towel wrapped around her. She smiled at Joe, that nice, flawless orthodontic smile. As Joe looked from her to Rick then back to her again, something occurred to him he hadn't noticed before—she was scared. He saw a desperation in the way she looked at him, a request, even. She wanted him around. He had no rational way of knowing this, but he knew. He knew from her eyes. She needed something.

"The question," said Rick. "Is do you really want to know?"

And the answer, they both knew, was no.

Later, after he'd eaten and walked for a while, thinking through this opportunity, this risk, Joe slid around to the back of the motel and counted off the number of windows to the room, then snuck up and stood on his tiptoes and peeked in to see if he could learn something. But instead of catching Kari and Rick talking, sharing secrets, they were on the bed, naked, Kari on her stomach with her face turned away from the window, Rick on top of her. He had the fingers of one hand curled into her hair, and held himself up with the other. He moved his hips against her, thrusting in and pulling out, and he was saying something in a low voice Joe could not hear over the air-conditioning. When Kari turned toward the window, Joe was struck by the passivity of her face. She looked as if she were dreaming, as if she were someplace else, but not at all excited or aroused; she made no noise. There was something sad about her that made Joe sad to watch.

Rick pulled harder on her hair, and she grimaced. He yelled something, and then Kari moved, lifting herself on hands and knees from the mattress and thrusting back against him, her generous breasts shaking and bouncing, harder and faster until Rick let go of her hair, gripped her hips with both hands, pulled her tight against him, closed his eyes and came with a yell Joe could hear over the AC and through the closed window.

Joe sat down beneath the window and listened as someone in the next room applauded. After a few minutes in the darkness, he stood and looked in again. Now they were both kneeling, still undressed, beside the bed, their hands folded together, heads bowed in what looked like mutual prayer. Maybe they were Jesus freaks, but these were like no religious folks he'd ever known.

It didn't matter right now. Joe was hooked and he knew it. He wanted that five hundred bucks. He wanted to pull what was turning into a disaster out of the fire, to deliver it whole and perfect, to get Terry on a plane and back home, and to do it himself, to make it work.

He made things work. That's what he did in life. The army had known that. The plants where he'd worked, and the wood shop owners now, they all knew. He could make anything work, given the right tools and some time. It was his gig. And he was going to make this trip work, one way or the other.

The lights were out when they let him in. Later he could hear them whispering in the dark.

2

AGENT LEANNE RED FEATHER LAY ON HER BELLY ON A FLAT SUN-warmed outcropping of striated limestone on the south slope of Evans Peak, outside Coeur d'Alene, Idaho, peering through a government issue Unitron 20 × 60 spotting scope. She was looking for guns, big illegal ones in particular, the kind that laid down seven or eight hundred rounds a minute. And explosives. She'd take those, too.

She was watching the ranch of a disgusting man named Big Bill Cooper who went five ten and three hundred pounds and ought, Leanne thought, for that reason alone, to be dragged out somewhere and shot. She didn't say anything though because the man lying next to her, Ed Simmons, newly assigned and transferred RAC—Resident

Agent-in-Charge—of the Boise resident agency of the Federal Bureau of Alcohol, Tobacco and Firearms, now her immediate supervisor, probably went two sixty, anyway.

Big Bill's ranch and house lay a thousand yards in front of and below them. Bill himself was just prying his bulk from the passenger seat of a white pickup truck in the driveway behind the house. Leanne's Unitron picked up every disgusting fold and crevice.

"How long you been here?" Simmons said. He was peering through a pair of binoculars.

"On and off for two weeks."

"And nothing?"

"Not so much as a twenty-two."

"Well, shit, then. What're you thinking about?"

"I think he's not running anything through here." Duh. She pulled away from the scope and glanced at Simmons, who was sweating so much it worried her. "But that doesn't mean he's not running anything," she said.

The information Leanne had received was skimpy, but good enough to lead her to believe Big Bill had got back into the arms business, and had built up a stockpile of weapons to move. Temporarily without a supervisor, she'd assigned herself the task of sniffing around up here, Coeur d'Alene way. And in sniffing, she'd caught a certain scent. She knew the smell. That was how she worked—she picked up trails with her nose and followed. She'd always done it; she was almost always right in the end. Besides, she loved this best of all, hounding some renegade free-market asshole with obscene amounts of blood and money on his hands.

"Wasting your time," Simmons said. His first order of business, he'd declared, was to determine which of various investigations underway were worth continuing and to focus the Boise agents on some central tasks. "He starts to move, we'll hear about it." Simmons sat up and wiped sweat from the lenses of the binocs. "And we'll hear where. That's what matters. I don't give a shit what he does from day to day."

"I still think—"

"I'll give you another day," said Simmons. "Then you'll get your ass back down to Boise."

She knew nothing would happen in the next day, but all she said was, "Yessir."

"Something'll break. We'll nail him," Simmons said, by way of offering encouragement, and squinted, which was, apparently, meant to be a smile. " 'Til then, you might as well be on something else."

When Leanne thought of the people who'd died at the hands of the weapons Big Bill sold, of her own fellow agents who'd gone down under a .50 caliber machine gun a couple years ago at the Koresh compound in Waco, a gun which was supposedly handled at one time, a few owners before the Davidians, by none other than Bill Cooper, she could taste her hatred, which was not unlike the sensation of chewing aluminum foil.

But at the same time, whether she agreed with Simmons or not, she knew he was a good agent. He'd been transferred up here and given charge of his first resident agency from the district office in Kansas City, after having helped supervise the ATF's share of the investigation of the bombing of the federal building in Oklahoma City in April, four and a half months ago. As everyone knew, the feds, FBI, ATF and Customs, had all shined in that one.

From the boardinghouse room she'd rented for the week, she called her number in Boise. It was busy, so she waited fifteen minutes and tried again, but still didn't get through. Twenty minutes after that, it rang. And rang eight more times before a man answered.

"Yeah."

"Calvin," she said. "It's me."

"Hey," Calvin said. "What's up?"

"That's my question."

"Nothing. Nothing. Just watching the tube."

"For nine rings?"

"I was in the can."

"Watching the tube in the can?"

"Hey—"

"All right," she said. Calvin was her brother, four years her junior. "Just wanted to hear you were OK."

"I'm OK," Calvin said. "When you coming home?"

"Soon, it looks like. Day or two. Nothing doing here."

"See you then," Calvin said, and hung up before she could say anything else. But Leanne did not like how he sounded and she did not trust him. Since he was eleven little Calvin had been in and out of treatment for alcoholism and other substance abuse problems, and in and out of jail since he was sixteen. Now, just six weeks ago, Cal had finished his first big time stint, six months at the state prison in Deer Lodge, north of Butte, Montana, for aggravated assault. In a bar fight in Havre, he'd clocked a man so hard with a beer bottle the man had been in a coma for two days. Even now, almost a year after the event, Leanne was told the man was not right, and would never be. His left eye and ear did not function quite properly.

So when Cal walked, she brought him over to live with her in Boise, to help him get started again, give him a roof while he looked for work. Actually, it was only because, when the parole board learned that she, a federal agent, had offered to take Cal in, they'd consented to release him at all. She knew he resented having to live with her. She also knew that he knew that if she hadn't offered, he'd have been kept down for another year.

And she liked having him around. He was a nice kid most of the time. He'd been nice when he was a little boy, sweet. And he still had it in him. But he had a bad time with anything that altered his brain chemistry, booze or grass or sniffed paint thinner, for which he was treated when he was eleven. When Cal got a little something in him, he turned into one mean asshole Indian. She knew. She'd been on the receiving end a few times.

Their father, Jimmy Red Feather, had been a full-blooded Native American, half Gros Ventre, half Flathead; their mother, whose maiden name was Anna Willingham, was an Anglo from Billings, the daughter of a cattle broker named Les Willingham. This white woman named Anna met Jimmy Red Feather one fall day at a Billings livestock auction and a month later had followed him west, across Montana, to the Flathead reservation.

The irony was that in later years, long after Jimmy and Anna had split up, it was Anna the Light, as she was called, who stayed on the rez, in an ugly little piss-yellow tract house, and Jimmy who'd moved away, first down into Butte, when you could still work for Ananconda Copper there, then into Missoula, and later up near the tourist town of Whitefish. Leanne and Cal had bounced back and forth some between Jimmy and Anna, but the times Leanne remembered best were from the reservation, where she had lived the most, with her mother, in a patch of cheap houses stapled down in some dirt outside the town of Arlee. There had been uncles and aunts, of course, but mostly aunts, relatives of Jimmy who helped raise the children, who taught them some of the Salish words they weren't allowed to use anywhere else but around the old people.

But mostly Leanne remembered the man people called Guts. Wolf Guts was his full name, he told her the first time they met, when she was eight. He was not a Flathead, she knew. Someone told her once he was an Apache from South Dakota, though she had never known if that were true, or even if there were any Apaches in the Dakotas. But Guts had been a friend of Jimmy Red Feather's, and had supposedly had his life saved by Jimmy once, when he went through some bad ice on the Blackfoot River. In any case, Guts had kind of adopted Leanne and Calvin, although Calvin wanted nothing to do with him. Leanne, though, spent as much time with Guts as she was allowed, sitting quietly and watching him carve or tie fishing lures, or listening to his stories. His great-grandfather whom he had known, he claimed, had been a boy in the times before the reservations, and had told the stories. Guts remembered those stories. In the summers and falls she followed him on treks up into the white-capped Mission Mountains, which bordered the rez to the east, and it was there, when she was eight or nine, that Guts began to teach her how to track.

He taught her to read the prints of deer and elk and coyote and bear, how to gauge the age and condition of a print, and the speed at which an animal was moving. They spent much of the time just sitting and waiting, watching whatever appeared. And to her amazement animals did appear.

"Being quiet is always the best way," Guts would tell her. "You'll never be as smart or as fast as your prey. Your only hope is if he don't know you're there. Then it will be him instead of you who will make the mistake."

Although she had never learned his patience, could never sit as still or as long as him, finally having to crawl off through the brush to search, to follow some fresh sign, tracking was still one of the things she'd learned best.

But Calvin had a different name for it. He broadened the category and called it "getting after people." Just before she'd left for Coeur d'Alene last week, she and Cal had another big fight in her living room. She'd been after him to clean up the place a little, to not live like such a slob. It pissed her off when people degraded themselves like that. It was part of his whole problem, she felt, which had to do with self esteem.

"There you go!" he yelled. "After me again. Nag and bitch. Bitch and nag. Fuck you."

"What's wrong with cleaning up?" she said.

"Nothing, Leanne. Nothing's wrong with cleaning up. Something's wrong with being told to clean up when you're thirty-one years old."

"So just do it and I won't say anything."

He shook his head. Angry out of all proportion to things.

"You don't understand shit," he said. "My whole life you don't understand. And now here you are, an anal-retentive, ladder-climbing, ass-kisser of the federal Indian-fucking government, you married a white man, and you want to teach me how to be a better person."

She was stunned for a moment. All this from a discussion of cleaning the apartment? Besides, she'd been divorced for a year and a half.

"Cal," she said. "Our mother was white."

"She turned Indian," he said. "And Dad was Indian. That makes me a hundred percent as far as I'm concerned. What about you, huh? What do you consider yourself?"

"Human," she said.

"Barely," he spit back at her, and slammed the door to his room. She'd had to leave then. She was going to miss her flight.

Now, after he'd hung up on her, she remembered that she hadn't told Calvin she loved him. That bothered her. It was something she thought he needed to hear these days.

3

TERRY CAME IN A PRE-DAWN DREAM VISION, HIS CUT AND BLEEDING HANDS open and reaching out to Joe, the look on his face saying, I need you, brother. In the dream, Joe had a fever, felt himself sweating and red-faced. They were working on a car together, Joe leaning in under the hood, Terry handing in tools. But he was getting blood all over them, from his cuts, and Joe couldn't hold on. Each tool slipped away and clattered down into the black, empty hole where the engine should have been.

The phone call had come a week ago, now, some girl who didn't even give her name, just started in about how Terry was so sick he was at this free clinic they had there, on some kind of IV or something, he was all dehydrated and couldn't breathe.

"Where are you?" Joe asked her.

"In our place. We got a room together."

"Is he working at all?"

"He done some work. Ain't working now. He's sick."

"Does he have any money?"

"Not much," the girl said.

"Look, I need to talk to him," Joe had said. And a day later Terry called, and he sounded like hell, and when he started to cry, Joe knew what was coming.

"What if I buy a ticket in your name, you fly yourself back here," Joe had said.

"I can't," said Terry. "I can't even walk, Joe. I got this lung abscess, and my leg's all fucked up."

"How'd that happen?"

"Got mugged."

"Mugged for what? What could they steal?"

"Look, I don't know. Some guy jumped me and beat my ass. He broke my leg, and a rib."

"You have a broken leg?"

"Kind of. I got a walking cast now. But it was three days before I got any help, before Lori found a place we could go."

"Why didn't you go to an ER, for Christ's sake?"

"I don't like those places."

"So you fucking lay around for three days with broken bones." And so it went on, the various versions not quite meshing. For one thing, the girl who called hadn't mentioned Terry's beating and the broken bones. Wouldn't that have come out first? Why just mention the dehydration? And why wait days for treatment? Anyway, Joe knew for fact that if he booked a ticket Terry would cash it in for whatever money he could get. And he knew the only thing to do was to get Terry back here. People died from lung abscesses, and who knew what had really happened, why the two guys had beat him, or what other things he had wrong, what diseases he'd picked up. With Terry it was always a lot of reading between the lines, and whenever Joe had thought he was reading in too much, that things couldn't really be that bad, he'd been wrong. It always turned out, in one way or another, to be worse.

Joe woke from the dream and saw the dim red Idaho light rising through the window.

An hour later, after they were dressed and packed, Joe and Rick both wearing jeans, boots and T-shirts, Rick said, "Well?"

"You said something about a hundred no matter what happens," Joe said.

Rick was quiet for a moment, then said, "You want it now? Like a down payment. All right." From his pocket he took a roll of cash, peeled off a hundred dollar bill and handed it to Joe.

"So, let's do it."

"Good man," Rick said.

While Joe and Kari loaded the car, Rick crossed the street to a pay phone and made a call, then hurried back and got them going. West of Coeur d'Alene, instead of heading for Washington, Rick turned off the interstate and drove north then east, around the outskirts of the city. Shortly he turned due north again, onto a wide blacktop road that led away from the city, into open country. They drove for fifteen minutes before turning onto a smaller road, then stopped at a café.

"Coffee," Rick said. "My treat."

Rick made another call from a phone outside the diner before going in. As Joe watched him from the car, he realized that there must be somebody else in on this, that Rick had other people working with him as well. Rick was calling in for some kind of information having to do with the man he was going to talk to. But if someone else was involved, what kind of a deal was this? Still, it might be nothing significant—a friend of Rick's who also knew the man Rick wanted to talk to, who knew where this man was and reported to Rick. Joe thought about it. There was still time to walk away. But he sat. As he did, he looked at the back of Kari's head, at her black-red curls.

After Rick came out and handed out the coffee, they continued to sit. Then a white pickup passed by in the road. Rick watched it, then put the car in gear and pulled out after it. Joe caught glimpses of it up ahead of them, coming into sight and then disappearing again around a curve. The word Ford was written in red letters across the tailgate. It looked like there were two men sitting in the cab.

Just when Joe's coffee had cooled enough to sip, Rick slowed, then turned sharply into the gravel parking lot of an isolated general store, with signs advertising everything from groceries to livestock supplies to hardware.

"Perfecto," Rick said to Kari.

Now Joe saw that the white Ford pickup was there as well, parked by the front door of the store. In fact it was the only other vehicle in the lot. As Rick pulled past, Joe watched a huge blubbery fat man in a white Stetson, tight jeans and a pair of black and white cowboy boots ease himself out through the passenger door of the pickup. The man glanced up at them as he headed for the store. Then he passed out of sight because Rick had driven around to the side of the building and stopped there, near a wooden loading ramp that rose up to a chained double door.

"You take the wheel," he said to Kari.

A breeze had kicked up, not hard but enough to stir the heavy air. From the trunk Rick removed a red-nylon windbreaker and put it on over his yellow T-shirt, in spite of the fact that the temperature had already topped eighty-five degrees.

"Come on," said Rick. "Don't say nothing. Stand with me."

"It's the guy from the truck we're seeing?"

"I'm seeing. You're standing and keeping your mouth shut."

"You're going to talk to him in the store, though?"

Rick stopped and looked at Joe. "Will you fucking let me worry about it?" he said.

Joe didn't like it now. The five hundred dollar gig had started to feel bad. He didn't like Rick's new attitude. He didn't like the fact that Rick had been calling someone else, that there was more to this than Rick let on. Still, Joe thought, they were here, now. What could he do? Run? He imagined that, himself bolting away from this place, out across the open gravel lot to the blacktopped road and back toward town. It was several miles before he'd reach anyplace. And then what? He'd just be in the same hole. Plus, he had Rick's hundred dollar bill in his pocket. He looked back at Kari sitting in the car. She was watching him, too.

On the way in, Joe got a look at the man in the driver's seat of the pickup, who had been staring forward but looked over at them now. Maybe Rick wanted this man out of the picture, so he planned on cornering the fat man somewhere back in the store for the talk. That made sense.

It was an old store, with a wooden floor and counter, a huge rack of cigarettes and only five aisles of food. Two packs of Merits sat on the counter; an old woman sat behind, reading a paper. "Morning, fellas," she said.

The fat man who'd come in was back in the store somewhere, out of sight. Joe started to walk back through an aisle, when Rick grabbed his sleeve and said, "Stay here."

"But the guy—"

"Help you gentlemen?" the woman said.

Rick took a pair of white cotton gloves from the jacket, and pulled them on, tucking them up under the elastic wristbands of the nylon jacket. Joe knew, then, that he'd been lied to, suckered, that this was going to be bad. He saw what was going to happen, but these insights seemed to come almost simultaneous with the events themselves. It was as if the images in his mind were being played out in the world, as if he were a projector that could only spit out the image but could do nothing to alter it.

"Take a bag and fill it from the cash register," Rick said.

"What?" said the woman.

"Take a paper bag—" He picked one up from the counter and shoved it at her. "—and fill it with cash. Everything in the register."

"I can't . . . Virgil!" the woman screamed. "Virgil!"

Joe felt his face go numb. His fingertips and the tip of his tongue tingled, as they did sometimes when he ran too hard and went into deep oxygen debt. His mouth filled with a faint metallic taste, of blood iron, maybe. "Rick," he said. "Jesus Christ."

Rick lifted a can from the counter and swung it overhand down onto the old woman's head, knocking her to the floor. He looked at Joe and said, "Don't you fucking think about moving." Then he leaned over the counter and started punching with his left hand at the buttons on the old, antique register, trying to get it open, but he wasn't looking at it; he was watching the store around him. Then the bell rang and the drawer slid open. As he shoveled bills into a bag, a man appeared with a rifle in his hands.

"Hold on there, son," the man said. He was older, too, Virgil this must be, the woman's husband. He held the rifle at his side, tucked up beneath his arm as if it were too heavy for him to shoulder and aim. His shoulders were stooped; he wore glasses. He had a gray mustache.

Without hesitation, without even looking at the man first, Rick swung a handgun up. It was a semiautomatic of some kind, stainless steel, expensive looking. Where Rick had been hiding it Joe did not know. Rick fired, hitting the man in the gut and knocking him backward. The old man's rifle clattered on the floorboards when it fell.

At the report Joe thought he had yelled. His ears rang so loudly he couldn't hear anything else. He noticed that Rick held the gun and fired with it turned parallel to the ground, rather than perpendicular in the normal manner.

Joe took a step toward the door. Rick pointed the gun at him and said, "I mean it."

As he said it a man ran in the front door. It was the driver of the white pickup. He held a gun of his own, a large squared-off semiauto, which he held as if he knew what he were doing, one hand wrapped around the butt, the other bracing it from the bottom. But the man had no chance even to orient himself to the scene, because Rick, who had surely been expecting him all along, had dropped into a crouch, pointed his own gun at the bright, open doorway which framed the man, and fired three shots.

The man dropped hard to the floor and did not move. He gripped his gun still in one hand. A moment of silence passed.

Joe was on his knees at the end of the counter, the air hazy with burned gunpowder and smells of sulphur and cordite. He opened his mouth and sucked air like a netted fish, because the air felt too heavy to breathe. But he forced himself back up to his feet. He must have dropped reflexively when the driver ran in and Rick fired. His head felt light, but clear, as if it were a glass bubble filled with helium. The store was brighter than it had been. Light poured in from the front door which now flapped open in the mild wind.

He could tackle Rick, Joe thought, and end what he feared was not over yet. But Rick held the gun, aimed out in front of him still, in case any other men decided to run in the door. Joe knew that he wouldn't get three steps before Rick shot him, too.

Then Rick left the money bag on the counter and, holding his gun up now, by the side of his face, shuffle-walked back into the store. Joe looked at the open door, and as he thought about running again, he was startled by another shot, then another, much louder and different sounding. Then one more, like the first, like Rick's gun. He found he had knelt down beside the counter again.

Rick came back, laid the gun on the counter and continued unloading the register. When he finished he cocked the gun and aimed it down at the woman on the floor.

This amazed and horrified Joe, somehow, more than the shooting of the men. To fire into an unconscious old woman was sick in some deep way Joe could not comprehend.

"Don't," Joe said. He stood up.

"She saw us."

"Just don't."

"She *saw* us."

"She won't know anything. Don't do it." He carried a good knife. He thought of threatening Rick, but again knew it would be futile against a gun.

Then the man in the doorway, whom Rick had shot three times already, cried out and kicked again against the floor. He'd lain as still as death after the initial shots, but was either regaining consciousness or entering the final throes of his dying. In any case, it ended the discussion of the old woman. Without another glance at her or at Joe, Rick stepped over to this man and fired a bullet into his forehead.

Joe felt himself yell again.

The man went into spasm then, his legs and arms bouncing, his cowboy boots clattering against the wooden boards. Blood poured out from his head.

Rick looked around at Joe, then put the piece into the side pocket of his jacket, folded over the top of the bag and said, "Watch out the front door. Yell if anyone pulls in." Rick disappeared once more back into the store.

Joe looked outside, at the brightly lighted air and the road and the blue-green Idaho hills. Run, he thought. If he took off now, going hard, he'd be out of sight and Rick wouldn't have time to look around for him.

But all these shot people. Christ, he thought. Jesus. He looked at the dead man inside the front door, his blood seeping into the old wood. Behind the counter the old woman lay curled into a ball. Joe shoved the drawer of the register closed, then bent over her. She was breathing, but weakly. Next Joe looked at the old man, who was much worse off. He bled heavily from his belly, and a line of blood ran from the corner of his mouth. He'd started to shiver, and he stared up at nothing. He would die, Joe was sure. By the time help got there, he would be dead. Unless they came right away—

Joe spotted a pay phone mounted on the wall by the door. He looked into the back of the store, but could not see Rick. Then he noticed something else: a pair of what looked like snakeskin cowboy boots sticking out from one of the aisles. He walked back toward them. The pattern was a swirl of black-and-white scales. The boots were connected to the huge man, who lay on his back. He'd been shot twice, once in the fat middle and once in the eye. Joe could only glance at the bloody face and the pool of blood gathering around the head, and then had to look away. Next to one of the man's hands rested a large silver pearl-handled revolver.

Joe walked back up front to the pay phone and lifted it.

He dialed 911 and was waiting for an answer when he heard Rick's boots whumping on the wooden floor, so he hung up.

"You won't believe this," Rick said. "Chicken feed in the register, but the old man must've been just ready to make his weekly deposit. Check it out." He held open a small strongbox stuffed with wrapped stacks of twenties and tens and loose piles of fifties and even some hundreds.

"Must be a couple grand." Rick shoved the strongbox into Joe's hands and said, "Come on." They left the store, having to step over the body of the driver of the pickup, and walked around to the side where Kari and the car waited.

"Hustle butt, honey," Rick said. "We scored good. Follow me around front." Rick dumped everything, the strongbox, the bag of cash and the jacket and gloves, in the trunk. He motioned Joe into the passenger seat, then slammed the door and ran back around to the front of the store.

Kari started the car and backed up and by the time she had pulled around, Rick stood holding a double-wide briefcase. The driver's side door of the white pickup was open. Rick threw this case into the trunk as well. "You drive," he told Joe. Kari jumped over into the back seat. As they were pulling out, another car turned in with a woman driving and two kids next to her in the front seat.

"Get down!" Rick said. "Shit." He and Kari ducked.

When they'd found their way back to 90, Rick had Joe stop the car. He got out and worked in the trunk for a few minutes. Joe could hear things clunking around and watched Rick throw a duffle bag into a shallow pond near the road.

Then Rick set the strongbox and brown paper bag of money on the front seat. He said to Joe, "You keep driving. I've got stuff to do. Keep your eye out for a car we can lift. We gotta dump this one ASAP."

So Joe drove them west at sixty miles per. He looked from time to time at the strongbox and bag next to him and thought about what they held. He did not want any of it. He had to get away from these two and was afraid now they would not let him. They were crazy.

"You had this all planned," Joe said at one point. "You should have just told me."

"It was fate," said Kari. She leaned up over the back seat. "Rick knew when we saw you you'd do great. Do you understand how much Rick can see, what visions? That he knew you'd be there, and needed help? Rick is blessed, Joe."

They rode quietly after that, as Rick counted out the money.

Joe had talent in his hands. Wood, metal, engines, electrical wires, it seemed he could work anything he touched. He felt the breath in inanimate material, sensed its life force. Things spoke to him through his hands. At only eighteen, right out of school, he'd gotten in, at $9.50 an hour, to the machine shop where the old man had been working for twenty-five years. He learned metal machining there, lathing and pressing, tool and die making, but after only six months saw there wasn't any real skill in the work.

He taught himself how to drop a transmission right in the street. Pull two wheels up on the curb, then lie down and slide under. The old man and his buddies sat on the porch and watched, admiring him he knew as much as they could admire anything. "Right on his goddamn belly," he heard them say. "Drops that tranny right down then slides out with it laying there." Then he'd put the replacement on and slide back under; he'd use two-by-fours and cinder blocks jammed under to hoist it up into place while he bolted it in. He must've changed a dozen transmissions that way. He'd had a pretty good side business going there for a while, at a couple hundred bucks a crack plus parts.

The folks had taken them in when Joe was two and a half years old, Terry nearly five, their blood father disappeared, their mother, from what they were told, a hopeless drunk and whore. Child welfare had had them in and out of foster homes for a year, and the old man and lady had been looking. They'd wanted a new baby boy, but when they saw the two brothers, the old lady started in to cry, Terry told Joe years later, and the old man couldn't say no, although Terry knew, he said, even at that age, that the old man hadn't wanted two kids, and hadn't wanted anything older than six months. "So he could mold it," Terry said. "But I was already hard-formed by that time."

Still, he and Terry owed them, Joe thought. The old lady had loved them as well as she could. The old man had never been able to show much of it, but there'd always been a roof and food and clothes, which was a kind of love. Joe had known that he was the favorite son, had been when he was little, and had stayed that way into adulthood. It was not a thing he and Terry had ever discussed, but it was always there, hanging, and with it a kind of gnawing guilt.

When he was eight Joe became an altar boy at St. Michael's. He liked helping the old priests, holding the sacraments or carrying the candles but never having to talk and feel embarrassed. The folks had been proud of him then. They were good Catholics.

He was an athlete in high school, still at St. Michael's, a fullback on the football team and a good one; he'd always been strong in the arms and shoulders and neck and that's what counted when you were running up the middle, having the strength to hit someone your own size or bigger and keep moving, keep driving until your helmet met the ground. He'd played baseball, too, short and third, and he could hit the ball a mile. He liked standing up tight against the plate and watching the pitcher, never breaking eye contact as the ball screamed past. He liked listening that first time even if it meant taking a strike, liked the sound of the leather whistling. Then he'd wait for his pitch and nail it. He was good. He could have been scholarship, his coach said, or gone to a good farm team, but he had a job waiting.

Some time later, Rick said, "We can get some chow, now."

"You're gonna sit around and eat?" Joe said.

"Hey, you join us. Splurge," said Rick. Because by now he'd finished counting; they'd scored $2,200, which came out to just over $700 apiece.

"I don't want it," Joe said.

"The money?" Rick laughed.

"No, thanks," Joe said.

"What, you think that lets you off? You think you can just walk away like you weren't there? You and me had a plan, bud. You were in on it. So it went a little different than you thought, it was still *our* plan. Kari heard us talking, right?" He looked back at her. In the mirror, Joe saw her nod. She glanced at him, then quickly away.

"So no bullshit about you didn't know nothing. It's two against one, if it comes to that. And you know the Man. You know what that means. It means your only choice is to not get caught in the first place, get your ass out of sight. And you need cash to do that. So take the fucking money and shut up."

A few minutes later, just at the outskirts of Spokane, they approached a roadside restaurant with a lot full of cars.

"Steak breakfasts," Rick said. "Stop here."

Joe did what Rick told him, slowed and pulled off on to the exit ramp. But he knew he had to do something soon to get himself away.

He just needed for them to leave him alone for a few minutes, and he'd be gone.

It struck him, then, that he had only the plain of central Washington to cross, and then the Cascades. By day's end he could be in Seattle, and with all the money he needed. The irony now was that he wasn't sure it mattered anymore.

4

LEANNE WAS UP ON THE MOUNTAIN JUST BEFORE DAWN, SETTLED DOWN IN the middle of a patch of boulders at the edge of a treeline from which she had a clear view of Bill's ranch. Her thinking had been that maybe Bill would move early, before anyone should have been watching, but as the sky grew lighter and nothing moved down at the ranch, she knew she'd been wrong.

Still, after the faint glow in the sky passed to near-daylight and the morning broke fully, with sudden spikes of sunlight shooting out over an eastern ridge and down onto the valley floor, she felt happy for having witnessed it and was glad she'd made the trip up. This was her place, in the mountains, out, away from cities and people, most of whom she had never been able to bring herself to care much for.

Trips like this invariably led to ruminations on her life—the common one of a divorced woman living in a smallish city apartment, working out of a generic office cubicle. It had been nearly ten years since she'd gone to work for the fed and, from day to day, it wasn't a thing she thought about much anymore. But, when she made it back into the mountains, where she had grown up, and could look down upon herself, as it were, when she could place it all in a broader perspective, could see what she had given up in her journey away from the poverty of the reservation and what little she'd actually gotten in return, she found the vision irritating, and also found then that she could not push it away. It sat inside her and pulsed, like a sore tooth, begging to be poked at over and over until she went home and fell back into the routine and the thoughts quieted again.

At eight she headed back down into town to grab some breakfast. Afterward, from her room, she dialed her apartment. And again, as when she'd called yesterday, she kept getting busy signals for twenty minutes or so. Again it bothered her. If she hit twenty-minute conversations just calling once a day at random, how many hours had Cal been on the phone? He didn't know anyone in Boise. He had no reason to be calling anyone in Montana.

She was getting angry when she heard the line finally ring.

"What now!" Calvin said.

She waited.

"What do you want?" he said. His voice shook.

"Cal," she said. "It's me. Leanne."

"Oh, shit," he said. "Leanne. I—"

She waited.

"Cal?"

"Yeah."

"You want to tell—"

"Nothing. Nothing's going on, Leanne."

"Something's going on, Cal. At least don't bullshit me." She could hear him breathing, calming down a little. "You're very upset," she said.

" 'You're very upset,' " he mimicked.

"I'm not the enemy, Cal. Don't get mad at me."

"Sorry."

"Will you tell me?"

"No. Listen, what happens in my parole if I take off?"

"Where?"

"Anywhere. What does it matter? What happens?"

"You're in violation. They catch you, you go back down."

"That's all? No extra sentence?"

"Maybe," Leanne said. "Depends. I bet you'd at least finish out the old one. Another year."

"If they catch me."

"They'll catch you."

"You'd say that."

"They will. I see it all the time. You think you're smarter than the system? You think you're faster than electronic signals over telephone lines? You're not, Cal. No one is. Why do you want to take off? You just settled in. Living with me can't be as bad as jail. Don't tell me that."

"No. Nothing. Just—nothing. When you coming back?"

"Probably today. It's dead here."

"OK."

"You won't do anything until I get back? Promise?"

"Yeah."

"I mean it. A blood promise?" Even Cal could not break a blood promise. They had agreed on that before either of them was twelve years old.

But a "Maybe," was all she could get out of him. "I'll see you. I love you." Silence. She placed the phone back.

Almost as she hung it up, though, it rang again and she grabbed it, thinking Cal wanted to talk after all. She'd given him the number. But it was a Coeur d'Alene detective who knew she was in town and why.

"Leanne," the man said. "You're not gonna believe this." And he proceeded to tell her of the incident in a general store fifteen miles north of town, a horrible thing, really, but common except for the fact that a man named Big Bill Cooper was involved, caught in some bad crossfire it appears, and killed along with his driver.

Leanne leaned back against the plaster wall and slid down until she was sitting on the floor. She felt her face flush and her stomach tighten to the point she thought she might be sick. This was bad. Not the worst kind of fuck up, not the kind that would ruin her, but bad enough, losing her man so he could go off and get killed while she stuffed her face. In the on-going war to prove who she was and what she could do, this was a major blow.

She'd worked for the tribal police force during the summers while she was in college, initially doing clerical work and then dispatching, but eventually, after making good progress on a dual degree in criminology and biology at the University of Montana, impressing a few people enough to be allowed to go out in the field and gain some practical knowledge of police procedures. So when, after she'd graduated and spent another two years working full-time as an investigator and forensics technician for the tribal force, she applied through the Boise ATF resident agency for Treasury service, she'd been considered because she had this experience on top of her degree. Yet, while her interview with the RAC at that time had gone well enough, she sensed an undercurrent of animosity from him, and asked finally what the matter was. "Nothing," he'd said, but she found out when she asked about taking the Treasury Entrance Exam. The RAC shook his head.

"What?" she said.

"You don't have to take it," he said. "You're a minority, and a woman to boot."

"So?"

"So, that's D of T policy for Customs and ATF. Unlike your fellow white, male recruits, who have to score in the top third to be considered, you have three years to pass the exam. It's called a Schedule A appointment. Congratulations."

"I don't want three years," she said. "I'll take it now."

"Can't," he said. "Policy. You want to work for the government, get used to it."

In New Agent Training School at Glynco, the Treasury Department's facility at the old Glynn County Airport outside Brunswick, Georgia, she ran into the same attitude from most of the men, who knew she was there on a Schedule A. She didn't really even blame them. Still, she performed as she needed to perform and won a little breathing room. After NAT and eight more weeks of Special Agent Basics, she was shipped back to Boise for a couple months of on-the-job training, before returning to Glynco for more specialized courses in such topics as automatic weapons, explosives and basic arson. In Boise, before she really knew much of anything, she realized the agents there were looking for an excuse to drum her out, that she wasn't and never would be protected by old-boy camaraderie, and that any serious mistake she made would be her last.

She knew this then, ten years ago, and even after she'd proved herself, after the RAC in Boise who'd first reluctantly hired her had promoted her and told her she'd turned out to be the kind of agent he'd never expected her to be, she knew it was still true. The ATF was an organization, by and large and for better or worse, of redneck white men. There were no people she'd rather have behind her in a firefight, no investigators whose judgment she'd trust more. But always, she knew, they'd gut her and hang her out to cure if they got the chance.

Idaho state police investigator Ry Hickey hated these calls, goddamned pointless deaths because some low-life greaser couldn't pull his own weight. But it was better than some in that there was a witness, at least of the car. A woman, Sue Green, had pulled in with her two kids just as the perp was pulling out. Her oldest, a boy named Pete, age ten and a half, knew it all: "A gray Chevy Nova, officer, 1971 or '72."

"How would you know that, son?"

"He's in that phase," Sue said. "You know how kids get into certain things, they learn everything about it. Right now with Pete it's hot rods."

"American muscle cars," Pete said.

"And the Nova was one of those?"

"Yessir. One of the last ones. After that they started making all that small stuff to save gasoline. But the '71 Nova SS was still a barn burner, standard with a .350 small block and—"

"That right? You say it was gray?"

"Yucky gray. It wasn't regular paint. Ugly, like—" The boy paused here and looked around. "—that," he said, pointing at a wooden ramp that came down from a side door of the store. The wood was painted with gray deck paint. "Only lighter, and not shiny," said the boy.

"Primer," someone said, and Hickey turned to see Leanne Red Feather, a BATF field agent out of Boise who'd been up here working on some unshared mystery for days now. It pissed him off when the feds didn't cut him in on a case in his territory. And now here they were at the scene of a brand-new crime, and no one to his knowledge had called them in. But the girl was originally from a rez over by Missoula, Montana, and so, even though he wasn't a big fan of Indians and plain didn't trust them, Hickey gave her some benefit of the doubt since she was a regional native. At least she wasn't like some of the asshole feds out of California or Salt Lake City or Denver he'd met.

Besides, she was better looking, too, with her dark eyes, her full mouth and long earth-brown hair. Her face was broad, as was her nose, which added strength to the look but without taking anything away. On top of that, Hickey noted, she fit a pair of Levi's just right.

"What's that?"

"He's talking about primer," said Leanne. "You know how people put it on, then get lazy and don't finish the job right away."

"Yes, I do," Hickey said, brightening. "Yes ma'am, I do. Bobby?" A deputy from the Kootenai County sheriff's department stepped over but kept his eyes on the sheet-covered body of Virgil Hyatt as it was wheeled from the store to the county coroner's van. The woman had been taken already in an ambulance. She had a broken zygomatic bone in her face and a minor concussion but she'd be all right. As all right as she could be considering her husband and business partner of forty-three years was now dead. The second and third bodies, one William Harwood Cooper, known to his friends and family as Big Bill, known to the community as one of the richest and most generous men for many miles around, and Kyle Greene, one of his employees, were still lying inside.

"What you got, Ry?" the deputy said.

"I think we might have the God blessed getaway car," Hickey said. He recounted the boy's story.

"Now if we knew the plate and the direction," said the deputy, "we'd just go pick it up."

"West," the boy said.

"What?"

"That's west, right?" He pointed up the road.

"Yes."

"And it was Washington plates. Blue and white."

"By Christ, son," said Hickey. "I think you might've just earned yourself a medal."

Hickey was already moving. "Put out a description locally pronto. And get me the Washington State Highway boys," he called out. "They could'a been headed toward 90, and they don't have much of a jump on us. I don't want this shitbag slipping away."

Within moments an officer handed Hickey a car phone and said, "Washington HP, sir. An officer Melrose out of Spokane."

Hickey took the phone. "This Dick Melrose?"

"Who's this?"

"Ry Hickey, over here outside Coeur d'Alene."

"Hey there, Ry. What's shakin'?"

"God blessed triple homicide. Looks like some of your scum offed a long-time local businessman and one of our VIPs and his driver about an hour ago, Dick. Armed robbery. I'll tell you what we got."

Dick Melrose listened, then hung up and got right on the horn to his boys out on the highway.

Leanne Red Feather found a phone, too, and dialed a number in Boise. People there, particularly her boss, Ed Simmons, were waiting to hear from her how she'd lost the trail of Bill Cooper for just one morning, and how that one morning was the morning Cooper had gone and got himself blown away. Then, when she'd brought them up to speed, she was going back in to look over the body of Big Bill some more. He'd snuck away from his ranch in the dark, early, apparently before she'd even gotten up there. He'd been gone the whole time she was watching, and then while she ate, he was out here buying it. That bothered her so much—not his dying, but that she'd missed it—she about couldn't stand it.

5

RICK AGULLANA AND KARI DOWNS HAD FOUND GOD. THE PROBLEM, THEY knew, was that anyone could find Him. It took a little travel, because He'd moved up north, to Alaska, but the directions weren't hard to follow: from Anchorage, you took State Highway 1 east along the Turnagain Arm, that great fifty-mile mud flat reaching in from the sea, and followed the road around south at the Arm's end. After making the turnoff before Seward onto the Sterling Highway, which ran back west to Soldotna, you headed south again through the brushy wetlands of the Kenai National Moose Range along the western edge of the Kenai Peninsula, on toward Homer, but not that far. Shortly after the little fishing village of Kasilof, on an unnotable gravel road heading east, toward the center of the peninsula, toward the Kenai Mountains and the Harding Glacier, you drove for fifteen or so miles, catching other dirt roads, passing badly painted one-story clapboard houses, or smaller plywood shacks, or even an occasional hand-hewn log home, past kennels of baying Malamutes or Huskies, past sleeping meadows where moose grazed amidst the collapsing hulks of old rust-red trucks and snowmobiles.

To the final turn-off, a dirt spur marked by a red-on-white DO NOT ENTER! sign that led a half mile back in to the compound known as Sanctuary.

It wasn't much to look at: three long plywood dorms, each of which housed thirty comfortably, forty-five when needed; a group of smaller, nicer cabins; some shacks along the river; and a central meeting hall made of corrugated tin nailed to logs of native timber. This was the temple. The grounds were all dirt and gravel. Dogs ran with the little children from spring into the late fall, when the snows came hard.

God was here.

Or a man-god anyway, but as close to God as the Family members believed you could get. He was called Father, actually, by most of the members, and he could be found more and more often in one of the three dormitories, sitting in the dingy, utilitarian group dining room with its pale green walls and dirty carpeted floor, incongruous, at the long linoleum table that came originally from some school cafeteria clear down in Idaho. Him, a holy man, sitting like that, a little stooped, his forehead and nose dotted with sweat, his belly sticking out. Of course, he would be waited upon. Girls would come and go, whispering questions to which he nodded or shook his head. He rarely spoke when he didn't need to, and until recently he'd rarely made appearances in the dorms anymore. Usually his people went to him, in the church or in his cabin, in groups or one at a time, as he desired.

He had at one time mingled with the Family daily, lived with them even, reveled in being surrounded by all of his women and children, rolling and playing with them on the wooden floors, laughing like any father. But lately, the worries had grown more enormous than usual, the good words harder to find. The happiness they came here for had abandoned them yet again. He needed time and solitude to think, to plan, to organize their third move in less than five years, what would surely be the final exodus.

Soon, Father and his Family would travel once more, to the ultimate Sanctuary. Then God would no longer be easy to find. No roads led to this new Sanctuary, nor anywhere near it, not within five hundred miles. It was accessible only by air or water, far away as it was out along the ocean edge of the Alaska Peninsula, west of the Katmai National Park, on toward the Aleutian Islands. It had mountains, and oceanfront where the Family's fishing boats could come and go. Those Family members who worked the canneries in the summer to raise money for them all would still be able to work. The boats would take them over to the plants on Kodiak or maybe clear out to Chignik or Dutch Harbor. Or, who knew? Perhaps the family would prosper so much there that it could buy its own cannery, run by, worked in by, owned by God and his Family.

He had always dreamt the apocalypse, Father told his women. When he was a boy he would wake up in the night, screaming at the horrors he had witnessed, reaching across the bed he shared with his mother until he found her warmth and curled into it, not caring that even his scream had failed to wake her. In the beginning, it was she who gave him courage to beat back the demons, to forestall the final death. Later it would be other women, by the dozens. Always, he won those battles, for Good, for his people. But in the end, he knew, the apocalypse would come.

"I need you. All of you," he would say, stretching out his pale, delicate arms. "You are all that makes me happy." He came to the dorms for this reason, to see them, to fill himself with his purpose, to gather the strength he needed to continue the series of maneuvers that would protect and arm them, bankroll them, and move them to their promised land.

Rick, already at twenty-seven on the outer fringes of the Inner Council —the small group of men who ran the Family and were the only members besides Father allowed to prosper financially—had always thought Father looked like a putz with his dark frizzy hair that bushed out over his ears and around the back. Father wore aviator-style glasses, tinted yellow, a short-sleeved flowered cotton shirt, blue jeans and sandals, and he needed a shave. How a putz would dress, a weakling, the sort of man you'd walk over in the street, the sort you wouldn't hesitate to take advantage of, threaten a little and easily get what you wanted.

He looked like that, but Rick had seen him when he was full of the fire, preaching or singing or counseling, or better when he was angry and plotting revenge or an attack. Then he was vital, more full of life and power than any man had probably ever been. Then he looked like how you'd expect a god to look. God, Father, was also known as Amon Ka'atchii, a name that came from the Earth, he said, as did their very faith, the faith that linked them together into a whole, a unit. A Family. They were the Amonites.

Rick had done some clandestine research once. Father Amon had started life as Fred Haines, born in Tucson, Arizona, in August, 1944, to a hairdresser and an auto mechanic who went off and got killed in the World War a year later, thereby gaining the distinction of becoming one of the last hundred Americans to do so. But Father had ceased to be Fred Haines when he became God, Amon, Father, a decade ago.

It had been two years since Rick Agullana had been recruited into the Family. In the beginning, he knew, it had started as a humble group of fewer than twenty believers scrounging out a life in a beaten-down church and house in a poor dirt neighborhood in Bellevue, Washington, had grown to a hundred and fifty during the four-year sojourn in the mountains of northern Idaho, to the present—Amon had churches in three states now and maybe four hundred followers, with the church in Bellevue, still, one in Berkeley, and a core group approaching two hundred when everyone was in, here at Sanctuary, in the isolation and beauty of Alaska. There was barely room for them all here anymore, in these buildings, when the fishing ended and the canneries closed and everyone came in for the winter.

But this place, to which they had come to escape the intruders, the law enforcers, the federal agents, the revenuers, which had seemed so perfect three dozen months ago, was no longer protection. Roads led here, and where roads led, so came enemies.

Amon Ka'atchii was a wanted man. But then, Rick figured, they were all wanted for one thing or another.

Almost a month earlier, in the beginning of August, some of the Council had gathered, and Rick this time had been invited. There was a problem, he'd been told. And an opportunity. One that called for a specialist. Rick was a specialist, they knew. And now they needed him again.

In the nice cabin Amon Ka'atchii had said, "My son," and lay his hand on Rick's head. There were four of them in the room: Father and Rick; the man they called Deacon, Amon's attorney, six three, lean, not old but with pure white hair, who was often away conducting business, second only to Amon himself in the hierarchy of the organization and the strategist who had overseen Father's ascendancy; and, Brother Omaha. Omaha was forty, a stocky, light-skinned black man from L.A. originally, where Rick was from, too, and where Omaha found him one fateful summer's day when Rick was fleecing tourists to buy the rocks of crack he needed to breathe.

Omaha said he'd known right off Rick was something special, someone with talents the organization didn't necessarily like to recognize but could use, needed to use. The Family was growing quickly, and with growth and power came opposition. With opposition came the need for many different types of strength. One of these necessary strengths was Rick's, the strength of the street, the strength of the cold, cunning mind, of the animal that reacts without empathy and smells danger before it arrives. Omaha saw that after a brief training period in the Berkeley church, Rick was moved straight to the still-new Alaska Sanctuary, where he fell under the direct tutelage of Father himself.

Brother Omaha and the Family were good for Rick, good to him, had, through their love, turned him from a dope-smoking petty con and hold-up crook into a man of respect, of spirit. And of power.

"You do understand what this is about," Deacon said. Rick nodded but Deacon went on anyway. "We have an opportunity, of which Father Amon wishes to take advantage."

"Opportunity," Father says. "You were with us in Idaho, boy, weren't you?" Rick feels his face flush at this ignorance, but says nothing, only shakes his head.

"Well, there's a man there, William Cooper. He sells guns."

But Omaha had already filled Rick in on the scoop that morning. The man was known as Big Bill. "Sloppy fat white man," Omaha said. "Fucked us once on a land deal, Brother Rick."

Big Bill Cooper was a former Marine supply sergeant, a rancher, a failed land broker, a sometime marijuana wholesaler, and a wholesale-level underground arms dealer, which is where he made all his money. The Family had bought weapons from him before, back when Sanctuary had been outside Moscow, Idaho, mostly rifles and handguns in bulk, but some special pieces, too. And then nearly everything had to be abandoned when they moved north.

"Seems Father or Deacon heard about some hot stuff Big Bill's just got hold of, GI Joe shit, kind of toys Father wants bad before the move. Big goods."

"How big?"

"Bunch of M-16s, military issue. Couple M-60 machine guns, bipod mounted, 7.65 mm. Ass-whippers. And then, get this, some kinda motherfuckin' rockets or something. You dig that?"

Rick whistled.

"Big Bill's a Golden Meaner," Omaha said then.

Rick understood. The Golden Mean Society was spread throughout western Montana, Idaho, and parts of Washington and Oregon. He knew of a strong branch up here, too. Where money was concerned, they believed only in the gold standard, that paper currency was worthless. They wouldn't spend it, wouldn't accept it. The view usually accompanied a parallel view that guns of any kind were the full right of the people, no exceptions. And that taxes, especially property taxes and any income tax over a few percent, were heinous crimes perpetrated by the government. So the Golden Meaners were often targets of agencies of the Department of Treasury: the IRS, Customs, the Secret Service, and the Bureau of Alcohol, Tobacco and Firearms. This, along with the fact that they shared most of Amon Ka'atchii's political (if not religious) beliefs, gave them a lot in common with the Family.

"But it means we got to haul gold clear down to the forty-eight, pass it over, and get the shit back up here." Then Omaha shrugged to say he had no idea how they were going to pull it off.

"How much gold?"

"Buck and a half."

"Which is?"

"Three ninety, four hundred an ounce right now. 'Bout twenty-five pounds."

"That's not bad."

" 'Cept we got to cross two borders with it."

But now in the meeting, listening to Deacon lay it out, it made sense to Rick. They'd fly Deacon and some others down, and send Omaha and another man with the gold, by car. The border crossing into Canada wouldn't be a problem, and when it was time to cross into the continental U.S., they'd figure a way to mule the gold across separately, on foot maybe, over the mountains. Or they'd pay a trucker to smuggle it.

After delivering it to Big Bill, they'd take immediate delivery of the arms, which would already be packed up in crates somewhere, rent a truck, and haul the pieces north to the top of the Idaho panhandle, where, on certain roads on certain private border-spanning properties they could, for a fee, cross into Canada without passing through customs. Then they'd head up to the Trans-Canada, over to the Yellowhead Highway and on to the coastal town of Prince Rupert, which was just across a small strait from the American soil of the southeastern Alaska panhandle and the string of islands called the Alexander Archipelago.

There, near Prince Rupert, was a small private fishing dock with moderate loading facilities they could rent, no questions asked, and use discreetly at night. Meanwhile, they'd pull the larger of the family's two fishing boats, which were both now working down off Homer, and head it south along the coast to Ketchikan, an eight hundred mile trip one-way.

When everything was ready, the boat would find its way across the international border, load the guns, and slip back over. This was the riskiest part of the operation, but hundreds of tiny islands peppered the coast on both sides of the border, and the boat had a captain who could run them at night with no lights.

"What about up here?" Rick said. "How'll you get them here?"

"We won't," said Deacon.

Father smiled. "They're going straight to the new Sanctuary. No one will even see the boat." They were often under one type of surveillance or another.

"But we have another problem," Father went on, and looked directly into Rick's eyes with the gaze that did not break, the look that paralyzed. Father did not blink. Rick once counted forty-five seconds between Father's blinks. He didn't understand how anyone could do that.

"The weapons will cost a hundred and fifty thousand dollars, in bullion and Maple Leafs. Add another fifteen or twenty for the transport operation. We move to new Sanctuary this spring, as soon after the thaw as we can. The land has been secured with partial payments but we still owe a lot. The cost of the move will be huge, since all the Family has to be transported, and we'll need caches of supplies and equipment."

Until now Rick assumed he'd be part of the party which transported the gold down and the guns back. But in a flash of intuition he knew that wasn't so, knew exactly where this was going. Revenues were down. Alaska was a hard place to make a living, at least the kind of living Rick was used to making. Fishing and cannery work was just that: work. There was no percentage in it. In Seattle, even in Idaho, he knew, the Family had been able to pull the bucks, sending the women out collecting, running whatever games they had to. But here, it was tough. And a hundred and fifty grand paid to a man who'd screwed them once before, that would be hard to take.

"I understand, Father," he said. "It's not a problem."

"Do you understand everything?"

"How does he handle the gold?" Rick said.

Father smiled, because that was the right question. He looked at Deacon.

Deacon said, "He rents space in the vault of a private bank in Coeur d'Alene. He moves it himself, with some protection, an armed man or two. There's not much for him to worry about."

"Until now," Rick said. "No one will ever know."

"That's the absolute key," Deacon said, his voice hissy and mean. "The exchange will be well north of the city, at a barn he owns. Afterward, one of us will shadow him; we'll have a cell phone so you can keep checking in. You'll know exactly where he is, then, until you pick him up yourself. Once you're on him, whoever we've had following will disappear. You'll be on your own. It needs to be this way. It's safest."

Rick nodded.

Deacon said, "You need to do it before he gets to the city. You'll need to seize whatever opportunity presents itself, or manufacture one. That's up to you."

Rick's scalp tingled. He could barely wait. Two years here in the bush with only a quarterly week or two in Anchorage to hit some pavement, the occasional small job down in Seattle. Now, shit, this was golden, this was heaven, this was a major piece of performance art. God, he thought, he was going to love it.

That evening, after dinner and a prayer session in the church, Father and Deacon walked in the growing darkness up the dirt road toward the entrance to the compound. It was a nice August dusk with warm air full of the good scents of the earth.

Father said, "I know there's talk that I'm foolish to risk so much for guns."

"That's not for you to worry about."

"We can't doubt that people will still come after us there. And not just the government. You know what can happen in the bush. Entire villages wiped out by marauders. Paramilitary madmen. We must be unassailable."

Deacon didn't respond. They'd had this conversation many times and there was really nothing left to say. It had been decided. Amon wanted big guns; he'd get big guns. He just had to work through his little moments of self-doubt.

"It'll work, don't you think?"

"You know what I think," Deacon said. "You've staked an awful lot on him." Rick, he meant.

"I'm talking to him again later," Father said. "I'll tell him about the girl then. His first reaction will be to insist on working alone. Then he'll think better of it. For cover, a woman is invaluable. Couples can cross easily. And I'll make it clear that he has carte blanche with her, that she's his during the job. He won't be able to resist that."

"Someone very reliable," Deacon said. "Rick will do the job, but afterward, it's a long way back here. Anything could happen with him. So it has to be someone strong, physically as well as spiritually. She may have to pick up that heavy load and bring it home herself."

"I know who it will be," Father said.

"You do?" Deacon was surprised at this unilateral decision.

"Kari Downs," Father said, and Deacon was surprised again. She was not only one of Father's current wives, but one of his favorites.

"You do sacrifice," Deacon said. "You are a holy man."

"It's too important not to," said Father. "For one thing, she'll be desperate to get back here, and she'll know she can't come back unsuccessful. When I told her about it, today, she wept for an hour, begging me not to send her." Father nodded. "She'll kill to get back here. But there's something else, which is what I wanted to talk to you about. I heard from Berkeley."

"Yes?"

"Men showed up there, probing. They had money to spend. They're trained, it seems." By which, Father meant, they were professional deprogrammers, anticultists who kidnapped church members and locked them in rooms and berated them for as long as it took to crush their spirit.

"They're after her?"

"Yes. And some idiot's headed up here."

Deacon nodded.

"So I just don't want her around. This will be a way of hiding her, and I trust her."

Deacon nodded again and said, "If you're sure."

"I'm telling Rick that if he succeeds, and if he likes her, I'll give her to him. She can be his first wife."

Deacon stopped. "Are you serious?"

Father shrugged. "I don't know. She's been with me for four years, now. Maybe it's time for a change."

So Deacon was surprised yet again. They walked on together, and when they were out of sight of the church Deacon lit a thin spliff of marijuana and sucked on it and passed it over to Father, who seemed to need it badly.

6

It wasn't exactly a truck stop, just a restaurant by the highway, but half the clientele were truckers. The food looked to be a little better than average road grease. Joe and Kari went in first, while Rick worked in the car. She ordered two beers, on Rick's instructions. Joe, who had brought his shoulder bag in with him because he wanted his belongings close at hand, ordered only coffee. Rick came in then, carrying his own bag, a black duffle, and without even glancing at them, headed straight into the men's room. Before he came out, Joe excused himself, picked up his bag, and went out a back screen door into a dirt yard which looked out over a wide golden field of wheat. Here the land had some roll to it but was just grain fields again, open and vast like the prairies of Dakota. Joe did not like the exposure, the sensation of being unbounded. He liked having something around him, a city or mountains; it didn't matter which.

He sat at one of the picnic tables out back and felt a nice breeze but could not enjoy it. He did not think he would be enjoying very much for a long time. His hands trembled slightly. His ankles burned; he felt the red sores swelling. He noticed some semis in the parking lot. A couple of drivers stood talking and spitting in the dirt.

"Hey, there." Kari stepped out the back door and smiled at him. "How you holding up?"

Joe shrugged.

"We needed the money, too," she said. "Our task has to go on. God always provides, even in mysterious ways."

"God," Joe said. He looked out at the ocean of wheat. "How long have you known him? Rick, I mean."

"Couple years."

"Has he done this before?"

"I don't know what he's done. I suppose what he had to do. He's a very spiritual person."

"Spiritual."

"Yes."

"I don't get you." Joe looked at her long enough that she couldn't hold his gaze and flushed and glanced away. He said, "What are you doing with him? You're not scum."

"He's not scum either."

"He's scum."

"He's one of God's children. And you don't know what I am."

"I do." He was angry, but he did not raise his voice. He felt the emotion down inside, but sealed off by some membrane that would not let it rise up and bubble on his surface. He spoke levelly as he always did. "Your teeth are too good, how you talk. Got that nice hair. What's your old man, a doctor or something?"

She looked startled for a moment, her jaw going slack and her eyes a little wider. Then she closed her eyes and smiled and shook her head. "My *father*," she said, speaking with her eyes still closed, "is my savior. My *dad*, you mean? No, he's not a doctor, but you're right; he makes money. I haven't seen him in years. He hasn't been my father for a long time." She opened her eyes now and looked at him. "You knew because of my teeth?"

He glanced again at the semi drivers talking and spitting, then back at her face. As he had in the motel room the night before, he saw the unspoken request in her eyes, a plea for something. He was trying to think of a way to ask her what it was without coming right out and saying it, a way to broach the subject from the side, when she said, "How is it you're so calm?"

"What?" he said reflexively, although he knew what she meant and that it was true. His coaches used to say he had no blood pressure. He'd taught himself a long time ago to appear calm, to hold his fear and nerves inside, to present no ripples. To just listen. The old man was a hothead. From way back Joe remembered him swearing and throwing things in the house, slamming doors or driving his fist into a wall. They'd had to take him to the ER once, when Joe was seven, with three broken bones in his hand. Once he'd shattered a mirror and took seventeen stitches in his head. Joe had sworn from the time he could remember, especially when he saw Terry starting to take on the habit of blowing up when something went wrong, that he would not be that way, so he went to the other extreme, forcing himself to maintain control. Eventually, he didn't have to try. The control was just always there.

"And you know a lot about stuff," Kari said. "You're kind of strange. I mean, in a good way, sort of. And you have weirdly cool eyes and strong hands." She picked up his hand from the table and squeezed it. "Rough, too. Those are all good signs."

He could only shrug, then said, "What are we going to do?"

She said, "Listen, Joe. What if I said you were right about Rick, that I wanted away from him? Whatever we had to do together is finished now, and he scares me. I want to get out of here."

"Now?" he said, a little suspicious of the sudden change.

"Isn't that what you're planning on doing?"

"Maybe," he said. "Alone."

"Couldn't I go, too? Couldn't you rustle us both up a ride?"

Although this talk of changing ships, as it were, the shifting of her complicity from Rick to himself, sounded contrived, it lifted Joe's mood, too, by giving him the first glimpse of how he might begin to mitigate the terrible trouble he found himself in. If it were true that she was throwing in with him, it meant there was a chance she'd support him instead of Rick if they got caught and had to give statements. Maybe, even, he thought, after the two of them talked it through, they could turn themselves in together, confess to what really happened, and fix the blame on Rick, where it belonged. If, on the other hand, she was just using him to get away herself, so she could disappear, well, that was all right, too. Because she was right—the important thing now was to just get out of here, to get away from Rick without his knowing.

"We just leave, like that?"

"I have to at least go back in, see what he's doing," she said. "Give me a minute. I'll buy another round of beers. Then I'll make up an excuse, and come back out here. You be looking for me. And be ready. Do you have your share on you?"

"Yes." He'd stuffed the money down in his bag, although he had not wanted it. He'd planned on slipping it back into the car somehow, when Rick wasn't around.

"I have mine, too. That'll get us a ways." She stood up.

"We shouldn't have it," Joe said. "We should just leave it here. Give it back to him."

"Joe, listen." She sat back down. "We have to get out of here fast if we're going at all. With no money, we're screwed. I don't have any other cash. And I know you don't have much. So let's just do it, OK? We'll discuss the money later." She got up again and went inside.

Joe wandered over toward the drivers and their rigs. He stood a respectful distance away, far enough that he couldn't quite make out what they were saying. When one of them noticed him and looked over, he said, "I'm headed west—"

"Company policy," one man said. "Sorry. Can't give no one a lift. They catch me I'm out."

But then the other driver winked, and lifted his chin. Joe understood. He looked toward the picnic table in back of the restaurant but saw no sign of Kari yet, so he walked around the rig and sat on the passenger side running board and dropped his head down between his knees. He felt half sick. He sucked in lungfuls of the dry, western summer air and tried to think again about what had happened, to understand how he'd gotten so involved, how it could be possible he might be considered an accomplice. Yet it was so. He saw the old man going down and lying bleeding on the floor. He saw the dead man inside the door. He saw the boots of the fat man, the bloody face, more blood pooled thick and dark around his head on the wooden floor. He saw Rick smashing the old woman, maybe killing her, too.

Five years earlier, at twenty, his probation satisfied, Joe felt something missing or maybe that he was missing something, so he joined the army. Terry had laughed and called him nuts. The old man wouldn't talk to him, acted like he'd betrayed something fundamental. The deal was that they'd train him and then after a few years, when he was out, pay for him to go to a voc school if he wanted for more training. And he couldn't imagine any possibility of his seeing action.

The army recognized the skill in his hands. After boot camp at Fort Benning, and advanced infantry training, in which he stood out, he reported directly to Army mechanic school.

Some months after that, George Bush's war in the Middle East began. Although Joe, twenty-one now, was not yet fully certified, because of his skill and his scores in AIT, he was assigned to a small company of ace mechanics which was to accompany Fort Benning's 197th Mechanized Infantry Brigade, which was in turn temporarily assigned to the 24th Mechanized Division.

Joe was chosen to be one of the special troops, although not a front-line soldier, who swept into southern Iraq, where sand was the worst enemy. It clogged filters and shields and batteries and carburetors and got into the fuel supplies. Joe and the other mechanics tore down machines and cleaned and reassembled as fast as they could. That's all it was supposed to be: maintenance.

But there in that oven desert, Joe was to see things few men outside of modern war have ever seen. Desert Storm had nothing to get in its way—no buildings, no civilian population, nothing but burnt sand around them. The easiest way was to just send down cluster bombs that exploded and scattered hot debris over a wide radius, cutting, maiming whatever it encountered. Sometimes a war chopper would fly low over Hussein's entrenched and pathetic troops, and spray a form of aerated gasoline that hung in microscopic droplets, saturating the air. And then, as it sped away, the bird would fire a small incendiary rocket from its retreating ass back into the cloud of particulates. When the rocket exploded, all the gas went up at once, a wall of flame that could be seen from twenty miles away, that sucked the oxygen itself up from the earth, and scorched everything in its vicinity.

And Joe the mechanic, tagging along at the rear of the force, had passed these scenes in aftermath, underground bunkers that had lain beneath the fire bombs, their tops sucked off by the vacuum, the scorched-black bodies of dead Iraqi soldiers, some exploded inside out, lying haphazardly about the surface of the sand. Joe was to see scenes like this again and again, or bodies dismembered and disemboweled by the force of shrapnel explosions, Americans as well as Iraqis.

Something else happened in that desert, too. A couple of times at night all the men's eyes began to burn and seep as if some invisible menace had crept in over them from the dark sand. A few guys lost their breath and clutched at their throats. Others screamed and poured water over themselves. Joe just lay on his back and squinted until the burning went away. There were whispers that this was nerve gas, or bacteria, or some fake thing to freak them out, but nothing official was ever said.

And it had all rattled him so that sometimes he thought he could not keep functioning. But he did, working, fixing, not complaining, not discussing, as had been ordered. All through that tour, and back home on the base, until his time was up, he was a good soldier. Later, at the VA in Ann Arbor, he received some treatments for his symptoms, and psychiatric counseling as well, but nothing seemed to help much, and he quit going.

He heard the driver's side door open and the driver pull himself up into the cab. Joe stood on the running board and looked again toward the restaurant. Kari had just come out.

"Hey!" Joe yelled. He waved. She saw him finally and started to run. She carried a black duffle bag and the wide briefcase Rick had in the parking lot after the shootings. Which was strange, Joe thought. She could barely lift it. It pulled her over to one side, so that she nearly dragged it on the ground.

The driver leaned across and unlocked the passenger door. He said, "I gotta run inside, take a leak. Where you headed?"

"Seattle." Joe tossed his shoulder bag inside.

"Your lucky day," the driver said. "That business about not taking on riders, hell, that's why I'm an independent. Good to have someone to talk to, you know?"

Joe nodded. "I got a friend, too."

The driver's smile faded. "Now, listen—"

"A lady. We just need a ride outta here."

The man watched as Kari got to the door, then smiled when he saw her. Joe leaned out and took the case, which he guessed weighed at least twenty pounds, and set it inside. Then he grabbed her arm and in a single heave pulled her clear up and inside the cab. The driver climbed back down and headed in.

"So," Kari said. "Tell me where we're going."

"He'll take us all the way into Seattle."

"Then to Alaska," she said. "That's the place to be."

"Really? Is that where you live?"

She didn't answer. A moment passed before she said, "Rick'll start looking for me. I snuck this stuff around the side, but he'll notice soon enough."

"Why would you do that? We're trying to get away from this, aren't we? So you bring that along? What's in it?"

"I don't know."

"Is this what Rick was after?"

"I don't know. He didn't tell me anything."

"Then why—" Joe started to say, but the driver opened his door and climbed in. He revved the huge diesel engine a few times before they finally started to move.

Somewhere from off across the rolling land Joe heard sirens, maybe two vehicles. The sound, although it came from some distance away, ran like ice up the back of his neck. His heart thumped. He felt Kari's hand on his, squeezing.

The rig swung around and as they headed for the exit the driver said, "Ho, lookee there. Someone bought some trouble."

Joe had been keeping his head down, listening, but now he sat up. There at the Nova stood Rick surrounded by two black unmarked cars and a highway patrol cruiser with lights flashing. Rick leaned against the car roof with his legs spread. A man in a suit patted him down while another held a gun at his ear. A patrolman stood off a few feet with his shotgun trained and ready.

Joe could not draw a breath. His throat had closed. All he could hear was the sound of the great diesel engine and the gears shifting as the driver headed for the access road and picked up a little speed. He smelled the familiar old scent of engine grease and oil. A white plastic Madonna prayed on the dusty dashboard. Kari's fingernails had dug into his flesh, cutting him, making him bleed.

What was odd, Joe noticed, was that Rick had changed clothes. Instead of the jeans and yellow T-shirt, he wore a white collarless shirt and gray suit. He looked different.

The empty strongbox sat open on the car's hood, next to another black duffel bag.

Then Joe heard the sirens again, closer now, the cops not bothering to come in quietly at this point. He saw a cruiser tearing in from the highway, and out beyond that, yet another, coming hard in the eastbound lane. Traffic had pulled over.

Joe sat back in his seat and looked at Kari, whose face had bleached white. Then Joe stared forward again through the windshield as they left the restaurant behind them. The first approaching highway patrol car bore down at them on the access road. The siren was screaming, now, so loud that the truck driver raised his left hand to plug his ear. Joe watched the patrol car come, surrendering himself to whatever was going to happen.

But the car simply hugged the berm of the road and slipped past them, into the restaurant parking lot. The second cruiser went by in the same way.

Joe felt like he did not breathe until they had gone fifty miles already.

"So lemme get this straight," said Ry Hickey, who'd driven over here to pump this shitbag, as he called him. "You mind we go over it once more?"

Leanne Red Feather sat in a back corner of this room in the Spokane post of the Washington State highway patrol, and listened. She'd ridden over with Hickey and invited herself in on this interrogation, and knew she'd have to give a little afterward, quid pro quo, but that was all right. She wasn't really supposed to be here. Simmons' direction, when she'd called from the carryout had been to finish out the Cooper investigation and then get home. Well, she figured, that's what she was doing.

The shitbag, Rick Damschroeder of Bellevue, Washington, according to his driver's license, nodded like a good boy. They'd had him sequestered in this small, stuffy room for two hours now, informed him that he was free to go if he liked, that he was not under arrest at this time, but they sure would appreciate any help he could give them. And the shitbag had just gone along fine with that, and had been talking ever since. He'd even agreed, already, to ride back to Idaho if they wanted him to, where the Kootenai County DA was standing ready to fill in the blanks on an arrest warrant as soon as Hickey called in the details.

But before any of that, Hickey and Melrose and Leanne needed to know fast what this was about.

The guy must've sweated off five pounds by now. Leanne felt like she had, and she'd been able to go back to the air-conditioned offices from time to time, while Hickey and Melrose took over the questioning. They'd alternated, tag-teaming, Hickey playing nice by bringing in iced teas or Cokes. And Damschroeder seemed to be holding together a consistent story.

He sat, his no-longer-neat white shirt plastered with sweat to his body, with his hands on the table in front of him, twirling a piece of paper.

Hickey said, "All's you know about the guy is his name's Joe. No last name."

"He's a ringer," Rick said.

"Ringer," said Hickey. Dick Melrose stood against the wall by the door, his arms folded across his chest, so there were four in the room and the temperature was rising.

"A scammer," Rick said. "A con. He set me up. I only wanted to get home. That's it. None of this. I told you, I was hitching out of Montana. He picked me up late last night outside Missoula. He was strange looking, kind of scary, with these freaky eyes. But, I needed the ride. We stopped alongside the road after midnight and dozed 'til sunrise."

"And you'd been distributing religious pamphlets."

"Missionary work. Up on the reservation. I'd worked the campuses in Bozeman and Missoula. Just talking to people, trying to get them to see the light of the lord."

Leanne knew about missionaries on the reservations. Someone was always handing out something to those people. Even after all these decades, she figured, white people still felt the urge to convert them to something. This notwithstanding the fact that most natives had gone Christian ages ago.

"Traveling by bus."

"Yessir. I have, or had, a Greyhound pass." Which was true; the pass, expired the day before yesterday, lay on the table in front of them.

"You a preacher?"

"No, sir. Just a missionary. For the Northwest Apostolic Church and Temple of Spiritual Rebirth, in Bellevue—"

Melrose said, "So today this Joe—who is maybe the Devil, no?—he made you walk right in there and shoot those three men at point blank range."

"All right," Ry Hickey said. "Let's let the young man talk."

"I didn't shoot nobody, Mister," Rick said. "I don't own no gun. I didn't have no gun with me." Here he started to choke up a little, and his eyes got misty. "I confess I was in the store. Lord Jesus Christ, it scared me. He said we was gonna get some stuff. We hadn't had breakfast, right? He told me to wait there in the car. He'd parked around to the side, you see. He said I didn't need to come in. But then I decided I wanted some orange juice. That was all. I hadn't told him to get me some juice.

"I didn't see much. When I walked in I smelled smoke and saw this old man just lying on the floor, bleeding. I didn't know what'd happened. I didn't see Joe. Then another man ran in fast, carrying a gun. I heard shots, only it wasn't this man shooting. He was being shot. By Joe. Just shot him dead. Oh, God. He told me to get back in the car, and pointed the gun at me. I wasn't gonna say no. After I was outside, I heard more shots."

"How many did you hear, in total?"

"Don't know. Seven, eight altogether."

Hickey leaned back from the table but kept his eyes on Damschroeder. "You didn't run away."

"No sir. I just froze. I went out and fell down and prayed. I'd'a left right then, though, if I'd had keys to the car."

"The strongbox?"

"When Joe came out, he was carrying it. We just left then. He watched me while he drove. He had the gun still on him. I just did what he said."

"All the way to this truck stop by Spokane."

"Yessir. I thought I could call someone. Do something—"

"All right," Hickey says. "Now what about this girl the waitress said she saw talking to you two. She said both this other guy and the girl disappeared, then."

"I didn't know her."

"The girl?"

"No, sir."

"She wasn't with you at the shooting?"

"No, sir. Like I told you, Joe first started talking to her in the parking lot at the diner. They were talking about a ride somewhere. They were laughing. I don't know if she had a car. But I didn't get the idea they knew each other. But maybe they did. Maybe it was set up she'd meet him there."

"But it seemed like they were strangers?"

"Yeah. He just took up talking to her out there. Then, later, he and she went outside to a table and kept talking. She came in to me and asked did I want a ride? I said, 'No.' "

"He just up and started talking to her."

"That's right."

"So she joined you for beers."

"Him. I didn't even sit with them."

"And they went off together."

"I guess. I didn't see 'em after a while. Which was fine with me. I just wanted to get out of there. When you found me I was getting my duffle out of the car."

There came a knock on the door. Melrose opened it and spoke with someone. He then motioned to Hickey and Leanne.

"You're not gonna believe this," he whispered. "There's an Idaho attorney calling, saying he's been retained in the defense of Rick Damschroeder. He's already yelling about due process and rights and every other damn thing, saying we better not say another word to this man before he has some counsel. And he said if Damschroeder agreed to voluntary extradition, it's rescinded as of right now. He's on his way over."

"You shitting me?" Ry Hickey said. He looked back at Damschroeder. "What the hell'd you do, boy?"

"I called my church from the restaurant," Rick said. "I knew I was in trouble, but didn't know what to do. I was gonna call the police anyway, if you hadn't shown up. The church must've arranged something. I swear I didn't call a lawyer. But, listen. I'll be glad to keep talking to you. I got nothing to hide, sir."

"Sonny bitch," Hickey said. He walked out, leaving Leanne and Melrose to follow.

7

AN HOUR EAST OF SEATTLE THEY PULLED OFF INTO A BIG-TIME TRUCK stop. It looked to Joe like fifty rigs were parked there, and men in jeans and cowboy boots and hats and vests sauntered all over the place, some smoking, most drinking coffee, some laughing, some dozing in a corner. Kari was back at the truck, still waking up.

A sign in the front lobby said SLEEPING ROOMS FOR PROFESSIONAL DRIVERS ONLY. To the left was a restaurant, to the right a store and a check-in counter for the sleeping rooms.

"Get some grub?" the driver asked.

"No, thanks," Joe said. "You take us on into Seattle?"

"Sure thing. I just want to stoke up, so I don't have to mess around in the city. Meet you back here in half an hour."

Joe walked back outside and sat on the low concrete wall which fronted the building. His head was starting to go again, precursors of the pain to come arcing across the side of his head like little bursts of electricity. His stomach churned, too. Sweat ran down his face. He stood and walked along the front of the low building and knew he had to sit down somewhere, but he also needed to be alone.

In the men's room, he just got himself locked in a stall before the real pain hit. He sat on the stool with his head between his knees and one hand on each wall, steadying himself, drawing deep breaths. He imagined men breaking in here, guns aimed at his stall door, and screaming at him to come out with his hands clear. And if he wasn't fast enough, them blasting away the door and piling in on top of him, dragging him out by the hair.

He did not lift his head for fear he'd fall off the toilet to the wet, dirty floor. He sat still, waiting for it to pass.

During the break in the interrogation, Leanne called her office in Boise and asked for Ben Regis, who had once been the closest thing to a full-time partner she'd ever had.

"Hey," she said. "I'm in Spokane."

"Everything all right?"

The son of a heavyweight Chicago commodities trader, Ben wouldn't have had to work at all if he hadn't wanted to, a fact the other agents in Boise had somehow known immediately on his arrival four years earlier. He'd gone to Loyola, pre-law with a major in criminal justice. But he hadn't wanted, really, to be a lawyer, preferring something more physically active. After finagling an internship as a ride-along with a Chicago PD tactical unit, he was hooked on that life, and took the Treasury Enforcement Exam over his family's protests. He wanted to be a federal agent, he said, and had once met, through his father, actually, the agent in charge of the ATF's Chicago district office. After reestablishing his contact with that agent and placing in the top one percent on the exam, Chicago hired him in spite of his minimal experience. He cruised through Glynco, and even completed the highly demanding Special Response Team training. Then, after a few years of knocking down doors and getting shot at, he'd requested transfer to a full-time investigatory detail somewhere in the great northwest. Because the other thing he'd always wanted to be, he told Leanne, was a ski bum.

So he came to Idaho to chase guns and investigate bombings and arsons, and to ski during whatever free time he had left. But he was and remained, in his way, as much an outsider to the culture of the bureau as Leanne. So, not many months after his arrival in Boise, he and Leanne found themselves drawn toward each other.

"Everything's fine," Leanne said. "Except it seems like we got the wrong guy. He claims to be a missionary from some church. Can you believe that? His bus pass expired. He was hitchhiking his way back over there when this bad man picked him up."

"So you still have to find the bad man."

"He's headed for Seattle. I shouldn't have called you, probably. I'm sorry, but I need a couple favors and there's no one else I really wanted to ask."

"It's all right, Leanne. Tell me."

"Think we can swing it so I can go over there?"

"Maybe. You in the tracking business now?"

"I'm still in the gun business and I know there's an angle here. I know a hit when I see one, Ben. And the only reason you hit an arms dealer is if it has to do with arms."

"Simmons won't buy it."

"I can be over there by late today, just to see what's up. I'll check in with District when I get there." The resident agency in Boise was attached to the ATF district office in Seattle out of which, technically, they all worked.

"Unless you think this guy is carrying crates of guns on his back, it's nothing but interstate flight to avoid. Maybe kidnapping. Those are FBI raps, last I checked. Why don't you let them handle it?"

"Since when have the fibbies ever minded an extra hand, Ben? They'll just have the Seattle cops running it, anyway."

"So?"

She paused, then said, "Unless you call over there and warm them up to the idea that it's such an important case, the best agent in Idaho is traveling all that way just to stay on it. Then maybe they'll actually send someone out to do some work. With your powers of persuasion?"

"I see," Ben said. He was quiet a moment, thinking.

"I'm sorry," she said. "I shouldn't have asked."

"Stop it. All right? I think I can probably do that."

"And you'll bring it up with Simmons later?"

"If you don't hear anything from me, just go."

It happened, a year and a half or so after they'd begun working together, while Leanne was still married but barely communicating with her husband, that she and Ben drove together one afternoon to Baker City, Oregon, to try to hire a man reported to be offering his detection-proof arson services around town. They didn't find the guy the first day, so stayed over, since it was a two hour drive. That night they had dinner together, and a couple beers. At the door to her room, as she was saying good night, Ben leaned in and kissed her. Leanne did not react—she did not kiss him back at first, but she did not pull away or stop him either. When he kissed her again, though, she put her arms up around his neck. She knew she'd come to love Ben, but had tried to believe there was no romantic element to it. With her marriage collapsing, her job the only anchor she had then, she could not afford this.

But she and Ben became lovers. At the least, one of them would have been transferred if this had been discovered by the agency, but because they spent so much time together anyway, and because they were both highly self-controlled, they had no trouble in keeping the fact hidden. Still, Leanne was racked by the knowledge that it was not a thing they should continue while they were working together.

So a month after they'd begun seeing each other in this way, she told him that she was scared, both of keeping him and losing him, but maybe they should cool things off until she knew what was going to happen with her life, until the divorce was final and they'd decided what to do about them both working in the same office. The next day, Ben, along with dozens of other Special Response agents from around the west, was drafted as part of the largest ATF operation ever mounted—the raid on the Branch Davidian compound at Waco, Texas.

When Leanne first heard news of the slaughter of agents there, she remembered, a sharp pain pierced her chest, as if her heart itself had seized. She learned quickly that Ben had not been one of those hit. But, although the FBI took charge of the surrounded compound, Ben stayed at the scene. It would be another five weeks before he'd come home finally to Idaho.

"I'm afraid that's not all," Leanne said, now. "What's your plate look like tomorrow?"

"Medium full."

"Can you clear it?"

"I don't know," he said. "Why?"

"I'm still thinking about Big Bill. I mean, maybe I am screwing this up even worse, leaving."

" 'Cause you should still be in Coeur d'Alene."

"Someone should. If Bill was selling, that's where it is. That's still what we have to know."

"But it's your case, Leanne. Your people."

"Person. I only ever had one direct source on this."

"That's not what Simmons thinks. He's under the impression you had a whole line of informants talking their heads off."

"Uh huh."

"You lie to him?"

"Not exactly."

"I see. Will this pochucker talk to me?"

"Probably, if I make a call first."

"Shit, Leanne. They had an arson bombing in Pocatello this morning. Somebody's got to go over there. And I've got to try to set a buy with this asshole from Casper. I don't want him disappearing." A man from Wyoming had reportedly been trying to sell some bags of cocaine and a thirty caliber machine gun in the bars around Boise.

"See what crap you'll be getting out of, then?" she said.

"Simmons is gonna blow when he finds out you're in Seattle. And then this—"

"I'll talk to him later. I'll make it OK. But, Ben, there's still one more thing. It's personal."

He went quiet, then.

She told him what had happened with Cal, how worried she was. Ben knew the situation, knew Calvin pretty well. They even seemed to get along, sort of, which surprised her. As far as Cal was concerned, Loyola was in the Ivy League and about as far from his world as you could get. But Ben said he'd swing by later, see what was up, talk to Calvin if he could.

Leanne said, "I know this is a lot. But there's no one else I could ask."

"Hey," said Ben, "you know I'm always here. You know all you have to ever do is ask. Right? You know that?"

"Yeah. Thanks, Ben."

When she heard he was finally returning from Waco, Leanne had felt giddy. She knew now that she'd been wrong in pushing him away, that she wanted him with her, whatever it cost, regardless of what the ATF thought about it or how long it took her divorce to be final.

But when she saw him in the office, and he just nodded at her and smiled, she knew he was different. His face had changed—he looked older, drawn and thin and beaten somehow. And she knew, although she did not let herself fully realize it yet, that he was not coming back to her.

She didn't go out of her way to talk to him that day, and when it was time for her to go home, he'd left already. They fell into a pattern of avoiding each other for that week. Then one day they went out for lunch together, and talked like old partners.

The only thing he said about them was, "You were right about pulling back. It's too much, us both being agents." She did not tell him that she'd been wrong, that it wasn't too much, although she felt like someone had punched a hole in her chest.

And when, six months later, Ben fell in love with someone else, Leanne told him she was happy for him. Six months after that, in the same month Leanne's divorce was finalized, Ben was married. At the reception, Leanne sat in the ladies' room and wept.

A year after that, six months ago, Ben became a father.

◇

It took fifteen minutes for the pain and the blurred vision that followed it to pass. Joe thought it must be about time to meet the driver back out front, but before he opened the stall, the bathroom door opened and two men came in.

"The hell the smokies doin' working the cafe like that?"

"Triple murder over by Coeur d'Alene. Two guys. They got one of 'em. Other one slipped off. Probably got a ride but he might be hitching trucks."

Joe listened as the men washed and left the room. Then he washed his face and hands and rinsed out his mouth. Outside the lavatory he stopped in the dark hallway which led to the front lobby and waited behind a pay phone mounted on the wall.

He saw Kari wandering, looking at things, killing time. He waited until she was looking in his direction, then caught her attention. She understood that something was wrong and did not approach him. He pointed toward the outside, indicating that she should get back to the truck.

Then he saw the driver in the lobby, glancing around and checking his watch. Joe waited, watching from behind the phone. Suddenly, as if some other sense than seeing or hearing had informed him of Joe's presence, the driver looked straight up at the phone and at Joe behind it.

"That you?" he said.

Joe stepped out, expecting cops to pull down on him with twelve-gauge shotguns. Nothing happened.

"Well come on then, kid," the driver said, waving his arm and heading for the door. "The hell you been doing? I got a schedule to beat. Just about to go without you."

On the way out, Joe saw two highway patrol cruisers parked in front of the building, but apparently the driver hadn't been in the café when the patrolmen started through.

It was a cool day for August. As he climbed into the rig Joe looked up. The sky was a beautiful cornflower blue, clear and hard and as deep as he could look into it. Puffed up cottonball clouds floated here and there, but left most of the sky open and free. Joe looked at it for as long as he could before he ducked in and pulled the door closed behind him.

"My gut says he's full'a shit," Ry Hickey said. He and Leanne sat in Dick Melrose's air-conditioned office. Melrose sat behind the desk. "Say anything to cover his ass, make it look like he didn't know nothing."

"Maybe," Melrose said. "But the gun's a problem. You say it was a 9 millimeter. If it was Damschroeder's, I say he'd have had it on him. We dropped on him cold. He had no time to think about it, to ditch it somewhere, unless he ditched it right after. We tore up the diner—nothing there. Hard to tell who fired without a weapon, but I can't say it was Damschroeder."

"Why's that?"

Melrose handed Hickey a sheet of paper from his desk, the results of the powder residue test they'd run. "His skin's clean. He hasn't fired a weapon today. Something would have showed."

"Could'a wore gloves," Hickey said.

"But there's the car," said Leanne. "The prints." The Nova turned out to have been stolen outside Yellowstone, just across the Wyoming line, two days earlier. The Washington plates had been stolen a week ago, in Spokane. The Idaho highway patrol technicians had dusted the car and were still dusting the store for prints. So far the only prints belonging to Rick Damschroeder were from around the passenger seat area of the car, which corresponded precisely with his statement. No prints of his were found anywhere inside the store.

"Shit," Hickey said. "We better find that other one, Joe Whoever. Then he can sure as shit blame the one we got."

"He's the one," Melrose said. "We can hold Damschroeder overnight, long enough to confirm his story with the church and the Montana rez. But this Joe fellow's prints were all over the steering wheel and driver's area of the car, the strongbox. And matches were found on the register and the pay phone in the store. We find him with the gun, that's it."

"And the money," Leanne said. Very little cash had been found on Damschroeder or in the car. "We'll find that on Joe, too, if we find him."

"We'll find him," said Melrose. "Now that the feds are in, that'll be some good manpower there. He's either on his way to Seattle with this woman he sweet talked or there already. Shit, she'll probably turn up somewhere raped with her throat cut."

Leanne said, "I'm thinking of heading over that way myself."

"Tell me something," Hickey said. "Dick here says, 'Now that the feds are in.' And with this girl involved, a hostage maybe, course it's a federal case, but evading across state lines and kidnapping, that's FBI, maybe the Marshals. Don't get me wrong, you're more than welcome. I want to catch this scum, and he's way out of my jurisdiction. But, first off, you're Treasury. Second you showed up at that murder scene not long after I did, and I got the call straight off. How's that work, that you were right there? They got the BATF investigating local murders now?"

Leanne shook her head and cleared her throat. "I'd been keeping an eye on Big Bill."

"You had Cooper under investigation?"

"Not exactly. Just some low-key surveillance. He might've been thinking of selling some weapons again."

"Again? You folks never proved it before."

"I don't know, Ry. As I said, we were just watching."

"And here he turns up shot to death right under your nose." Hickey laughed. "And just a random low-life robbery. Pure chance. Some scum out to score a few dollars. Ain't that something. Huh? You accuse him of selling big ol' cannons and here he can't even defend himself from a little 9-millimeter handgun."

It turned out that one of the highway patrol investigators was headed over to Seattle on other business, so he agreed to give Leanne a lift. Before she could leave, though, the receptionist buzzed back into Melrose's office and said Ed Simmons of the BATF was on hold and wanted to talk to his agent, Leanne Red Feather.

She shook her head at Melrose, and told him sotto voce that she'd already left. She was torn, though—a strong part of her wanted to get back to Boise to find out what Calvin's big problem was. But the urge to stay on this trail would drive her nuts, she thought, because she knew there was something worth finding.

"Tell him she's gone," Melrose said, keeping his eyes on her. "Just left for Seattle. She's riding over with one of our boys."

"Thanks," Leanne said. "He wants me back."

Melrose nodded. "Just catch this SOB, will you? I want to see you with him back in an Idaho court. I want to be there when they thread that noose."

"Amen," Ry Hickey said. "I like a little girl who'll lie to her boss so she can go off and chase some bad murderer." He laughed, and looked at Melrose, who laughed, too.

The fall she turned ten, in the same month the divorce between Jimmy Red Feather and Anna Willingham Red Feather was finalized, six months after Jimmy had moved away, Leanne was suspended from the Catholic school for a week because she'd gotten in two blood-drawing fights in three days and then swore in Salish at the nuns. Speaking in Salish was forbidden in the school, as were, of course, fighting and swearing. For two days she came home after spending the morning cleaning at the local Mission Chapel, which was the punishment her mother had decided upon, and took the two dogs out for long walks, the dogs running happily ahead, sniffing and then marking or chewing what they could find, Leanne dragging along behind, nursing a long, good sulk.

On the third day, she kept going.

In Arlee a few people called to her, but she ignored them. The dogs had gone on home by then. She got on the paved road headed south and kept her head down and walked.

What surprised people when they heard the story later was how far she got, clear to Evaro, at the very edge of the reservation, where huge signs advertised cut-rate cigarettes and booze—sold tax free because it was reservation property—where the road rose up to pass through the mountains before descending into the long, hazy valley that held Route 90 and the city of Missoula.

She'd come ten miles on foot, cold and chapped but showing no signs of stopping until a dusty old International Harvester truck crawled past her and pulled over. She walked by without even a glance, then stopped, went back and got in the passenger seat.

"Long way to Butte," Guts said.

"Highway down there," she said. "I'll get a ride."

"I'll give you a ride. That's what I come to tell you."

She considered this for a minute, then, suspicious, said, "What you want, old Guts?"

"Problem is, your dad ain't there right now. I been callin' to tell him you was on your way. I mean, when you turned up gone, I figured that's where. But you know Jimmy Red Feather. He might not show for days or weeks."

She sat hunched up and looked out the window. After a minute, she took off her boots and showed him the bloodstains on her white socks, from the blisters that had been rubbed raw. She smiled when he shook his head.

"Sometimes you only find peace by lettin' things go, Leanne."

"Not me," she said.

He started the truck to get the heaters working. "Hey, I forgot," he said. "Look here." He pulled a rifle up from behind the seat, a short Winchester lever-action. "Thirty-thirty," he said.

"That ain't what you shoot."

"Not me," he said.

She looked at him.

"Talked to your mom. Told her you been gettin' pretty good up there in the woods, thought it was time you learned to shoot."

"She said yes?" Leanne's head spun at the thought of it but she allowed no emotion to show.

Guts said, "See, though, the rut's here in a few weeks. Barely got time now to see if you can handle this. Your mom's worried you're too little for it."

"Shit," Leanne said. "Hey, Guts, this gun big enough to kill an elk?"

"It'd be tough. Deer, though."

"I'm getting me an elk," she said.

"Blister Foot gets an elk," said Guts.

They stopped at the café in Arlee on the way back home and had a burger.

8

In the camp called Sanctuary, on the Kenai Peninsula, with Deacon away overseeing the mission, Father found himself playing the role of enforcer.

A man just drove up in the morning, pretending to be lost. The gate guard, a sixteen-year-old boy, panicked and pulled a gun on the man, who easily disarmed the boy and then—oh, mover in defensiveness and desperation, thought Father—grabbed the boy around the neck and pressed the muzzle to his head.

One of the women screamed.

Father saw the situation, but he did not panic. He smirked, put on his prescription sunglasses and stood watching the scene from his cabin doorway, a distance of fifty yards or so. Then he walked very slowly toward the gunman and the boy hostage.

Someone else come to make demands and threats. They were all so smart, such clever men.

But Father had known about this man's coming for weeks now. And for the past few days he'd known the man was lurking about in the woods around the camp, snapping pictures and taking videotape, confident in his mistaken belief that he remained undetected. In a sense, Father had been looking forward to this moment of confrontation.

When the interloper heard five rifle breeches simultaneously crank five rounds into five chambers, and looked around and saw five men and women behind five trees, each with their scopes trained on his head, he shrugged and threw the small gun into the dirt. So maybe he wasn't quite as stupid as he seemed.

"I insist you search everything," Father said. They sat at the wooden table in Father's very comfortably appointed cabin. An air conditioner hummed. Father sipped at an iced tea, the gunman at a gin and tonic. A girl worked in the kitchen. "She's not here."

"You got her stuffed somewhere."

"I don't. If she were here I'd let her talk to you, so she could tell you that she's here of her own volition."

"After your brainwashing."

"That's propagandistic shit," Father said. "Do you know how hard it really is to brainwash someone?"

The man shrugged and said, "It can be done." Beneath his camouflaged coveralls he wore a pink flowered Hawaiian shirt, the fabric of which had been sewn inside out. It was a Reyn Spooner, Father knew, and cost some money. Father knew because he had seven of them in his own closet. Reyn Spooners, especially the linen ones, which cost even more, were his favorite summer clothing.

The gunman was tall, too, and slender. He wore round eyeglasses and a mustache. His hairline had receded; his eyes were brown going on black. He looked Germanic, Father thought.

"Do you deprogram?" Father said.

The man shook his head. "I can. I used to help out. Didn't have the stomach for it. Now I just grab and deliver. The big-time head guys, they come in later."

"Well, it's not something you can count on, brainwashing," Father said. "Let's put it this way. People go where *they* want to go, and they stay with whom *they* want to stay. The twist is that sometimes they don't understand what that is, even though they may already be acting on it. So you help them see, you clear their eyes. But you can only ever count on that one element—their desires. I just give people what they want."

"You sound like an intelligent guy," the gunman said.

"You sound surprised," said Father. "What's your name?"

"Roy Jameson."

"All right, Roy Jameson. I'll tell you where she is. She's in the lower forty-eight, on a job for me. Believe that? It's true, and she's doing good work from what I hear. Sooner or later she'll be home. But the point is, there are only two ways for you to get her back, and one of those, kidnapping, is a virtual impossibility in a place like this. I mean, look around. We're alone. We'd just kill you. We could do it now."

Roy nodded, aware, undoubtedly, of the situation.

"But I have something much more pleasant to suggest. I like the girl; she's been good to me. But people have been coming after her since she found us back in Idaho, and frankly I'm tired of it. I mean, one day one of you will get her, anyway, right? So—her pop's what, into computers?"

Roy nodded.

"Small company in Silicon Valley," Father said, and elicited another nod. "Privately held. Worth some serious cash."

"How much?"

"You want to make an offer?"

"Fifty grand."

"Oh, stop," Father said, and dropped a hand loudly on to the table top. "It ought to hurt at least a little. I'd take a quarter of a million, nonnegotiable, to arrange a situation wherein you would find her away from camp with little protection. You don't get hurt by us, and, just as important, it still looks like a grab. Understand? I'm not involved."

Roy shook his head. "I understand. But I don't know if they'll swallow that."

"They'll swallow it," Father said. "She's still their daughter, even after all these years. And I'll tell you something else. If you help convince them to swallow it, on top of what they're paying you—what, maybe ten grand after expenses?—I'll give you ten percent of what I get."

Roy's eyebrows raised. Father could see him spending twenty-five thousand already, a boat or a car, a trip maybe. Tough guy like this, hustler, former cop maybe, could use a couple months in the Caribbean. Finding people was a hard life.

"Hmm," Roy said.

"Strictly between the two of us, of course."

"Of course."

"If you make the delivery—it'd have to be in cash, and I prefer gold—you could take your cut before you even deliver. I get two twenty-five, I'm satisfied. I'll turn her over. Then Daddy can sic his deprogrammers on her and fuck up her head forever. Personally, I know she'd be a lot happier and better off here, but I'm tired of these hassles with her family. Her former family, I should say."

Roy smiled.

If he was really smart and good, Father thought, he'd get three or three fifty from Daddy, and turn over the two twenty-five. Then he'd really have a vacation ahead of him. Father wrote down the name and number of the motel in Kenai where Roy Jameson had a room, and said the girl, Kari, would be back soon, in a matter of days. He'd be in touch. Then Father handed Roy's .45 back to him.

But before Jameson could stand up, Father said, "On top of that, Roy, my friend, I'll do you another favor. See that girl in the kitchen?"

Roy leaned forward and looked just as she bent forward over a counter to reach something in a cupboard, just as her short shorts rode even higher up the top of her very attractive thighs.

"You've been traveling," Father said. "It's been a tough day. There are women here who look that good who'd help you, what, relax a little, shake the dust off. Hot bath, back scrub, whatever comes next."

"Her?" Roy said, jerking his thumb toward the kitchen. His throat felt thick.

"If you like. But take a walk around. Take your time. Have a look. There're lots of fishies in my little sea."

Roy smiled again, and nodded at first, then shook his head. "I don't think so," he said.

"We're not evil, Roy," Father said. "People have this preconceived notion. You want to know why we're here, the simple, stunning reason? Because it's *enjoyable,* Roy. That's the whole secret. We pray, we sing, we make love, we raise babies, we fish and we hunt. It's Eden, Roy. Shangri-Fucking-La. Know what we don't do? We don't browbeat each other, we don't work nine-to-five, we don't pay taxes, we don't get caught in traffic, and we don't hate our neighbors. If you ever get tired of shagging runaways and kidnap victims, I'll tell you something, you can come right up here and make yourself at home. I could use a man like you. Any damn day of the week."

Roy Jameson smiled again and shook his head. He could understand how people got sucked in; this guy was too good. He saw right through to what you wanted the most, to what you needed. And he made it his job to provide just that thing you were missing, whatever it was—love, self-respect, discipline or just a soft woman. Amon saw and Amon knew and Amon provided. Roy laughed and shook Father's hand and excused himself. He had a good mile-long walk back up the dirt road to where his truck was hidden, a half hour to pack up his camping and surveillance gear, and an hour drive from there to the room he was keeping in Kenai. And he knew exactly about what he'd be fantasizing on that long trip.

"How'd they tumble so fast?" Rick spoke in a low voice and leaned over the table toward the old man across from him. This man, a defense attorney, seemed sometimes to know the truth, sometimes not to know, and sometimes to wish he didn't know anything. "Hadda be some kind of fluke."

The lawyer was a Golden Meaner, Rick knew. Deacon, who'd been all the way up at the border with the weapons, which the men had collected at some remote upstate spot, drove back down and delivered

$2,000 in American Eagles so the attorney would get his ass moving on this case, just in case the scam developed a snag. But Rick knew it wouldn't. They had nothing on him. And they didn't have his true ID, so they had no idea of his previous arrests. When they let him walk, Rick Damschroeder would vanish.

The problem was, if they did suspect him, and turned anything at all, they'd never even set bail.

"A young boy ID'ed the car," the attorney said. "He was a hot-rod buff, I'm told."

"No shit."

"That's why people like you take precautions. That's why you were careful. I don't think we're in bad shape."

"We secure here?" Rick looked around at the small tiled room.

"Yes," the man said. He looked like an Idaho attorney in his nice prairie-tan suit and bolo tie, crisp white shirt, and cowboy boots.

"What about Amon? He know?"

The lawyer leaned closer, and lowered his voice. "I don't know. I was told that *if* there was a girl with you, she has not been picked up. *If* she was carrying a certain package, it has not been confiscated. So as of now, nothing's been jeopardized. You should get some credit for that."

"It worked out right," said Rick. "She was gonna split, anyway. It was time. It was almost fucking perfect. They'd just left, and I'd just changed, and had gone out to the car for one last going-over when the heat came tearing up. I couldn't believe it. Another minute, I'd of been out of there. But then a couple minutes the other way, I'd be having a lot harder time explaining my way out of this. It actually works out better this way."

"You don't have to tell me these things."

"I'm not saying I killed anyone. What the girl and me were up to, that's our business. That's not why you're here. You're here to grease the wheels. You just tell them you've advised me not to say anything else. Then I go in and sing some more. They love that shit."

"I know quite why I'm here," the attorney said.

Fuck you, Rick thought. He hated the attitude of these rich bastards. But if Kari set it up right in Seattle, as long as she kept it anonymous and fast when she made the call, as long as word got back here soon, this shyster wouldn't even have to work for his money.

The man shook his head. "Considering the bad luck, you're in fine shape, really. If they can't arrest you tomorrow, or at least declare you the focus of the investigation, you're fine. I don't think they have a shred of physical evidence against you. Assuming your story's not contradicted by anyone."

"That's not a problem."

"Then you'll be out."

"And then I fade."

The lawyer shrugged. "You understand that if they find this other man, and make an arrest, they'll want you—"

"Don't make me think you're stupid. I won't be anywhere near here by then. Besides, this Joe, if he's arrested, will not thrive in captivity, if you know what I mean."

The lawyer averted his eyes and cleared his throat. "That's not my concern."

Rick said, "I just meant it's rough in here. That's all. He didn't seem like the type that would handle it very well."

"What do I say about the girl?"

"Tell Deacon she'll turn up, with a package. She's scared. Give her a day or two, she'll show at the Bellevue church. Then they better get someone to her, and get her home."

The attorney nodded, and slid back his chair. "I'll tell them." But before he could stand, Rick's hand snaked across the table and pinned his wrist. "Just a second. Worse case. We didn't discuss that. They don't buy the story. They charge me and don't set bail."

"They'd have to present evidence at a hearing."

"Say this Joe somehow turns it around, either slips off or manages to put doubt on my story, in the next few days. Say some evidence is manufactured."

"You're paranoid. Right now—"

"Humor me. It's my ass in the can. Say he does. Say they don't like the evidence against him. Say it's Bum-fuck, Idaho, over there and they snuff whoever they want."

"That's too hypothetical. I can't give you an answer."

"I'll give you an answer. When you talk to Deacon, tell him this: tell him he better take care of it, one way or the other. A door's left unlocked. A ride's waiting. Poof." Rick let go the man's wrist and spread his fingers into the air, like dust rising, like smoke. "I disappear."

"I can't discuss this with you," the attorney said.

"Don't. Discuss it with Deacon. Just make sure they know."

"That's not my job—"

"Remember, I disappear," Rick said. "Like holy magic."

The attorney turned and hurried from the tiny room.

9

IN THE DARK, IN ONE OF THE TWO MUSHY DOUBLE BEDS, JOE LAY LISTENING to Kari's breathing coming from the other, irregular and shallow now so he knew she was awake. A thin light bled between the vinyl curtains onto the floor-mounted air-conditioning unit that rattled and leaked in the night. This was their second motel room of the day. The truck driver had dropped them in front of a Holiday Inn adjacent to the airport far south of the city, and watched them walk inside. Kari paid cash and used a false name to book a room. Once inside, though, as she started to pull clothes from her bag, Joe stopped her.

"Call a cab," he said.

"What? Why?"

"I heard some guys at the truck stop. Cops are looking for me. They think I might be hitching trucks. They're all over. If they find that driver, he'll lead them right here."

So they snuck out a back door and cabbed north into downtown Seattle, where, almost directly alongside Interstate 5, they spotted Sam's De-Luxe Motor Inn with ground floor rooms that opened directly to the outside. Joe didn't want to be trapped in any hallways.

They hadn't spoken much to each other. She seemed angry at him. Probably just stress, he thought. He felt angry, too. After a fast, tasteless dinner, for which Kari ate only undressed salad, they both collapsed on the beds and dozed. That was three or four hours ago.

"Kari?" he said into the night, now.

"What?"

"Are you really going to Alaska?"

"Maybe so," she said. "Listen, you said those guys in the truck stop only said it was you they were after. They didn't say anything about me, nothing about a woman?"

"No."

"Maybe they don't know."

"Maybe."

"Joe, there's someplace I have to go here in town, someplace you shouldn't go."

"You can do what you want."

"And . . . maybe it would be better, now, if we split up. Safer, you know."

"If that's what you want." He felt stupid then for having imagined an alliance with her, for believing they might work their way out of this together, that she needed him. He was just lonely and scared, he knew, and reading into things. And she was just a woman he barely knew and in fact would probably be better off without. He heard her breathing grow deep and regular again.

I have taken the money, Joe thought. He tried again but still could not comprehend how easy it was to be suddenly guilty of such a crime. He had the foggy sense that everything around him had conspired in the process, even this cheap room with its rust-stained ceiling and matted, smelly carpet, its very seediness a necessary link in the chain that would either lead to his destruction or his fading back into anonymity.

To be unknown, to be nobody, seemed the greatest luxury the world could offer. And just yesterday morning such luxury had been his.

But it wasn't anymore. And he thought again about what he'd thought this morning, at the restaurant, with Kari—about going in, taking his chances with the cops, laying it all out, explaining every detail. They had ways of knowing if you were telling the truth or not. They had lie detectors and interviewers who could tell. They'd interview him and they'd interview Rick, and weigh the two against each other. He had a good shot, he thought, of convincing them. But what would Kari say? In a sense it came down to her word tipping the balance one way or the other.

He'd bring it up to her tomorrow. They'd have to just have it out, the two of them. His ankles burned.

As he sank into sleep, his last thought was that they didn't know his last name. The cops would have prints, which could be matched to his file prints in Detroit, but who would know to look there? He didn't know if they could match anonymous prints to an old local police file halfway across the country. He guessed not. The sure thing was that, if he decided against turning himself in, he could never get busted again.

When he was barely nineteen and angry and drunk one night, in the days before he knew anything of death or fear or sickness, he and his buddy since sixth grade, Scott Piasecki, tossed a cinder block through the driver's side window of a cherry 1968 Pontiac Firebird, what some called the ultimate street racer, because they'd both always wanted to drive one. They'd worked on cars since they were thirteen. One summer, at fifteen, they'd torn down the engine to a Volkswagen Rabbit, re-bored the cylinder shafts, replaced a cylinder which the arm had punched through when the engine blew, rebuilt the whole thing and dropped it back in the Rabbit. It ran just fine. They knew some things about cars, so hot-wiring a relic ought to be easy.

Still, when the Bird coughed and turned over, throaty and muscular, they looked at each other wide-eyed. "Hot shit!" Scott said. Joe was in the driver's seat. He pulled the T-handle automatic back into gear and they motored.

They lasted a couple hours, until a cop cruised on to them in the parking lot of a cemetery in Ferndale, rapped on the window and shot his light into the back seat on the seven empty Strohs cans, then caught a whiff of Joe's breath.

"You guys ain't makin' out?" the cop said.

"Hell no," Joe said, and he and the cop laughed. No big deal. Until the cop radioed in and found out the car was hot, phoned in half an hour ago. He came back up with his gun out and ordered them out of the car. A backup unit arrived. The boys spent the night in jail.

At home, as soon as they walked in the front door, Joe's dad kicked him so hard in the ass it knocked Joe down and made his right leg go numb. The old man laced his knuckles and brought both hands down on Joe's head, knocking him the rest of the way to the floor. Then the old man turned him over and started slapping him in the face. Joe covered as best he could until his mom started screaming and the old man let up.

The thing was, through it all Joe knew he could take him with one punch. The old man was strong, working all those years throwing sheets of metal, swinging rivet guns, lifting barrels. But he was old and he'd had a lot to drink over those years. One good upper to the jaw, Joe knew he'd go down and not get back up. But Joe only lay still and took the beating.

"You ever do something that stupid again, you'll rot in jail," the old man said. "I won't bail you out after this. One screw-up is enough in this family."

Two weeks later he and Scott did it again, this time to an '82 Le Mans, another GM car, because everyone knew GM steering columns were made for thieves. They drove it into the city, parked it at Cobo, walked away and caught a bus back home. In all they stole four or five more cars, never vandalizing them more than they had to, never joy-riding around the city, never trying to sell them or using them to hang out like the first stupid time.

By the last few, they could get in without breaking glass, and could break the steering lock and turn the engine over inside thirty seconds, using nothing but a hammer and a screwdriver. They'd leave the cars nearly as good as they found them, just fifteen or twenty miles away.

Kari was different in the morning, full of bustle and haste, for one thing, instead of the lethargy of the night before; she was already dressed when Joe woke up. For another she looked different. She had applied no makeup. Without the heavy black mascara she'd worn for the past couple days she looked younger, and the intensity of her eyes, while still there, was changed, too, muted, asleep. Instead of jeans, she wore a kind of shapeless gray cotton skirt which hung nearly to her ankles, a plain collarless white blouse, and ugly black leather oxfords. Her hair, rather than bushing out in its glory of natural waviness, had been pinned down until it lay vanquished against her skull. She'd managed to make herself plain.

The first thing she said to him was "Mother the Earth and Father the God will bless you." He could not think of a response to this—it was not how he had imagined beginning this conversation—but when she said, "I'm going out for a minute. Would you like something, a coffee?" he said, "Thanks." She smiled, but her eyes were flat and empty.

"Will you wait for me?"

"Why not?" he said.

She shrugged.

"If you need help—" he said.

She chewed her cheek in the doorway. "No," she said.

He said, "We should talk. We need to."

"Why?" she asked, and left.

He pulled on his jeans then lay, shirtless, back on the unmade bed. It was quiet in this city, on a Thursday. Some traffic but not a lot. Terry was out there, a cab ride away. The reason he had come all this way. But now, if he found Terry and the authorities found him, it could bring the world down on Terry as well, Terry, who might be arrested for harboring, even, and who could in no way withstand the abuse and hardship which would result, even if it were short-lived. What sense did it make to travel here to save his brother, only to bring disaster to his doorstep? Joe didn't know yet what he could do about Terry.

So Kari wouldn't be helping him. Maybe, in a way, that worked out better. He was the outsider; he didn't know either of them, Kari or Rick, nor did he care about them. He wanted just to save himself. So if he turned himself in alone, under no pressure, no duress, without them knowing his last name or who he was, it had to look good, had to work in his favor. He'd tell his story. If it went badly for Kari as well as Rick, well then, that would just be too bad for her.

Then he thought about Alaska, where she seemed to be aimed, about whiteness and ice, about the millions of miles of which no one had yet taken the measure. He had no real idea of what it might be like up there, but he decided then, in that moment, that if he were to run, it was where he would go, too. But he did not think now it would come to that.

He sat up again. She'd been gone five minutes. Maybe she was skipping already. He wouldn't be surprised. He knew that when she went, she'd just disappear. But no, he spotted her black nylon shoulder bag where it had been tossed on the floor and left unzipped. Then he noticed some money sticking out of the top, the corners of a couple of bills. Careless, to carry loose cash like that. He knelt to stuff it back in. Anyone could run by and reach right in—

Then, in the bag, he saw not just a little money, but stacks. Her cut had been seven hundred and thirty-three dollars, just like his. But this was more than that. He pulled it out and counted over two thousand dollars. How could that be? He opened his own bag, where he had stashed five hundred of his cut, but the money was gone.

She was ripping him off. And Rick, too—she must have taken his share. What a pro! he thought, impressed and angry and embarrassed all at once.

Still, he'd caught her. He counted out his share and stuffed it in his pockets, having lost his concern for the moment at carrying around this blood money, evidence which, if he were caught with it, would prove beyond a doubt his complicity in the crimes, would put him beyond the hope of any argument any lawyer could come up with. But he didn't care. The twice-stolen money was here either to be left or thrown away or spent, and it really didn't matter which, as long as it eventually disappeared. So it might as well do him a little good in the process. Then, inspired, he pulled off an extra three hundred and pocketed that, too, before putting the rest back. If he decided to turn himself in, he'd just ditch the money first.

When he put it back, he saw something else that stopped him. The butt of a gun. *The* gun, the silver semiauto which he watched Rick use to kill two men, and heard him use to kill another, stuck down in Kari's sack here in their cheap Seattle room. He pulled it out by its wooden grips. He popped the clip from the butt and saw that it was still loaded. He tossed it on the bed and looked further. In addition to the money and the gun, stuffed down beneath some of her underwear and jeans, he found the red jacket Rick had worn into the store, his white cotton gloves, and inside one of those the keys to the Nova. She'd stiffed Rick, even taking the car keys, and left him to hang there until he got nailed.

He remembered something from the night before, after they'd left the Holiday Inn and were on the street, waiting for a cab. Kari had thrown some clothing, denim and some yellow material, from her duffle bag into a curb-side trash can. Only now did Joe realize he recognized it as the clothing Rick had been wearing during the crime, his jeans and T-shirt. Had she stolen everything from him? But Rick had only just changed in the restaurant before she left. So this black bag was the same one Rick had brought with him into the restaurant just after they arrived. Why would she take that? Joe couldn't answer.

Finally, down in the bag, he found a rubber-banded stack of business-sized cards which had printed on them the words Northwest Apostolic Church and Temple of Spiritual Rebirth, and an address in Bellevue. He took one, then wiped the gun with the bedspread, stuck it back into the bag, and tucked everything else inside on top of it.

Next, he wanted to see what was in the thick, heavy briefcase. But he saw now that it had built-in combination locks. He didn't feel like prying it open and having her know what he was up to. Then he heard her key in the lock.

She was sweating. It was unusually hot for Seattle, even for the last day in August. And the sky, he could see, was clear. Not a rain cloud in sight.

She handed over a cup of black coffee and a cinnamon doughnut. "I didn't know if you took anything—"

"Black," he said. She had nothing for herself but a glass of ice water and a plain unbuttered roll, and she only ate two bites of that.

"I'm seeing some friends," she said. "A cab's meeting me down at the Pike Street Market in half an hour. I didn't think it was smart to have it pick me up here."

"Can I walk there with you?"

"Then that's it."

"All right."

"I have to clean up," she said, although she had already washed once that morning, and took her purse and the duffle bag into the bathroom and closed the door. Her whole personality seemed to have shifted in the night, from loose to rigid, from kind of nicely weird to just weird. Besides her stealing the money, something else was up. He just couldn't figure it yet. While he waited, he sipped the coffee and packed his few belongings into his own shoulder bag, the one that'd brought him clear from Detroit. He felt no fear right now. His scalp tingled; his nostrils were so open they seemed able to scoop gallons of air at a time. His eyes were sharp, seeing. He felt strong.

Before shutting the door he walked through again to make sure they hadn't left anything. In the bathroom he saw only a pile of white towels she'd left on the floor by the base of the toilet. He set the key beside the bed and they left.

The weird, atypical heat wrapped around them like a cocoon. Joe liked the sensation of a strange new city, in spite of the anxiety that chewed at his stomach. He smelled something new, then realized it was ocean. Not what you got in Detroit. Instead of the dirt and the acrid fumes that blew off exhaust stacks, instead of the rot of Lake St. Clair and hot tar and smog, here it was fish and brine.

After they passed beneath the expressway, she entered an enclosed phone booth and made another call, then led him first past a courthouse, left past a library and a string of large hotels, then right and into increasingly narrow and congested streets, by a row of shops set in two different stories along a narrow hilly side street that rose up and away from the sidewalk where they stood.

She was dripping sweat from the strain of carrying the heavy case, but he did not offer to carry it for her. He smelled the fish market before they got there. Here was the heart of the city, he could feel, the core from which it all spread out. He slipped his hand around her elbow as they approached.

"I took it back," he said. He felt her arm tighten against his as she tried to pull away, but he held her.

"What?"

"I counted the money. You left the bag sitting open."

She walked faster, pulling at his arm. "May Mother the Earth and Father the God bless you." Her voice was loud. People glanced at them.

"I don't care," he said levelly. "It's all shitty. I saw you took Rick's money, too. So I took back what was mine and borrowed a little of his, too. Fair's fair."

"Mother the Earth and—"

He jerked hard on her arm, spinning her so she faced him. The market was just across an open square from them now. He could see boys carrying wooden boxes of iced fish and crabs over their heads, people picking through the day's offerings.

"Fuck you," she said. Back to the old Kari. Her voice had an edge again, like before. He liked it better this way. "Fine. Good. Take the money."

"I'm turning myself in. You ought to ditch that gun."

"What?"

"They can tell, you know, if that's the one that killed those people." He'd been wearing his dark glasses, but removed them now and squinted at her. "You don't want them to find it on you."

She twisted her face and sneered at him. "What are you talking about? Killed what people?"

"Little store in Idaho. Three men that Rick shot. You know?"

She shrugged. "I just know he did whatever he had to do. For Father and the Family. Now we have to get back. It's our ordained task. We can't—"

"Who gives a shit about that?" Joe said. "You really don't care about this? You can just let this go? I don't believe that."

"Believe what you want."

He pushed closer to her. "Or does the fact that it was for your church magically make it all OK? So what if a few folks get knocked off."

She looked off toward the market and recited: "Mother the Earth and Father the God will bless us all."

"Stop it," said Joe.

"You're lying," she said. "No one got shot."

"You didn't hear gunshots?"

"A few. But no one got shot. Rick told me what happened when I went back in the restaurant, before I met you at the truck. He said he shot into the ceiling, to scare them. He said there was nothing to worry about. He'd promised Father he wouldn't kill anyone if he could help it."

"And did you really believe him, Kari? Are you really that brainwashed?"

She recited, "We cannot fail for Mother the Earth and Father the God rely on us. If we need to break man's law for the law of God, that is not a sin." Then she looked at him again, and he could see that her eyes had gone sad, now, that she knew well enough Rick had killed people, had prayed for it not to be true, knowing that it was. That all along she'd been helping and praising and having sex with a stone killer.

"He said he tied them up, Joe. I swear. He promised." She sounded frightened. She was in shock, her facade cracking. "But it can't matter. I can't let it matter. I have a task, and that's all I can care about."

"Why'd you take the gun and that other stuff, the keys and that coat and his money? How'd you get it?"

She just looked up at him. He watched a range of expressions cross her face, from disbelief at what he had just told her, to fear, to pained comprehension.

"I don't know what you're talking about."

He tore the black bag from her arm and unzipped it. Inside he saw her underwear and the pair of jeans and the stack of cards. Some of the money was there, too, but not all of it. And there was no handgun or car keys, no jacket, no white gloves.

His face went numb, then hot from flushing. It took him a moment to work it out, then nausea washed through his gut.

She said, "There was a pen, too. With the name of the store on it. Some of the cash. I threw the gun outside, in a garbage can, where they'd find it. The car was stolen. We wiped it clean but for your prints, and a few of Rick's on the passenger side. He had a story all ready. It's all part of the task. You can understand that."

The pile of towels in the bathroom. That's where she hid everything. And the call she'd just made, as they were walking, had to be to the police. She'd set him up.

"Why?" he said. But he knew the answer.

She looked stunned still. This had all gotten bigger suddenly than she thought it would, much more than a robbery cover-up.

He said, "It was set up all along, wasn't it, from the moment you saw me sitting there on the highway, waiting for a ride? You two were probably out looking for someone, weren't you? People who thumb never have much money."

"I was . . . Joe, I'm sorry." Her eyes filled and tears spilled over.

"What's it about? What's in the case?"

"I really don't know. All I know is I have to get it back to Sanctuary. The sad thing is, it would have worked without you. There didn't need to be a real person, just someone Rick made up. We ministered around the area to lay alibis. We had expired bus passes to explain the car, hitchhiking. If we needed, we had a story about a mystery man, a driver who took off, but having someone real would be better. Like I told you before, Rick knew we'd find you. He is blessed. But he should never have shot anyone."

"Goddamn," said Joe. He dropped the black bag at her feet. She did not move or respond. She was not looking at him anymore.

"Let it go," she told him. "All you have to do is disappear. That was the idea. No one meant to hurt you. Just go and don't look back and it will be all over. You have Father's blessing. You are blessed, now."

But he turned and ran.

"They don't know you," she shouted. "You're nobody!"

He sprinted back along the streets they had walked down, toward Sam's De-Luxe Motor Inn, where Kari left a weapon and the keys to a stolen car and evidence from the scene of a murder. Where Joe left prints that would match those found in the store and the car, and skin cells and hair and his signature, albeit of a false name, on a registration form, and God knew what else because he never would have guessed this room would get turned over before the maids had had a chance to clean it.

He got lost, had to turn back, drenched in the dense, humid air. As he ran, his lungs burned and his eyes watered, and startled people leapt from his way. He ran hard, so that soon he could not breathe at all in the unusual heat of the morning.

In the hot saltwater air and the closeness of the city streets he couldn't maintain both pace and anger, and slowed from a sprint to a steady run. And then nearly to a jog. Spent, he began to think sensibly again, and so slowed down even more when he saw the expressway, and walked finally the last block between himself and Sam's Inn, so he could catch his breath and avoid barging on to the scene sucking air with a foaming saliva mouth and red face. And before he even turned the corner from which he could see into the courtyard of the motel, he knew that he'd dodged it yet again.

He found himself on a moderately sloping hill at the base of a T formed by two roads, in the juncture of which lay the motel. The scene was quiet, almost hidden, but he could make it out: a beige sedan parked directly in front of the room, backed urgently up on to the walkway, trunk open, and off to one side a squad car, but no lights flashing, no sirens. Everybody calm. A cop stood out at the street, looking up one way, down the other. A man in a sport coat walked from the room, plastic bag in hand.

Joe walked toward the scene, fascinated. He couldn't see the items in the bag from this distance. He stopped behind a thick electrical pole in front of a dry cleaners which smelled of petroleum. Another man, this one in rolled-up shirt sleeves, came out of the room. He said something to the first, who picked up the radio in the car. The manager of the motel and the girl who worked behind the desk both watched from the parking lot. A uniformed cop talked to them, made a note, walked away.

Joe worked his way closer, until he was about halfway down the stem of the T, within fifty yards of the entrance. Here he found a doughnut shop with a few wobbly tables inside, and open windows. He sat by a window, ordered an iced tea, and watched.

For all they'd be able to tell, he thought, they still wouldn't have his name. But he saw what had been accomplished. Whatever happened now, Rick was much closer to being a free man, with a world of reasonable doubt now built up in his favor. If Joe went in, this would make it much harder for him to convince them of his story. What would be standing between him and a life sentence? Or death—it was Idaho, after all.

Details fell into place, came clear: Rick had cleaned the car. That's why they stopped shortly after the killings, when Rick knocked around in the trunk. He was wiping it down. Kari must have begun wiping down the car's interior while he and Rick were in the store. That's why they'd had Joe drive afterward, so his would be the only prints to show up. Then, Rick was slow coming into the restaurant from the parking lot—he was finishing the clean up job, and loading the black duffle bag for the setup. Joe had even told Rick about his record for auto theft. It really was perfect, as Kari had said.

Even Kari's pretending like she needed his help to get away from Rick, those looks of fear and need. All one huge con. And it wasn't over with her, he now knew. She'd testify; she'd lie on the stand, say anything they wanted, how this Joe killed those people, forced her to come with him. Kari of the nice hair. Oh, the statements she could give them.

He stood and was about to head into the street, when more cops arrived, another squad car, this one with lights flashing, then another. Then another unmarked car with detectives. One, he could see, was a thin, dark-haired woman. She wore a light, khaki colored jacket and skirt and looked out of place among all the men in their dark grays or blues. It was a busy place now, bristling with police. They'd realized what they had—the still-warm footprint of a triple-murderer on the run.

From the doughnut shop he turned left, back toward the market and the downtown. Already his brain was remarkably cool. His skin was cool, too, even in the heat.

10

SIMMONS HAD REACHED LEANNE IN HER MOTEL ROOM WEDNESDAY EVENING. "I had to get the number from District," he said. "How does that make me look?"

"I left you a message when I got here," she said.

"Yeah, with Ben, who I find out called some FBI schmuck to *ask* if you could follow this case with them. If we want to investigate a case, we'll fucking investigate it! We don't ask those pencil-dicks!"

"That wasn't the point—"

"So why haven't I heard from you?"

"Ed, a few things've happened since then. After Cooper got hit—"

"Hit my ass. It was a random hold up–related homicide."

"Who told you that? The Kootenai County sheriff? What does that mean?"

"It means you're in deep shit with me."

"Bill's driver was lying two feet inside the door, Ed. Hit four times, with one in his head. Somebody was standing in that store waiting for him. Waiting. Does that sound like your average heist? Bill took one in his left eye. Sound like a panicked robber spraying a store?"

"Leanne," said Simmons. "Forgive me here. But what the *hell* does this have to do with us?"

"Ed, listen. When I was little, I learned how to hunt pretty well. The guy that taught me, he used to say, 'Leanne, if you step in elk shit, you can be sure—' "

"Don't you fucking patronize me."

"I want to follow this out. I want to help find this guy. In the end, it's going to be about weapons. I promise you. Give me a couple days."

"You're coming back tomorrow. If you want to investigate this, investigate it here."

"What can I do by then? Let's at least see where we are."

"Stay in touch with me, Leanne, often. Not with Ben. Not with District or the goddamn FBI. With *me*."

"Yessir," she said. "And listen. Speaking of investigating, I think Ben should go up to Coeur d'Alene."

"He told me. So now two of you will be tied up in this."

"Will you let him?"

Simmons grunted. She could hear him adjusting himself in his overburdened chair. "He's leaving in the morning."

"Thank you, Ed," she said. "You have real vision." But he'd already hung up on her.

A little later the phone rang again. This time it was Ben.

"You're going," Leanne said.

"Yeah," he said. "I talked to Cal."

"Thanks, Ben. Again, I'm really sorry to put you out . . ."

"Stop apologizing, Leanne. Listen: he took off. He said he'd be back when you got home, but for now he was going under."

"Under where?"

"I don't know. Those were his words. Someone's after him, you know."

"In what sense?"

"In the sense that they want to do major bodily damage."

"What's going on?"

"Did you ever look much into the guy he bopped?"

"Other than to find out he's permanently damaged, no."

"Well, I called around. He lives in Billings, and worked for an outfit called DF Enterprises. Not so easy to discover was the fact that DFE is owned by a Denver shell corporation called Florence, Inc. Know what else? Treasury has files on them."

"Why?"

"Theory is it's also a front for a sort of finance company, the kind that loans at 3 percent a week. They run book, too, outfits all over the west. Your brother likes to gamble, Leanne. Did you know that?"

"No," she said. She felt her heart sinking hard and fast.

"He's got a problem. I think he's in deep debt."

"Then it wasn't just a bar fight in Havre."

"The guy that came after him was a collector and strong arm. Calvin knew he was coming, and sucker-sapped the guy in the john with a beer bottle instead. I'm sure they tried to get to him in prison, but you know how strong the Indian gangs are in there. I'd guess Cal had pretty good protection. Anyway, now these people are after him."

"Shit," she said. "You don't know where he is?"

"Nope, and that's good. Right now, hiding is the one thing he needs to do very well."

Thursday morning, Leanne watched Seattle PD investigators work the motel room at Sam's De-Luxe. The print man seemed especially meticulous, moving painfully slowly over certain areas, using three different types of fingerprint powders, red, black and white. He was around sixty, with copious amounts of gray hair in his ears and his bulbous nose. After he'd looked at a couple of the prints he'd lifted under a mobile scanning scope, he told her he was pretty sure they had a match to the prints from the car and the store that had been faxed over.

Whether because Leanne was here or not, a real live, working FBI agent showed up, an Oriental man named Mark Truong. Outside in the sunny heat of the parking lot Leanne leaned over a car hood with him. She knew after a few minutes that she'd got lucky in that he was a pretty decent guy who didn't seem to mind too much being called out of his air-conditioned office to look at an empty room.

Whenever she traveled, even undercover, as she had been in Coeur d'Alene, Leanne carried a basic suit for contingencies—in this case, a light poplin jacket and skirt and a white blouse—and was relieved now that she had. Truong of course wore the typical conservative FBI suit and tie, and she'd have felt like a clod in jeans.

"We're an hour or two behind him at most," Truong said. "Looks like the woman was still with him last night."

Leanne nodded. She'd seen the two used beds, longish dark hairs on one pillow. "But she had to be the one who called."

"We put out notices in truck stops all over the region. A driver outside Portland, headed down from Seattle yesterday, said he picked up a man and woman in the Spokane joint where the car was found. In fact, they saw the state guys come down on Rick."

Leanne knew this already. She was told early this morning by Simmons, who had his own FBI sources. But she said, "Really?"

Truong told her more of what she knew: "Must be the same woman Rick Damschroeder talked to you about. Doesn't seem like she's under any duress, though. Driver says they were a nice enough couple, had no idea they were on the run."

"But if she's the tipster, she wants him caught for some reason."

"So." Truong squinted at her. "Here we stand. What are you thinking? Three guys whacked in the mountains, a killer who runs cross-country to the coast with a woman. What's behind it? Anything? Or just a scared fuck-up robber running away, trying to find someplace to hide?"

Another man who needed to quiz this Indian woman agent. But she was over here on the thinnest of theories and probably beyond her authority, so all she could do was play their game, answer their questions and not piss them off so they'd let her keep following.

"I don't know, Mark," she said.

"Listen, I'm not saying you're wrong to read into this. I checked up a little. You get high marks. But I don't know where to go with it. I'm not sure I can even justify the bureau's involvement beyond this point. So you think . . . what, exactly?"

"I think we have a dead arms dealer. I think there's an odor to it I don't like."

Truong nodded and looked off at the buildings up the street. "All right," he said. "In any case, whatever it turns out to be, we've got a guy on the run. Does he know he's being chased?"

"He knows he will be," she said. "Does he figure he's only got an hour's lead? No. He thinks he has some time."

"So he's careless?"

"No. But he takes his time. Doesn't make any sudden moves. He just eases on out."

"He's leaving?" asked Truong.

"Depends on whether he's from here or someplace else. The Nova was lifted in Wyoming, and it turns out there was an armed robbery down there, too, small store in West Yellowstone, no good description of the perp other than his being a single white male, but a similar MO except for the shooting."

Troung said, "But the plates were stolen in Spokane, I'd guess when the guy was on the way over in the first place."

"So you think he's from here."

Truong shrugs.

"A crime spree," Leanne said. "He drives all the way from here to Yellowstone and back, over fifteen hundred miles, just to knock off two carry outs. He's lucky if he covered gas money."

"These guys aren't brain surgeons. People have done stupider things. But, anyway, tell me what we go on."

"I don't know," Leanne said. "Except that something went badly wrong, and our guy has to get out of the sticks, fast, to a city where he can hide and from which he can travel anywhere."

"Back to the traveling."

"I think we should act as if he's running, try to cover the exits."

Truong leaned into his car and pulled out a brown paper portfolio, from which he handed her a copy of a sketch made by the FBI artist who'd interviewed Rick Damschroeder last night. She didn't tell him she already had the sketch in her purse. She'd been looking at the face of Joe all morning.

One could only rely on sketches to a degree, since the likenesses were filtered not only through memory, but through the hands of an artist as well, double-distance from the real thing. Still, elements, sometimes essential ones, came through in uncanny ways, she'd found. This face was narrow and a little elongated from top to bottom. The narrowness continued into the individual features, the nose in particular which was sharp and prominent, beaklike, as they said. The hair bushed up on top, but had been nearly shaved on the sides, which made the face look narrower still. In contrast to all this, however, were the eyes, which appeared unusually wide-set. And they were nearly white in the black-and-white sketch, so pale and washed out as to have a kind of albino effect. But Rick had been explicit in this description even before they brought the artist in. "Weird eyes," he'd said. Still, overall, Leanne decided, the man was not bad looking. The contrast between the eyes and the rest of the face remained interesting.

"Say we distribute these at the airport, car-rental agencies, bus stations, truck stops again," Truong said. "Does that work?"

"Aren't there ferries out here that go all over?"

He shrugged and nodded. "I guess we can hit those, too. I don't have unlimited resources. The airport and truck stops seem more likely. You think?"

She nodded. "Maybe the border."

He shook his head. "If you were being chased, would you try to cross an international border?"

"I might," she said.

"From another country," said Truong. "Here, you'd be safer and less exposed staying in. There's lots here to get lost in."

"Still," she said.

"OK. I can send copies up to Canadian customs and the RCMP. That make you happy?"

She nodded, then said, "Meanwhile, we have matching prints from the room here. You'll see that somebody calls the points in to the NCIC?"

"Of course," Truong said. "But we'd have to get real lucky to hit." The FBI's National Crime Information Computer held data on every person arrested in the country. Among other things, it could match a full set of prints and provide an ID in minutes. But loose prints, Leanne knew, unless they included a palm with several fingers, were tough to match in this way.

11

BEN REGIS HIT COEUR D'ALENE AT TEN THURSDAY MORNING, HAVING LEFT his house just before six. He'd thought about asking Simmons to approve money for an airline ticket, but after watching Simmons fume the afternoon away, convinced himself an eight-hour round-trip drive through Idaho scenery would be a good thing, a break. Actually, he'd never minded driving. When he was in college, each spring break he drove from Chicago out to the Rocky Mountain ski slopes.

In a granola-bar health-food restaurant, where he had a cup of some purple tea he couldn't drink, he was met by Leanne's contact, a young woman who called herself Georgie and who turned out to be the girlfriend of Kyle Greene, Big Bill Cooper's driver who was killed in the store. The girl's face looked swollen, either from tears or hangover, or probably both, Ben thought. The story was that Kyle had started making big money suddenly, and Georgie, suspicious, fearing drugs, went through some of his things and found some lists, strange sounding things she couldn't identify. So she showed them to her uncle, a former cop, who thought they sounded like guns. It was he who called the ATF office and got Leanne.

"I was scared, but after I met her, I liked her a lot," Georgie said, of Leanne. "She's a good person."

"She is that," Ben said. "So where does it stand now?"

"I really went through Kyle's stuff after he died, and I found more of those lists. I can give them to you."

"Good."

"And I found this." She handed him an envelope with an address scrawled on the back. "It's up by Lake Pend Oreille, like thirty miles from here. There's a friend of his who worked with him and Bill Cooper sometimes. I ran into this guy in a bar and asked him what this place was. I was half drunk anyway and didn't really care. But he got all weird on me and was, like, 'Shut up, bitch, don't tell anyone about that.' "

"When was this?"

"Last night," she said.

"What type of guy is he? I mean, is he strong and real dumb. Or is he smart enough to be nervous if, say, a federal agent surprised him one morning and told him if he didn't cooperate he stood a good chance of being named in a firearms indictment tied to a murder case? Know what I mean? Is he the sort who'd tell me to fuck off, or the sort who'd kind of pee his pants a little?"

"Pee," she said. "Why?"

"Without a warrant, I can't go up there and look around. To get one, I have to show a judge evidence that there's a reasonable chance I'll find something illegal. One sort of evidence is if someone who had seen what was there told me I might be very interested in it. Signed a statement to that effect. See?"

"He works part-time for the John Deere dealership, when he's not running around with the Big Bill crowd being a terrorist."

"Lot of terrorists spend their down-time selling tractors," Ben said. "You'd be surprised."

It was nothing but an old barn, once red, now weathered wood, leaning a little to one side. Ben arrived first, then was joined by three Idaho state cops, backup he requested after his warrant came through.

"Pop it," he said to one of them, indicating the lock and chain looped through the handle of a high sliding door, and the man did, with a long-handled pair of bolt cutters. Ben slid open the door and found a dusty light switch. When he flipped it, the impression of a falling-down old barn disappeared. First, a whole series of lights came on, three straight lines of double fluorescent fixtures. Any trace of hay or animal debris had been cleared. The inside was all clean concrete and beams, much of it covered with new tarps or plastic sheets. And on these tarps and plastic sheets, stretching in three rows corresponding to the lines of lights, sat stacks of variously shaped wooden crates.

He and two of the state policemen stepped in. One had brought a crowbar, and they chose a large crate in the first row and pried it open. Inside, sealed in plastic, they counted ten black-Ryanite-stocked assault-type rifles.

"M-16s," one of the cops said, peering over Ben's shoulder. "That's straight military."

Ben said, "You know military weaponry?"

"I'm in the National Guard, sir, second lieutenant," the cop said. "I was active army from '85 to '88."

"Good," said Ben. They worked down this first row, prying open random crates. One contained green metal boxes of .223 ammo for the M-16, thousands of rounds. Another, boxes of an older-style fragmentation grenade. "Vietnam era," the cop said. "Still see them around, but they're not really used anymore, except for training."

Another crate held mortar shells and launchers. Another sealed bags of small rifle parts.

Then, off to one side in a darker alcove, what might have been a horse stall once, they found two tarp-covered mounds. Ben and the cop pulled one back, and the cop said, "Whoa." He shined his light on an uncrated, heavy black bi-pod-mounted machine gun.

"M-60," Ben said.

"Yessir."

In the next stall over, then, and in the two after that, they found long wooden crates, the top of one of which was loose. Inside was a weapon Ben had not seen before, and he had been trained extensively in weapons. It took him a moment to make out that what he was looking at was a kind of shoulder fired bazookalike gun, at least five-feet long, and black, with complex electronic attachments and cords, a hi-tech sighting scope, and some sort of sensory vanes folded along the barrel.

"Antitank?" Ben said.

"Antiair," the state cop said. "Infrared. Heat seekers."

"Where—" Ben said.

"Look here." The cop held up the crate cover, on which had been stenciled in black letters, PROPERTY OF US ARMY, FORT LEWIS/YAKIMA FIRING CENTER, WA. "Lewis is a big base," he said. "And Yakima's not far from here. Couple hundred miles."

Ben said, "You and your buddies sit tight, keep an eye on this place. I have to make some calls. And then it's going to get crazy around here."

12

"HEY," TERRY SAID, WHEN HE CAME UP BEHIND THE BENCH WHERE JOE sat. "I can't believe you're here."

They were not far from where Terry said he lived, in the northern part of the city on the shore of a pretty round lake that seemed incongruous to Joe, situated as it was in the midst of apartment buildings and houses. Even on this weekday plenty of people walked or lounged on the grassy shores.

Joe had not wanted to see Terry's apartment, or to be seen going there, and had not wanted Terry's girlfriend to see him.

"What's not to believe?" Joe said. "I'm always here."

Terry walked with a single crutch. He wore a fiberglass cast on his left leg from the knee down and he looked much too thin, as if he'd suffered some long, persistent illness. He breathed heavily, and when he sat down on the bench next to Joe he started to cough and could not quit for a full minute.

"Abscess," he said. "They say it's clearing up, but it still hurts."

"You're getting better, though," Joe said, "if you could come out here to meet me."

Terry nodded. "First time I've been out alone other than going to the clinic. Feels good, but I can tell I'll be tired." Up and down Terry's pasty arms Joe could see faded red marks that looked like the scars of healing cuts.

Joe let Terry talk for a few minutes, Terry going on about what had happened to him, how he'd come to be in this condition, which was just an embellished version of what Joe had already heard. Joe wasn't listening, really, anyway. He was more interested in watching the happy people around the lake.

When Terry grew quiet, Joe said to him, "How about whoever jumped you? How'd it happen?"

Terry shrugged.

"All I want to know is whether this is still a problem or not."

Terry shook his head and made a face. "It was in a club," he said. "No one I even knew. Some asshole I pissed off."

"Cause if it's a problem, I'll take care of it," Joe said. "I just want it finished now, today."

"It's over, Joe. He waited for me outside. He had a bat or a pipe or something. What's the big deal?"

Neither of them spoke for quite some time. They sat together, watching the people around the lake, fathers with kids, women pushing strollers, one couple walking arm in arm, all these people on a Thursday morning at the end of summer. This was a good city, Joe thought. It felt fresh in ways Detroit hadn't ever in his and Terry's lifetimes.

Joe said, "I'm in some trouble, Terry. Things happened on the way out here, and I have some decisions to make."

"What trouble? What could you get into?"

Joe shook his head. "I don't think I'd better say, for your own sake. But tell me this: can you get yourself home? Are you capable of that?"

"What do you mean—"

"If you had the money, and you could get on a plane, could you get yourself home?"

"I'm not an idiot, Joe."

Joe nodded. "But would you do it? Do you want to go home?"

Terry worked a finger under the top of the cast and scratched. He bit off a fingernail, then said, "Yeah. I guess I do now. This bitch I'm with here, Jesus—"

"And will you stay there this time?"

Terry nodded. "I think I will."

"Will you work?"

Terry shrugged. "I always work, on and off."

"That's not good enough," Joe said. "You have to get a real job and stay there. That's the only thing that keeps people going. You can't be on and off."

"Joe, what the hell's wrong with you?"

Joe shook his head again. "Listen to me. If anyone comes to you and asks if you saw me, you have to say no. Do you understand? This conversation didn't happen. Does your girlfriend know I'm here?"

"No," Terry said. "She was out when you called."

"Don't tell her either. A lot could depend on it. Trust me on this and don't screw it up. Lie through your teeth. You haven't talked to me in days."

"Joe—"

Joe turned on the bench so he was facing his brother, and gripped Terry's upper arm in his strong hand and squeezed. Terry's arms were thin compared with Joe's.

"Ouch."

"It's time to grow up, Terry. This is it, right now, this minute. The big time. The real world. Heavy-duty." He let go of Terry's arm, but could see the impressions his fingers left. "You have to change, because I'm going away, maybe for a long time. That's what I know now I need to do. I thought it could be some other way, but right now it can't. When I can work things out, then I'll come home. But I've got to have some time and distance to do it. I'll call you when I can. I'll stay in touch."

"Joe, what the—"

"Shut up. I mean it. It's time right now. It's all going to change in the next few minutes. You're going to get your sorry ass back home and get a job. And I'm going on."

Terry had stopped trying to ask. He stared at Joe's face in a kind of horror, because he knew now that his brother was telling the truth, whatever it was. And he had begun to sense that they really might not see each other for some time. Because this was Joe who was talking, serious Joe who never screwed around and never made a mistake and never over-reacted to things. If Joe said he had to go away, then it was so.

Joe said, "I can't save you this time, Terry. That's what I'm telling you. That's what you have to believe." He took a wad of bills from his shirt pocket and set them on the bench. "Five hundred dollars," he said. "Listen to me: for about two fifty you can fly, seven day advance, to Detroit. Or, if you don't want to wait, catch a bus out. Then you'd be on the road for days, unreachable. That's not a bad idea. Anyway, right now, I want you to go straight from here and get a ticket of some kind. Later, if anyone asks—and they will ask, I promise—you tell them it was your money, you saved it. And you were waiting for me to come and get you, but I never showed. You called, but I'd left home. So you decided you'd come home on your own. You can fill in the rest, but you get the basic story. Understand?"

Joe looked at Terry until he nodded. Terry's mouth hung open a little, as it had done when he concentrated on something since he was little. Joe remembered him watching TV like that, the mouth hanging open, the lower lip drooping and sometimes a little spit hanging there. He felt himself tearing up, and closed his eyes against it. It was bad luck for people to see him crying. They'd remember that, a guy weeping in public. It would be just one more thing that might leave a trail.

Terry had not moved to touch the money, so Joe picked it up and stuck it in Terry's pocket, along with a ring of keys. "Those are to my apartment. It's paid through September. If you want it after that, you'll have to keep up the rent. Three fifty. The black Taurus out front on the street is mine. Drive it."

He hugged his brother, put his face into Terry's neck and squeezed hard. "I'll talk to you," he said. Then without looking at him or saying anything else, he stood up and walked away. They'd see each other again, soon enough, he thought. This just had to be worked out, the mistakes he'd made rectified. It wouldn't be much different than when he went off into the military—the letters from home, calls, the occasional visit. It just would be like that, he told himself, although he knew it might not be so.

When he got to the street, he risked a glance back. Terry was still sitting. Joe could see his face quite clearly. It had changed, he thought. Already, Terry had begun to look older.

Northgate was big as malls went, a place so various and huge, so oversupplied, you could live your entire life inside, where the corridors were high and wide enough to drive a semi tractor through, and where it looked clean and rich with its white stuccolike walls and polished floors.

At first, Joe just cruised, looking up at the potted trees and the skylights and the fountains, getting his bearings, until he noticed a Lenscrafters store advertising cheap eyeglasses WHILE U WAIT. He stepped in and asked about nonprescription contact lenses. Tinted. Had he had a recent eye exam? No. He'd have to have one to make sure he didn't need prescription lenses, and be fitted for the contacts. How long would that take? Half an hour for the exam and fitting, an hour or so while they made the contacts. He asked if they had dark brown. They didn't, but they had a color they called Walnut, which was a kind of hazel, which he said would be fine, if they could do the testing right away. They could, it turned out.

After the fitting, while he waited, he bought a map of the city along with some travel books and a notebook and pens, a pair of reading half-glasses, nylon straps with buckles, rolls of packing and clear tape, binoculars and an expensive assortment of tools, and a Supersonics sports bag in which to carry everything. He transferred some of the clothing and toiletries from his old bag and threw it away.

Next he found a hair stylist and had her cut the long, moppy hair off the top of his head—a businesslike cut, he'd said. He found a bathroom and shaved. He bought an outfit, a sport coat, short-sleeved white shirt, blue print tie, and slacks, and some cheap wire hangers.

By then it was time to pick up the contacts. It took a few minutes for the optometrist to teach him how to put them in, how to clean them so he avoided infection, all that. But when he walked back out into the mall, his eyes were no longer an unusual, memorable silver.

It was getting late. He mall surfed a little longer, thinking things through, but knowing now exactly what he was going to do. It would either work or it wouldn't, and too much thinking, he knew, could be worse than not enough. His coaches used to love to bark that jock truth at the new underclassmen: Think long, think wrong, boys.

Out in the vast mall parking lot, Joe walked briskly so he didn't appear to the cruising security guards to be casing. It wasn't long before he spotted what he needed: a big, white, mid-seventies Bonneville with a cavern for a trunk, a simple engine, peeling vinyl on the roof, and rust around the fenders, parked a little ways out and jammed in next to a pickup truck, which blocked a lot of view. The doors weren't even locked. Old cars like this were ridiculously easy: forty-five seconds to pound a screwdriver through the plastic around the steering column to break the lock, then to strip the right wires from under the dash and cross them, turning the engine over. And it only took that long because he was rusty.

It was rough, needed a tune-up and wasn't far from needing a new muffler, but it ran. A beater like this probably belonged to an employee, some stiff working for the minimum wage mopping or selling pretzels. If so, and the stiff was on day shift, the car wouldn't be found missing until five. If Joe was lucky, the stiff had come on in the afternoon and would work until the mall closed at nine. If it belonged to a shopper, it could be called in at any time. In any case, he only needed it for a few hours.

Farther south in the city again, near the bridge which crossed Lake Washington east to the city of Bellevue, Joe drove into a beautiful arboretum, exotically green and dark, past a sort of museum with people passing in and out, until he was alone among the trees. There, with a hammer and chisel, he punched out the trunk lock, then taped the trunk closed again with packing tape.

By six the city had settled some, taken on a dusky aura, and had grown noticeably cooler. The road he had been looking for in Bellevue turned out to be gravel, and passed east through a poor-looking section of small two-bedroom tract houses into a more open area of industrial warehouses, then past a wide and active landfill over which flocks of sea gulls circled, growing narrower until it ended at a sign announcing The Northwest Apostolic Church and Temple of Spiritual Rebirth.

It was a compound of sorts, with the church, or what passed for it—a low, flat-roofed brick building which didn't look much like anything holy except for the cross on its roof—on one side and a huge clapboard rooming house off to the other. The center of the compound was an open gravel lot which held several cars. A few more were parallel parked out along the road.

Joe parked the Bonneville behind these cars on the road, so that he had a shielded view of the rooming house. This way, if anyone wanted to ask questions, he could take off. But no one seemed to even notice him. The lenses had begun to irritate his eyes, so he popped them out into their little storage cases. He wouldn't need them yet, anyway.

Half an hour passed before a man came out of the house and got in one of the cars in the lot. As he started it, a girl stepped out and watched him. She was large and wore a shapeless ankle-length gray dress. Then, through an open window next to the door, another head appeared, only for a moment. But it was a long enough moment for Joe to catch with his binoculars the red-black hair, the oddly attractive face, the same white blouse she'd worn that morning. He slid down farther in his seat.

There was more activity now. People were leaving the house and walking toward the church.

When Kari came out, she was with two women, the large one and another, a black lady dressed in the same long gray skirt and white blouse that Kari wore. They walked together to the church, then a man in a sport coat followed, then another, larger group of women, all dressed in the same drab gray. It must be some kind of after-dinner service, Joe thought.

On the back of the church's card he'd taken from Kari's bag he printed, in block letters:

K:
I'm here. White Bonneville. Bring the case. Hurry.
Rick

Joe folded it over and taped it.

He walked along the road and onto the gravel, where a man standing at the church door noticed him.

"Hey," Joe said.

"What do you want?" the man said.

"A woman," Joe said. "Kari Downs. Dark hair. She just got here today."

"Yeah," the man said. "She's in there."

"Right. You new here?"

The man shrugged.

"My name's Rick." Joe waited. It could have been that this man and Rick were old buddies, but the man just looked at him, showing no signs of suspicion. He wore the same collarless white shirt and gray suit Rick had been wearing when he was arrested.

"From Alaska," Joe said.

"Oh, yeah?" the man said. "She's from up there, too, right? That's what people are saying."

"Can you get this to her?" Joe held out the card.

The man took it but said, "Why don't you just go in? Or wait in the house?"

"That's all right," said Joe. "She'll find me."

Forty minutes later, from the Bonneville, which he had backed a hundred yards farther down the road, he watched people begin to file out of the church. Some left in cars, but most headed into the house. When it grew quiet again, he thought he saw Kari run into the gravel lot, pause to look down the road, then into the house. It was nearly dusk, the sun lying low in the sky, but not quite low enough to hamper vision, which was too bad, but now it would just have to happen when it happened.

Joe started the car, then untaped and opened the trunk. He watched around the side of the trunk lid until he saw her trying to run with the heavy case bouncing against her leg and her bag over the other shoulder. She was alone. He stuck his head into the trunk.

"Rick?" she said. "What're you doing here? I thought—"

Joe stood up. For a moment neither of them moved. And then, when she turned to walk away, before she was able to run, he slipped his left arm around her neck and pulled her back toward him, back behind the car, out of view. She dropped the case and opened her mouth, but he slapped a piece of the packing tape over it, cutting off her scream.

"More you fight, the more it'll hurt," he said into her ear. He half lifted, half pushed her into the trunk. She kicked at him, catching him once in the mouth with her heel, and he felt his lip open and begin to bleed.

"You want to get beat?" he said. "Is that what you're used to?" Then, forcing her head down inside the trunk, he managed to tape her hands behind her and get the lid closed. He leaned on it to hold it shut against her kicking while he tied the rope, which he'd already threaded through the hole where the trunk lock used to be, and then around the bumper, to secure it.

He lifted her bag and the heavy case and was surprised again that she had managed to carry it as far as she did. Then he saw the large woman in the long gray dress standing in the road. He hadn't noticed her following Kari. She stared, hand over her mouth. Their eyes locked, then Joe turned and set the case and bag on the front seat.

As he did this the woman began to scream.

Joe got in, dropped the car into gear and U-turned in front of the screaming woman. Soon it would be dark. They could chase, but they wouldn't find him now.

The first thump startled him. He jumped and looked in the rearview mirror. Then he realized Kari was pounding on the trunk, as he knew she would. But she'd get tired of that. He'd drive for a while, let her wear herself out. She'd just better hope this old car wasn't sucking too many fumes.

13

IN LIGHT OF BEN'S DISCOVERY, SIMMONS AND THE SEATTLE FIELD DIVIsion had approved another night for Leanne. But now, having run nonstop for two days, she felt the trail of the man named Joe growing cold, and she knew Truong felt it, too. Late Thursday afternoon, he'd dropped her at her room and told her to get some rest, saying they'd pick it up in the morning. She ate a sandwich and grew sleepy thinking about how exposed to ridicule she'd left herself by coming over here, about how Guts would have shaken his head and said, again, "You're chasing after. You gotta wait. You gotta let it go before you find it."

In the next hunting season, after she'd learned to use the .30-.30, when she was eleven, her impatience blossomed.

One snow-brushed day late that fall, which had produced little game, as they hiked up a fresh, raw clearcut, she saw a set of new elk prints running up along the treeline.

She looked back at Guts, then put her head down before he could say anything and strode off up the slope.

The tracks led up over the clear-cut ridge and down into a draw. Leanne, who was skinny anyway, moved with no noise and soon noticed that Guts had stopped following her. This did not surprise her. She did not turn back, though, but followed the tracks to where they headed into a dense patch of skinny-trunked Aspens.

She dropped down farther into the draw, until she was below the Aspen grove, from which no tracks led. The elk was in there. So she climbed back up into it, knowing as soon as she was in the heavy brush that she was making too much noise now, stepping on branches and shoving saplings angrily aside when they swatted her cold cheeks. By the time she'd got herself into the dense middle of the stand, where the trees were so close together she could barely move, she'd begun to feel foolish.

Then, from up on the ridge, in the direction from which she'd come, she heard a rifle blast, then another. When she'd freed herself and climbed back out of the draw, she saw the elk, a royal bull with a rack that was taller than Leanne herself, lying near the crest of the ridge, blood smearing the snow around his muzzle.

Guts stood on the ridge, holding his rifle in his folded arms, waiting for her. She walked slowly up past the elk, taking the measure of it, a twelve hundred pound animal, inhaling its pungent odor. When she got to Guts, he only said, "The herds must'a come down early this year. Gonna be a hard winter."

"F'I hadn't gone in, you would'a never got him," she said.

"I was just waiting," he told her. "I thought I'd let the old bull go, but you chased him right back up."

"I wanted to get him."

"Old Elk didn't know he had Blister Foot after him. He never would'a stopped if he'd known that. Good thing though. You'd both be clear in Wyoming by now if he'd kept going."

"Shut up, Guts." She felt embarrassed but glad at the same time. He was right, she knew. It was stupid to go in like that. But, then, here was a bull elk, probably six hundred pounds of meat to give out because she'd done it. Was that a bad thing?

The phone woke her at seven-thirty that evening. She'd slept for an hour.

"It's Truong. I'm there in ten. Be ready." He hung up.

She was waiting in the parking lot when he bounced in and braked hard in front of her.

"So tell me while I've been napping you caught him."

"No," he said. "But I have news. No calls were made from the room at that motel. But we ran the pay phones in the vicinity—there were a dozen within a quarter-mile radius."

"*You* ran them?"

"Seattle PD, OK? One of them, from the phone right across the street, at eight this morning, was to the Black & White Cab Company. They have no record of any pick up at that motel today. But they had six pickups in or near the downtown logged in in the hour after that call. Two were single women. Three single men. One couple. Then we checked the destinations."

She waited for him to continue, then said, "Well?"

"One of the single women went to an address out in Bellevue." He hit his brakes hard and slid up to a stoplight and swore.

"What address? What's wrong with you?"

"I was putting a report together on all this, updating things. I had some notes a Seattle PD detective had faxed over. He was at the motel this morning, and yesterday he'd run a check in connection with the same case for the Kootenai County, Idaho, DA's office, at a church compound."

"Rick Damschroeder's church. The Northwest Apostolic something. Right. They wanted to make sure it was legit—"

"Same Bellevue address as the cab," Truong said.

"What? Oh—" said Leanne. "That's cozy."

"I called the DA over there right away, of course." Truong glanced at her. "Damschroeder was cut loose earlier today."

Leanne pounded the side of her head against the window.

"Nothing pointed to him," said Truong. "No physical evidence. No witness. The church corroborated his story. And so did all the stuff we found in the room today. DA had no way to charge him. Guy had a decent lawyer, too, to expedite things."

"But Damschroeder knew this girl after all."

"So, you were right. Looks like more than an armed robbery. When I told you, I figured you'd go through the roof."

"Inside, I'm tearing my hair out. Really, I am. I just don't want to embarrass myself in front of you. So who're we after now, Rick, Joe or this woman?"

"Whoever the hell we can find," Truong said.

"You going to tell me where we're going in such a hurry?"

"Out to the church. I thought we should talk to them."

The sores on his ankles had finally flared up again. He felt them burning and seeping, but did not look at them. Somewhere in the distance he heard sirens, whether for him or not he couldn't know. He drove north on I-5, back toward the great mall and its thousands of cars.

But it was going on eight o'clock, so the mall would be closing soon. It occurred to him that any car he stole would be reported in under an hour, and possibly sooner. Then he spotted a multiplex cinema with seven theaters and a full parking lot of its own. He pulled in over some speed bumps, as far to the rear as he could, to a dark corner, and watched the cars beginning to arrive for the later movies. These interested him, because they'd give him nearly two hours of lead time.

He wanted something newer looking this time, but not too new, so he wouldn't have to get around computers. He chose a dark red mideighties Chevy Cavalier, still an old GM product with that easy steering column, from which he'd watched two women hurry without locking the doors. Late for their movie. When traffic abated, he hopped in.

This time was different; this job had to be neat. First he needed to make a hole on top of the steering column above where the lock would be. Instead of breaking it, he used a heavy cutting blade to score the plastic first, so the hole punched out clean. After retrieving the punched out piece of plastic, he inserted a screwdriver and hit it with a hammer, breaking the lock. Then, using clear tape, he replaced the plastic piece. At a glance, it didn't catch the eye; it didn't have the usual ripped apart look of a stolen car.

Next he lay across the seat and stripped wires from under the dash and found the two he needed which, when touched together, turned the engine over. With one hand he pressed on the gas. The engine caught and sounded like it was in good shape.

He drove around to the Bonneville in the dark back corner.

The Chevy had an inside trunk release, so he wouldn't have to punch the lock and tie it.

Kari's eyes burned out at him. She slammed her head back into the floor of the trunk a few times, and then she lay still and cried some.

He said, "I was going to say, I guess north is as good a direction as any." And at this she settled down, nodded, grew peaceful even. He lifted her out and lay her in the Chevy's smaller trunk.

He said, "When we cross, if you make a sound, I'm fucked and you're hung up for a long time, if not worse. If you want to go north, keep quiet, and pray I'm not the one they pick out of the line for a random check."

She nodded again and closed her eyes as he closed the trunk.

He tore open the packaging on the new clothing he had bought, took the pins and cardboard out of the shirt, and laid the clothes out on the back seat. Then he drove, north again on 5.

More little surprises awaited Leanne at the Bellevue temple. As she and Truong pulled into the gravel lot, with the low church building at one end and a large house at the other, even though it was by now pretty much dark, with only sunset back-lighting and a few white yard lights, she had the sensation of knowing this place, as if she'd seen this silhouette before. Yet she knew she'd never been here. She didn't have time to ponder the thought for long, though, because there were two Bellevue PD squad cars, lights flashing, parked in front of the house and a small group of people gathered there. One of the cops broke off and intercepted them as they walked up.

"Federal Agent Truong," Mark said, holding up his badge. "This is Agent Red Feather."

"What're the feds doing here?" the cop asked.

"What're you doing here is the question."

The cop shook his head. "These goddamn Jesus freak weirdos. Twenty minutes ago we get a call that there's been a kidnapping. Dispatch says the woman is hysterical, she witnessed the whole thing. We get here, some bozo tells us it was all a mistake. Mistake? What the hell? I ask him where's the woman who called us. 'She's not here,' he says. No kidnapping. No witness. But what're we gonna do?"

"Nothing," Truong said. "Not a thing you can do."

"Freaks're probably high on something," said the cop. "So, how'd you hear about this already?"

Something had happened, that much was sure. Leanne left the cop to Truong and walked out on the grass of the front lawn, past the group of people talking to the other cops, telling what maybe happened, how the mistake could have been made. If something bad had really happened here, it would have left a mark somewhere, a trace. Bad always left a trace. The trick was in finding it.

As Leanne stood, still and quiet, listening, waiting, she caught, in her peripheral vision, a movement, a body moving away from the group surrounding the cop. Leanne followed, and saw that it was a young black woman, hunched over a little. When she passed beneath one of the yard lights, Leanne saw the shine off the tears on her face. The woman moved along the front of the house and into a side yard full of trees.

It was dark now. Leanne herself walked away from the house, circled around and came into the side yard from the opposite direction, so as not to be seen if anyone were watching from the house. She found the woman sitting on a lawn chair.

"Can you talk?" Leanne said, startling the woman, who sat up and wiped her face.

"No," she said. "I mean, there's nothing to say."

"Someone was grabbed here tonight. I know that's the truth. Someone else doesn't want anyone to know about it. A girl got taken. She's in great danger. The trail's fresh. I'd love to get on it and help her."

"I don't know," the girl said. "God."

"What's your name?"

"Lou Ann."

"Yeah? You won't believe this. Mine's Leanne."

The girl smiled.

"Lou Ann and Leanne. Sitting in the dark. Who called the police, hon?"

"Mother the Earth and Father the God," Lou Ann whispered, then looked around, judging the darkness, and added, "A girl named Sunny Carson."

"Sonny, like Sonny and Cher?"

"Sunny, like the sun."

"What's she look like?"

"About two hundred pounds. White girl."

"And she's gone now."

"Father help me, for I am lost."

"*I'll* help you," Leanne said. "I'll help your friend. Think of me as being sent right here by God Himself."

"But Father says . . ."

"Lou Ann, who's your father?"

"They took her," said Lou Ann.

"Your father?"

"To Sanctuary. Sunny. She's already on her way, now."

"Wait a minute," Leanne said. "Start with Sanctuary."

"The holiest place, where they all—look, I can't talk about this. Father bless me; Mother help me."

Leanne knew she'd seen this compound, now. She still couldn't place it, and didn't have time to think, but the name Sanctuary set off all her alarms.

"Back up, baby, quick. Sunny, who witnessed the kidnapping, has already been taken away to a place called Sanctuary."

"Sunny called the cops. You can't ever do that."

"So there actually was a kidnapping."

"Sunny got scared. She figured least the cops could find her fast. Sunny loves her; they've been together a long time. Sunny came down to get her."

"Who, Lou Ann?"

"Kari Downs."

"Spell."

"K-A-R-I. Downs like it sounds."

"What'd Sunny see?"

"I was inside when she ran in and picked up the phone. She was crying so hard. White car, she said. Old and big. License number SK then some numbers."

"You're sure? That's what she said?"

Lou Ann nodded. " 'Cause they're the same initials, see? SK. Sunny and Kari. Christ Lord. Father and Mother," she said. "It's all connected. Everything's connected. Father tells us that. Why don't we learn? Why don't I learn?" Lou Ann moaned and ground her knuckles into her teeth. "They were supposed to go up together." Lou Ann shook her head.

"Sunny and Kari?"

Lou Ann nodded.

"Where had Kari been?"

"Don't know."

"All right, baby. All right."

A heavy-set, crew-cut man in a white collarless shirt emerged from the shadows by the house. Leanne did this girl a favor. "Listen," she said, loudly. "I'm sick of this stone-wall. Someone had better talk soon or we'll just get subpoenas."

Lou Ann looked surprised.

"Get your subpoenas," the man said. "And leave us alone."

"Hey, *son,*" Leanne said. "You called us, remember?" She huffed and walked back to Truong, who was still chatting with the cop, grabbed his arm and said, "Let's go, and I mean now."

From the car he called in the partial plate and description.

"Let them hurry, please," Leanne said. These were not random happenings, she knew. They were all connected to one thing. She needed to find this girl, Kari Downs, and soon. Even more than Joe or Rick Damschroeder, maybe, the girl was a key. Leanne had caught a trace of that old familiar scent.

14

OUT ON THE PLAINS OF CENTRAL WASHINGTON, NEAR THE BRIDGE ON U.S. Highway 90 which crosses the Columbia River, just before ascending into the foothills of the Wenatchee Mountains of the Cascade Range, the man who had called himself Rick Damschroeder picked up a pay phone and dialed a number in Alaska.

"Me," he said, when Father answered.

"Stay out. Get lost. Feds are all over Seattle."

"What happened?"

"The bastard grabbed Kari."

"Who?"

"Who? I don't know who. The guy you set up. Who else would it be?"

"He grabbed her? He *took* her?"

"Yes." A sickening pause. "She had the case."

Rick watched as the clear glass of the phone booth glazed over red. He squeezed the phone so hard he expected the plastic to crush. He focused on his heart beating wildly, painfully in his chest and imagined the pleasure when he found Joe.

"Get safe for now," Father said. "Then call again. We'll regroup and plan. They can't just disappear. We'll find them."

"Oh, I'll find them," said Rick. He hung up and walked back to his car. Not too far up the road was the town of Ellensburg, where 90 crossed U.S. 97, a north/south route. Instead of continuing west, as he had planned, he'd turn south on 97. To Portland, he figured, where there would be no heat. From there he'd begin to make his way north.

And then he would figure a way to get the girl back. And to slit the throat of the man who stole her and the gold, who should have been killed right away, when the job was done.

At Bellingham, on the edge of the ocean, an hour north of Seattle, maybe twenty-five miles south of the Canadian border, Joe pulled off the highway and circled around until he found a dark spot beneath an overpass where he dressed in the shirt and slacks and tie, making sure the tie was straight, the hair neat.

When he leaned forward to change from white socks into dark, he saw his ankles in the dim interior light of the car, and he was shocked still for a moment. The sores were not only all open and bleeding, they'd begun to spread now, up his calves. The white socks he took off were soaked wet from the seepage. The ankles burned and itched worse now that he'd irritated them, but he could do nothing except bear it as he put on the dress socks.

He slipped on the sport coat, then, using the rearview mirror as a guide, managed, after a couple minutes, to get the tinted contacts back in his eyes.

Before leaving Seattle, he'd taken the registration from the glove box of the car and found a pay phone. He called information, first, and then the number of a woman named Mary McGuire, who owned the car. And heard an answering machine pick up and Mary's voice say, "Hi. I'm not here right now—" This was as good as it could be, Joe knew.

Now, in the shadow of the border, it was set, it was all done but the doing. It would either work or it wouldn't. He might as well try, he thought. If he went down, it wouldn't matter what happened, regardless of how they caught him, girl in the trunk or not. He was a murderer. What was kidnapping on top of that?

So, take a breath. And go.

Back in Seattle, somewhere along the series of canals and small lakes that connected Puget Sound with Lake Washington and bisected the city, in a brightly lighted strip-mall restaurant, Leanne sat across an orange Formica table from Mark Truong.

Although the decor looked like an average diner, this was a special restaurant, he'd told her, serving a type of southeast Asian food he bet she'd never heard of—Hmong. He explained about this tribe that had been nearly wiped out in the war, how many of the survivors had immigrated here, to the northwest U.S., because of the similarity of its terrain with that of their birthland.

When he told her he was part Hmong himself, by his mother, who'd smuggled him out of Vietnam through Laos and brought him here when he was a young teenager in the mid-sixties, and that old friends of hers owned this place, Leanne decided she didn't have the heart to remind him that there were probably more Hmong in Idaho and Montana than here, that she'd eaten in half a dozen of their establishments. She just smiled and nodded, to be nice.

Truong, after all, was just being nice to her, by bringing her here, showing her a little courtesy before shipping her back home. They were finished working together, she knew. The odds of finding a stolen car this night in Seattle, with only a color and two letters of the license plate to go by, were worse than slim. Her presence here, two days of expense and time lost, had proved to be a folly. She'd added nothing to the pursuit, no information, no insights, that Truong didn't have already. She'd just been baggage; she deserved whatever reprimands Simmons dished out.

She'd spoken with him before coming in here to eat, to bring him up on the late developments, and then told him about how the sight of the temple compound and the name Sanctuary had resonated with her, how he should really think about getting someone going tonight on the computer and archive files to see what came up, how she wanted to call the Field Division here in Seattle to see if anyone knew of this place, or had something on it. But Simmons only grunted a few times and told her not to call anyone, to wrap things up and make sure she had a flight booked out for tomorrow.

They'd just been served a dessert called by some, Truong said, Dog Eye Soup—translucent berries with dark irislike spots on one side, floating in cream—when Truong's cellular phone rang. He listened, then shook his head and covered the mouthpiece. "They got it," he said to Leanne. "White Pontiac Bonneville, mid-seventies. License SK 244."

"How could they?"

"Our boy Joe traded up for a newer model."

In the parking lot of a movie theater only ten minutes from the restaurant, they were met by Seattle cops, and two more young ladies, one with a tear-stained face.

"Mary McGuire," a cop said. "She and her friend stopped after work to see a flick. Let out just before ten. Found her car, '86 Chevy Cavalier, missing. We get here, look around, right, we notice this boat back there with a punched out trunk lock, the trunk lid's open a few inches. We can see in without touching it, so we shine some light, take a peek—spot some heavy-duty tape, a crowbar, wire hangers. Tools of the trade. Called in the plate. Came right up, with a tag to call you."

He'd crossed the Ambassador Bridge from Detroit into Windsor, Ontario, dozens of time, as a kid with the folks, then later when he and his buddies started hitting the strip joints that made Windsor such a popular destination for state-siders. Quite a few times, with three or four guys in an older-model car, some of them dressed in slop like army jackets or ripped denim, some with long hair, the customs agents would pull them over, make them all step out and run the dogs over the car. It was all about drugs and no one was stupid enough to try to smuggle. Beyond drugs, though, and handguns, he never thought the customs people cared much. They went by appearance. You looked good, or had a family, they'd only glance in, then nod you through.

Joe had thought for a while about the driver's license. He had no immediate way of getting a false one. Out-of-state would attract attention, especially because it was a different state than the license plates, but all he could do was wing it and hope that the name Joseph Michael Curtis had not been uncovered yet.

The lights were brilliant at the border, the agents frightening in their dark uniforms and hats. German Shepherds lurked somewhere, he was sure, as he pulled up behind a large flatbed truck. He felt his heart rate rise, his palms begin to sweat. He took deep breaths and willed himself to be calm, casual, so nothing would appear unordinary.

He slipped on the half-glasses and straightened his tie.

And then he was up.

"ID," the woman said. Bleached blond hair. Too much makeup. He handed her his license.

"You're from Detroit?"

"Yes, ma'am," Joe said.

"Whose car?"

"Belongs to a friend of mine, Mary McGuire." He offered her the registration, which she glanced at.

"Do you have a letter of permission?"

"No, ma'am, I'm afraid not. I have her phone number, if you need to call." Just so old Mary McGuire hadn't gotten bored and left the movies early.

The woman shook her head. Without saying anything else, she stood up and came out of her booth. Joe felt his pulse rocket as he watched her walk around behind the car and stop there, at the trunk, inside of which Kari lay curled and bound. The woman stood for a moment, jotting something down, then went back into the booth. Still without a word to Joe, she picked up a telephone and said something into it. Then he heard her reciting the license plate number of Mary McGuire's car.

When she hung up, she said to him, "What's your purpose in coming into British Columbia?"

"Job interview."

"How long are you planning to stay?"

"Couple days."

She looked at his license again. "You came all this way to look for work?" She seemed genuinely curious about this.

He nodded.

"Long way to come, isn't it?"

"You ever been to Detroit?"

She looked at him a moment and then cracked a half-grin and handed the license back. "Any handguns or drugs of any kind?"

"No, ma'am."

"Liquor?" As she asked, she glanced away, at the opposite wall of the booth where, Joe now noticed, a sketch had been pinned up—the newest U.S. FBI wanted sketch, distributed only this morning. A deep shock ran through him as he realized he was looking at his own face—not a perfect facsimile; he looked too thin, for one thing, and the nose wasn't quite right—but he knew it was supposed to be him.

The woman paused. Something in the wide-set eyes, Joe imagined, had caught her attention. But the eyes in the sketch were bleached, so pale as to have been drawn nearly pure white—not the nut brown eyes of this driver. Still she looked for several seconds at the drawing before turning back toward him again and studying his face.

"No. No liquor," said Joe. He smiled again and looked over the top of his glasses directly into her eyes. See how relaxed and confident? Nothing going on here.

"I'm waiting," the woman said. She looked at her phone and back at him again. "I might ask you to pull ahead up there." She pointed at a concrete tarmac next to a small building.

Joe knew that if he were stopped there, it would all be over. His crossing depended on their passing him straight through. Nothing could deviate from that scenario.

He looked out ahead into the blackness of Canada and thought for a moment of gunning it, of tearing off and seeing how far he could get before they caught up with him. But it was silly and he knew it. If he ran now, they'd have helicopters and searchers here within minutes. He needed a window of time. Not much, but something through which he could get lost.

But now the agent's phone was ringing. She snatched it up, listened, and hung up.

And when she looked at him again, he could see that her face had relaxed in some way. The license plate had cleared—Mary McGuire had not yet reported her car stolen. Perhaps if this agent had stopped to read the memo attached to the FBI sketch, and had seen that the fugitive went by the name "Joe," and this driver's name was Joseph, that and the similarity in the face might have been enough to make her pick up her phone again. Maybe. But she did not stop, in any case.

She smiled at the nice looking, nicely dressed man from Detroit who had borrowed his lady friend's car, and said, "You're really supposed to have a signed letter of permission if you're driving someone else's car. Next time, bring one."

"OK."

"Good luck."

"Thanks."

He drove.

It was black ahead, beyond the lights. Canada. And after Vancouver it would be even blacker, and bigger, and emptier and colder.

But here he was, out, away. When some distance had passed between the car and the booths at the border, when the bright lights were tiny in his rearview mirror, he allowed himself a smile, but did not whoop or pound the steering wheel in celebration. This was only one small unlikely victory in what would need to be an incredible chain of them.

Still, it was a victory. Oh, Canada. Oh, freedom.

Joe could not have seen, twenty minutes later, the phone ring again in the booth of the customs agent he'd just passed, nor as she received a verbal FBI/RCMP priority from her supervisor about a wine-red Cavalier, just reported stolen, just now typed into the system, registered to a Mary McGuire, driven by a suspect named Joe or some variation thereof, a sketch of whom had been circulated earlier. It was the consonance of Mary McGuire that clicked first for the agent. And then the names Joe, and Joseph. Joseph from Detroit. How many Josephs do you encounter on a slow night?

What about that plate she'd had run a little while ago? she asked. Did they still have the number?

They did. They checked. And it matched. It was Mary McGuire's plate. It had just gone into the system too late.

Then the agent remembered thinking that something in the sketch had resonated with the man's face. She remembered pausing for just a moment, to think, then passing it off. Joe did not see the agent look up and after him, now, as if he had just driven away, as she realized with a sickening shock what had happened, as her supervisor picked up his phone and telephoned the Royal Canadian Mounted Police, who in turn called the FBI and the Vancouver PD. And Joe was long out of sight of the lights of the border when the flashing lights of squad cars began to arrive, when an FBI chopper landed on the concrete tarmac on the U.S. side.

He could not see, would not have recognized if he did, the face of the darkish skinned, brown-haired woman named Leanne Red Feather, of the Salishan speaking tribes of Montana, of the Federal Bureau of Alcohol, Tobacco and Firearms, did not see her complex expression—not only of frustration, but of a kind of amusement, too, and even of triumph. To have come so close to him, this running man named Joe, across the expanse of Washington State, into and out of a city of millions, to have tracked him to within a few minutes at the border into Canada, for which she alone predicted he might head, was a feat of nearly impossible odds. She was not angry. She knew that she and Joseph Curtis would meet one day. She felt it.

Joe also could not know what a monumental storm had begun to brew around him. But he'd been a fugitive now for a couple days, and already he'd begun to learn to think like an animal, sniffing death at every turn.

As a result, when, well after midnight, a Mountie chopper spotlighted a wine-red Chevy Cavalier, Washington plates, hidden in a copse of trees and high grass alongside a dark road twenty miles inside the border and a mile off of Highway 99, when RCMP agents sped in and surrounded the car, flood lights burning, guns trained, they found it empty. In the trunk were a single nylon strap and some wadded-up strapping tape. In the front seat they found clothing, a cellophane wrapper, a dirty black T-shirt and a wet pair of tube socks.

Where, in this darkness, in the country, could the man and his hostage have gone? There was no place to steal a car, or catch a bus or a cab. It was another fifteen miles into the city of Vancouver. The mounties organized a sweep of the area. Hours later, when the sun rose on the west coast, they would figure out that the man and woman walked, or ran, along the pavement of the road for a half mile or so before cutting across a muddy field. The tracks led to another small dirt road, then along that and across another field to a busier surface road which fed back on to 99, where they could have thumbed into the city, or even walked a good part of the distance. The mounties will realize all of this, finally, with the morning, but by then of course the trail will have gone cold.

Up the Archipelago

15

ON FRIDAY, IN ARLINGTON, VIRGINIA, IN AN OVERHEATED, WEST-facing office in the Pentagon, an army lieutenant named Bliss sat down to brief Colonel Johnson Rozsa, head of the Domestic Intelligence and Threat Analysis Center (DITAC) under INSCOM, the Army Intelligence and Security Command. Lieutenant Bliss was a liaison from the Army Criminal Investigation Division Command, CRIDCOM, up at Fort George G. Meade in Maryland. CRIDCOM of course ran Army CID, the Criminal Investigation Division, which had a post on every army base in the world for its vast and largely invisible network of military investigators, many of whom worked plainclothes assignments off-base.

Bliss said, "I know it's a Friday and possibly this could wait. I tried reaching Major White—"

"Not at all, Lieutenant," Rozsa said.

It was not unusual for CID investigators to uncover situations of interest to DITAC. Rarely, though, in Rozsa's experience had such a situation actually turned out to be a direct threat to civilians or national security, and usually these were passed along through channels in non-priority written reports.

Bliss settled in, then said, "I'm sure you'll be getting a call from Simpson today." Simpson was the deputy head of CRIDCOM. "But I heard this and wanted you to know."

Rozsa nodded and smiled. Bliss said, "CID sent three men up into the Idaho panhandle this morning, sir, after it learned of a discovery by an ATF agent of an arms cache there."

"Army property?"

"Apparently. Much of it, anyway."

There had been for years increasing amounts of military surplus parts, small weaponry and other equipment finding its way on to the black market, into public gun shows, the hands of private gun dealers. Most often it stemmed from National Guard bases where inventory clerks, supply sergeants, and drivers would band together to ship supplies off the base and cover up the disappearance. CID, in conjunction with ATF and FBI agents, routinely set up sting operations at suspected leak sites to make purchases, identify the members of the theft ring, both inside and outside the military, and make arrests.

"When?"

"The agent made the find yesterday afternoon. For some reason, ATF notified directly the Fort Lewis Base Commander, Major General Ed Shaw. That's where the bulk of the material seems to have come from, or rather from the Yakima facility in south-central Washington. Shaw didn't notify his CID until today. They scrambled some men up there and briefed CRIDCOM immediately."

This was serious, then. The Yakima Firing Center, while it did serve as a National Guard base, was also a training ground for, and under the command of, Fort Lewis, in western Washington, a very large and complex regular army base.

"Shaw wanted to see if he could cover his ass," Rozsa said.

"Apparently so, sir."

"Apparently he couldn't. Well, shit, Bliss. What's this have to do with us?"

"Sir, Shaw ordered an immediate general inventory check to get an idea of what was missing. They worked through the night and found quite a list. It hasn't been cross-checked with the find in Idaho yet, you understand—"

"What's gone?"

"Mostly rifles, M-16s, as well as crates of ammunition and parts. Various small explosives, grenades."

Rozsa watched Bliss, waiting for it.

"Also, sir, they're missing ten M-60 machine guns, and about forty thousand 7.62-caliber rounds."

"Jesus."

"And, sir, I'm afraid that's the good news."

"What?"

"I said that's the good news, sir."

"I heard you, Bliss. What do you mean?"

"There also appear to be a dozen Stinger missiles gone as well. They were being stored at Yakima for training exercises."

"Good *Christ,*" Rozsa said and stood up from his desk. "Someone sold twelve of our Stingers into the goddamn black market? Are you telling me that?"

"Possibly. I mean we haven't heard yet if the missiles were found in Coeur d'Alene. But they're unaccounted for."

"Lieutenant—"

"Fort Lewis is re-running the inventory as we speak, sir."

"Bliss, listen to me. If we're missing Stingers, I want to know about it today. You understand? If they're up there in that warehouse, I want to know. If they're not up there, and they're not in the Yakima inventory, I'd better be the first to hear.

"The next question CID has to answer, the big one, is whose hands have they fallen into? If they're being sold offshore, which is probable, then it's no concern of this office. You understand. But if they're in the possession of someone who might use them here, I'll have to issue an immediate Level Three p.r." Colonel Rozsa's superior was the head of INSCOM, Brigadier General Thomas Parkins. Among those Parkins reported to was the Chief of Staff of the Army, General Hargrave, who in turn answered to the Secretary of the Army, who answered of course to a suit, the Secretary of Defense. Level Three priority reports from DITAC, which red-flagged possible threats to the military or civilian populations or property on U.S. soil, moved rapidly up that command chain.

Lieutenant Bliss stood to salute and leave. But Rozsa remained seated for a moment and looked up at him, then said, "Impress upon your people, son, although I'm sure they know it, what havoc just one of those Stingers could bring to bear."

At the same hour, across the Potomac from the Pentagon, another meeting was taking place, this inside the Justice Department building, which took up the entire trapezoidal block bordered by 9th and 10th streets and Constitution and Pennsylvania avenues, in the wood-panelled office of the Attorney General of the United States. It was nothing unusual—the biweekly briefing between the AG and her special troubleshooter, the former chief U.S. attorney from the Miami office, who'd known the AG for some years.

This had been a quiet week, generally, and the special troubleshooter ran through his agenda quickly until there was one item left, a nonitem, really, but one which, because of new protocols the AG had established, had to be mentioned. It was a summary of the shooting death of a suspected arms dealer who had been under active ATF surveillance in Coeur d'Alene, Idaho. The reason it came up at all was because it contained two elements: ATF and shooting. Since the debacle at Waco, Texas, two and a half years earlier, which had been the baptism by fire of the current administration, especially those in Justice, the AG had insisted that any "situations" involving ATF agents—that meant any incidents other than routine investigations—be evaluated directly by Justice. The Treasury Secretary had complied, ordering ATF to forward copies of any such reports via E-mail to the special troubleshooter's office.

In this case, however, the special troubleshooter pointed out, the

ATF agent involved had not done the shooting, nor was she even present at the time. While the agent was investigating a man with regard to illegal arms sales, the man got shot to death in a store robbery, apparently as a bystander. The ATF agent had only shown up on the scene after the fact.

"What about the arms?" the AG asked.

The troubleshooter shrugged. "None found, that we've heard."

The AG nodded, thus ending the meeting.

Amon Ka'atchii felt the dark forces closing in on him. He'd been feeling it for some time, ever since, nine months earlier, a helicopter had appeared over the compound and hovered there for ten minutes while someone in the open doorway shot rolls of film as the women screamed and ran and the men loaded rifles and prepared to fire into the sky on Amon's command. He did not give it. Rifles were not any good against choppers and surveillance planes. They'd have brought down nothing but retribution.

But, just like that, these invaders thought they could violate anyone's privacy. The chopper had been unmarked; no one had been able to find out who it was, whether Treasury or FBI or even some nongovernment enemies. Father had many. Any number of them could afford choppers and surveillance equipment.

The appearance of the chopper marked the end of a brief period of peace for the Family, and Father had known that very day what he had to do. Although it was midwinter, he began shopping for land the following week and by June, three months ago, had found what he was looking for: an extremely remote two hundred and fifty acres, bounded on either side by natural walls and with narrow ocean access to the south, a federal wildlife refuge to the north and undeveloped native land to either side. It was owned by the Koniag Corporation, one of the tribal companies formed by the original people of Alaska, the native Indians and Eskimos, and granted huge tracts of wilderness by the government. Many criticized the natives for selling some of this land, but, they argued, they needed to make money, too. After flying out with Amon to look at the rocky isolation of the place, Deacon had struck a deal with a Koniag lawyer for the land and fishing rights in certain tribally controlled waters, in exchange for a percentage of income and half a million dollars—40 percent up front in cash and the rest paid with interest over ten years. This was a lot of money to pay so soon after the previous move, especially for remote, inaccessible land, but there had been no choice.

Father lay on his back in the woods beyond the Kenai compound, within listening distance of the running river. It was a good river, big enough to support a decent salmon run in the spring and summer, but small enough not to be too well-known. The Family had fished successfully each summer and had rarely seen outsiders. Father listened to it talking, saying its good-byes.

Deacon had called two days ago with news: good about the arms, which were where Bill Cooper had said they'd be, in a barn on a deserted piece of property near the lake. The men and truck were now already over the border and skirting westward, across lower British Columbia. Soon they'd cut north toward Prince Rupert. The *Maribel S.,* their purse seiner, which left Homer a week ago, had arrived this morning in Ketchikan.

But when Deacon had told about Rick and the three dead men in Coeur d'Alene, Father felt himself going blind with the pressure inside his skull.

"It's under control," Deacon had said. "Rick covered himself. We retained an attorney, for insurance, who thinks he'll be out in a day or two. The girl has the gold, all of it. She's headed for Bellevue." That calmed Father down, some.

Until yesterday, when someone from the Bellevue outpost, a preacher named Karsten had called and told Father Amon of the kidnapping of the girl and her package, of the visit from the authorities, of news stories of a chase to the border, of the escape of the kidnapper and his cargo.

Now, lying among the green alders, which would soon be shedding, listening to the water, watching the sapphire sky overhead, Father felt himself open to the world as he had done before, felt himself merging with the Earth, his body decomposing into its basic elements, which filtered into the dirt and the water, which evaporated into the air. He ceased to see and hear, felt only the dissolution and merging of himself with the One.

He was One. He was Amon Ka'atchii.

He did not know how long he remained thus before his cells rushed back toward each other and reformed into organs and skin and blood and hair, whooshing into the vacuum their absence created. The reformation was as painful as it was disconcerting, but Amon knew, now, what was required. There was no time left, and he would have to begin instructing the Family today.

On his way back into the camp, he stopped for a moment to watch some of the children, who'd organized a rough game of softball in the central dirt yard. He smiled as one boy—one of his boys, Daniel he thought was the name—smacked a long, booming hit that rolled clear to the front gate of the compound. Good, strong children they were raising here.

He locked himself in his cabin, and dialed a motel in Kenai. "Roy," he said, when the man answered, "this is Father Amon. We have a problem." Father described what had happened, then said, "The sooner we get her back, the sooner you can have her. Also, there's a package worth a lot to me. You deliver that, too, it's another ten grand."

Roy Jameson said, "They got across?"

"It seems so."

"There must be roadblocks. If no one's picked them up, they gotta be in the city. Anyone know who this guy is?"

"I haven't heard that."

"They'll ID him soon enough. I know a Seattle cop who can get me whatever dope they have. I can get around Vancouver, but I'm going to have to hire leg men. It'll be expensive. Some of it I can bill back to her family, you know—"

"Anything, Roy," said Father. "Just please find her before anyone else does."

16

FRIDAY MORNING, LEANNE PACKED HER SUITCASE AND STUFFED IN THE FEW extra things she'd bought in Seattle: a pair of panties and hose, a white cotton blouse, a tourist T-shirt for Calvin. She was booked on a flight back to Boise that left after noon, three hours from now. She'd been briefed in detail the night before by Ben on the findings at Lake Pend Oreille. From Boise, she hoped Simmons would let her go back north to join Ben in shaking down whomever they could turn up that had had ties to Big Bill, to find some trace of a lead on who had bought arms, and what they'd used to transport them, and where they were headed. But Leanne doubted whether any of Bill's functionaries they could find would know much. As for the man, Joe, and Kari Downs, they were in Canada now, subject to pursuit by the Royal Canadian

Mounted Police. If they crossed back into the states, then the FBI and federal marshals would make chase. But she knew the FBI and the RCMP were working together on this, trading intelligence at least. Mark Truong had flown to Vancouver earlier that morning to give brief and to help sift and interpret leads.

Although the sky was growing cloudy, the weird heat had yet to break. From her air-conditioned room, she watched businessmen loosen ties and sling jackets over their shoulders as they walked. It came to her again that she'd heard somewhere of the Temple of Spiritual Rebirth, that it had some meaning to her.

In the distance to the east, through the haze that overhung the city, the green foothills of the Cascades rose up. Leanne could not quite see south far enough to make out Mt. Ranier's massiveness, but she'd get a good look from the plane, she knew. She liked that view, heading east, first of Ranier and then of the caved-in crown of Mt. St. Helens.

She lifted the phone and called her apartment, hoping again that Calvin would answer, knowing, as she knew every fifteen minutes when she called, that he wouldn't, that he had bolted in fear for his life, and had dug his hole, from which she had thought he'd begun to climb, all that much deeper.

The cab was due before eleven. She didn't want to do anything until then, or think, so she turned on the television. She hadn't seen daytime TV in so many years, it felt exotic to her. Phil Donahue was talking with a woman who'd been implanted with her brother's infertile wife's sister's egg, fertilized by her brother. Leanne rubbed her eyes with one hand and her belly with the other, and was rising to turn the set off when the phone rang.

God, let it be Calvin, she prayed. It was Simmons. "Pat yourself on the back, smart ass," he said, by way of a greeting. "I'd do it but I'm not going to see you for another couple days."

"Ed," she said. "Give me a clue here. I'm in a frightening mood."

"Don't be. You pulled one out, hit a home run. Two, really."

"What? Come on." She could picture him in his glass office, wedged in behind his desk so tightly it would take him minutes to pry himself loose. She'd wondered what would happen in a fire, if fat Ed would make it out in time. She thought of all the ways she knew how to set one and make it look like an accidental burn. Poor fat fucking Ed, may he rest in peace.

"The Northwest Apostolic Church and Temple of Spiritual Rebirth," he said. "All your nonsense about how it looked familiar to you. And how the name Sanctuary set off vibes. You were right. You must've seen pictures of the Bellevue compound somewhere. It was the first church of Fred Haines after he became Amon. Sanctuary is what Haines calls his main compound. That place in Bellevue was the first Sanctuary. That's where the Amonites started, Leanne, before they left for Idaho, before we got involved with them. Seems Haines still has a finger in there now. There's some affiliation. And old Fred, you may remember, was a kind of associate of your buddy Big Bill."

She sat back down on the bed, holding the phone to her face with both hands. "I remember," she said.

"Fred had his own big stash, too," Simmons said. But he did not need to tell Leanne the story. Unlike Simmons, she'd been there when they raided the Idaho Sanctuary and recovered all those arms, two fifty-caliber machine guns, grenades, enough explosive to bring down a skyscraper. She waited until the Special Response Team boys—Ben among them—in their fatigues and heavy bulletproof armor had secured the buildings, before she went in and found that Fred himself had skipped days before with some of his women, that the other men had gone too, north, to some land Fred had bought in Alaska, that Fred had already sold part of the Idaho land to some other isolationist group up there. Only some women and children were left in the camp. They were detained but later released for lack of any specific charges. Leanne had advocated going north right then and finding the new camp, but since they got what they were after, the weapons, higher-ups said let it go. They'd establish new surveillance eventually in Alaska.

"So these people I was chasing, Kari and Joe," she said, "are Amonites. And Rick, too. He lied about not knowing the girl. She was probably with them the whole time." Alaska. Big Bill. It all made fabulous sense that Fred Haines was behind it, but she never would have put it together.

"Still chasing," Simmons said. "The Canucks are crying over the fact that not only a murderer and kidnapper, but maybe some arms as well, have crossed the border. A Ryder panel truck, rented three days ago in Coeur d'Alene, was found abandoned alongside Highway 3 in BC. Rented on stolen cards. Wiped clean."

"What arms, exactly?"

"Army's still running inventory at the barn up north. But the way this has drawn down, with Haines involved, I'm telling 'em it doesn't look good, that you were right—there's some firepower floating around out there. Don't know what, yet, but we think Kari Downs or your man, Joseph Curtis, might."

"What did you just say?"

"Oh, yeah," said Simmons. "FBI nailed down his ID this morning, based on the customs agent's statement and the prints. Curtis is an ex-con, ex-military head case from Detroit. Fits. His family said he was driving to Seattle to help move his brother back home. They don't know what could have happened. The brother's gone, too. Woman he lived with said he moved out yesterday. FBI hasn't found him yet.

"Anyway, the RCMP is convinced Curtis and the woman are in metro Vancouver. Speed's the issue, they say. They've asked for help, someone with feel for the situation, background on the mentality, Fred's people. You're booked on a one-fourteen to Vancouver, Air Canada. Be there. They said they could put you up in the barracks if you didn't mind. I said you did. If they want you, they can treat. You're in the Hyatt, downtown. Nice, I hear."

"Thank you, Ed."

"No, I owe you one. For uncovering Bill Cooper's newly stocked toy box, the Army's kissing our ass right now. I was on with our handlers in D.C. this morning. They're giddy. You're probably looking at a citation. Meanwhile, don't get cocky. Division's messengering you over as much background dope as they have on Haines and the Family, so you can refresh."

What was funny, Leanne thought, was that she remembered the time of that raid on the Idaho Sanctuary, three years earlier, with a kind of fondness. It had been July of '92, in the year before Waco, so ATF agents were still operating with great autonomy—without politicians and reporters breathing down their necks at every step. And Leanne and Ben were at the apex of their partnership, best buddies, best back-ups, best sounding-boards. Calvin hadn't gotten into his big trouble yet, either. Even the Amonites and their peer groups had seemed innocuous, in retrospect, little more than mountain people selling sawed-off shotguns.

Randy Weaver's wife would not be shot to death for another month. It would be six months still before Ben kissed Leanne, before the stresses of that new relationship and her crumbling marriage and Waco would turn them into mere colleagues again, who nodded politely to each other when they came into the office each morning, before the catastrophic raid on Koresh and his .50-caliber gun. It would be two and a half years before some homegrown fascists found the gumption to blow up a federal building.

Now, here they were, the country on constant terrorist alert, the ATF fighting for survival, Leanne divorced, Ben a married father, Calvin running for his life, and the Amonites involved in multiple murders and probably the theft of military arms. Amazing how a brief three years could complicate everything so profoundly.

When someone knocked a little later, Leanne assumed it was the messenger, so she was doubly shocked when she opened the door.

"Cal," she said.

"Hey, big sis." He tried to smile when he stepped in and closed the door behind him. "Ben told me where you were."

She only nodded at him. She was careful to rein in her urge to chastise or lecture or pump for information. She sat down in the desk chair. When he sat across from her on the bed, she said, "What do they want?"

"I only lost ten grand," he said. "But they wanted fifteen before I went in. Now it's twenty-three plus an extra twelve for the douche bag I clocked. Where am I gonna get thirty-five Gs?"

"They don't want your money, Cal."

"They do. They said thirty-five will stop it. Or I can pay the nut every week. Three per cent."

"You think they think you can get thirty-five grand? Or, what, a grand a week?"

He sat forward on the couch and held his head in his hands.

"They don't want your money anymore."

"What do they want?"

"Didn't they tell you? What's the alternative?"

"They didn't say, exactly."

"How well do you know these people? What do they do?"

"I don't—" He stopped, his breath caught, then he said, "One guy in Denver, they cut part of his leg off. From the knee down. They used a chain saw, Lee—"

He started to cry then, painful reluctant sobs that ripped themselves upward and out of him. She hadn't heard him cry, and did not think he had cried, since he was a little boy.

When he was thirteen, he'd come home drunk and beat her up. Wolf Guts had heard about it, had looked at Leanne's cuts, and came over and kicked in the door of their mother's home. Calvin was sitting at the table, eating dry cereal, but he knew immediately what was happening and broke for the back door as Guts came in the front. But Guts, though he was fifty years older and eighty pounds heavier, caught Calvin in six steps, grabbed him by his long hair and twisted his head down to the ground. He took a huge bladed knife from his belt and held it against Calvin's face.

"Before anything," Guts said, "understand that I'll kill you if a time comes when it is necessary. Do you believe me?"

"Yes," Calvin whispered.

"For now, you have to pay a punishment for what you did to your sister. She's your blood, and she did nothing to you. You hit her out of plain meanness. I gotta take that out of you."

Guts was pressing the point of the knife into Calvin's face below an eye, hard enough that the point had cut him and blood was running up into this eye, burning him. But Calvin did not cry out or whimper or say anything. He held that eye closed tightly, but the other open so he could see Guts kneeling above him.

"Shave your hair off," Guts said.

"What?"

"Your hair. Shave it off. All of it, until you're bald as a rock." Calvin loved his hair. Unlike Leanne, who'd inherited the Anglo-brown of her mother, Calvin's hair was glossy black and straight and thick, and he wore it down his back.

"Fuck yourself," Calvin said. The knife flicked, and the point beneath his eye became a gash half an inch long. Blood poured out and into the eye. Still he did not cry out.

"Hair grows back, fool," Guts said.

Leanne, who was watching with fascination from the doorway, said, "That's enough." But Guts did not acknowledge her. And finally, when the blood burning in his eye was too much to take, Calvin agreed. Guts stayed until the head was bald.

But even then Calvin did not cry a tear. He stood baldly before the people, walked to the store in Arlee and back, took the taunts of the boys and the snickers of the girls without so much as a sideways glance.

Later, Guts told her she should be proud of Calvin for how he handled himself that day. He had some honor, after all. But now here he sat, sobbing, choking, on her bed.

"Cal," she said. "I can help you."

"You got the money?"

"Even if I did I wouldn't pay them. It's not what they want. But these are the kinds of people I go after every day. Don't you know that? Don't you think you could have come to me?"

"It's my fight," he said.

"You want your leg gone? Or worse?"

She had only an hour now before she had to leave for the airport, and she felt that if she left him here or sent him home, it would go bad before she got back. He'd come for her help, finally. And who knew who'd followed him, who was watching?

Then she knew what to do. She picked up the phone and dialed the 800 number of Air Canada.

17

IN PORTLAND ON FRIDAY, RICK AGULLANA, AKA RICK DAMSCHROEDER, looked up an old girlfriend of his named Angie Morales, and was surprised to find her living alone in a pricey apartment in a nice, new eight-unit building, on a wide paved street of a dozen other identical buildings in one of the better sections of that city. Rick knew she was here in town, and had found her name easily enough, but in addition to the digs, there was something else about her he didn't know, so after the surprise of the nice neighborhood and building, he had another one waiting. When she opened the door for him his eyes popped open.

Angie had once been a fully-clothed waitress in a topless bar in LA, which is where Rick met her, and where they started hanging around.

Not long after Rick left there, Angie met a guy and fell in love and moved north, too, to Oregon. The guy had since moved along, but she'd liked this midsized city of green lushness a lot better than smoggy, hot LA, so she stayed. And in time she'd waitressed enough to save a couple extra grand for breast implants, which in turn led to her becoming a dancer herself, and a very popular one, so that she found the money and tips to be surprisingly good, good enough for her to keep this nice place and a Mustang convertible in the car park downstairs and to even take the occasional trip now and then.

"Angie, Angie," he said, staring at her double-Ds. "What the hell happened to you."

"What're you doin' here, Rick," she said. He was trouble all the way, she knew, even if she had liked him once and missed him when he was gone. He was trouble and he wasn't here because he had some burning desire to see her.

"I need to use your phone," he said.

"My phone? You go to all the trouble of finding me so you can use my phone?"

"And maybe to crash."

"Right."

"Come on, Ang. I'm kind of in a tight spot, here."

"What else are you gonna want?"

He shrugged and pushed past her into the apartment. "I don't know. Man, you are looking well and doing well." He glanced around the place and nodded his approval before opening the refrigerator and grabbing a beer, then sitting down in front of the phone in the living room.

He dialed, and when he heard the phone picked up, but no voice, said, "I'm in Portland."

"We think they're in Vancouver."

"Yeah? How—"

"There's someone else on it."

"Is this someone else going to take care of things?"

"He just finds them."

"So I better get up there."

"Quickly but carefully. Don't make any scenes on the way up. Try not to expose yourself."

Rick hung up and was about to say, "Angie, baby, how'd you like to go for a drive," when a key slid into the door lock and a man let himself in. He was thirty maybe, geeky looking, short and a little heavy. He wore tinted glasses and his brown, kinky hair needed to be trimmed around the sides. He wore a sport coat and an open-collared shirt with the points of the collar outside the collar of the jacket, in true dork fashion.

"Who are you?" he said when he saw Rick.

"That's my line," said Rick.

"Rick, this is Gerard."

"Gerard?"

"My boyfriend."

"Boyfriend?"

"Gerard, this is Rick. We been friends for a long time. He was just passing through town and stopped by."

"Good," Gerard said. "So now you stopped. Be seeing you."

Rick nodded and smiled and leaned back so he could put his feet up on the table. "Sit down, Jerry. You too, Ang. We got things to talk about, here. Like I said, I'm in a little bind."

Gerard made it three quick steps across the living room toward Rick before Rick had drawn the .38 revolver he'd picked up in a strictly cash, strictly off-the-books deal in central Oregon, on his way over. The cash he had picked up in a strictly too-easy, unarmed knock-off of a self-serve gas station just before he crossed the Washington-Oregon line. He cocked the pistol and aimed at one of Gerard's eyes.

"Keep coming."

Gerard stopped.

"Now sit the fuck down," said Rick.

"Rick," said Angie. "You never change."

"No, but you sure did. And I have to say, Ang, I like it. I like it an awful lot."

That night, Roy Jameson sat strapped into his seat on a turbulent Alaska Air Anchorage-to-Seattle flight, the first step in his renewed search for Kari Downs. There was still enough light from over the Pacific for him to make out, to the east, a series of sharply peaked mountains extending above the blanket of cloud cover below. These must be somewhere along the eastern panhandle, around Juneau maybe, he thought, although his sense of the geography of this area was sketchy.

He pulled out a photo of Kari Downs, which Amon had given him, a much more recent one than her family could provide, considering they hadn't seen her in over four years, and studied it again. She looked good. Intelligent face, bright eyes. Someone he wouldn't have minded getting to know, and there weren't many people he felt that way about.

Friday evening, Colonel Rozsa received a call at his home from Lieutenant Bliss, who was working late.

"Sir," the lieutenant said. "Fort Lewis reports that they've recovered almost everything."

"Almost," Rozsa said.

There was a long pause between them, and Rozsa could hear Bliss shuffling papers on his desk. Then Bliss said, "According to their inventory records, four M-60s and three ten-count crates of M-16s are still outstanding."

"Outstanding."

"Unaccounted for."

"And the Stingers?"

"They recovered nine of the twelve in Coeur d'Alene."

"So someone has three missiles. Each one capable of dropping an airliner."

"Yes, sir."

"I have to know who has them. You'll tell your people that's an absolute priority?"

"Yes, sir."

"All right," Rosza said. "I have to talk to General Parkins about this, but I'll hold off on any written reports for another day. Hopefully the situation will clarify."

◇

In the morning, a working Saturday, after a brief but intensely pleasant exchange of elevator greetings with the AG, the special troubleshooter would find himself thinking about that dead suspected arms dealer in Idaho, enough to make him call up the file on his screen. To his mild surprise, he would see that the file had expanded during the night. First, arms had been found after all, and serious arms, guns and missiles, many of them stolen from the Army's Yakima Firing Center, some possibly still missing. Second, the suspected murderer, after pursuit by both the ATF and FBI, had apparently fled with a hostage across the western Canadian border. The troubleshooter chuckled at the drama. It didn't concern Justice, really. After all, the barn-warehouse had been secured. Now it was just a manhunt in Canada. But he drew up a short memo to the AG anyway, just in case it turned into something.

The special troubleshooter was a thorough man, and he hated leaving himself exposed to any sort of oversight.

18

After abandoning Mary McGuire's car, they had jogged and walked, Joe carrying his pack and the heavy case, Kari now unbound. She didn't complain, and he admired that, jogging in the dark in a strange country with her kidnapper, not talking at all but to say she had to stop somewhere to relieve herself. He was going to tell her to just go in the grass, but they saw the lights from a service station. They needed to get away from these open fields, anyway.

"Don't think about running," he told her.

"Where would I go?" she asked.

He'd planned on stealing another car and driving north, but just in the time she was in the ladies' room two police cruisers sped by. Then a large truck from a landscaping firm pulled in for gas. The back end was enclosed with rubber webbing instead of doors. When Kari came out, she watched with Joe until the truck driver went in to pay. Joe led her around behind the truck, out of sight of the register, and undid a corner of the webbing so they could crawl in.

The truck went north on 99, toward the city. After some warehouses and a long stretch of expensive-looking neighborhoods, where 99 became a two-lane, surface street, they passed into a congested area of storefronts and apartments buildings. At a red light, they slipped out.

"What are you going to do with me?" she asked him.

He didn't answer.

She said, "You don't have any idea."

They walked west on a busy cross street called Broadway until they saw a Traveller's Econo-Lodge. Joe had Kari register. It was that risk, or the one of exposing his face. He didn't think she wanted to get picked up any more than he did.

He still had the tools he'd bought in Seattle. In the room, with a hammer and screwdriver, he pounded off the hinges of the case. He expected cash first, but realized the case was too heavy for just money, so documents, maybe, he thought, or photographs. But he was not prepared for the dull shine of gold bullion.

There were two Englehard bricks, one hundred ounces each, wrapped in blue tissue paper, and boxes of rubber-banded stacks of coins, one ounce Maple Leafs mostly, with some Krugerrands and a few American Eagles mixed in as well. Joe counted a hundred and seventy coins.

When Kari was finished eating, he told her to lay down on her back on the room's only bed. He straddled her as he fitted the straps around her wrists again, his knees pressing on the sides of her rib cage.

"You're not keeping me like this," she said.

"You'll run," he said.

"No, I won't." When he didn't respond, she said, "Don't—listen, Joe." He could feel her beneath him, moving, pressing up against him. In a new voice she said, "Tell me something. When you tie a woman down like this, to a bed, don't you want to—don't you feel power, that man thing? Don't you have the urge, sitting up on top of her?"

"What?"

"She's helpless. You're poisoned with anger, fury. You hate her for what she's done to you. At the same time she's not bad looking . . . You could do anything you wanted."

"Shut up."

"And what if she'd let you? All I mean is, I think there's a way to work something out here." She was moving more now, up and down, trying to rub her body against his.

And she was right—his face burned. He felt his dick pressing down against her belly as he strapped her hands, one to each corner of the bed frame, his belly against her breasts.

"I just want to know if you want me."

He swallowed and did not answer.

She laughed up at him, her breath warm and sweet-smelling until he pressed a piece of strapping tape across her mouth.

He slept on the floor. During the night he found himself waking every hour or hour and a half. Each time he got up and leaned over her, checking to make sure her nasal passages were clear, that her breathing hadn't grown labored. He checked the straps, too, in case they'd begun to cut into her skin. But she slept soundly from what he could tell, with little movement or distress. He did not think he could ever have slept tied to a bed with his mouth taped shut.

Saturday morning he allowed her up for a half an hour of walking around the room, cleaning up in the bathroom and so forth. Then he ordered her back onto the bed. She cried this time, but he felt little mercy.

"I don't mean to hurt you," he said. "But you understand."

"Until when?" she said. "How long?"

"We'll see," he said, and taped her mouth.

She sniffed and blinked, which made a couple of tears run out the corners of her eyes.

It was cooler here than in Seattle, but still unusually warm, maybe in the low eighties. He turned the air conditioner on low. "I'll try to hurry." He picked up the day pack, into which he'd transferred the gold, and grunted at its weight. He thought of her carrying it, wordlessly, through Seattle.

Now she was lying with her eyes closed, apparently waiting for him to leave so she could meditate or pray or whatever she did to take herself away. Then, as he left, she looked at him, her eyes wide open and bright and as dazzling as they were when he'd first seen her, back in Montana. After she'd left him, in Seattle, he'd found that he could picture only her eyes. And today, as he worked this new city, he knew it would be the same.

It was just after 9 A.M. He hung the DO NOT DISTURB sign on the door when he left.

From a city map, he figured out that they were on the south side of an inlet called False Creek, just across from the downtown proper, which was set apart from the rest of the city on a peninsula. So he called a cab from a pay phone and had it take him in, to an address he'd copied from the Yellow Pages, under "Gold, Silver and Platinum Buyers and Sellers." He sold two thousand Canadian dollars worth of Maple Leafs, then, at a second nearby store, two thousand more. From the rate he got, he calculated that all the gold was worth almost $200,000 Canadian, about $145,000 U.S. In addition, he still had a thousand or so dollars left, between his take and Kari's, from the store in Idaho.

In spite of how clean and organized this city seemed, he figured that it must be like other cities in the ways that mattered to him now. So after studying the map again and asking a few questions, he made his way east out of the downtown, through an old section of the city called Gastown, toward Vancouver's Chinatown, and passed eventually through some blocks of boarded up storefronts and flophouse hotels, with men standing on every available corner, throwing out glances which told exactly what they were selling.

Joe stopped at the curb. A man slid out to him from under the awning of a closed-up theater. "You looking for, man? Little smoke, hey?"

"I need a good ID," Joe said.

"A what?"

"ID. Driver's license."

"Shit," the man said. Joe handed him a twenty. It would take three more conversations and more twenties, but Joe ended up on a certain tucked-away block of sleaze theaters and porn shops on the north side of Chinatown, close enough to the waterfront that, between buildings, he caught glimpses of the docks and ships there. He could smell the ocean. A few shop windows, in addition to advertising RED HOT CHICKS, hawked IDs. He began at one end of the street and worked his way up, until he found what he was looking for, in the fifth store he tried.

In the dark, behind a cracked linoleum counter which held a glass case of dildos, sat an Oriental kid, seventeen maybe, watching a tiny black-and-white television.

"Sort of IDs you have?" Joe said.

Without looking away from the screen, the kid slid a sample across the counter. As Joe had expected, it was a cheap-looking fake, a grainy blank run through a dot-matrix printer, with a dusky picture glued on, designed only to get juvies into dark nightclubs where no one really cared as long as they had an excuse.

"What if I want quality, something that looks real?"

The kid shrugged until Joe set two twenties on the counter. The kid glanced up at Joe, then at the bills, slipped them into his pocket and pressed a buzzer on the edge of the counter. After a minute, an old, bearded man shuffled out through a curtain behind the counter.

"I need two good IDs," Joe told him. "Canadian driver's licenses. Professional quality."

"We got driver license, photo ID card, wha'ever you want." The old man pointed at the sample the kid had already shown.

Joe shook his head. "I need a forger. Thanks anyway."

"Mi' know someplace," the old man said.

Joe took out another twenty.

The old man shrugged, and continued to shrug until there were five twenties on the counter. Then he said, "You want register?"

"What?"

"You want ID in a computer? You know, like real."

The kid said, still without looking up from the TV, "You can get the phony numbers put into the system. Then it's like a real ID. It holds up, you know. Cost you, but it's high quality."

"I don't think so," Joe said. "Just good fakes. I've got a picture for one already." He'd cut the photo out of Kari's driver's license.

The old man picked up the phone, dialed, and said something in Chinese. Then, to Joe, he said, "You want in-a system, take two week. One thousand each, U.S."

"I said I don't need them in the system. I just want good-looking counterfeits."

"OK, OK," the old man said. "Birth certificate, too?"

"What?"

"Second ID," the kid said. He showed one to Joe, a laminated wallet-sized reproduction of a birth certificate. "We all got 'em here. You need two forms."

"All right, those, too. Tomorrow?" said Joe.

"Tomorrow?" The old man laughed. Then he spat Chinese into the phone again. "Picture no matter," he said to Joe. "Cost three hundred each, for rush-job license. Nice real look. Two hundred each for birth certificate. Thousand dollar, U.S. No in-a system. Just fake, made-up."

"Fine."

The old man hung up and said, "You cop?"

"No."

"How I know?"

"I'm American."

"You prove it. You got license? Lemme see."

"I'm here looking for fakes. Why would I show you my real license? Why would I even have it with me?"

The old man shook his head and sat down.

"Jesus, come on," Joe said.

The old man shook his head again. There was nothing to do, so Joe laid his Michigan driver's license on the counter.

The old man read it, then said, "Not far, guy name Dan Sim." He studied the license again, tossed it on the counter and went back into the recesses of the store. The kid wrote down Sim's address and slid it over to Joe, all without ever looking up.

After visiting Dan Sim, Joe walked south out of Chinatown, beneath some high overpasses, then came upon a railway terminal and bus station set well back from the road. It gave him an idea. He was tired of carrying the heavy sack. In the back of the building, outside, on the concrete pavilion where the trains boarded, he found a bank of large pay lockers, inside one of which he cached the day pack with the balance of the gold.

It was going on three, now. He'd left Kari alone too long.

When he got back and let her up, she swore at him and rubbed her arms and her mouth, which was raw from the tape. She slapped him once in the face and pounded him in the chest, which he allowed her to do, until she'd spent some anger.

On this same late afternoon, Roy Jameson thought about the man named Joe Curtis, who'd stolen Kari Downs from Seattle and spirited her across an international border. He knew they were in Vancouver. It would have been too stupid for Joe to expose himself on the open roads. And Roy couldn't believe that Joe would hike with the girl up into the mountain wilderness. Joe was a city boy, so it had to be Vancouver, or one of the smaller cities bordering it, North Vancouver, Burnaby, Horseshoe Bay or Tsawwassen, from which the ferries to Victoria, on Vancouver Island, left. Somewhere here in this metropolis hid the man Joe, the golden girl Kari, and some mystery package worth thousands.

All Jameson had to do was find them and hold on until Amon's people arrived to take the package. As for Kari, he had no doubt that, after a few weeks in a locked room with the specialists her father was waiting to send, she'd come around.

So he sat in the city and thought. He thought like a man who was running hard, dragging the dead weight of a hostage. That they hadn't been caught yet was some kind of testament to the guy's street sense or some amazing luck. But the answer, Roy knew, was to lie low, to stay hidden until the worst of the storm passed over. On the other hand, he would want to be getting ready, preparing himself. So how would he go about that?

He thought about it some more. Later, he called a Vancouver PI he'd met once on a job in Denver and arranged for five local legmen to do some work-intensive questioning and surveillance. Roy had decided that if he were in Joe's situation, he'd focus, before trying to ride out of here, on money and identification. Money, who knew how much Joe had? At least a couple grand from the store knock-off. But it would be tough to travel without a cover. The press even knew the feds had made this guy, and were pushing for the information, which had not yet been released, but would be very soon. So he'd have to work something out. And that gave Roy Jameson an approach.

The five men he'd hired knew the city, of course, and started on all the logical places, but they had a lot of ground to cover. Still, he had an advantage: his friend on the Seattle force had, for a fee, slipped him a copy of Joe's full name and a print of his military ID photo. Roy had the photo copied five times, one copy for each of the legmen he hired.

Joe's face, actually the police sketch made from Rick's description, stared out from the front page of the *Vancouver Sun.* Two articles accompanied it: one, an AP piece, rehashed the triple murder in Idaho; the second, a local tie-in, concerned the fact that the sole suspect and a possible kidnapping victim had probably crossed the border into Canada and could be hiding in the Vancouver area. U.S. and RCMP officials believed they had identified the suspect, but were not releasing this information yet, pending its confirmation. A reward for any information leading to the apprehension of this man would be offered.

Joe sat on the bed in the dark. The AC and the lights were off, the window open. The only light in the room came from the security light in the parking lot of the motel, which spilled in and illuminated a rectangle on the floor at the foot of the bed. Kari sat there, on the floor in the rectangle of light, leaning against the bed, sipping bottled water, which was all she'd have. She'd eaten only some rice cakes and dried fruit for dinner, even though he'd brought back Wendy's burgers and fries.

"Why don't you eat?" he had asked.

"Processed foods are impure," she said. "Father teaches us to eat purely, direct from the Earth."

"You ate normal when we were driving, back in Montana. Was that all just for my benefit?"

"If you have an ordained task, you do whatever is necessary to fulfill it, even if it means poisoning yourself. Afterward, you re-purify. That's all."

"I ask you something?" he said. "What religion are you?"

"It's called Amonism."

"One of those weird cults."

"You're an ignorant ass," she said. "But Mother the Earth and Father the God will bless you." After that, she wouldn't speak of it, or even acknowledge his questions.

He took a long pull of his Jack Daniel's on ice and held it in his mouth until his eyes watered from the burning. He could feel his momentum waning, dying out from beneath him, the energy, the panic that propelled him from a bloody store in Idaho clear across the state of Washington in one blur, the anger and hopelessness that engineered and fueled his kidnapping of this woman and drove them, law hounds apparently snapping at their heels, across a border and into the world of international pursuit, dissipate in the emptiness of yet another room, all laid bare in the little rectangle of secondhand light.

What he had done was so profoundly stupid. He should have just stopped it in the very beginning, tackled Rick and not let it happen, or, barring that act of bravery, just left the two of them and called the authorities himself, as he'd considered doing, explained the whole thing and taken the penalty whatever it would have been. In his mind, that way, he would at least have been clear. They could have convicted him if they wanted; he would have known the truth. This way, though, he wasn't sure anymore. Who had the money? Who was the evader? Maybe he really was as guilty as they believed him to be.

Even now he could end it. He could call them to him, and live inside a jail. But that image, of incarceration, of bars and men and darkness for years, blew breath on the tiny waning flame of his desire to continue to run, breath enough to make the flame burn a little brighter, enough at least to keep it alive, to keep away a panic attack, to keep his hand from the telephone.

"Why don't you leave," he said, to her dark back.

"What?" She turned toward him, hope brightening her face.

"I can't keep you. I'm not tying you down again." He shook his head. "You're a lot of things, but you're not an animal."

"You noticed."

"But the gold stays," he told her.

She settled again, having risen slightly at his suggestion, as if she were ready to fly. Of course she would be ready. She must hate him. But she wouldn't give up the gold. That was the key to all of it. The task she talked about was nothing more than getting the gold back to her master. That's what this had been about from the beginning. Steal a man's gold and take it north to Alaska. And unless she could fulfill this mission, she wasn't going anywhere. He saw now that the straps and tape and cruelty had all been unnecessary anyway. She was tethered to him more surely by the gold than by any straps he could buy.

"What will you do?" she asked him.

"Hitch. Bus. Steal a car, maybe. Or even buy one."

"And then?"

"Head north, still, I suppose."

"How many highways do you think there are out of Vancouver, going north?" she said. She turned on the floor in the light to face him, crossed her legs Indian-style and set her water bottle in front of her ankles. He didn't answer. He watched her face in the blue-white light, watched how this light made her red-hued hair look ink black, how her wide slanting eyes caught it when she turned her head in a certain way, how it played off her perfect teeth.

"One two lane road runs due north, one highway and one road east, which merge before they turn north. That's it, Joe. Two roads. You're a fugitive with a pretty good likeness of your face in all the papers. What do you think they'll do with only two roads?"

She was right, of course. He was slipping more quickly, and what surprised him was he didn't care. It could happen; he could go down. He felt heavy again, in the eyelids and arms, felt a pressure in the center of his forehead, as if someone's thumb was pressing there. He set the drink on the bedside stand, lay back on the bed and closed his eyes.

"What do you even want?" she asked. "Do you know? Why did you come back to get me?"

He didn't answer her. It had had something to do with using her to expose Rick again, and then to turn Rick over to the cops. Also, she was a link, the last person who'd known him when he was nobody, the only one but Rick who knew the truth of what had happened. But now, facing her, he recognized that he had no specific idea as to exactly how he'd planned on using her to get at Rick. And he knew she wouldn't ever acknowledge the truth of what had happened.

So what good could she really do him? As it turned out, strangely, she'd delivered to him a fortune in gold. But he hadn't known about that when he grabbed her.

"Joe?" she said.

"Yeah."

"We could help you, you know."

"Who?"

"The Family. We have power, connections. I could make a call; we'd get help."

"Your family?"

"The people I live with. The people of my religion. The Amonites." She smiled. "All we have to do is get out of here. If we can get to Sanctuary, in Alaska, they'd never find us."

Her voice had changed. She sounded sweet again, cajoling, seductive, like she had outside the restaurant near Spokane, when she'd asked him to take her away.

"If you do things right, we can both get north. That's what I want. That's what you said you wanted, too. If that's still true, we can help you get it. You can disappear up there."

He laughed at the thought of turning for help to these people who'd killed and stolen and left it all on his shoulders.

"What I want," he said, "your people can't give."

"What's that?"

"I want my life back."

She got to her knees and came from the light around to the shadow beside the bed, and leaned over so she was looking down at his face. He could just make out her features. "Would you give up the gold to get that?"

"Sure," he whispered. "But who could do it?"

She gripped his face between her hands, and pushed her nose in so close to his that, even in the dim light, he could see the green of her eyes sunk into her pale, unpainted face. He could feel her breath. She squeezed, pressing his cheeks into his teeth until they burned and then, in her best-trained voice of renewed camaraderie, said: "Father."

And at that moment, out of the tumbling fog inside his head, it began to come clear. He saw how he could use her to suck Rick back out from under his rock. She was right; he did need her help and that of her family, of this man Father, of Rick himself, even. He must give himself up to them, through her, allow them in on this run of his. He must allow Kari to make the plans, to decide where they'd go, and how they'd get there.

Because what she would do, he knew, was to work it so her people, Rick, probably, could steal the gold back from him, and probably kill him in the bargain. But his knowing that, knowing she'd be leading him to his slaughter, knowing that she believed he was following her plans, would give him the edge he needed. And then, along with Rick and Kari, he could turn over the gold, or a part of it at least, and information about the cult, into the hands of the authorities. In exchange for himself.

He'd have to feel his way along in this, and didn't know yet if there were really any hope of it working, but he could feel that this was the one way to play it that had a chance.

"Father," Joe said. "He'd help me?"

"Oh, Joe." She held his face still between her hands. "People don't understand. All you have to do is ask, and a hand will be offered."

She had real tears in her eyes, he could see, before she flung herself upon him in an embrace of pious passion. Maybe she really believed it, he thought, that the Family would just welcome him in. He believed she hadn't known, or let herself believe, that Rick had killed people in the store. Maybe it was true, too, that she hadn't known the suitcase was full of stolen gold. These facts, that someone so obviously intelligent could be so misled, so taken in and corrupted and used, surprised him as much as anything that had happened so far.

Whatever the reason, her desperation matched his. The difference was that his was to evade, while hers was to return. Whatever force drew her back to what she called Sanctuary was powerful enough that she would commit any act, form any liason to get there.

Again, he found himself wondering about her true self, and how she'd come to lead such a bizarre and tenuous life.

Eighty miles to the south, at roughly the same hour, Rick Agullana rode through Seattle and north on toward the border in the back seat of a six-month-old, still new-smelling Acura Legend. His old friend, the dancer Angie Morales, sat in front of him in the passenger seat. Angie wore cut-off jean shorts and a halter top Rick had picked out of her closet. He had only to look up over the seat at her, inadequately restrained as she was by this halter, to feel newly energized and inspired, capable of great deeds. He had only to think of himself and Angie in a room together later that night. He did not sully these thoughts with thoughts of Angie's boyfriend, Gerard, although it was no one other than Gerard at the wheel of the car.

Gerard, it turned out, was a CPA and made pretty good jack, hence this bitching Acura. He was stewing away up there, all white-knuckled and mumbling profanities under his breath, him pulling down seventy-five grand and being made to drive his car and his girlfriend north in the service of some wolf who'd just slunk in off the plains. But, hell, Rick thought, a guy like that, all tight-assed and organized, needed an unplanned break now and then. It'd do him good, blow some dust out of the corners. And Angie, well, Rick knew what scratched her itch. Angie liked power, which explained in some ways this dork accountant. Seventy-five Gs a year was power to a girl like her. But right now, in the old hand-to-hand, Rick had power to burn compared with this eraser head. And he could see that light in Angie's eyes when she looked at him. And he could see the mild disgust when she looked over at Gerard. Already they'd had three good hissing matches, Jerry accusing her and her bad associations of screwing up his life, her telling him to go fuck himself and get out if he didn't like it (Rick said, no, not yet, since they still had some driving to do). But it was a great thing, sitting here in this all-beige-leather, sweet-smelling back seat, listening to Angie and the accountant build up some hatred between them, anticipating the moment when he undid that halter and got his first unhindered look at her new assets, oh. And then, for the final cherry, he thought about tomorrow, or the next day, when he got his hands on Joe the

Fuckface and shoved a knife up into his belly. When he got his hands back on Kari again and made her pay some penance, too, for being a screw-up in her own right. When he got the gold back and scraped 10 or 15 percent off the top for his personal account. Then, by God, he'd be one happy and satisfied man.

He could take his wife-to-be and his gold and get back on home. And, since he was fantasizing, he thought, why not Angie, too? Maybe she was tired of the boring life, maybe she was ready for something real. Imagine the look on the faces of the Inner Council men when he strolled in with a hundred-plus Gs and two fabbo broads, one on each arm. He'd let Father have at Angie, fair was fair, but in the end he knew she'd be his own second wife. Rick and Kari and Angie, sitting in a tree.

And then, not too much farther down the road from that, before this Family move out to the true middle of nowhere, well, Rick figured the religious life was wearing a little thin now, after two years. It was almost time to choose his best girl and collect the cash he'd saved and head back to civilization, and a new life all over again.

It was just too damn much to think about all at once.

19

UNITED STATES DEPARTMENT OF TREASURY
Seattle Field Division of the
BUREAU OF ALCOHOL, TOBACCO AND FIREARMS
456 Delray Plaza
Suite 335
Seattle, WA 80092

EXTERNAL MEMO

DATE: SEPTEMBER 2, 1995

TO: Various (for limited, classified distribution to specified US and foreign law enforcement agents, US military and Justice, State and Treasury Department officials.)

RE: Fred Haines, aka "Father," aka "Amon Ka'atchii," aka "God"; the religious extremist cult known as the Family, aka Amonites; the religion known as Amonism.

. . . .

Fred Haines (b. Tucson, 1944) founded his first church in Oakland in 1977, as an offshoot of a congregation of Seventh Day Adventists, and, after demonstrating from the first a remarkable ability to attract people, soon moved it and his "family" of fifteen, to a residential commune farther north in California. The church was still oriented toward Christianity, however non-traditional. In 1981 Haines was arrested on felony narcotics charges and served three years in the California State penal system. In prison, according to informant statements, he underwent training in Islam, and studied other Eastern religions, particularly Hinduism.

In 1985 he began a new residential church, in Bellevue, Washington, which, by late 1987, housed thirty to forty members. This was no longer a Christian sect, although it involved elements of Christian fundamentalism. It was also believed to include practices of some Eastern and occult religions and tenets of the general religious/spiritual orientation known as "Earth Worship." This last element would grow to become the dominant theme in later incarnations of the new "religion," called Amonism by followers. Haines was now known as Amon, or Amon Ka'atchii. ["Amon" (also spelled Amen, historically, and pronounced AH-mun) was, in ancient Egyptian mythology, the god of reproduction and life. "Ka'atchii," while claimed by Haines, according to ex-family members, to be a native American term, is believed to be an invention of Haines'.]

The Bellevue church was issued a series of warnings and citations for various infractions ranging from building to health code violations. In June of 1988, Bellevue City police, accompanied by Washington State child welfare authorities and health department examiners, served search warrants. In the process of inspecting the living quarters of the grounds, police uncovered unregistered handguns and semi-automatic and automatic rifles. Haines was not present at the church at the time the warrants were served and, apparently, never returned there. Ten members were arrested on various charges, but all were released. The church was charged with health code violations and fined. A report from child welfare stated that "as long as health code violations were timely corrected, no grounds were uncovered which would warrant consideration of removal of any children from the custody of church dormitory residents." Still, the fines went unpaid and by mid-July the grounds were abandoned. The property was then and is still registered to a non-profit corporation in Oakland believed to be controlled by Haines.

Haines and about half of the family members from Bellevue eventually established a new communal church in the mountains of northern Idaho, between Moscow and Coeur d'Alene. It was during this time, 1988 to 1992, that Haines became linked to William Cooper, a suspected arms and narcotics dealer, once convicted of felony tax evasion (two years served). The Amonite's Idaho commune was on land purchased from a company owned by Cooper.

Haines has proved to be a surprisingly aggressive businessman. In Seattle, he had women on the streets soliciting donations. Some suspicion, but no proof, existed that some of them were prostitutes as well. In Idaho, Haines allegedly received payments from Cooper for using Family members to transport guns, and is believed to have trafficked in arms himself. Sources also indicate that Haines may have dealt in narcotics again as well, and that certain of his women worked as prostitutes in Moscow and Coeur d'Alene. Haines eventually owned a service station and a trucking firm, both based in Coeur d'Alene, but paid no tax on any income from these businesses. The Internal Revenue Service moved against him in 1991. Haines' attorneys contested on the grounds that he was a religious leader and the cult was a wholly religious, non-profit, organization and so exempt from any tax burden. The Idaho property alone was valued at over a hundred and fifty thousand dollars, the legitimate businesses at a net of another two hundred and fifty thousand. IRS estimates put his and the cult's total worth, based on property and cash holdings and rumored gold reserves, in 1991, in excess of half a million dollars.

Testimonial evidence held by local law enforcement agencies indicated that quantities of arms, including automatic weapons, narcotics and bullion were stored on the grounds. In April of 1992, ATF agents in Spokane purchased three modified automatic AK-47 rifles and two sawed-off twelve gauge shotguns from two Amonite men, and made arrangements to purchase more. On the strength of the testimonial evidence and these purchases, the BATF, utilizing an informant within the cult, planned a raid on the compound for July of 1992 to exercise arrest warrants for Haines and three other men, and search warrants for the grounds and buildings. When agents went in, however, only eight women and five children were present. All other members, they said, had moved days earlier to a new "sanctuary," as they called it. No gold, currency or drugs were found, but a substantial store of arms, including two fifty caliber machine guns, was recovered. It was later discovered, when the IRS moved to impound the land and buildings, that months earlier part of the property had been sold to a small, non-religious separatist group, and the balance deeded over to the Northern Idaho Land Trust, one of William Cooper's real estate corporations.

Haines and his followers—at this time believed to number at least a hundred, including up to fifteen children under the age of five—are known to have moved to property in southern Alaska owned by an Anchorage-based corporation registered by an attorney named Samuel Reed. Reed is believed to be Haines' principal "advisor," known by the name "Deacon." This corporation also owns and operates two commercial fishing boats, a purse seiner and a smaller gill netter, from the port at Homer. The two boats and their licenses, valued at roughly $550,000, and financed by the Fifth Third Bank of Anchorage, are capable of generating estimated gross annual revenues of between $125,000 and $200,000. Family members work in canneries during the summer months, generating an estimated additional gross income of $75,000-$100,000.

In settlements negotiated by Reed, the Anchorage corporation—as distinct from Haines or the Church or the

> Amonites—agreed to pay, and actually paid for one year, income tax on fifty per cent of net income from commercial fishing. The ATF informant was withdrawn just prior to the attempted raid in 1992. Subsequent ATF activities have been limited to surveillance. No movement or possession of any controlled firearms, munitions or narcotics has been documented or is suspected by the ATF to date, but the warrants issued in 1992 are still in force.
>
> Estimates of the number of family members are rough since, after the move to Alaska, many members seem to live away from the commune. Up to 150 have been counted in the commune, of whom 70% were women and children. Another fifty to seventy five live in the Bellevue compound. There is also recent evidence that Haines may control a church in the San Francisco/Oakland Area.
>
> In summary, the Amonites differ from other known religious cults and/or separatist groups, while exhibiting tendencies of both. For one thing, the Amonites, and Haines in particular, are able to generate and control a substantial amount of wealth. Second, the religion is motivated not by Christian fundamentalism, nor a desire for racial purity, but rather a belief in and facility for so-called "natural-living," surviving on the Earth, and living as a "tribe." While little is known of Haines' psychology, he is thought to be intensely paranoid, fearing and preaching that the "family" will someday suffer badly at the hands of authorities or society if they don't maintain "discipline, isolation, respect and, above all, vigilance." Haines also is a known polygamist, having had up to six wives at one time.

A fax of the ATF memo, along with an FBI report on the same topic from the NCI computer in Washington, sat front and center on Colonel Rozsa's desk. He'd read them both twice, and picked one up every other minute or so, looked at it and set it back on his desk. Next to the faxes about the cult was a brief put together by Lieutenant Bliss, based on Army records and the reports of FBI field agents in Detroit, about an ex-soldier named Joseph Curtis, who received psychiatric treatment after his discharge.

Rozsa had a teleconference in fifteen minutes with the heads of

INSCOM and CRIDCOM, General Shaw of Fort Lewis, a Major Wecht who was in charge of all western U.S. Army CID posts, and a special assistant to the Army's Chief of Staff. Rozsa was preparing himself; it was his pitch, since, in light of this new information, he'd convinced General Parker to call the meeting.

Bliss sat in the low chair, watching him.

"It's all here, Bliss," he said. "Every detail needed to put the larger picture together. There's a lot to fill in, which we'll do, but the big picture, it's here. Do you see it?"

"I'm not sure what you mean, sir. Curtis was a loony—" It was right there in the report, that Curtis had been treated by psychiatrists at the VA hospital in Ann Arbor after his discharge.

"Exactly," Rozsa said, holding an extended index finger out toward Bliss. "And what else was he?"

"A felony convict."

"And?"

"A mechanic, sir."

"Ah. Not just a mechanic. He hadn't even been certified. No one else in his company had that little experience. Why?"

"Because he was good, sir."

"He was a whiz kid, some kind of genius on machines. And there he was, out in that sun-fucked desert getting his brains scrambled, but putting that genius mind into our weapons, our systems, Bliss. Not just machines. He had access to every goddamned piece of hardware the army had out there, which was, to put it mildly, a mother-lode of cutting edge military technology."

"He learned it, are you saying, sir?"

"Yes," Rozsa said. He liked this young man, Bliss, who kept right up. A good soldier here. "He learned our weapons. The fried-out mind of a mechanical genius studying, learning the intricacies of our weaponry."

"That's a bit of a stretch, if you'll excuse my saying so."

"How so, Bliss?"

"There's no indication. All we know is that he worked on machinery, mostly engines. He wouldn't have had access to weapons systems. He had no clearance."

Devil's advocate, Rozsa thought. Good, Bliss. Keep me on my toes. "That's the point," Rozsa said. "Of course he didn't have clearance. He just did it. He *could* have done it. How long would a mind like his need to study a system to know how it operated?"

"I don't know, sir. I'm no weapons expert."

"But think about it. Not long, that's the answer. Remember, he had been through AIT and weapons school."

"But for what—"

"He comes home and goes psycho, then whines like these other slackers that he's got this mysterious Desert Storm Syndrome. He develops 'symptoms.' Who's to blame? We are, Bliss. The damn army, who forgave his criminal record and trained the SOB and made him a man. The army's at fault. And then, one day, he meets someone who offers him some religion, the kind of made-up, mumbo-jumbo religion you can sink your life into. The kind of religion a guy like him would eat up with a spoon. Psycho-babble; black magic. Next thing you know he walks out on his job and his loving, heartbroken parents, tells them he's driving out west to bring his brother back home. Didn't the feds find the brother?"

"Last night," Bliss said. "On a Greyhound, headed home. Claims his brother called before he left Detroit, then he never heard from him again. He didn't see him in Seattle."

"Yeah. So, instead, this guy, Joe, snaps, has a vision or something, or he was lying and never planned on getting the brother in the first place. Whatever—he abandons his car and hitchhikes the fuck into *Idaho,* spiritual home of the antigovernment freaks, right, where he proceeds to murder three people, and where our weapons disappear."

Rozsa wiped his mouth. He could feel it coming, the good place he got to inside when he knew he was right, knew he was on and pumping. He had powers of persuasion they couldn't imagine. And now, he was getting there. Inside his head he heard a hum.

"It's too perfect, Bliss. This Amon Whatever is a gun nut from way back. These guys are all nuts. Look at Jim Jones, Koresh, Randy Weaver—that was Idaho, remember? Canucks had one, too, in Quebec, man named Rock something. And the Oklahoma thing, that started in Michigan. I mean, it's too perfect! But Amon wants to get his hands on something more than a machine gun or a farmyard bomb. And he's got a knowledgeable vet who's pissed off at the army. Sound familiar? What better way to rub their faces in it than stealing their weaponry?" Again Rozsa wiped spit away from his mouth.

"How'd they hook up?"

"Who knows?" Rozsa says. "They each have needs. They find each other. That's how history gets written. Alaska, Idaho, Montana, Michigan. Come on. These places are at the heart of this kind of shit."

"All right. So then what?"

"That's where I get frightened," Rozsa said. "What's a group like this going to do with three Stinger missiles? Defend themselves? From what? They've got automatic weapons. Wouldn't surprise me if they have a .50 cal or two still knocking around. But infrared, guided, heat-seeking missiles? Shoulder-launched antiaircraft weapons? Unless this: They want something, Bliss."

"What?"

"I don't know. Something. They want some of their people sprung from jail, or they want ten million bucks, or they want us to fix the hole in the ozone layer and save the goddamned whales by next Tuesday. Who fucking knows? But now, now, Bliss, *now* they have some teeth."

"With three missiles?"

"Think about it. How can they leverage those three hot little missiles? Here's a scenario: 'Dear Motherfucking Establishment. Unless you meet our demands, we're going to park someone near a commercial airport and wait for a fully-loaded 747 to come over. And we're going to blow it the fuck out of the sky, killing all four hundred people on board. So listen up.' "

"A terrorist threat," Bliss says. "Or hostages! Holy shit."

"There you go!" Rozsa says. "What's the range of a Stinger?"

"Over three miles. Flies at Mach 2. And not that difficult to fire, I think."

"What'd they have in Oklahoma, a hundred and sixty eight dead? These guys could make that look like a minor skirmish. Three times four hundred—they could do twelve hundred civilians in one morning. Unless these people are caught soon, and the fireworks recovered, we've got a situation here."

"What are you going to do?"

"My job is to convince the brass as I've convinced you. We need information. FBI and ATF are fine, but I want CID going full force after this, too. And when we locate the missiles—well, let's find them first, Lieutenant."

Across the river at Justice, they'd just received the ATF memo, and now, suddenly, the distant little Idaho drama had become a very different situation. An emergency briefing of the AG by her special troubleshooter took place in a limo as she rode to the Winchester Hotel to address a civil rights group.

"You handle this for now," she'd said. "Our job is to contain it, whatever that requires. Draw up a memo today from me to all involved agencies. And keep monitoring. Under no circumstance are we going to have another Waco or Randy Weaver on our hands. No civilian deaths, whether cult members or bystanders, under *any* circumstance, and particularly not women and children." The woman's soft voice, with its rounded edges, had always startled the man a little because he expected someone so tall and big-boned to sound large. She didn't. But when she meant something, by Christ, she could be fearsome. And she meant this.

"No one is to go after these people directly," she said. No one meant, first, the FBI, which was directly under their control, and then the ATF and locals. "If need be, I'll call the Treasury Secretary myself. All efforts should be made to find the fugitive and locate those weapons. Agents can set up long-range, clandestine surveillance of the Kenai property. But no one is to enter the camp, or surround it, or even be visible. There will be no warrants drawn or assaults planned until I give explicit, specific approval. Which I will not do as long as women and children are at risk."

"It's in Canada now, anyway," the troubleshooter said.

"Then let's hope the RCMP can wrap it up. If not, everyone had better understand—these people are to be left alone until we have a much less cloudy picture than we have right now."

That afternoon, the office of the special troubleshooter made it clear to all involved agencies that if there were any sign of noncompliance with the AG's order, the discussion would immediately be escalated to Cabinet level.

20

JOE WATCHED KARI WORK THE PHONES, MAKING IT UP AS SHE WENT ALONG. Airline schedules, first, to dummy destinations, for which, at various travel agents' offices, she'd pay cash. Ferry tickets north. A reservation at the Marine View Hotel in Ketchikan, Alaska, which she picked out of one of the tourist books Joe had bought, and arrangements for four packages to be delivered there shortly, which they would pick up when they arrived later this week. She gave the names that would be on their new IDs, Eric and Susan Delray.

It was up to Joe, she said, to retrieve the gold and package it for shipping by Federal Express from Sea Island, near the airport south of the city. This was how they'd smuggle it back across the border. Kari was explicit in her description of how he must do it—buy four thick loose-leaf notebooks, one each for the two bars, two for the remaining coins, wrap the gold in paper and then tape it securely into the notebooks, then pack the notebooks into Federal Express shipment boxes and label the boxes as business documents, with no declared value.

It was a smart plan. The only thing wrong with it was that it was hers.

On this Saturday morning, with the temperature back down to a more seasonable seventy-some degrees and no rain in sight, the city preened itself in the sun. With its spotlessness and order and the mountains rising up just beyond the narrow inlet, it looked more beautiful than any city Joe had seen.

While Kari was still making calls, he cabbed it back to Chinatown to pick up the IDs. Then, from the motel, the two of them walked west on Broadway to a nearby strip of car dealerships Joe had found, and met Mel Stone of Mel's House of Cars, who had some kind of rash on his face, scaly looking blemishes along the jaw line and across the forehead. He combed his hair back, too, so they could see every flake. When he smiled, his teeth looked like they were too big for his mouth.

"We have a problem," Joe said.

"Yeah?" Mel's eyes lit up.

"We're Americans."

"Not a problem," said Mel Stone. "People come up here to buy from me all a time. Exchange rate, see. I can give you a thirty day tag, get you back where you need to go."

"We need something now. *Right* now. Cash and drive."

Mel Stone scratched his ear and looked around at his cars.

Joe said, "We'd be willing to pay, say, an extra five hundred over what you're asking. . . ."

Mel Stone nodded and looked a little happier. "Hey, one of you got your Washington driver's license with you?"

"Michigan," Joe said. The key to her idea, Kari had said, was for Joe to buy the car under his real name, not the fake one. They'd argued about this. She explained it to him in detail, why the car had to be sold to Joe Curtis, and he understood the reasons, but it scared him.

Still, after he'd thought through it, he had to agree that her plan was actually pretty good.

"Michigan, whatever," Mel Stone said. "You're gonna have to pay for temporary Canadian insurance. But I can take care of it over the phone with a guy, you just drive over and pick up the form when we're done."

"OK."

"Come on," he said, leading them across the gravel lot toward where his string of colored plastic flags snapped in the breeze.

Half an hour later Joe leaned in toward Kari through the window of an old Honda Civic, rusted along the door frames and over the wheel wells. Joe could see that parts of the body had been rebuilt with Bondo. The car wasn't worth a grand, and he'd just given Mel Stone $2,500 in cash. But it ran. And it said Joseph Curtis, of Detroit, Michigan, on the title and temporary registration.

He handed her three thousand dollars, to buy the tickets and whatever else she thought they'd need.

Across the street, at the edge of an empty lot, a woman and her child sat beneath a tree, rolling a ball back and forth; a guy sat in a car, talking on his phone; a bum in a dirty overcoat, the first Joe had seen in Vancouver, sat on the curb.

Kari ground the gears and drove away in a cloud of blue oil smoke. The car needed rings and gaskets. It made Joe feel bad, that someone could let a car go to hell like that.

He watched her drive off in a vehicle registered in his real name, in the city where probably dozens of local, national, maybe international law enforcement agents were looking for him. He thought about it, but he didn't think about it too long. Thinking about something like that too long could lead straight into a fit of paranoid paralysis, and that he could not afford.

But some paranoia, if not paralysis, might not have been a bad thing; it would have been justified, anyway. Because while Joe was leaning into the Honda, talking with Kari, the driver of the car parked across the street leaned across and opened his passenger door so the bum in the overcoat, who was none other than Roy Jameson, could slip in.

The false ID canvass hadn't panned out, but that morning he'd checked in with Amon in Alaska, who'd just received a call from Kari Downs. He hadn't asked her where she was staying, for fear she'd realize someone was right there looking, but he had gotten her number. Did Jameson have access to a reverse index? The PI whose men he'd hired did. Sweetness. Jameson and one of these hired men got to the motel in time to watch Joseph Curtis and the woman just stroll on out and up the street.

From Mel's House of Cars, Jameson told the driver to follow Kari in the Honda. She was his concern, not this guy she was with.

But what was interesting, Jameson thought, as they trailed the smoking Civic through city traffic, was how Joe and this woman seemed to be getting on. Chatting, strolling, buying a car for her to drive off in. Funniest way for a kidnapper to treat a hostage he'd ever seen.

In the train station men's room, after pocketing fifteen coins, Joe divided the rest of the gold between four notebook packages, as he'd been told. But he did not ride all the way south of town to the FedEx office, and he did not ship the gold to the Marine View Hotel in Ketchikan. Instead, he found a post office and mailed two of the packages to Eric Delray, c/o General Delivery in Juneau, not Ketchikan, where the PO would hold them for up to ten days. The other two he sent Priority to Ketchikan, as agreed, but not to the Marine View. Instead, from a guidebook, he'd copied the number for the Front Street B&B, which he called to make his own arrangements.

He also wanted to arrange something different for their transportation north, but didn't know what until a bright poster outside the station gave him a wild idea. There was no way it would work, he thought, but he found a pay phone with a phone book and started making calls. It took nearly a dozen before he finally hit, but hit he did.

Afterward, he sat on a bench up in the elevated monorail station across from the train depot, and thought again. He held this morning's *Sun,* which contained a copy of his military ID photo, and his full name and a story all about his conviction, his psychiatric discharge, even his job in the cabinet shop. The feds had nailed him down, after all. Time was growing very short; he couldn't risk being seen on the street any longer. He had bought a baseball hat and pulled the brim low over his eyes.

He was wearing the tinted contacts again, as well as sunglasses, and had grown the beginnings of a beard, which helped cover, but his eyes, tinted or not, and his snaggled front tooth were the sorts of things people noticed and remembered.

Kari, he knew, would already have been on the phone to her people, asking for instruction, reporting her arrangements, letting them know where the gold would be, and when. Joe saw all that and how to circumvent it, but what he could not see yet was what difference it made, how he could use it to turn things around without having to go in and talk to a million cops. If he could just talk to one person, alone—and then he had another idea.

Vancouver RCMP headquarters answered after three rings.

"I have information about Joseph Curtis," Joe said. He was put on hold, then someone said, "Where are you calling from?"

"I want to talk to a U.S. agent. I know they're here." The *Sun* article had mentioned that fact.

"Yes. There are some here. Who did you want?"

"Who are they?"

"Why don't you tell me where you're calling from?"

"You got about three seconds," Joe said. "Then I'm gone."

"Uh—" the man said, then covered the phone. Joe could hear him talking to someone. Probably they were trying to put a trace on the call. Then the man was back: "Agent Red Feather is here but she's in a meeting right now. And Agent Truong—"

Joe hung up. Red Feather. He liked that name. It was different. And it was a woman. He liked that, too. Red Feather it would be.

The monorail train slid up, and the doors hissed open. Joe stepped in.

Near the waterfront at the northern edge of the downtown, on the top floor of an open-air parking garage, Roy Jameson and his hired man had scootched down in their seats, the better to stay hidden as they watched Kari Downs park the Honda. They followed as she walked toward the elevator, but could only watch as she entered and the doors closed. They ran for the stairs, and reached the ground floor breathless but ahead of the elevator.

But when the elevator opened, it was empty.

Roy Jameson stared in astonishment. Then he ran back up the stairs, as his partner took the elevator.

"Try two!" Roy yelled.

They met again on two. Nothing. Three, nothing. From four, Jameson leaned over the concrete wall and looked out at Granville Street. He saw her at the curb, waiting for traffic to clear so she could cross over to what looked like some kind of luxury mall.

"Shit," Roy said to the hired man, and bolted again to the staircase, and down. His man yelled, "Hey, we got her car, man! All we gotta do is sit here."

"She made us. Follow me in the car!" Roy yelled back. He was already two flights down, then out past the check-out window and into the sun. He saw her, dressed in the nice skirt and high heels he'd watched her buy at a downtown shop.

Her legs flashed out of sight around a corner, in between two taller buildings. He'd follow her through, and then, if his man had brought the car around, it would be just a matter of muscling her into the back seat.

Jameson dodged two old lady shoppers and tore around the corner, and there she was. Talking to a shorts-wearing bicycle cop, plucking his sleeve, the original Lady in Distress, and pointing back. There, officer. That's him. The bad, bad man.

Shit, again. Roy Jameson turned and hustled it back, but the cop was peddling after him, now. "You! Hold it, there." Jameson picked up speed when the cop yelled again, "Freeze!" But what was the cop going to do—peg him in the back on a crowded city street? And for what, some woman whining to him? No, he was tooling now, half a block away already, when another bike came right off the damn street and onto the sidewalk in front of him, his momentum carrying him into it and him and the bike and the cop on it going over and down hard onto the cement, everything spinning out there for a second. When he could focus he saw the goof with a bleeding scrape on his cheek, blood running down his hairy leg and a sidearm drawn and pointed at Roy's face, and the other, the chaser, frisking him and finding the ankle holster with the little .25-cal Beretta backup pistol he carried, licensed in the U.S. but smuggled illegally into this country.

Shit again, again.

"This is called you're busted, asshole," the injured Canuck cop hissed. "This is called you even breathe wrong, I'm gonna fuck you up and like it."

"Hey," Roy Jameson said. "I'm on your side, friend. Let's just go talk this over."

From a downtown pay phone, Joe called the RCMP again. It was only a matter of lying well, of convincing the woman who answered that he was a relative of Agent Red Feather calling long distance, and that he needed to talk to her right away.

The woman told him Agent Red Feather was out, now. He'd have to leave a message, she said.

How could he reach her quickly, he wondered. "It's about her Father," Joe said. "Kind of an emergency."

And, just like that, for the asking, the woman gave the name of a downtown hotel, the Hyatt Regency.

"What is your name?" she said. "Why don't you leave—"

Joe hung up and called the Hyatt, which even supplied the agent's room number, 1225, before they rang it for him. Although he only planned on stopping at the front desk, he did not want to risk running into this agent who undoubtedly knew what he looked like. After seven rings, he figured she was out. The Hyatt was only a few blocks from where he stood—he could see its red sign now, up on a tall modern building right in the densest part of the downtown.

He felt little pings in his head as he got closer. He was walking right in to the lair. But this was how he'd decided it had to be played. He needed to make a contact if this plan were going to work, if he were going to turn this mess around and screw the people who had screwed him. So this had to be done. And no time for panic. No time for tight breathing and weak knees. Adrenaline was pumping like mad now; that should keep the panic away. He'd noticed that—in action, he did all right. It was the quiet times, when he thought, that it got so bad.

In a small park near the hotel he stopped to write on a piece of notebook paper:

Agent Redfeather:
I want to end it. I'll talk to you alone. Be in your room tonight. I'll know if you're trying to trace, and I'll be gone again.

JC

In Fish & Co, the restaurant on the Hyatt Regency's second floor, Leanne and Calvin sat across from each other at a small window table overlooking Burrard Street. She had returned a few minutes before, after a morning full of meetings, and gathered up Calvin for lunch. They were just ready to order when her RCMP-issued beeper sounded off and she ran for a pay phone.

The message was from the laconic, stiff-backed RCMP sergeant named Connor whom Leanne met the night before, and who had been assigned to escort her around, sticking with her, as much, she assumed, to keep tabs on her as to help.

"Sorry to disturb you, Agent Red Feather," Connor said.

"Leanne," she said.

"Yes. We just learned that Vancouver police arrested a man downtown this morning. A woman approached a patrolman and said a man was threatening her. The man was apprehended, and found to be concealing a Beretta. The woman disappeared. This man, Roy Jameson, is a U.S. private investigator, licensed to carry his gun in the states, but not here, of course."

"Yes, Connor," she said. "So what?"

"He had a picture in his pocket, a black and white ID photo. It didn't take long for one of the interrogating officers to recognize it, since there've been so many copies circulated."

"Joseph Curtis?"

"Yes, ma'am."

"This PI was following Curtis?"

"He claims not. He claims he was following Kari Downs."

"Why? And how did he find her?"

"He was hired, he said, by her father. And he seems to know this Amon Ka'atchii—"

"I'm there, Connor."

"I sent a car. It should be waiting already, at the valet entrance."

"Don't let anyone else talk to him."

"No, ma'am."

Calvin stared out the window. It made her suddenly sad, again, the aimless way he sat, waiting for her so he could order some food. And now not even that.

"I'm sorry, Cal, hon. I have to run. It's an emergency."

"What about lunch?"

"You'll have to order room service again. I'm sorry. We'll have dinner."

He turned back to the window.

"Go back up to the room now. Just wait there. You've been doing a good job."

He smirked and shook his head. "Good boy, good boy," he said.

"I mean it. Just go back up to the room and stay there. I'll call."

"Woof," he said, and stuck his tongue out and panted.

The Hyatt was only about five blocks from the Sinclair Centre, in front of which, not much earlier, Roy Jameson had been arrested for threatening a certain frightened, anonymous young woman with dark red hair. But Joe had not seen any of this, of course. As he passed from bright daylight into the coolness of the hotel lobby, he found himself directly in front of a short hallway with two banks of elevators. To his left an atrium filled with potted trees and couches for the guests stretched upward. It took a moment before he was oriented enough to find his way past the elevators to the desk, where he planned on leaving his note. Only one clerk was on and a large, loud man stood arguing with her about something on his bill. Joe waited, hands crossed, note folded between his fingers, when a Vancouver policeman slid past and leaned on his arms against the check-in counter. And then, to Joe's horror, the cop was joined by another officer, wearing hat and trousers with wide golden-yellow bands—RCMP.

To appear the more natural, Joe studied his watch, glanced toward the entrance leading from the hotel lobby to what seemed to be an underground mall, then wandered back in the direction of the elevators, past the rich-looking sofas, waiting for someone to stop him and demand to know why he was here, dressed in his dirty jeans, who he'd come to see, but no one did.

Before he could think himself out of it, he pressed the up button and entered when the gold doors slid open. The agent was out; he knew because he'd called.

The twelfth floor was quiet but for a cleaning lady pushing her cart. "Can you put this in a room?" Joe asked her, holding up the folded note, but the woman shook her head.

So he walked down the hallway until he saw 1225, listened, then slid the note under the door. But as he stood up, bracing his hand on the door handle, the door swung suddenly inward, pulling Joe off-balance and into the room. He froze face-to-face with a shirtless, well-muscled man with long tied-back hair.

A moment passed as the two men looked at each other. Then the one who'd opened the door said to Joe, "I know you. Yeah." He shook a finger in Joe's face. "From the pictures. You're the one the porkers all looking for. Who killed those people in Idaho, Joe."

Joe turned to run but the man's hand came down on his shoulder. He said, "She ain't gonna be back for a while. And they'll *never* think to look for you here, right?" The man laughed. "Stick around a minute. Close the door. No one will know, man. Come on."

Joe pressed himself against the wall beside the door, with his fingers holding it open a few inches. The room was large and cool with heavy maroon drapes, pale green wallpaper, and a dark wooden highboy for the TV. Not cheap veneered stuff, Joe could tell, but real wood. Beyond that sat a glass writing table with a phone, and a separate sitting area of upholstered chairs and a table. He'd never seen a hotel room like this.

"I'm her brother, Cal. I'm in almost as much trouble as you. Some guys want to cut my legs off. So she brought me along for safekeeping.

Baby sitting. And I'll tell you, it sucks a big one. Sit in the damn room all day, staring at the boober. Hey, glad to meet you, Joe." Cal reached out and picked up Joe's clammy hand and shook it. Then he said, "That a note for Leanne there?" He laughed again, a high-pitched, rapid sort of barking, which didn't fit at all with his appearance.

Joe nodded.

"You confessing? You're not gonna make it that easy for her. If she don't gotta work for it, she gets all pissy."

Cal picked up the note and, after reading it, looked up and said, "You didn't do it, did you? Can you talk?"

"I can talk," Joe said. "No, I didn't do it."

"I told Leanne that. I said, 'Why would he go back and grab the chick? Don't that make you stop and think? It just does not fit.' I aced three people and scored cash, I'd be on the next plane to fucking Brazil, man. I would not be cruising around Seattle with some female. But she can't think like you and me, for one thing, and beside that she's obsessive, you know, like a bird dog with a hard-on; she should'a been a man. You can't tell her nothin'.

"Anyway, she'd never go for this." Cal waved the note. "She'd have you traced. Listen: what're you thinking? You tryin' to set a meet or something?"

Joe nodded.

"I stay with her down in Boise, but I have this message service I use there, you know, 'cause she's nosy and don't need to be hearing my business. I call it a couple times a day. You call that number, leave a message when you're ready. I'll pass it on. I'll be, you know, your contact." He walked to the table.

Joe thought it had gone over-the-top crazy now, but all he said was, "OK."

"This is cool, huh?" Calvin laughed the laugh. "I ask you something? You scared?"

"Yeah. Sometimes I'm petrified."

"You don't look like it. You're, like, weirdly calm. Here." He shoved a piece of paper at Joe. "Listen: take care, man." Joe left and walked in a daze of disbelief down the quiet hallway.

21

THE PREVIOUS EVENING HAD NOT GONE AT ALL AS RICK HAD FANTASIZED. When he and Angie and Gerard stopped for the night just short of the border and took a room with two double beds, Angie lay down on one with Gerard, leaving the other to Rick alone. He drank a few beers and fumed, then got up and tried to order Gerard into the bathroom.

"What do you want from us, Rick?" Angie said. "You needed a ride, you got a ride. You want the car? Take it. Gerard can report it stolen when we get back. What else?"

Then Angie and Gerard got into it again, about losing the Acura this time, and finally Rick locked himself in the damn bathroom where he could think in some kind of peace. When he came out, they were both asleep on their bed.

The morning saw them across the border, Gerard deciding to play along, using Rick's story that the three of them were relatives going to a funeral, because it seemed the easiest, safest way. Who knew what Rick would do if Gerard tried to attract some attention? Besides, as soon as they got to Vancouver, Rick promised he'd turn both of them and the car loose.

But Rick knew it wasn't going to play that way.

Before the outskirts of the city came into view, Rick had Gerard pull off the highway onto an empty rural road and drive a mile or so. Then he leaned forward and said, "Pull over here. I gotta take a leak."

"We're almost there, for Chri'sake," Gerard said.

"Can't wait," said Rick. "Where'm I gonna go in the city, the sidewalk? Stop here. We got some things to discuss anyway."

"What things?" Angie said.

"Jerry'n me," Rick said. "About how to work it with you guys turning loose. I don't want anybody knowing about this."

"What?" Gerard said, pounding the steering wheel. "Knowing what?"

"This whole thing. I got a way you can drop me off in town and I'll know for sure I'm away clean. I mean, face it, you guys could cause me a lot of trouble by going to the cops."

"We're not going to any cops," Gerard said. "I just want to get the hell home and forget it ever happened."

"Still," Rick said. "I want to tell you how we're gonna play it. Pull over and hand me the keys."

So Gerard did, on a long straight stretch of open road with only the occasional passing car. Off to the right about a dozen yards in, through some high brown grass, was a small stand of trees. Gerard and Rick both stepped out onto the berm.

"Come on," Rick said. "Let's take a walk."

"I don't have to pee. I don't see why—"

"Come on," Rick said. "Don't piss me off now. We're almost there, buddy."

They plowed through the tall grass and into the trees. As Rick peed against one of the trunks, Gerard crossed his arms and looked up at the branches overhead, then shifted and crossed his legs, then put a hand into his front pants pocket. Finally he could stand it no longer, and went behind a bush to another tree and unzipped himself as well.

Rick waited until he heard the stream of Gerard's urine before he stepped lightly around the bush and looked at Gerard's back and bowed head.

"Hey," Gerard said, when he heard something snap behind him. "What're you doing?"

"Sorry about this, buddy," said Rick. He stepped forward, pressed the .38 to the kinky brown hair, and fired a bullet into Gerard's brain, a good portion of which ended up on the tree. Rick jumped sideways to avoid the initial hard spurt of blood out the back of Gerard's head as his body collapsed against the tree and slid to the ground, but some of it got on Rick's sleeve and one of his shoes.

In the car, Angie, who'd heard the shot and knew exactly what had happened, cried quietly into her lap.

"Sorry," Rick said. "You know how it is, Ang." He looked at her, pathetically weeping down onto her balloon boobs, and shook his head. "Let me see, Angie."

"What?"

"I want one look, then I'll leave you alone."

"Jesus, Rick—"

"Come on." He jerked her T-shirt out of her pants.

"Rick!"

"Pull it up. Take off the bra." He checked his mirror—no traffic—then cocked the gun and pointed it at her head. Angie pulled the T-shirt over her head, and leaned forward to undo the triple snap.

"Stop crying," Rick said. "It ruins the effect." She let the bra hang when it was unsnapped. He pulled it away from her and said, "Look at me, now. Turn this way." She did.

"Oh, man," Rick said. He reached over and pinched her nipple. "Can you feel that, with all the crap they put in there?"

"Stop it."

"I need a piece bad, Angie. What do you say?"

"You said just a look." She pulled the shirt back over her head. "You're a fucking animal, Rick. I'm getting out of here." She opened the passenger door as a car came up behind them and sped past.

"Let me give you a ride into town, then you can take off."

"I'll thumb," she said. "I'll be safer that way."

Rick nodded. He gritted his teeth and looked in the rearview mirror at stupid Angie with her thumb stuck out, although there wasn't a car in sight. If anyone did stop, it sure wouldn't be because of her thumb.

Rick watched another car approach and slow when it got close, then continue past. Angie turned to watch it go. This was enough nonsense. Rick jumped out of the car and hurried back toward her.

"No," she shrieked, and ran off into the tall brown grass. He went in after her, following the trail she left, and came on her quickly and shoved her in the back, knocking her down. She lay looking up at him.

"Do it if you have to, you shit, you *fuck,*" she said. "Just get it over with so we can get out of here."

He thought about it. He shook his head and looked over the top of the high grass, which would hide everything, and saw there were no cars in sight in either direction, and said, "Angie, I would love to. But I got business to take care of. Mother the Earth and Father the God."

He took the .38 from the back of his waistband and shot her once, in the eye, just exactly where he'd shot old Big Bill Cooper. As Angie convulsed, Rick walked back out to the road.

After he got into Vancouver, Rick found Gerard's wallet full of credit cards tucked into the Acura's glove compartment. This would make life much easier, especially since Gerard wasn't going to be reporting the cards stolen in the next few days. Rick pocketed several of the cards. At a Radio Shack he bought a hand-held scanner for monitoring the police. Then, from a motel in Burnaby, he called Father and learned that Jameson had found Joe and Kari's motel, and was at that moment tracking them. He should be checking in soon, Father said. Father, in turn, would call Rick with that information. Rick's fingertips tingled. He waited for the call until, by two that afternoon, impatient, he again called Father, who'd heard nothing. The only other information Father had was where Jameson was staying, which he gave to Rick.

So Rick drove to this hotel, a Holiday Inn in Vancouver proper, south of False Creek, and found the room and knocked. No answer.

He stepped back and kicked the door twice before the lock splintered open. There wasn't much inside, however, but some clothing and a phone number on a piece of the hotel stationery. Rick dialed, and a woman answered with the name of a Vancouver investigation firm.

"I'm looking for a man named Roy Jameson," Rick said. "He's been using some men from your firm here—"

The woman put him on hold. A man picked up, then, and said, "Who is this?"

"Who's this?" Rick said. "I want to know where Roy Jameson is. I'm working with him."

"He's been arrested," the man said.

Rick went quiet.

"We just found out," the man said. "If you want to help him—"

Rick hung up, wiped off the phone, and left. From a pay phone, he called Father to tell him the news. Father took it surprisingly well, Rick thought. He did not yell. He simply said, "Well, we know where they're staying," meaning Joe and Kari. "All you can do is wait there for them to show up again."

Not long after Rick had gone from Jameson's room, a Vancouver police detective running leads for the RCMP showed up with a search warrant, noted the kicked-in door, and called the RCMP complex in the Shaughnessy district, where Jameson was being interrogated. "Whoever was here is gone now," he reported.

The next thing, he was told, was to check out a local PI firm Jameson had been working with.

The detective wrote down the address. "On my way," he said.

From the Hyatt Joe's cab took him out of the downtown over the Burrard Bridge, past the Molson brewery a few blocks, and back to the Econo-lodge on Broadway.

It happened that the driver who'd been following Kari with Roy Jameson until Jameson's arrest had eventually driven back hours earlier to this Econo-Lodge to wait, since there were no other leads to follow. Although Jameson was busted, the guy figured he was still being paid to follow this woman and, if her room was here, eventually she'd show up.

So, he was sitting in his car in the parking lot, watching, when Joe climbed out of the cab and hurried inside with his hands pressed against the sides of his head. The man, recognizing Joe from that morning, followed him. Before Joe could close the door to his room, the man heard him moaning in agony.

The man listened outside the door as the phone rang six times before Joe answered it.

Outside, from his car phone, the man reported his location to the PI who had contracted him out to Jameson. He didn't know, of course, that a Vancouver PD detective was sitting in the PI's office at that moment, impressing on him the importance of passing along any information relevant to this case. The PI knew bad stink when it wafted by, and he knew this one had gone way bad and so wasn't about to piss off the cops on top of it. When he hung up, he gave the detective the address of the motel and the news that Joe Curtis was there now.

The Vancouver Police detective in turn called the RCMP investigators, who were with a U.S. FBI agent named Truong and a woman agent named Red Feather.

But while this was going on, as the PI's man watched, a rescue squad arrived at the Econo-Lodge and the EMTs carried Joe out on a stretcher. The call Joe had received was from Kari, who'd been trying all afternoon to reach him, to tell him she'd been followed and he might have been, too. But he was having one of his headaches when she reached him, though he said he'd be all right soon. And even as they spoke, he began to sound a little better to her, as if the pain were easing. But it gave her an idea. "Just lay on the bed and wait," she told him. "I know how to get you out of there and lose the tail."

The PI's man tried to follow but couldn't cut lights and traffic like the ambulance. When he got to Vancouver General, over on 12th Avenue, a mile to the east, he saw the unit parked beneath the ER portico, and approached the attendant.

"It was strange," the attendant explained. "This guy, who couldn't breathe when we found him, insisted he was suddenly all right, aye? And he did sound normal when we got here, but he still hadda be checked out, I said. He refuses to go inside. Then a woman meets him here and just walks away with him. 'Hey,' I say. They can't leave. But the woman hands me a couple hundreds for our fee, she says, and they do leave, like it's nothing, right down the friggin' avenue."

When the PI's man got back to the motel, which again he figured he might as well watch in case they returned—it had worked twice, now, after all—he was greeted by squad cars and cops and Mounties. Since the officers were busy watching him, they did not notice as a late model Acura Legend with Oregon plates pulled away from the curb across Broadway, slid past the motel, slowed, then sped around a corner.

Leanne Red Feather, standing with Agent Truong and some RCMP investigators in the abandoned motel room, knew that it had happened again, that she had been left clutching air. But when the PI's man was brought in and told the story of the hospital, and one of the RCMP agents said, "Damn, that's right here," and pointed to the east, Leanne stood up. "They're on foot," she said. "We know what they look like. Can we cordon off the area?"

"They could be on a bus or in a car by now," someone said.

"They could be sitting at a goddamn bus stop, too," she said. "All your men are just down the road! If you move—"

"OK," he told her. Within minutes, two dozen RCMP officers and trainees, some uniformed, some in street clothes, poured from the barracks in the beautiful Shaughnessy compound down on Heather Street, tucked in as it was at the edge of a lush botanical garden. Some rode west and then north up Granville, others east, then north, up Cambie, the two major roads which crossed False Creek into the downtown, and between which lay Vancouver General. By then, the Vancouver police had set up commercial vehicle search points on all major roads leaving the area around the hospital.

In fact, Joe and Kari had walked east from the hospital until they came to Cambie Street. Just to their north was the Cambie Bridge, over False Creek, to the downtown, but they knew that to try crossing the long, open span on foot would have ended it. So they turned south, past pretty, tree-lined streets of prosperous looking homes.

Down a few blocks, Kari slid off her heavy backpack, stuffed with new clothing she'd bought them, and stopped for a minute to rest. Joe stepped out to the curb to see what he could, and what he saw scared him.

"Kari," he said. "Listen. There're lots of lights down there, coming this way. And up the other way it looks like they've got the bridge closed now. Something's happened."

Joe put on the pack now. They crossed the street to a small pizzeria. Before entering, they noticed a police cruiser well to the south, turning off of Cambie. What they did not see was the new Acura coming toward them from the north, nor did they see it pull a U-turn and stop at the curb in front of the restaurant.

Inside, Joe said to the kid behind the counter, "Bathrooms?" The kid pointed at a hallway leading toward the rear of the building.

"Hurry," Joe said to Kari. "There'll be a back door."

Kari had been watching outside. She turned to follow Joe, but, when she took one last look back before entering the hallway, saw Rick's face peering in through the plate glass. She screamed. Rick stepped back and fired his .38 at the window, at Joe. The glass exploded and collapsed with a cascading crash.

Joe pulled Kari to the floor and crawled, leading her by the hand, down the hallway then through a swinging door marked NO ADMITTANCE. The kid behind the counter dropped, too, and covered his head with a pizza paddle.

In the rear, in a kind of open office area, Joe stood to make for the back door, but Kari put her hand on his arm. She shook her head and pointed back toward the front of the store.

"What?" he whispered.

She yanked his hand. He followed her through the swinging door again, and into the restaurant. Then he heard wood splinter as Rick kicked through the locked back screen door, and knew that Kari had saved his life.

The kid was behind the counter, still cowering beneath his paddle. Joe motioned Kari behind the counter, too, and pointed at another of the flour-covered wooden paddles resting there, on the counter. Kari lifted it and handed it over to him. Then Joe stepped back over beside the entrance to the hallway and waited.

Quiet. A dead moment passed, until the hinges of the swinging door squealed slightly. Joe pressed himself against the wall, and raised the paddle over his head. He heard Rick's shoes ticking on the tile floor. Then the ticking stopped.

They waited. Five seconds passed. Ten. Then Kari stood up behind the counter and shouted, "Rick, hurry!"

Rick ran in, looked at her, and swung up the .38. Joe, who'd hit baseballs more than three hundred feet, brought the paddle down on Rick's head. The paddle split in half with a deep crack, as pleasing a sound to Joe as any bat on ball had ever made.

Rick dropped to the floor like so much ballast. His gun clattered away.

Joe nodded at Kari. Composed as he had ever been, Joe knelt and rifled Rick's pockets, and found a key to an Acura.

Rick, however, who hadn't been knocked completely out, but simply stunned by the blow, was already stirring and grunting.

"Move," Joe said.

Rick pushed himself to his hands and knees. He let loose a kind of moaning yell, the cry of a wounded, pissed-off animal.

Joe and Kari broke for the front door. Outside, a nice big car waited there at the curb. Joe went in first, through the passenger door, and said a quick prayer before fitting the key in the ignition and turning it. It started nicely.

While Kari tuned in the police scanner Rick had used to find them, Joe dropped the car into gear and slipped around a corner on to a side street as they heard sirens converging.

The first cops in found a young man curled into a ball behind the counter by the ovens, and beneath a pizza paddle. Another paddle, this one broken into two neat pieces, lay in the middle of the floor, next to a small fresh puddle of blood.

But a thorough search turned up no one else in the restaurant. Units continued to arrive. Cops and RCMP trainees spread out through the neighborhoods behind the pizzeria and into the new condominium complex across the street, and beyond that into the grounds of the St. Sacrament church and school compound.

◇

Later, in the burned-out neighborhoods between Gastown and Chinatown, in a wino hotel room that smelled of disinfectant masking sick human odors, Joe sat at the wobbly table while Kari rested on the bed.

"Why'd you go against him?" Joe said.

"My loyalty's not to him. I have a task," she said. "He's jeopardizing it at this point."

"You saved me twice today, with the ambulance and then in that restaurant."

"Father is with us, Joe. We have virtue. This is our test. Everything's set for tomorrow. I even thought to move the Honda again, after that man got arrested."

They'd kept to the smallest side streets in the Acura, and got clear to Main, where there were no checkpoints and which led north past the train station and beneath the overpasses back to Chinatown—neighborhoods Joe was familiar with. He'd left the Acura parked on the street with the keys in it, knowing it would be gone soon.

Kari said, "If we make it through tonight, God will put it all into place in the morning. Then we'll just go on home."

He shook his head and settled in on the floor with a pillow and blanket. He felt better, now, like they might really be on the verge of something, but thought he'd better rest while he could.

Rick had run, disoriented and bleeding, up the alley behind the pizzeria for three blocks, when he caught a woman with two children getting into a minivan and impressed upon her the urgency of getting him to the hospital, what with his bleeding and all. He'd hate to lose control and hurt the children. Too frightened to resist, the woman did what he asked, crying in relief when he really did get out at Vancouver General.

He didn't go in, of course, but cut through the grounds north to Broadway, stopping at a water fountain to wash the blood from his face and head, to the Vancouver Holiday Inn, which he knew about because he'd been there earlier that day, in the room of Roy Jameson.

Rick still had Gerard's credit cards in his pocket. He figured he could use them for another night or two before they'd have to be ditched.

After renting the room and cleaning up some more, he went to the Gap across the street, where he bought some nice new clothes.

The search went on until dark, when the major road and bridge checkpoints were called off. Still, extra cruisers were ordered to stay in the area through the night.

Leanne Red Feather, in an unmarked RCMP sedan parked on Cambie Street in front of the shot-up pizzeria, felt her face burn at the thought of it. But she knew anger was not the emotion she needed now. In the mountains Guts used to say, "Have no mind, Leanne. Like your prey, have no mind, no pride. Only senses; only instinct."

"We still have the APB out," Connor, her escort, said in an attempt to lift her spirits. He was referring to the used car dealer, Mel Stone, to whom Roy Jameson had directed them, who had cooperated fully, saying he knew something was fishy with that couple, who had shown them the paperwork and the photo-copied Michigan driver's license of Joseph Curtis and given them the temporary Canadian license plate number.

"If they run, we'll have them," said Connor.

Instinct, Guts said. More than the fact of the car, what stuck in Leanne's mind was Jameson saying it wasn't just Joseph Curtis who bought the car, but Kari Downs, the kidnap victim, as well. And that it was she who drove away, alone. What did instinct say about that? That Curtis was after all a cult member, that the kidnapping was another ruse, that maybe Curtis and Downs were splitting with the gold themselves. Hard to say. It was just hard to say.

She nodded and smiled at Connor, then said she was tired. Connor started the car and drove north across the Cambie bridge to take her back to the Hyatt, where her brother, Calvin, lay waiting with a sly smile on his dark and handsome face.

22

MILE MARKER A 21 ON CANADIAN HIGHWAY 1A EASTBOUND, HALF-way between the towns of Abbottsford Junction and Hope, lies on the lee side of a steep rise, surrounded by rich fields of ripe alfalfa and, beyond them, an exceptional view of the rocky peak of Mount Baker. The spot is usually tranquil, even with the passing traffic, and especially so on a Sunday morning. But on this rainy Sunday morning a part of one of the alfalfa fields was beaten flat by the blades of a RCMP helicopter as it came in from Vancouver, bearing, among others, U.S. agents Truong and Red Feather.

Mile marker A 21 itself was surrounded by RCMP vehicles, and traffic was backed up the steep hill because of a surprise roadblock that had been in place since the night before.

Now, at this roadblock, surrounded by three officers pointing twelve-gauge shotguns, sat an old Honda Civic sedan with temporary plates, the driver of which, an eighteen-year-old, soon-to-be college student, had urinated in his pants. He sat, hands on head, staring out through the windshield in blind terror until an RCMP officer grabbed him by the hair and dragged him out onto the highway, and then knelt on his back as the boy was locked into handcuffs and leg manacles.

At this, the poor driver, although he was not an uncourageous young man, began to weep. His deal with the Hasty Vehicle Delivery Service of Vancouver was that he'd be paid a hundred dollars plus expenses to drive the car to Edmonton, where he was to begin his studies at the University of Alberta. Free transportation and a hundred bucks, you couldn't beat, he figured. He did not understand how something this simple could have gone so horribly wrong.

On board, high up on the mighty ship, passengers threw colored streamers into the air and watched them unfurl toward the tiny people below in Vancouver's beautiful white Canada Place terminal. People inside waved back and wished they, too, could be going on the luxury liner *Winter Princess,* which would sail in moments from the mist of the Burrard Inlet north between mainland BC and Vancouver Island, through the Strait of Georgia, then through the Queen Charlotte Strait and into the labyrinth of the thousand tiny glacial islands known as the Alexander Archipelago that pepper the coastline of British Columbia and the southeastern panhandle of Alaska. This route, which passed through one strait after another, sometimes cutting between islands so close together it seemed as if the ship had entered a river, never veering out into the open ocean, was called the Inner Passage, and ran through some of the most majestic scenery—glaciers and frozen mountains, vast evergreen rain forests and ice floes—on the earth.

The ship's first stop, tomorrow afternoon, in thirty hours, would be Ketchikan, Alaska.

Joe knew Kari was angry at his jettisoning her plans so completely, and at his misleading her. But she was also rendered speechless for the moment by her surprise at this new arrangement.

Of all the cruise lines he'd called from the bus station, only one ship, the *Winter Princess*, made port each summer Sunday. And it happened that at this time of year, the next to the last run of the season, this first week in September, the ship had a vacant stateroom, and could take them on as standbys. He'd had to agree to buy the whole package, 4,000 U.S. dollars for a round trip all the way north to Glacier Bay and back to Vancouver, when all they wanted was a one-way ride to Ketchikan, the first stop. And he'd had to agree to pay cash before boarding. But what was four grand in cash when you had more than a hundred in gold?

On deck, Joe and Kari stood arm in arm, sunglasses and hokey straw hats hiding their faces, waving to the ever-smaller crowd on the dock. They were just Canadian tourists Eric and Susan Delray now, out to see the wide world.

The only thing left from the Roy Jameson lead, after the blow-up of the night before, was the location of a printer named Dan Sim whom Joseph Curtis had used for his new driver's license. Jameson had mentioned he'd had local PIs trolling the city to find whether Curtis had purchased an ID. Jameson said nothing had come of it, but when they questioned the men he'd hired, it turned out one had turned a lead after all, an old man in Chinatown, but hadn't said anything because by then Jameson was already on to Curtis and Downs. Sunday morning, while Leanne was flying out to watch the arrest and later release of an innocent driver, RCMP agents were detailed out to find Sim, and failing that to break into his shop and execute a search warrant. He was not found, however, and the search revealed nothing. A neighbor said Sim often disappeared up into the mountains on the weekends. He'd be back in the shop on Monday morning.

So, from her room in the Hyatt, Leanne watched the sky change colors, watched the rain roll in that morning and hang all day. Calvin was strangely content, happy to just lie on the bed and read papers or watch television.

"I got a feeling," he said to her at one point. "I got a feeling, sister Lee."

"About what?"

"I just got a feeling." A couple times Calvin dialed a long distance number, but she did not ask him who he was calling and she did not look over his shoulder when he dialed. He said nothing during these calls, and nothing to her afterward.

At one point the phone rang, and an excited agent told Leanne they'd uncovered Northwest Airline standby tickets purchased for Joseph Curtis and departing that day for Denver and San Francisco, and Canadian Air tickets to Calgary for Kari Downs. Leanne thanked the man and asked to be kept up to date, but she did not sound happy because she knew what had happened, that Joe Curtis had laid an elaborate and false trail that had pulled them all off and allowed Joe and the girl easy passage out of the city. She knew that they had new identities and were gone now, had been gone since morning, and were somewhere far away, but most definitely not in Denver or San Francisco or Calgary.

When Cal went down to work out in the hotel gym, Leanne, before she could talk herself out of it, picked up the phone and called Ben Regis in Boise.

"The wandering agent," he said. "How you doing?"

"Bad," she said.

"You're depressed. I know that voice. Curtis slipped away?"

"It's not just that. To be honest, I'm feeling weird about this guy. I don't know."

"You think he's innocent?"

"That's not the word for it. He's something. He's laying down big-time vibes."

"Leanne, you are the strangest, you know that?"

"Yeah. Thanks. I couldn't figure out why I was calling you, of all people, but now I know. It's because you always say such nice things."

"Glad to help. So you're depressed because you're getting vibes from Curtis."

"I don't get depressed over one guy. I get depressed over my life."

"Oh, brother."

"Yeah. Forget it," she said.

"If you want to talk about something, talk."

"No. I shouldn't have called you."

Ben waited. She could hear him breathing at the other end of the line, waiting for her to drop the hammer or not. But she felt ridiculous, then. Why would she call him like this? It was as if she'd had some lapse, some memory wipe-out. She could feel him dreading what she might say next. Then he said, "You really want to talk about this?"

"I don't know."

"What about your life?"

"Have you ever been to Vancouver?" she said. "The mountains, they come right down outside the city. Big, new mountains, just across the bay to the north. Gorgeous."

"So?"

"So I think about Boise, the office and the apartment and the car and all the bullshit, and I don't even want to come back. You know?"

"Yeah," he said, but she could tell he didn't. He loved it there. He was happy. He had a family, something to care about.

"I'm sorry," she said.

"I told you to stop saying that."

"Well I am. You don't need to hear this."

"Why don't we talk when you get back, OK?"

"Sure," she said. She hung up. He could never help her, she knew, because what she wanted from him was himself. She wanted him back, the way she'd had him once, and that wasn't ever going to happen. So it was stupid and unfair to pretend like talking to him did any good at all. She covered her head with a pillow until Cal came back.

By evening the sky cleared again, fingers of rosy light reached down toward the western horizon, which she could just glimpse between buildings and over the mountains.

"Did anyone ever come by here for me?" she said to Calvin at one point.

"What? Like who?"

"I don't know. It was strange, I got a message that someone had called RCMP HQ about my father. Guy said he was a relative. I guess they told him I was staying here."

Cal shrugged his shoulders.

"Hey, you want to try that fish place downstairs again?" she said. "No interruptions this time."

After dinner, when she had paid and gone off to the bathroom, the waitress laid Leanne's credit card and the sales slip on the table. Calvin just had time to write the credit card number and expiration date on a napkin and stuff it in his pocket before Leanne came back and signed and they went upstairs for another night of lying awake and waiting.

In midafternoon, when they had been underway for six or seven hours, Kari came in and sat in a chair across from the bed where Joe lay. She'd been on deck most of the day, away from him.

"You should go up and look before dark," she said. "You're the one who decided on a cruise. You've never seen anything like it. It's beautiful."

"You a little pissed?"

"I have to admit," she said. "I was thinking about it, and I went back and looked at the schedules. If we'd taken the ferry system up, like I planned, it would have taken us over three days to get to Ketchikan, way too far past when they grabbed the car. I mean, they'd figure it out while we were still on board. We'd have cornered ourselves. But now we'll be in Ketchikan tomorrow."

"They still might figure it out."

"They won't," she said. "This was brilliant."

"So why're you mad?"

"You're never what I think you are. I mean, I told you that before, when we stopped after the store, that it was strange. You're so controlled all the time. I mean you never crack. But now, I see how you think about everything. You're always working things out in your head."

"Not always."

"You do. You get something going in there and you turn it and turn it until you get it to come around the way you want. You make it so it works out. And you just stay ice-calm until it does. It's bizarre."

"It's not how it looks."

"Last night," she said, "in that gross room, I kept expecting to see Rick's horrible face peeking in, for him to shoot us both to death. Then something occurred to me—I've never thought of him as horrible before. It's strange how you just suddenly see someone differently."

He liked her talking this way, real talk, not all full of the passion and craziness. Sometimes, at odd moments, when she didn't think about it, she showed herself.

"You wash your mind," he said.

"What?"

"You go out into a new world. All this stuff happens, it washes your mind. You see things differently. You're different."

"I—" And at that she shook her head and shut her eyes tightly. Her shoulders drew back, as if a cord were pulling them together, and she looked away from him. "Mother the Earth and Father the God. It still doesn't change the fact that you lied to me." She was gone again, back into her madness.

"We agreed," she said. "We had a plan. If you just change it behind my back, it'll never work."

"No? Look around."

"You should have told me. What about the gold? Did you send that like we agreed?"

"Don't worry about it."

She took a breath. "You're Family now. Stay with our plan."

"I need to make a call," he said.

"I read that they have a communications room. I'll help you look, if you want."

He followed her through the labyrinth of the ship's interior straight to the phones, which she found without hesitation or wrong turns. As if she'd been there already, making surreptitious calls while he dozed, keeping in touch with the world.

In the evening they changed and sat down for a fat wine-soaked dinner in the ship's main dining room full of its groaning surreal tables of meats and shellfish and desserts.

At first she refused to eat, asking only for some sliced fruit and unbuttered bread. But Joe reminded her she was on another task, that this was just another act she had to play and that meant eating the food. It didn't take much to convince her; he knew she was starving. And once she started to eat, she didn't stop until long after he had finished. They'd trained her to starve herself, he realized. Food was a powerful tool.

He remembered in boot camp once, they had a long morning training march in boots and full gear, and the sergeant leading them didn't let them stop for lunch because he said they were too ragged and didn't deserve to eat. A couple of them had passed out by midafternoon. By dinner time they were all weak and broken. Still he didn't let them eat, not until he was satisfied they'd learned how to march like soldiers, which was around ten that night. But then the sergeant led them into the mess and a special late night meal he'd arranged of prime T-bones and potatoes and salad and pies, and the men had fallen on it like animals. Joe remembered that sound, not one voice speaking, just the noise of thirty jaws chewing and ripping. Afterward, he noticed, all those men looked at that sergeant differently, with a mixture of fear and respect and even love. The way Kari talked about Father Amon.

When they returned to the tight, buttoned-down, single-windowed cabin that had become their fourth shared residence in the span of a week, Joe flopped on one of the hard twin beds, crossed his legs at the ankles and watched as Kari peeled off her new sweater, and stood in blouse and skirt, considering the remaining outfits she'd bought. The sun still sat well up in the sky, so light poured in through the small window, illuminating her back and hair in such a way that Joe couldn't help but rise up on his elbows to watch her.

He felt sad, suddenly, that it was necessary to carry on this deceit, for her to think, in her desperation, that he'd joined forces with her and her handlers. When she was herself, he'd begun to feel a bond with her, affection, even. But at the same time, having seen her in and out of her cult mind-set, he felt sorry, too. He wanted to stand up and squeeze her until all the poison flowed out of her brain.

And she, in that moment, as if he had spoken out loud, faced him.

"What?" she said.

"Will you tell me something?"

She shrugged.

"Where'd you grow up?"

She flushed a little at this, and shook her head.

"No, come on. Where's your real family. Your dad."

"California, outside San Jose." He hadn't expected her to say. But she had that voice again, the real one. Her appearance changed with it, he'd begun to notice. She seemed to loosen up, to relax. And she looked at his face in these moments. It was the meal, he guessed, that had broken her spell for a bit.

"Rich?"

"Mm, not rich, really. Comfortable. He ran a small software company."

"Do you ever talk to him?"

She came over and sat on the edge of the bed next to his feet. "I haven't seen him in years. Or my sister."

"Your mom?"

"Died."

"Is that why you left?"

"Oh, no, I was thirteen when it happened." Kari folded one leg up under the other and turned more toward Joe, who had pushed himself up so he was sitting now. "But I got married young, eighteen. Moved away, you know. Divorce, the whole thing. I was back home by the time I was twenty-one. That was a mistake. I should never have gone back. I hated them. They hated me."

"I doubt that."

"And you'd know?"

He shrugged.

She said, "My dad remarried when I was fifteen, a real work of art that woman was. Phyllis. She was beautiful. Smart. Frighteningly organized. A psychologist, private practice, rich clients who needed to unload. A very hot woman, by appearance. And ice-cold inside. There was a Mexican restaurant we went to a lot where they served fried ice cream. You ever had that? They batter and deep-fry it really fast, so it seals and doesn't melt, but the outside's sizzling. We, my sister, Jenny, and I, started calling it Phyllis. We'd whisper, 'Let's have Phyllis for dessert.' And we'd laugh. Phyllis knew it was about her but she didn't know why, so she'd just glare."

"Where's Jenny?"

"She's a nurse in Oakland. Doing fine as far as I know."

"Younger?"

"Three years older. She was pretty much on her own, away at college, by the time Dad and Phyllis tied the knot."

"But not you."

"We hated each other."

"You and Phyllis."

Kari didn't answer; she stared down toward the floor at something far away. He didn't want to lose her again, yet, but he wanted her to talk about this, to remember. He could sense that this mattered, that it had mattered for a long time.

"What happened?"

Kari shook her head. "Let's say I just had to leave."

"Which is really why you got married."

She didn't answer.

"So how'd you end up in the Family?" He watched her remembering, thinking back through it.

"They found me in the city, in San Francisco."

"They took you in?"

"Yes." Her voice was different again, still her own but farther away. "I was twenty-five. I'd been in school. Berkeley. The first time I went to an afternoon workshop with a friend of mine, I didn't even know it was a church then. The topic was something about developing personal power. I liked it, so I went back for more, a series of longer workshops. Some lasted several days. And gradually I came to understand that what I was being taught was the way of God. And the new Messiah who had come into the world at the same time as nuclear power. You see, the world received both its ultimate threat of destruction, and its ultimate hope of salvation, simultaneously! That's how God works. The Messiah was Father. He started as a student of the world, who studied Christianity and Buddhism and Islam, ancient mythologies, philosophy and psychology, biology and ecology. And from all that knowledge, and through intense prayers and fasting, he learned how people in the world should be, and founded Amonism—it's about purifying ourselves by eating and drinking correctly, living in nature, untainted by civilization, and about True Motherhood and the myth of the nuclear family, how people are really tribal. All kinds of things. It really is amazing."

"No doubt. But, I mean, don't you think it's like mind control. All that isolation. Starving people."

She stared at him, and he saw the light go out of her eyes, and knew the voice had gone with it. She had been trained well in how to clamp it down when it came back, and she'd lasted far longer than he'd expected, than she'd ever lasted with him before. She stood up from the bed, went back to the closet and started looking through her clothing again.

"What about Rick?" said Joe. "Are you, you know, his girlfriend or something?"

"No." She stopped. "I'm, I was . . . Father married me."

"*Married* you? You're Father's wife—"

"One of them."

"I see," Joe said. "One out of how many?"

"Eight, now."

"Then what about Rick? I watched you with him, in that motel. Was that a rape?"

"No."

"You just let him."

"It's not for me to question these things," she said, her back still to him.

"You were just following orders. Rick needs some relief, you have to give it to him. You were kind of on loan, huh?"

"Father took me in a long time ago, when I had *no* one. The Family loved me and taught me and took me with them to Alaska, where only the chosen got to go. That's a great privilege."

"The frozen chosen," he said. He didn't know why. He knew he'd already sent her over and the best thing was to lay off for now, to shut up and let her rest. But it pissed him off, the thought of her, brainwashed, out in the bush like that, getting fucked by who knew how many of these men whenever they wanted her, of her risking her life to mule a suitcase of money back to them.

"Are you still with us?" she said.

He sat up and leaned forward to look out the window, but the light inside the room was too bright so he couldn't see. His breath fogged the glass.

"You should pray, Joe. Let me teach you."

"I'm a Catholic, and that's enough religion for anyone."

"Shhh." She stepped across to him and touched his hair, ran her hand down the back of his head to his neck. "Don't be angry. Listen to me. I'll teach you the first prayer." She dropped to knees at the edge of his bed and clasped her hands and began: "I am sin, Father. I am darkness and impurity—"

"Hail Mary, Full of Grace," Joe said to the window. "The Lord is with Thee."

"—but the Earth is my womb and You are my salvation."

"Blessed art thou amongst women—" recited Joe.

"Shut up!" she screamed. He lay back down to watch her as she slammed the door of her closet and stormed from the room.

Later yet, still alone, Joe found an empty fore deck and stood against the railing.

It felt odd to him, but time was beginning to stretch out again. It had only been seven days since those lonely hours on the road in Montana, a week since a time when he had never known Kari Downs, which had seen him become a fugitive from the federal law in two countries, and go from broke into the possession of a hundred and fifty thousand dollars. Lifetimes packed into those seven days. But now, by late evening, time had slowed again. And what would happen next, and in the days and weeks to follow, would happen more slowly, more deliberately, under more control. He felt it in his hands, which had mastered so many physical materials, which had mended engines and weapons and buildings, which had shaped wood and metal, and stolen cars and gold and a woman. Now in these hands he began to imagine a different sort of control, over his life, over the events which would save or ruin him. He did not know why, what would lead him to believe this was so—perhaps the headiness of continued freedom, or perhaps something larger than that, a glimpse, maybe, of what awaited him. But he could not see that yet, could not begin to imagine where he would end up, other than to feel that these mountains which tore upward from the sea, blue-black and green and frozen white, that this land of endless ranges of mountains, would make a difference.

Somehow he had avoided, twice, the forces chasing him. And he was gone again, lost to them this time, until he chose to make contact. Which he would do soon. But for right now, he had only to lean, drink in hand, against this railing near the bow of the great ship. He wore the good new clothes Kari had bought him, corduroys and a heavy Pendelton shirt and a dark wool jacket because it was cool this evening. The air carried the chill of the north, of the end of summer in the near Arctic. He listened as the ship cut water far beneath him. He watched the shadowed mountains to the east as they caught the last flushed rays of the sunset, and the vast darkening ocean to the west, which rolled away and away forever until it exhausted itself, finally, on some wondrous, distant beach.

23

Again, just three weeks since the last time, Father was in the dormitory. The women had grown unused to such exposure, such access; the newer, younger ones had never experienced it. For the last year Father had resembled more and more a hermit, a religious isolationist, a monk in the throes of prayers so intense and important they would take years to complete. It had only made them love him more, only made him that much more authentic. Because when he did say words to them, the words were magic, the words made them feel that heat, that blinding, flashing moment of self-knowledge. As if by withholding himself from them most of the time, the few minutes he spent with them were condensed, concentrated, purified into the essence of his message, of his meaning. Often many of them wept openly at his mere touch.

But, now, so soon, he was back, lingering, almost unsure of what to say. The older ones, his early wives, the mothers of the older children, remembered him like this, from California, from Bellevue, from Idaho. They remembered those unsure, dangerous times, and they did not like it that he was here now. It reminded them of then, of when he had warned them that men would come and try to kill them. He had been right then. And so he would be right again. He was always right.

He stood on a folding metal chair. He needed no formal pulpit. This was only another small sign of his authenticity. And he spoke:

"My Family," he said. "We know that to live the honest life, the valid life, is a struggle, a fight against nothing less than the world. We know that, we are reminded of it, but sometimes, when we have succeeded, when the life we have constructed and fought for is good, we forget. We believe that the goodness, because it is so good, will last of its own accord. While such a belief is understandable, it is also dangerous. So I am here to remind you that the fight is not over, that the fight will never be over until we reach the ultimate Sanctuary."

Here the women nodded and smiled at one another. Some held small children on their laps. They sat around the long folding tables, faces turned upward toward him. The ultimate Sanctuary, they murmured. Out there, along the peninsula, past the last road and the last town, past the mountain ranges. That place. This was where they thought he meant. But he said:

"I do not just mean the next physical place we will live, which will be the last physical place, because I will not run anymore. There we will stop and we will stand and we will fight our fight. And there, later or sooner, we will become a part of the Earth, which is truly the ultimate Sanctuary." He waved a hand out in front of his face, toward an imagined horizon.

Some of the women, the younger ones especially, gripped their children more tightly, for they now understood his meaning.

"I'm telling you that this fight, for which we are preparing, for which other events in other places are even now helping us prepare, could be terrible. To be blunt, I'm telling you that, for some of us, it may be our last fight. I am sorry to say that. I am overjoyed. For we are worthy. We are prepared. And we know, each of us, that the rewards to come are so great, so beautiful, that we cannot imagine them. But we are entitled to those rewards. We have earned them. They shall be ours.

"So prepare. We were to move to the new Sanctuary next year. Now, it may happen sooner, and on an instant's notice. So plan accordingly. If any of you wishes to see me in private, I shall make myself available, in my cabin, today and tomorrow."

He smiled at them. Someone reached up to help him down from the chair. Tears wet his cheeks as he moved around the room, embracing each of them in their turn.

The first part of Colonel Rozsa's argument, that this was, potentially, an issue of civilian security, had been conceded. He was told the Secretary of the Army grabbed his ulcer-ridden stomach when he read Rozsa's scenario of an army Stinger missile killing a planeload of civilians.

But his second point—that the army should be prepared to move immediately to confiscate or destroy the missiles if an opportunity to do so with a minimum of loss of civilian life presented itself—was rejected out of hand. Federal agents would carry out any necessary police actions.

"Federal agents aren't trained in antimissile counteractions," Rozsa spit out, when he was briefed on this decision by General Parkins. "The last time someone used a military machine gun against them was Waco. We know how that turned out. Only this time, *we'll* be held responsible. Did you tell them that? If innocent people die, it'll come back to haunt us. It's our hardware. Property of the U.S. Army."

Parkins didn't say anything. There was nothing to discuss.

The Army Chief of Staff, General Hargrave, had cleared CID to maintain a full-scale field investigation, to be coordinated with, but remaining independent of, the efforts of the ATF and FBI investigators. INSCOM and Rozsa were to be kept fully briefed. Other than that, they were out of the loop.

◇

West again, into the dark night, to a wooden pier in Prince Rupert, the town on the British Columbia coast which lay directly across from the southernmost point of the eastern Alaskan panhandle, the beginning of the Alexander Archipelago. A boat, a fifty-two-foot purse seiner, had tied up, its wooden clapboards squealing against the pier's rubber bumpers. The pier was away from the many crowded docks off the town's center, up the coast a little, around a bend in the bay. Other private piers jutted into the water here and there, not too many but enough so they weren't unusual sights. Most, though, were well lighted by sealed all-weather lamps, a few by old-fashioned-looking strings of plain white bulbs. But this pier was nearly dark. The only lights were flashlights, held by the men unloading two unmarked yellow vans.

So it was some time before any of the working men noticed another man standing on the pier, watching them. One of the men, in describing something to the ship's captain, used his light to point toward the shore. As he did, it passed over the face of the observer.

"Shit," the man said. "You scared the—Rick?"

"Hey," Rick said.

"How long you been standing there?"

"Little while."

When Deacon stepped out of the cabin of the boat and saw Rick he smiled and said, "Come on. We have a lot to discuss."

"What?" Rick said. "They're gone again."

"They'll be in Ketchikan," Deacon said.

"How do you know that?"

"Kari made the reservations. This Joe person shipped the gold there from Vancouver. She's been calling Father Amon all along, when she can."

Rick and Deacon sat at the galley table, an old kerosene lantern lighting the space between them, and Deacon and Omaha laid out maps of Ketchikan, the surrounding topography and the ocean floor. They'd cross the border later that night, hopping first from island to island on the Canadian side until they'd come to within three miles of U.S. waters. Then, without benefit of running lights or navigational sonar, using only stray light from the islands, and moonlight, creeping at five or six knots in order not to generate noise and to avoid disaster if they should strike something, they'd cross.

Once there, they'd drop Rick on a dark beach a few miles out of Ketchikan, then would guide the boat back out among the smaller islands to wait, to lie low until they received a radio message from Rick saying he'd recovered the gold and Kari. Although Deacon did not like risking the exposure, it would be best if they could just pick up Rick and the gold, and head out to sea. Assuming Rick pulled off the job cleanly, and wasn't pursued.

Father didn't like the idea because it put everything, the weapons and men and gold, all into one tight little package. If anything should happen to that package, the whole mission would be a loss and the Family out not only its money and its best men, but would still have no real protection. Still, Deacon said, as long as Rick did his job, this was the best way.

24

THE PASSENGERS WERE BRIEFED ON THE WONDERFUL SIGHTS TO BE SEEN IN the old gold-rush town of Ketchikan. Eric and Susan Delray disembarked with the others, looking a little nervous or excited, perhaps, but not so much so that they drew particular attention. They carried with them only a bag with some extra clothing, and an empty backpack. For souvenirs, Eric explained to the U.S. customs agent. Of course he'd be glad to declare them when he came back aboard. Joe silently thanked the old Chinese man in Vancouver, when, after they presented their licenses, the agent asked to see a second form of ID. They showed the bogus birth certificates, stated that they'd only be ashore a few hours, and were passed through.

But he was not well, this tourist. His head felt as if the arteries in his neck had been squeezed so that the blood had to increase its pressure many times in order to get past the stricture into his brain. His face felt flushed. The ankle sores were so red and inflamed that he could see the swellings through his socks, more like little tumors than swollen sores. His skin itched all over his body.

On the dock, Kari handed Joe a slip of paper with the address of the Marine View Hotel, but Joe crumpled it. She said nothing, and followed him along the dock and into a taxi, an old late-seventies Cadillac with dented doors and a driver with three or four teeth left.

"On break," the driver said. "Not open."

"Front Street B&B," said Joe. Kari looked at him, but still did not ask any questions.

The driver laughed. "I'm on break. But maybe I can work you some native magic."

"What?"

"Abracadabra," said the driver, and pointed. There, right on the other side of Front Street, which they were on, was the entrance of the B&B.

Inside they spotted the packages in a small room behind the wooden counter, stacked one on top of the other.

"There're only two," she said, but he did not look at her. He set his license on the counter and pointed at the packages.

"Yessir," the woman said. "Right here. And you weren't sure how long you'd be staying."

"Two nights," he told her, and handed over a handful of cash. He had no plans to stay here even one minute, though, and when she handed the packages across, along with a room key, he picked them all up and turned back toward the door.

But Kari led him by the arm to the staircase. "We've got to go," he said. "There's no time."

"I want to know what's going on," she said. "This isn't where I arranged for you to send the gold. And this isn't all the gold. I'm not going any farther until you let me in. We're supposed to be together, but you haven't done one thing we agreed on. I want to know why. Besides, I can tell you're getting sick again."

"Kari—"

"It's either this or I start screaming. You choose."

He followed her up the staircase and down a narrow wallpapered hallway to a small room with more wallpaper, large red roses, and a double bed and a dresser. He dropped the two packages of gold to the floor, sat down next to them and squeezed his temples, but the pain was hitting fully now, tearing through his brain so he thought he might go mad.

He got on his hands and knees and pressed his head against the linoleum.

"What's wrong with you, exactly?" Kari said. She knew he had these episodes, from witnessing them, but he'd never said anything about them.

Now he said, "I know you've been calling them . . . giving reports —where we are . . . where we're going, how we're getting there." He spoke without lifting his head. "I've known it all along."

"Joe—"

"I don't care, Kari." He turned so he could see her. She sat on the bed.

"I knew you knew," she said.

"What?" He sat up, steadying himself against the wall.

"I mean, part of me did. Maybe I hoped you did." Her face was pink. "Maybe I prayed somehow you'd make it all work. You're hard to read. I couldn't tell if you had that in you. But when you took me to the ship, I knew, then, what you'd done."

He exhaled hard and squeezed his head again. She said to him, "Will you tell me what's wrong with you?"

He didn't answer.

"Come on," she said, and she knelt next to him, lifted his arm, and helped him to the bed where she laid him face down so she could sit up on his back. Then he felt her hands along the tops of his shoulders, kneading, then on the back of his neck. And it helped some, blunting the pain's edge a little.

"I'll tell you what I think it is," she said. "You keep everything, every emotion—fear, desire, relief—inside. So they build up and come out like this, your brains trying to explode. You are so repressed."

"It's all my fault," he said so softly she had to lean in toward his face to hear. "All the way from Bozeman."

"What do you mean?"

"I went along just to follow you. All the way. I should have left when I knew there was going to be trouble, when we hit Coeur d'Alene. But I had this fantasy that you were desperate, that you needed me. And later, in Seattle, I shouldn't have grabbed you. I think all along I just wanted to end up like this, in a room, with you, alone."

She'd stopped massaging to listen, and smiled as he spoke.

"I should have let you go."

"I am going," she said. "I'm on my way right now."

"Alone."

"With you. We're together."

"You were right, though. I've been lying to you."

"Your note, in Bellevue," she said. "I knew Rick didn't write it. I knew it had to be you out there. But I came anyway. I pretended it might really be Rick, but I knew."

He turned so he could see her face. "Why?"

"When I first saw you, on the highway in Montana, looking in through my window, I felt it, too," she said. "I said to myself, this one could be different. This might be the one that saves you. Or kills you. But I played safe—I used you and I left you. But when you came back with that note, I knew I had to look at you again. When you tied me up and stole me, then when you took care of me even after I'd ruined your life, I knew it. I knew you were the one, that you'd been sent. One way or the other—whether you were going to ruin me or deliver me—I knew I was gone.

"It's dangerous, deciding to care, Joe."

It was her own voice speaking, not the voice of the Family. He lay back down so she could rub his neck again. Her hands were as strong as a man's, and they rubbed so deeply he thought he would have bruises. If he were wrong, if this were another con, a setup so she could call someone in to finish it, then he knew she had won already, because he could fight no more, he wanted so badly to believe her.

But he'd only know it when he took a bullet in the head. What was strange was that that felt less disappointing than would the knowledge, in the millisecond before he died, that this had all been another act on her part, the caring for. It would mean there was no self left inside her manufactured facade. Both of them would be gone, forever.

As for himself, now, he was gone already. And if it were only ever to be that she would rub his neck when he panicked, he supposed that would be enough. As long as she stayed.

"I have to know something," he said. His headache had faded, his vision blurring now.

"Ask."

"It's not what you think."

"What do I think?"

"I don't care about the Family or Father or Rick. I mean, I care about what they've done to you, but I can't help that now. What I want to know is more about you, the parts you can't talk about."

"Such as?"

"I want to understand, in the beginning, how someone like you goes into a cult, or whatever you want to call it. You come from money. You were married. You go to Berkeley. And then, when you're twenty-five, you just fade out. Now you're what, thirty?"

"Not for a few months yet, thank you."

"So how did all this happen to you? You hated your father that much? Or was it about your step-mother, Phyllis?"

He was lying flat on the bed. She moved off him and propped herself up against the headboard, her arm pressing against his face. "What about her?" she said.

"Is that where it begins?"

"More like where it ends."

"Tell me."

Kari hugged a pillow to her chest. "You have to understand. When Mom died, that was the end of our family. I mean, my dad just stopped being there. He worked all the time. He let Jenny raise me, what raising was left to do. We might as well have been orphaned—maybe it would have been easier somehow, that way. In any case, he wasn't my father anymore. He was just some guy who showed up from time to time.

"And then when Phyllis came into it, it changed again. Daddy tried to start acting like we were a family again. He wanted me to do stuff with him and Phyllis. But she didn't want me there, and I certainly didn't want to be there."

"So you left at eighteen and got married."

She nodded.

"You tried moving home again after the divorce. It didn't work out."

"God," she said. "Didn't work out. It was horrible. I could never go back there again, after the things they said to me. It was finished. They weren't my family anymore."

"Except for paying for college."

"Oh, no," she said. "There was no contact, no support. I put myself through. Grants and loans and work."

"So what then? You graduate? You're twenty-five? And—"

"I told you before. I went to these meetings. It was so brilliant, what they were talking about."

"No, no," Joe said. He turned and propped himself up on his arm, so he was face to face with her, their noses only a few inches apart. "Not the bullshit line," he said. "Not the crap about the new fucking messiah and all that. Really, what was it that made you go in like that. What is it in a bright, beautiful, rich girl that makes her sign her life away? That's the question, Kari. That's what I want to know."

She looked at him for a long time, her face so close he could feel her breath on him. She did not move or change her expression. But her eyes grew wet and red. Then she said, "I've been taught not to think about it. Trained. But I have thought about it, some. A lot recently, since I've been with you. And you know, I don't think it's complicated. I don't think it's some big cosmic answer. School was done so my friends, you know, were all off in different places; I didn't have a relationship or a real family or a job yet. And I think I was just so lonely, Joe, I couldn't stand it. Then these people I met, from the Family, they liked me. I mean really liked me. And they were nice to me. Supportive. Generous. And that's important. To belong. To be nurtured. It's a big thing."

"The biggest," Joe said.

◇

For as dreary and depressing as the rainy, no-action Sunday in the hotel room was for Leanne, Monday had dawned different. The sun came, for one thing, burning off what thin cloud cover had held through the night. And the day began quickly, when Connor called to say that the printer, Dan Sim, had opened his shop a few minutes ago. Connor was on his way to pick her up, and a squad car would meet them at the printer's shop.

In the end, after a long morning of interrogation, of threatening and cajoling and promising, the printer didn't have much to tell except that, yes, he'd made the IDs, not knowing of course that this guy was a fugitive, certainly not a wanted murderer, and no, he did not keep records of any kind, either of the transaction itself or of the documents he printed. So he honestly wasn't sure what the names were. And why would he lie? What'd he have to gain now? He'd just as soon see them caught since they'd got him in this jam anyway. Susan was one name, he remembered. The man's first name he couldn't. As for the surname, Ray something. Rayner, maybe. Or DeRay. That sounded closer. DeRay. Or Delray, maybe. He wasn't sure, exactly.

Joe packed the gold in the backpack, with the extra clothing stuffed in around it.

"Are you going to tell me where the rest is?" Kari said.

"Do you want to know?"

She considered this a moment, then said, "It depends. What are we doing? How is this going to work?"

"Just the same. You keep telling them what we plan together."

"What I said earlier, I meant it, but it doesn't mean I can let you turn against us."

"What?"

"I mean I still have to take the gold to Sanctuary."

"Kari, why—"

"It doesn't matter why. I have reasons. I'm telling you that in the end I'll need the gold."

It was wrong still. Right, but wrong. They could leave, go together anywhere they wanted. Buy real IDs, tickets, new faces, even. It was her eyes he loved, and no surgeon could change the way they looked.

He thought to tell her all this, but knew she'd thought it all already, considered making the big run with him. And that she'd decided against it. So, OK, he thought. He said, "Who're they sending? Rick?"

"Yes."

"What if you didn't take it all. Maybe, say, fifty grand."

She thought, and said, "That'd probably work."

"What if Rick takes the fall."

"Fine."

"Will you help? For my sake, he has to go down. That's what I've been after, to turn him over along with some of the money."

She smiled, the beguiling grin that hurt him in his heart. "Then I can go back with my share of what's left of the gold?"

"Yep."

"So, you got a deal, Joe Mechanic." It was still her real voice, her true self, talking. He knew it. She'd stayed with him all the way this time.

Leanne got back to the room late. Cal was lying on the bed.

"We're finished here," she said. "They're out of Canada, somewhere. Time to go home and figure out what to do with you."

"You're just gonna give it up?"

"What can I do?"

"Leanne, you are so full of shit. When was the last time you let anything go just because it was time? Have you ever done that? You can't let up on anything."

But he was wrong, she knew. She'd let Ben go. She was the one who suggested they cool things down. And she'd been wrong about that. She'd ruined what was good.

"Why are you doing this?" she said.

"There's another trip we can take," he said. "Tonight. It's already arranged."

"What trip?"

"You can't ask a lot of questions. Get packed. We have to be at the airport in an hour."

"What is this about, Calvin?"

"I'll tell you what it's not about. It's not about me. It's not about my trouble or money or about me running. I'm doing *you* the favor this time, Lee. But you can't ask me a lot of questions or I'll get mad. I'll tell you as we go along."

"And what am I supposed to tell them at my office?"

"Nothing. That's part of the deal—you can't call them at all. You're just going to vanish."

"Deal? I'd like to know who you're in a position to make deals with and what it has to do with my office."

"Will you just shut up and get ready. Think of it as a little side vacation I talked you into."

The phone rang. The RCMP had figured out the names Susan and Eric Delray. They'd booked passage on a cruise ship, which had docked three hours ago in Ketchikan, Alaska. Alaskan state troopers were boarding the ship now. Leanne hung up and started to run, when Cal grabbed her arm.

"Ketchikan," she said. "That's where they are."

"But that's not where the action is. They'll be gone before anyone gets there. In fact, they're gone already."

Leanne froze, then lowered herself into a chair. "Oh, my God, Cal," she said. "What have you done? How are you in this?"

"I said no questions." He wagged a finger at her. "We're going to the airport and we're flying north. But not to Ketchikan. Now, if you're ready?" He held the door open for her.

At the Ketchikan airport, a little earlier, as night fell, Kari paid cash for tickets, as Joe instructed her to do, using newly invented names, the Delrays having been retired. Behind the one-story terminal, on an apron to the double runway, they found their ride, an old corrugated metal trimotor prop job, two engines on the wing, which ran over the top of the square boxy fuselage, and one on the nose. Inside there were only twelve rows of seats. It made the Markair milk run twice a day, morning and evening, up the Archipelago, Ketchikan to Wrangell to Sitka to Juneau, which was their destination.

When the engines revved it was impossible to hear anything but the roar. To communicate they would have had to yell. So they didn't talk. She slid her arm through his and hugged it to her, held it as her support, and leaned her head on his shoulder. They'd no sooner reach their altitude and level out when a descent would begin. Down and up and down, and it got to her. She felt nauseous and dizzy. Strangely, Joe thought, he didn't feel anything the least bit unpleasant. He felt fine.

When they'd touched down for the last time and taxied to another one-story terminal, when the engines finally died, she whispered, "I don't know what to do anymore."

"What you've been doing," he told her. "Nothing else."

In a larger, newer plane, a 727 also enroute to Juneau, Leanne and Calvin sat with their arms touching on the armrest between them. A thought struck Leanne. "These tickets," she said. "How did you pay?"

"Your Visa."

"No. Cal—"

"Relax. I'm not stupid enough to charge them," he said. "I had the front desk send up cash."

After this, Leanne did not speak. She was fighting so violently with herself, with her nature, that she didn't have any energy or concentration to converse. Calvin was right to think she'd want to take this gamble, whatever it was he'd arranged, to have a final shot at finding the killer and the arms, a last chance to win although the cost of failure now would be wickedly high. She was surprised at how well he knew her, after all, well enough to have no trace of doubt that she'd go along with this madness.

And she thought about his question, about whether she'd ever let anything go just because it was time. What struck her was how much that sounded like a question Guts would have asked her.

In any case, she thought again, she'd let too much go. Almost never willingly, perhaps, but she'd lost too many people from her life just the same.

On the day she turned eighteen, in November of 1977, home from her first quarter of college for Thanksgiving break, Leanne awoke early, long before sunrise, and dressed in gaiters and wool leggings and sweaters and a hide coat one of the tribal women had helped her tan and cut and stitch together. She waited in the snow outside the door to her mother's house. Guts met her there in his '60 International Harvester that had enough four-wheel drive torque to climb walls, and they drove farther than they should have up precarious, switched-back logging roads into the Missions until they were miles in.

They stopped when they could pass no farther. A ten-foot drift covered the road, but they were nearly at its end anyway. Leanne knew this place. They'd been here before, in the summer, scouting, hiking, tracking just for the exercise of it. The road ended a quarter mile ahead. Then there was a foot path that led up to a ridge peak. From there, Leanne remembered, a wide game trail wove its way back deeper into the heart of the range.

For some reason, as if the snow in itself wouldn't be difficult enough, Guts strapped on a loaded backpack he'd brought.

It took them three hours to hike what hadn't taken half an hour a few months before. But finally, two hours after sunrise, they stood together on top of the ridge, at the head of the trail. Guts dropped his pack under a tree.

The snow was so fresh that nothing had marked it yet. As they moved down in, though, along the trail, the tracks of a large animal, a buck, crossed from one side to the other.

"He will be nearby," Guts whispered. "These are new. Should we do things your way? Should we follow him?"

Leanne nodded. She was itching to go.

A hundred yards into the timber the line of tracks became two. Two animals? Guts shook his head, and drew a circle in the air. The animal had circled back on his trail, which meant he'd caught some wind of them, knew something was behind him and had come back around to see. It also meant they were very close. The buck could well have been watching them at that moment.

Guts made another sign, pointing his flat hand out across the snow, drawing a line perpendicular with the slope they were on. Then he pointed at Leanne, then down the slope. He meant he would work across, while she could drop down a ways. The idea was that he might push the buck downhill, where it would run into her.

She headed down. The snow here on the lee side of the hill was at least two feet deep, and with each step she had to pull her foot up above knee-height to clear it. The bad part was that too much of this would bring exhaustion quickly. The good part was that she could move silently as the trees. If she stayed slow, she knew, she could creep up on anything that lived.

Then she saw the tracks again, coming from her left, across her trail. How, she wondered, did the buck get over there? They had seen no tracks leading down this way. She followed his trail with her eyes, as it angled back up the slope, and then she caught her breath. There, fifty yards over, watching her with his head held low, almost touching the snow, stood the biggest mule deer she'd ever seen. Ten, twelve points. She couldn't count. It didn't matter. There was a moment of mutual fascination, a frozen millisecond when they each just looked into the other's eyes.

She felt her rifle come up automatically to her shoulder, felt her cheek snap against the cold Maple stock in just the right spot, so her sightline was clear. She saw the deer now through the V-cut iron sight, watched as it began its spin into retreat. Her motion triggered its motion, and it was already halfway around and leaping up from the heavy snow when her gun fired of its own accord, and in the snow and trees made little noise. The sound was a pop. Then nothing.

The deer was gone. She hiked up to where it had been, but saw no blood in the snow and knew she'd missed.

Then Guts was next to her, nodding, looking around, kneeling.

"He was a big animal," he said.

"You saw him?"

"No. But I heard him. And I felt his presence."

"Goddammit," she said. "How could I miss?"

"Did you hold on steady, and squeeze?"

"Yes."

"Were you in the right spot, in your mind?"

"Yes."

"Did he move?"

"Yes, but I still thought I had him. I knew I did—"

"Then why doubt yourself?"

"Well where is he? Where's the blood?"

Guts stood up and walked through the snow, to a small crest that dropped into a ravine.

"There," Guts said, and he was right. The animal lay on its side not fifty yards from where they stood.

"He held his blood inside," Guts said. "He is a big animal. They can do that sometimes. Still, it did him no good."

Later, when they'd dressed the buck and dragged it, one holding on to each antler, out to the head of the trail, and were about to hike down to the truck, Guts took Leanne's shoulder in his hand in a way he had never touched her before, in all the ten years they had known each other.

"You go," he said. "It's downhill. You can handle the animal yourself from here."

"What do you mean?"

"I am not going back," Guts said.

"Why?" She sounded indignant; she spoke to him the way she spoke to her mother sometimes, full of disrespect.

He gave her the keys to the truck. "You drive it out. Be careful on the road. The snow will give out under you if you don't watch. Later, I want you to give the truck to your dad. He always admired it. I signed it over to him."

"Guts—"

"I am going to die," he said, as if he were announcing his plans to go get breakfast. He held his hand over Leanne's mouth. "Cancer they say. Blood comes out of me. I been to the clinic in Missoula, been going there for six months. They been tracking it with machines. I don't like the machines. They want to give me poisons. I won't take 'em. Now, I can feel it pressing on my heart. It is close to killing me, and I will not let it kill me that easy. More important, I will not let them kill me in their hospitals. I will die as a hunter dies."

She cried, the tears freezing on her cheeks. She knew she had to stop or she'd get frostbit, but she could not. They'd hunted together so many times she could never begin to count them. She knew him, and she knew that she could not change his mind in this, and that he was telling her the truth, that he would never come out, that she would not see him again. But she couldn't say good-bye. She couldn't say any words.

"You are a strong woman," he said to her. "The world is lucky to have you. Go on. Tell your father I say so long to him, and I'll see him sometime again. And tell your brother I will be watching over him. He needs someone to do it."

With that, Guts strapped on the pack, then turned and walked away. He listed to one side a little, as if he were tired in some way she hadn't noticed before. He adjusted the rifle he had slung over his shoulder, and passed through a line of aspens and was gone, down into the valley beyond the mountain where they stood.

25

"SHE'S DROPPED OUT OF SIGHT. SHE CHECKED OUT YESTERDAY. AND SOMEone was staying with her. A man," Simmons said. Ben was in his office, just the two of them alone. Simmons had already been over it on the phone with everyone, though, from District in Seattle all the way to D.C. He was at a loss.

"I don't believe it," said Ben.

"You'd better say that. Since she used you to get around me before, you'd better come clean now, if you know anything."

"Ed, I'm worried about her. If I knew anything I'd tell you, because I think she's making a mistake, whatever she's doing."

"Do you? I'm not sure I do."

"You think she's doing the right thing, going off like this?"

Simmons shrugged. "She's been right all along. I bitched at her for doing it the first time, I'd ordered her off the case, and look what she found. She made my first big break here, and less than a week after I came in. I have to love her for that."

"So you're going to let her run?"

"I have no choice, do I? The question is, if she's after Curtis and the woman, why didn't she go into Ketchikan last night? We know that's where they disembarked. Or is she there and not telling us? Is it just because she thinks I wouldn't have let her go up?"

"I don't think so. She'd have let us know, at least. She might not have waited for clearance, but she'd have let us know. Like Seattle."

"I think so, too," said Simmons. "And I don't think she's in Ketchikan at all. She found something else. So the second question is why isn't she calling for back-up? That makes me nervous. And not just me. I'm waiting for a call from the director himself. That's where this has gone. They're all shitting their pants. Justice is raising hell, I guess. Treasury Sec's in on it. They want us shut down."

"The arms are still out there. They still need to be found."

"By 'us' I mean this office. FBI and the ATF will continue to track. But not us. Not Leanne. What's funny is that she was a hero to them just a couple days ago. Well, they're all political shitbrains. See, that's what I think Leanne knows. That if she makes contact, she'll be ordered in not by me but by the guys in D.C."

"If you were to tell them she called."

Simmons nodded and smiled, then said, "Still, I worry about back-up. If she knew someone was coming in she could trust, she might act differently."

Ben saw what it was, then. "I'll go," he said.

"You guys were close, I hear."

Ben nodded.

"Too close? Should you do this?"

"It'll be fine," Ben said. "We don't know where she is, anyway. I might not even get to her before whatever's going to happen happens."

"We'll get you into Ketchikan. That way you'll be close when we hear something. If there's any way to put you in touch with her, we will. But my guess is she'll try to call you, first."

He was right, Ben knew. What worried Ben, what he wasn't saying, was his last conversation with Leanne, how depressed she'd sounded. He hadn't heard her like that in a long time, but he knew that the bottom, for her, was a long way down.

Early Tuesday morning, after Leanne Red Feather's disappearance had been confirmed, the RCMP, at the FBI's request, had arranged to trace out all the calls made from her room at the Hyatt. Which led the feds to Calvin's automated answering service in Boise, nothing more than a rented room full of phone lines and recording machines. Agents swept down on the place with warrants, drilled the lone woman working there, identified the correct tape, and found that all messages older than twenty-four hours had been taped over. So the tape was flown to a west coast sound lab where it arrived before noon. Without too much difficulty, the technicians were able to lift some of the messages that had been erased.

In the late afternoon, on the east coast, Lieutenant Bliss handed Colonel Rozsa a single sheet of paper, with the transcript of one of the taped messages, which simply informed the listener to check in at the Holiday Inn in Juneau.

"Juneau," Rozsa said. "What's ATF running there?"

"They're swearing she's AWOL," Bliss said. "She disappeared; they didn't know where she was. ATF and FBI believed Curtis and Downs were in Ketchikan, and they both have agents there now. They thought that's where Red Feather had gone."

"No. She's their ace. She's onto something solid," Rozsa said. "And it's all back on U.S. soil. You're people better get on to her and fast. Wherever she is, that's where it's going to happen."

"They're flying in now. FBI's flying agents in, too. They're in close touch with us. We may have resources up that way they want to share."

"You might think to have CRIDCOM remind all those bright boys that if they're really smart, they won't pick her up, or let her know they're there. They'll just watch and see who comes along."

◇

A day earlier, on Monday, at the twelve-story Marine View Hotel in Ketchikan, Rick Agullana asked at the desk about Eric or Susan Delray. He was told they had not yet checked in or made a reservation.

Had any packages arrived for them?

"Are you Mr. Delray?" the woman asked.

"No," Rick said. "An associate."

"Nothing's come in, sir."

So Rick took a room. Later that afternoon, he checked again with the desk about the Delrays.

"Nothing yet," the same woman told him. "But someone else asked, too. Two men."

"What men?" Rick said.

"I don't know who they were. They looked like businessmen. They waited in the lobby for a while. Who are these Delrays?"

Through a front-lobby window Rick noticed two "businessmen" sitting in their car. It made the hairs on the back of his neck stand up. Fucking feds, he thought.

He left the building through a back door, and cabbed to the end of the city, where he checked into a motel. He called Father to find out what had happened.

Father said, "That's where she said they were going."

"Is she setting me up?"

"I don't know," Father said. "I've told you everything I know. I don't know!"

"Are you setting me up?"

"Rick. Stop it."

Rick stopped. He calmed down. He felt better hearing Father say "Rick" in that killer tone of voice.

"Give me your number," Father said. "And wait there."

That night, after eleven, Father called back. "It's Juneau, now," he said. "They're in Juneau. She called me when he went out to get them some dinner."

Into a hand-held VHF-band marine radio, Rick said, "Wolf to Base. Wolf to Base. Over."

Seconds passed; he wasn't sure this would work, whether the signal would carry or the boat had even remained. If anything at all looked out of place their orders were to not look back. Now with the feds crawling all over, Deacon may have bailed. Not that Rick would have blamed him. Then the radio crackled and Deacon said, "Base here. Over."

"Wolf to come in, over," said Rick, and the answer came back, "Roger and over." They'd meet him in one hour at the same desolate spot up the beach where he'd come ashore. He'd float out in a dingy and they'd be northbound not too long after midnight. It was two hundred miles, though, and they were traveling along the Marine Highway through straits and channels, so the going would be slow. It would be well into tomorrow, Tuesday, before they reached Juneau. Whatever Joe had planned, Rick hoped it wouldn't happen before he could get there.

26

THE CITY OF JUNEAU IS BUILT ON A SHELF WEDGED BETWEEN THE MOUNtains of the Boundary Ranges to its immediate east, and the narrow, deep water Gastineau Channel to its west. Its residential areas, as is true of many of the coastal towns of Alaska, crawl uphill from the downtown, at the ocean's edge. The hills of Juneau, though, are so steep that wooden staircases had to be built as well, to allow residents and visitors direct access instead of having to walk the tightly switched-back roads. Behind the city, to the northwest only thirteen miles and reachable by roads, the Mendenhall Glacier empties into Mendenhall Lake. The glacier begins twelve miles farther up into the mountains at the Juneau ice field which lies just east of the city over the first ridge of mountains and which, at 4,000 square miles, is one of the largest permanent ice fields in the world, outside the Antarctic.

Although the glacier's face is accessible on ground, the best way to see it, and the only way to see the ice field, is from the air. Best of all are the commercial helicopter services based at the airport north of town which not only provide a view from the sky, but, weather allowing, deposit tourists directly onto the surface of the glacier or the ice field. In many years, these helicopter rides stop after the Labor Day weekend, but this year, because temperatures and the weather have stayed moderate, the choppers are still flying.

On Tuesday evening at six o'clock sharp, Rick boarded such a tourist chopper, a Hughes 500D, at Epoch Flights, which ran up to four birds in peak season when the cruise ships were in and the crowds heavy. Today, though, only one was running, lifting off once every two hours.

Father said Kari had been insistent in her call that day. Joe was meeting someone at six P.M. to hand over the gold. She did not know who it was, or why, but she said they were going up on the glacier to do it. Whoever he was meeting said it had to be someplace isolated, away from the city.

"He's passing it off," Father had said. "He ripped us off and he's passing it, and he's going to get away."

"We'll see," said Rick.

Now, to the chopper pilot, he said, "Is there only one place where you take people up there?"

"What do you mean?" said the pilot.

"On the glacier. Is there one particular spot tourists always go."

The pilot shook his head. "Depends on weather and where there's a flattened, level area. It changes. Past month, though, we've been going to one general area."

"Good," said Rick. There was a couple aboard with him, retirees from Storm Lake, Iowa, they explained. Their daughter lived in Juneau, now. Rick grunted, then ignored them.

Rick couldn't see it, of course, but when they lifted off and headed up over the ridge, a second chopper, this one privately chartered, lifted off to follow. That was the deal. The pilot had been told to wait for two passengers, a man and a woman named Red Feather, and then to follow as closely as possible the tourist flight that went up at six. The pilot didn't know the name of the man who had paid, but since he doubled the normal charter fee, the pilot didn't care to push the issue.

Calvin, following instructions left for him at the hotel, had Leanne at the charter company at a quarter to six. The pilot waved them over, ID'ed them, and said, "Get aboard."

"Where are we going?" Leanne asked.

"I don't know," said Cal. "And I don't know when or why. But we're going."

Joe's other instruction had been that Leanne should be armed. Cal didn't mention this, because he didn't want to alarm her. But then he didn't have to mention it because he knew she carried a nickel-plated S&W .357 Magnum in a holster under her shoulder. Instead of declaring it, though, and having to identify herself, he watched her pack it in a suitcase, which she had checked at the Vancouver airport.

The choppers wound back through the valley of the Mendenhall, half a mile apart and only a few hundred feet above the glacier, angling around broad turns past cliff faces and evergreen slopes. Leanne gripped her armrests and didn't care to look out, but Cal, who was sitting up next to the pilot, pressed his nose against the glass so he could see straight down. At times they turned so sharply that Leanne thought they must be completely sideways. She could glance to her side and see nothing but blue ice.

As the bird circled to land, she saw that another helicopter had just landed, and she saw people climbing out of it.

"You can walk on that?" she said.

"Every day," said their pilot. "Lot of money in that glacier. Look out there." He pointed. And there, beyond an opening in the mountains, stretched an endless white and blue expanse that frightened Leanne for its vastness.

"That's the Juneau ice field," the pilot said. "Over a hundred miles long and forty wide in some places. The glaciers are that ice field pressing itself down through the canyons. Like toothpaste. I'm gonna put you down on the glacier itself, near those others, where it's smooth. You stick close by, though. Don't get off, because there's lots of crevasses and covered tunnels in this ice. You get down one of those, you're never coming out."

"What are we doing here?" Leanne said to Cal.

But the pilot answered. He said, "You're here to see the ice, right?"

It was all blue. Some huge chunks Leanne saw in the near distance were amazingly dark, as deep blue as sapphires. Imagine finding ten-ton sapphires lying about, here and there. Just go over and chop yourself off a chunk or two to take home.

"Density of the ice," the pilot said. He was a regular tour guide, full of bits of information.

"Has to do with reflection and refraction. Glacial ice is incredibly dense, way more than regular ice. The density traps all light waves except blue, which are reflected. Of course, the density varies, so the ice is different shades." But it was all blue, Leanne could see, of one shade or another. And beautiful.

Her boots slipped a little on the surface. Out around her spread the ice. In one direction were huge chunks as big as houses jutting up from the surface. In another direction the surface seemed to be smooth all the way to its edge.

They were a couple hundred yards from the others, of whom there appeared to be four.

"Come on," Cal said, heading toward these others.

"Why?"

"Maybe to meet someone? You think we came just to enjoy the view?"

"I have no idea, Cal," she said. "I have no idea why we're here. I wish you'd tell me."

They walked, sliding their feet in spots. She was glad they'd bought the boots, water-proof Wolverines, in town. Cal had talked her into it. He was going to bankrupt her before he was through, she figured.

This was horseshit, Rick thought. He'd moved a little distance away from the others, twenty yards or so.

He'd watched the other bird come down, a private charter. He liked this one, with its all-glass bubble enclosure, better than the clunky Hughes he'd flown up in. Two people approached from this bird. As they got closer he began to feel on-edge. Something about them bothered him, but they weren't close enough to see much. He could tell one was a woman. She had dark hair.

At the same moment warning lights were about to go off in his brain, he was distracted when two other people stepped from behind a boulder at the glacier's edge.

The couple that was approaching stopped midway when they, too, noticed this other couple, who had on hats and parkas which hid their faces. One of them carried a package.

Rick walked in the direction of this couple.

They were spread out over a rough equilateral triangle, fifty yards on a side. At the apex stood Leanne and Calvin. At one corner, toward the tourists, was Rick. At the other, having just emerged from the spot where they'd been waiting since the chartered helo had deposited them here half an hour earlier, were Joe and Kari, who walked across the ice toward Leanne and Calvin.

When they were closer, Joe stopped and pulled back his hood. He threw his heavy package, a red nylon daypack. It slid on the ice toward Leanne.

"That's a hundred-ounce Englehard gold bar. Forty grand," Joe said. "Stolen in Idaho."

"Who killed them?" Leanne said back, as she knelt and lifted the pack and slung it over her shoulder.

Joe pointed to his left, at the man approaching.

Rick recognized Joe and Kari first. He knew these faces well; he had expected them to be here. But it was a terrific shock when he placed the face of the other dark-haired woman, the one closer to him. She had helped interrogate him in Spokane. This he had not anticipated, that Joe the fuckface would be meeting the feds.

"Shit," he whispered, and reached into his coat for the gun he'd picked up on the boat, but Leanne saw the move and had her .357 Mag out and aimed.

"Hands! Where I can see them," she yelled. "Don't fuck with me." And it was then that she recognized him.

"Rick Damschroeder," she said.

"It's Agullana," Kari said. She and Joe were close to Leanne now, a few yards away. Leanne glanced over, but kept her eyes toward Rick. "Rick Agullana."

"Why were you running?" Leanne said.

"Still running," said Joe.

"Doesn't add," said Leanne. "The room in Seattle. How'd that stuff get there?"

"I don't know," Joe said. "That's why I'm still running. I just want to make a deal."

"You in a position to deal?"

"I think so. You got the gold and a killer. I'm just looking for a head start."

"How do I know about this?" Leanne said. "How can I judge?"

"You can't," he said.

"I want you both to come in. Then we'll sort this out."

"Can't do it. Pull off Rick, he'll run or shoot you. Keep on him, I walk."

"Rick was an Amonite," Kari said. "But something happened to him. He went bad. He planned all of this, everything. Even I was taken in. He killed those poor people."

"You're Kari Downs?" said Leanne.

"I'm an Amonite, too. I'm going home. But don't blame the Family for this. Blame him. He's a killer and nothing more. We didn't do this. We didn't want this."

Rick watched in amazement, eyes darting, brain spinning, watching for the least opening. He noticed that the couple from Storm Lake had wandered in his direction, thinking, perhaps, he'd found something interesting to see near these other folks. They hadn't noticed, apparently, Leanne's gun.

And that stupid bitch Kari, mouthing off, supposedly kidnapped. She'd probably run the whole thing from the beginning. Forty grand was not even half the gold. This would net her a nice profit.

"Why here?" Leanne said to Joe. "Why like this?"

"Open," Joe said. "I can see. No one's hiding."

"Believe me, you're getting a good deal," Kari said. "You're getting the whole thing."

"Why use Calvin?"

"Shut up, Leanne, and take it," Cal said. "I just happened to be there when it mattered. It's a damn gift. Take it."

"I want the arms," Leanne said.

"There's a boat in the harbor," said Kari.

"Shut up!" Rick screamed at her. "What the *fuck* are you doing?"

"We don't need the guns, Rick," she said. "Not where we're going. Not out there. Father's mistaken. Those guns are causing all the trouble. They'll get us all killed. So I'm making a judgment. I'm selling you out, and giving the guns over. Then we can just live. I'll deal with Father when I get back there."

"What boat?" Leanne asked.

"The *Maribel S.*" Kari said. "A seiner. It's down there, somewhere. Maybe not in the harbor, but around. Waiting."

"For what?"

"To pick up Rick after he recovers the gold."

And so Leanne had to make her choice, but she knew already who would be her prisoner, knew in her bones who was guilty and who was telling the better part of the truth. She stepped toward Rick, not wavering in her focus. He had nowhere to go.

And then a terrible mechanical whine sounded from the east, from over the ice field, as a gray SH3H Sea King Coast Guard rescue chopper screamed out from behind a ridge down the valley. The ship pulled up and hovered, its side door open, men looking down, the wind from the spinning blades now tearing at them all.

A voice amplified to be even louder than the blades, so loud that it could have been the voice of God, commanded: "Federal agents. Drop your weapons!" The Sea King settled to the ice.

So Rick had his moment. He ran toward the Storm Lake couple, who had crouched and frozen in their shock and disbelief, grabbed the woman by her hair and dragged her backward toward the tourist chopper. But Rick could see that his pilot had kept the rotors feathered, so he could rev up and go. Good for him.

◇

When the Sea King touched the glacier, four men leapt out, one in military fatigues, carrying an M-16, the other three in boots and jeans and coats, with handguns. The man in fatigues knelt and aimed off to one side of the man holding the woman hostage, and pulled off three rounds. The bullets ricocheted from the ice and out into the mountains with high, singing whines.

Chips flew, some striking the man and woman, and the woman screamed, but the man did not stop. They were getting close to the bird, now. The man in fatigues flopped belly-down on the ice to better aim and hold his rifle. But with a hostage held like this, he knew he had no leeway.

It wasn't easy walking backward with his arm around the neck of this screaming woman, but they were almost there now. Until the woman's feet slipped out from beneath her and she sat down hard, slipping from Rick's arm, and then curled into a fetal position. So Rick dashed for the far side of the bird. He was almost there when he heard shots, but felt no pain, no tugging at his flesh. Then he'd made it.

He tore open the passenger side door, aimed at the pilot, and said, "You better gear this bucket up and get me back down before they're off the ice, or your fucking brains will be all over."

Already he could hear the blades picking up speed. He got in and slammed the door.

Leanne ran. She wanted Rick alive. She didn't want these idiot agents, whoever they were, killing her link. As she ran up behind them, the men in street clothes swung their guns toward her. The rifleman on the ice rolled and aimed at her, too. She held her own gun up in the air, and her badge in her other hand, and yelled, "Federal agent! Federal agent!"

Now they saw the badge, and lowered their guns. But in this break, the tourist chopper lifted off in a fresh rush of wind and wound back down the canyon toward Juneau. Out on the ice, the man from Storm Lake was slipping and crawling toward his wife, who lay curled in a ball.

The four men ran toward the Sea King. Leanne followed, and was glad one of them dragged her aboard just as it lifted off.

"I had him," she yelled over the noise at the men. "I had an arrest 'til you showed up! You blew it!"

The man in fatigues shrugged.

"Who ordered you in?" said Leanne. "You look like army. How is the army conducting domestic maneuvers against civilians?"

One of the men in street clothes held up his own badge, and said, "Van Doren. FBI." A second man was FBI as well.

The rifleman in fatigues was Army CID. He hollered into Leanne's ear, "Just part of an investigation." He patted his rifle and said, "Brought my baby in case we ran into any shit. Name's Cunningham, ma'am." He held out his hand to her.

The fourth man, in plainclothes, who had been hidden in a hat, a collar zipped up over his lower face, and dark glasses, uncovered himself and looked at her now. "Ben Regis, ATF," he said, and laughed.

"Hey," Leanne said. "I should've figured it was you screwing up my collar. Always after my crumbs."

"The hell," Ben said.

"You two know each other, then?" said Van Doren of the FBI.

"We've met a few times," Ben said, and laughed again.

The side of the Sea King was still wide open, the wind fierce and frigid. Leanne's face felt as numb as her brain.

After so much noise, the silence was overwhelming. Joe sat on the ice, arms on his knees, and took stock.

"Calvin," he said. "Kari Downs."

"All these famous people," Calvin said, and chuckled.

"You think it's funny?" said Kari.

"Funny?" Calvin said. "No. I think it's insane. It's wacked out. It's psycho-fucking-delic. But, man, you gotta laugh at it. No one got killed or nothing."

"Not yet," she said.

The chopper Joe chartered was still on the glacier. The pilot had walked over now, as stuporous as the rest of them. No one spoke for a few moments, then Cal said, "We should get back down there, see what happens. See how Leanne makes out."

"I can't go in," said Joe. To the pilot, he said, "You have a plane ready, right?"

"All set," the pilot said. "Cessna 182 outfitted with a stol kit so she can pull up a lot of weight. Got long-range tanks on her, too, so we can go where you want. How 'bout them?" He pointed back at the couple from Storm Lake, huddled together.

"Just send someone else up," Kari said.

So the four of them boarded.

As they lifted off they saw the older couple crossing the ice toward them, now, looking up and waving, not in panic or an attempt to make them wait, but as one waves to say good-bye.

27

DEACON WAITED. THE *MARIBEL S.* WAS TEMPORARILY DOCKED IN THE south public harbor, tied loosely to a pile. The captain had slipped the harbor master some cash to let them wait for a crew member who was meeting them there.

North from here not too many miles, in the middle of the ten mile wide Lynn Canal, were a series of tiny islands, one of which held another pier. At the shore-end of this pier was a boathouse, used for winter repairs and re-fittings and for storage. Deacon had arranged to use it to hide the *Maribel S.* and its contraband for a few days before setting out to run nearly the entire rim of the Gulf, to let pass the busiest of the activity which would come after Rick finished his business.

But when Deacon saw a helicopter heading directly into town, instead of to the airport, he had his first inkling that the firestorm wasn't as far behind as he had anticipated. And when this chopper came right down toward the harbor, landed in an open parking lot across the street, and Rick leapt out and sprinted toward the boat, he knew something had gone badly wrong.

"Start her," Deacon said to the captain.

"Go!" Rick yelled, as he came. "Get the fuck out of here!" Down the pier he ran and leapt up over the bow and onto the deck.

"What happened?" Deacon said, and then he heard, then saw, the Sea King coming out of the northeast and toward them. "Jesus Christ," he said. "What have you done?"

"Just get out of here, now," Rick said. "What are you waiting for?"

"You have the gold?"

"No, I don't have the gold."

"And you led them to us. Are you that insane? We've got all the guns in the hold."

"Then what are you waiting for?"

"You want me to lead them out to sea where they can pick us right off the water."

"I want you to get this boat going."

"Get out," Deacon said. "You get out of here. You're going to ruin it all."

"What?" Rick said. And he could see that Deacon had a long gutting blade in his hand. Deacon stepped toward him.

"You're gonna cut me?" Rick said.

"I will," said Deacon. By now the ship's captain and one of the hands had come up on board to watch.

"OK," Rick said, and turned, then turned back with the gun in his hand, and fired, hitting Deacon in the shoulder.

"Rick," Deacon said, and stepped backward and dropped the knife. Rick fired again, the bullet this time passing through Deacon's throat. He wheezed out a bloody mist, and gagged, and staggered backward to the deck's edge. Then Rick fired again, killing Deacon and sending him tumbling overboard into the oily waters of the harbor.

Then Rick pointed the gun at the captain and said, "You listen. We'll do what we have to do. Right now, get us out of this harbor."

Omaha stepped out from the cabin and said, "You take it easy, there, Rick. We gonna be all right. You just don't need to kill any more your friends."

"Then help me," said Rick.

"All right," said the captain. The hand stood, staring.

"Have you been helping with the weapons?" Rick asked him.

He nodded.

"Can you get something up here, one of the big guns or a missile?"

"Yeah," the man said.

"You know how they work?"

"Stinger's what you want. Surface to air. I was looking over one. Even had instructions with it. Seems easy, once it's set up."

"This isn't the time to experiment. You sure you can make it work?"

"Pretty sure."

"Then get one up here fast."

From the Sea King they could see the Hughes tourist chopper in the parking lot, and the pilot waving them in. The coast guard pilots tried to take them into the lot, too, but there were buildings on three sides and a few scattered parked cars and so not enough room. They lifted again, circled, then dropped toward an open concrete loading dock a couple hundred yards up the shore.

On the ground, Van Doren waggled a finger at Ben and Leanne, then jumped off. Ben jumped next. Leanne grabbed the red daypack and followed them as they ran back toward the parking lot, but not before she saw Cunningham flash her a thumbs up and grin from the bird.

The tourist pilot had run down on to the road and jumped up and down, pointing at the docks.

"Where?" Ben yelled.

"The boat!" he hollered. "Look."

And they saw it, heading toward the channel, a white seiner moving much too quickly for the closed waters of the harbor.

"He's on that?"

"Yes! Yes!"

Van Doren said something into a hand-held radio, and then the Sea King lifted and headed out over the water.

"No problem, now," Van Doren said. "They'll just tail. We'll get a couple Coast Guard cutters to pick 'em up."

Only now, from the edge of the road alongside the harbor, did Leanne notice the body of a snow-haired man starting to sink into the water off one of the piers.

The bird carrying Joe and the others had just wound out of the canyon when the Sea King crossed out over the water, so they had not seen what happened on the ground, or even that the Sea King landed and lifted off again.

"Look!" Calvin said, and pointed as the Sea King closed on the boat.

"Wait a second," Joe said, and touched the pilot's shoulder. He hovered the bird so they could watch the chase.

Although the boat captain had his engines at full throttle, the Sea King picked it up in moments.

On board the *Maribel S.*, the deck hand armed the Stinger and pointed at the sights. "Look through here. You hold this tracking button. When you hear a sound, it's locked on. Then you fire, here. It's heat-seeking. It can't miss."

"What sound?" Rick had to yell, because the chopper was getting close.

"Dunno." The hand shrugged.

"Fine," said Rick.

The hand disappeared into the boat's cabin.

The bird was close enough now that the men on board—Cunningham, the second FBI agent, and two Coast Guard pilots—could see details on the deck of the ship. Still, it took the pilots a moment to see that the man on deck was holding a rocket on his shoulder.

Cunningham, who was lying on his belly on the floor, watching through the open side door, recognized the missile immediately, switched his M-16 from semi- to intermittent auto, and tried to take aim, although by now the pilots had begun to pull hard away.

In the same instant that Rick heard a rapid high-pitched beeping and released the Stinger, Cunningham squeezed the trigger of the M-16 and tried to steady it in the direction of the man on the boat.

From their vantage, Joe, Kari, Cal, and the pilot had a spectacular view of the impact and explosion of the Stinger, of the Coast Guard's Sea King chopper erupting into a brilliant ball of flame, of its remnants and its dead occupants falling like so much debris into the Gastineau Channel.

"Oh, my God," Kari whispered.

Calvin yelled, "Leanne! *Leanne!* I killed her!" He slid forward off his seat onto the floor, and squeezed his head between his hands as if it would burst. "I killed my sister," he wailed in his amazement. "I killed her."

"Go," Joe said to the pilot.

They pivoted in midair and flew.

What they couldn't see from the chopper was that, in the moments before the missile hit the Sea King, jacketed .223 caliber rounds from Cunningham's M-16 strafed the fore end of the *Maribel S.* One three-round burst was dead on; one hit Rick in the right chest; two more tore through his abdomen. When Gary and Omaha and the captain came back out, after hearing the scream of the missile discharging, and the explosion, they found Rick lying on his side on the deck, holding his belly together with his hand, through which blood poured.

"Get us out of here," Rick said. Bright blood coated his teeth.

"You gonna die," said Omaha. "We got to find a hospital."

"Fuck that," Rick said. "We'll find someplace else."

"Ain't no place else," the captain said.

"I'll take my chances," said Rick, and with that he passed out.

"He's either gonna die or he ain't, and I ain't letting him lay here and die, damn what he wants. 'Least in there he'll have a chance. Go back in. Quick, now." Omaha pointed at the docks.

"What about—" the captain started, but Omaha cut him off.

"We'll get away just fine. First we gonna lay Rick up there on the dock so they can get him in where he belongs."

And that's exactly what happened. Crowds had gathered by now around the harbor. After lifting Rick from the bloody deck and laying him on a dock, Omaha looked up and saw some of these onlookers pointing at him and Rick. He heard sirens. So he leaned over and kissed Rick's forehead and said into his ear, "You hang on, now, Brother Rick. We'll be together again 'fore too long."

Then he stepped back on the boat, and the captain opened his throttles and pulled away from the dock.

Ben was on his radio, trying to reach someone. Van Doren sat on a dock with his head in his arms, and wept. Leanne rubbed his back and told him, "Shhh."

He was a young agent, twenty-eight, who had gone straight in after college. He worked out of Anchorage and was well trained in special procedures, which is why he'd been brought in here. He'd seen a man shot once, and had seen any number of dead and mangled bodies. But he'd never seen anyone actually die, let alone watch a fellow agent and three other good men go down in a blown-up chopper, had never come a moment's decision away from dying himself. What made him jump up and out of the Sea King first? No one had discussed it.

He was in shock now, so it was up to Ben to find the harbor master and tell him the classified emergency Treasury Department number to call to report what had happened. Within minutes of his call, Justice and Defense had been notified as well, and eventually the local Coast Guard. But given the shock and confusion, and the isolation of this place, some time passed before any new authorities other than local police showed up.

At the airport, Joe carried the remaining gold—the two packages from Ketchikan and one of the two others he'd picked up here and which he'd kept stored in the chopper—to the Cessna and stowed it in the plane's tail. Cal helped Kari haul the other provisions she and Joe had bought in Juneau, and load them as well.

"Where you going?" Calvin asked them.

"Just away," Joe said.

"Take me," Calvin said.

Joe and Kari both stopped and faced him. Kari said, "We're going into the bush, Calvin. Deep. To get real lost, for a long time."

"Where?"

Kari shook her head.

"Listen," he said. "I got nothing left. Men will kill me if I go back down. I mean, I'm fucked I show my face anywhere in the forty-eight. And now Leanne's . . . man, I don't know."

"It wasn't your fault," said Joe.

"It's both our faults," said Cal. "Yours and mine, guy. Now I just want to get lost somewhere, too. I'm good in the woods. I grew up there, listening to my bossy big sister. She didn't think I listened, but I did." His throat thickened, and he stopped and cocked his head and looked off into the hills for a moment. Then he said, "You can fucking use me out there."

"We're going to the Kenai," Kari said.

"You're nuts."

She nodded at him.

"Why now? It's loaded with people."

"You see anybody trying to arrest us?" she said, waving an arm around the empty airport. "Through brains or damn dumb luck, it seems we got ourselves a little window. Don't know how. Don't care. All I know is we're going through it as fast as we can. It won't be open long."

"Then go somewhere out, where they won't be concentrating. Go up to the Yukon or something. Your people are on the Kenai, right? That place'll be crawling with every fed in the western hemisphere."

"Ever been there?"

"No."

"It's not a huge area, but it's dense as hell. I mean you can hide. And, you're right, for Alaska there are a lot of people, which in a way helps us. Then, in time, I'll be able to sneak back in to Sanctuary. And Joe, or you and Joe, if you want, can clear out, get yourselves as far away from people as you need to go. Up the Yukon if you want. Now, though, we think the thing is for him and me both to get into the woods, any woods, as fast as possible and just lay low. The Kenai's where I need to be. Plus it's accessible from Anchorage."

"Anchorage?"

Joe said, "It's the only way to really cover our tracks. Anything else—charters, commercial flights, boats—will be traceable one way or another. You fly up north, they'll just follow. So we take the gamble—get into the city, find some cover, then slip as deep into the Kenai back country as we can. It's equal parts balls and planning and luck in the end, anyway. Any one of the three fails, we're screwed."

The pilot, who'd run into a nearby hangar, was coming back now.

Joe looked at Kari. She nodded.

"I sure got nothing to lose wherever you go," Calvin said. "So let's get there."

When the *Maribel S.* pulled away from the dock, after depositing Rick, a few people pointed and watched them go, but most were preoccupied with the bodies and the wreckage of the helicopter.

By the time the mess had been sorted out, and new agents and military officials had visited the scene and discussed their next move, the boat had already reached its hidden mooring on the Lynn Canal island, her cargo and crew off-loaded and stashed away.

A fierce and angry search ensued, involving military, Coast Guard and even customs planes and boats, and dozens of FBI, ATF and CID agents questioning hundreds of residents of the areas surrounding Juneau, and randomly searching nearly two hundred fishing craft in the vicinity.

But the *Maribel S.* remained undetected in the boathouse, and would remain there for many weeks.

28

As for Leanne, it would be quite a few hours of questioning and debriefing, of conversations with every manner of agent and investigator, including not only Ben but old Mark Truong as well, who was very nice to her, before it struck her that Calvin was missing. He had never come back to their room, and when she asked, no one seemed to have seen him.

The Storm Lake couple said everyone but the two of them had come in together from the glacier. At the airport, Leanne learned that the charter pilot Joe had hired left immediately in a Cessna after landing the helicopter, but had not notified anyone of how many passengers he was carrying, and hadn't filed a flight plan.

They waited another thirty hours—although the FBI checked every airstrip within range—before the pilot finally showed up. He was immediately corralled and interrogated. But he said simply this: "I took three of 'em, two men and a woman. No one give me their names. They paid me a lot of money. We flew up the coast to a private strip in Dry Bay, then to Yakutat, where they paid me to fly around a while before coming back here."

"But you don't know where they were going," she said.

"Nope. That was the point."

Truong leaned down into the man's face. "Aiding and abetting," he said. "Besides the felony, for which you could do time, I can pretty much guarantee you'll be one old man before you ever get licensed to fly again."

"Hey," the pilot said. "I didn't know they were wanted for nothing."

"You watched a Coast Guard chopper get taken down."

"Right. The people I was flying didn't take it down. They was with me. What crime'd they do? They was payin' me to fly. Shit, that's my business."

"Still, I can be a real pain in your ass."

The pilot nodded his head. "OK. Listen. I did hear somethin'. The woman said it wasn't long 'til they got to Sanctuary. So wherever that is—"

"My God," Leanne said, looking around at Truong and the other agent who was with her. "He's going along. Calvin's going with them to see Amon."

The other agent just looked at her, then made a note in his book when she turned away.

Later, in her hotel room, alone with Ben, she said, "He was desperate. But he doesn't know what could happen up there, with those people. He has no idea."

Ben took one of her hands, held it in both of his and said, "He can take care of himself. He'll probably split off from them along the way. Then he'll contact you. You don't know."

But she did know. Cal wasn't much of a loner. He liked company. He'd stay with them all the way to Sanctuary, not knowing he was walking into the camp of mad people who would do what they could to make him see their strange light.

She leaned forward and pressed her forehead against Ben's chest. He was wearing only a T-shirt and jeans and she could smell him, his aftershave and his deodorant, the same one's he'd used since she'd met him. And he felt good to her. She felt his arms come up around her shoulders and hold her there, like that, like she wanted to stay for a long time, to not think, to not be afraid, to not be so, so lonely.

But she pushed herself away from him. "I loved you," she said. "I was wrong to question it."

"Leanne—"

"No, listen. I'm not some hard-luck case crying about what might have been. But I've never told you this, and I've wanted to. I knew when you came back that I'd made a mistake, that I loved you and wanted us to be together. I was wrong."

"You weren't wrong."

"I was. Love's love. And nothing else should matter."

"But it does matter. I never told you what it was like down there," he said. "Cornered, with us getting all shot to shit. Nowhere to go, no one to pull us out. Watching my fucking buddy take a round in his throat, me holding him, him blowing blood all over me, bleeding out in the dirt, and those fuckers still shooting so I couldn't even pick him up and run with him. All I could do was sit there and watch him go. I could not come back and fall in love with you, and someday maybe it's you lying there like that."

She touched his face. "We should have said this a long time ago," she said. "I thought that was why, but I never really knew."

When he had gone, Leanne sat still and gathered herself. She knew now what she was going to do. She called her bank in Boise and arranged to have them wire north, the next day, the bulk of her savings, some of which she withdrew as traveler's checks, some as half-ounce Maple Leaf coins and some as currency. She mailed three months rent to her landlord, three months worth of utility payments, and three months car payments to the bank that held that paper.

Other than this trip to the bank, she was careful not to do anything unusual—she knew she was being watched, and none of the observing agents looked familiar to her.

Then, two mornings after the pilot had shown up, the day she and Ben were scheduled to fly back south, Leanne did not appear at her normal time for breakfast, and she did not answer her door. The FBI agents who'd been watching her used a pass key to open her room. There they found a khaki business suit and a pair of dress shoes in the closet. On the table she had laid out all her notes on the case to date, and her purse with all her credit cards and ID, including her badge, still inside it.

And they found a note to Simmons and Ben, informing them that she'd gone undercover, and whether the ATF sanctioned it or not she was going into the camp of Father Amon Ka'atchii to pose as a new recruit. She had a head start on them and she knew her way around the back country better than any other agent they cared to find, so they shouldn't bother trying to track her. She'd consider herself still an employee of the ATF and would file reports when she could, but above all no one, no one, should jeopardize the situation by trying to make a raid on the Family. Her goal was to find Calvin, she said, and to find the weapons. When she had done both, she would contact them and they could come and get her. Until then, she warned, they'd better keep their distance.

When the Attorney General's special troubleshooter got a copy of this letter, he passed it to her immediately.

She, in turn, had the deputy AG suggest to the heads of the ATF, FBI and CRIDCOM that, right or wrong, if this agent Leanne Red Feather actually got herself into the camp, then she had called the shot they were going to take as regarded the cult directly. Red Feather, after all, had been right so far—the AG had read the synopses from Treasury; she knew what had gone on, and felt this woman had earned the right to be trusted.

Then, assuming it was Amonites who had the weapons and had fired on the Sea King (and there was still not much in the way of concrete evidence supporting this), the essential thing, far more important than retribution, was to capture the weapons, not to mention the smugglers and the murderer from Idaho, before another, bigger, disaster happened. So either the boat and guns would be picked up in transit—the ideal solution—or they'd surface at some point in the camp of the Amonites. The latter would happen only if the water was not rippled. So no one ought to make a move, other than extremely discrete surveillance, directly on the commune itself, unless and until Agent Red Feather made contact to say the weapons were in, and the AG approved it.

To underscore the suggestion, the Deputy AG mentioned that the Secretaries of Treasury and Defense had already been briefed by the AG, and had agreed with her.

That afternoon, Colonel Rozsa received a call from General Parkins. As he listened, Rozsa's face turned bright red, and he grew so angry he thought he'd have a stroke. But when he hung up, he did nothing but sit down at his desk and fold his hands in front of him. For now, Parkins had said, that was all he, or any of them, was allowed to do.

But Rozsa had been vindicated, Parkins added, for as much as predicting just such a disaster. The Chief of Staff, General Hargrave, knew exactly where things stood. The Stingers were still missing, Rozsa had been right, and Justice and CRIDCOM had fucked up badly. In light of this, Hargrave did not agree with the AG's hands-off policy, despite what the Secretary of Defense thought. Furthermore, Hargrave held that several other of the joint chiefs, who had also been briefed, were inclined toward the same sentiment.

"Be patient," Parkins counseled Rozsa. "Just be patient."

The End of the World

29

THE CAMP, WHICH THEY'D PITCHED ON A LEVEL, SPRUCE-CONCEALED SPOT on the lip of a knoll up from the shoreline of Lake Tustumena on the Kenai Peninsula, 550 air miles from Juneau, had turned to running mud. The tent stakes held somehow, lodged, maybe, between rocks or roots in the soup, but mud poured over the lip and down toward the lake. The fire pit Calvin dug had long ago filled to its rim with water. Each of the two tents had its own single-burner Peak 1 backpack cook stove, and that is how they ate, sticking a pan outside until it filled with rainwater, then heating it over the Peak 1 and pouring in a packet of freeze-dried whatever. It all came quickly to taste the same.

Joe and Kari were both oddly well-equipped for the situation, Kari because of her conditioning by Father Amon (through solitude and deprivation, she told Joe), and Joe because he had the sort of mechanistic mind that was able to click into a lower gear than normal and idle for as long as it took.

They lay on their backs in a very expensive hooded-fly Tru-Leaf camouflage backpack tent, on their very expensive North Slope goosedown bags, listening. The tent fly was a drum skin on which the rain beat. And now, after three solid days of the rain, three days of lying inside the tent and listening, a complex rhythm had begun to reveal itself to them. Kari heard it first, for her conditioning had schooled her in the ways of such things. It was sometime during the second day, around the thirty-second hour of rain, that she first heard it. She lost it then, until that night, when, in the deep blackness of the moonless Alaskan outback, she awoke, and heard it again: a regular shifting in the patterns of sound, steady beats, then fewer, then a millisecond pause, then steady beats again. And then a sub-rhythm within the measures of the steady beats themselves. She woke Joe and told him, but he couldn't hear it and fell back into sleep. The next morning however, on the dawn of the third day, he began to hear it, too. They lay all that morning, not moving, letting the rain cradle them in its cadence.

The "No-Mind," Kari called it.

Calvin, on the other hand, had passed from impatience the first day, to anger the second, to a futile rage on the third. He stood in the mud outside his tent and howled with clenched fists against the sky.

Joe and Kari looked at each other.

"You'd better go," she said. Joe ran out in only his T-shirt and underwear, threw his arms around Calvin and squeezed as Cal jumped and struggled and pulled them both over into the mud. But Joe held on until Calvin stopped fighting and lay still.

"Try listening to it," Joe said. "She's teaching me."

"I been listening to it for three goddamn days! At least you've got someone with you, to talk to."

"Doesn't matter. You have to let yourself hear it. Of us all, you should be the best at it."

" 'Cause I'm an Indian? Fuck you."

"Because you're experienced. What would Leanne do?"

"She'd—" Calvin laughed then. "She'd do this," he said, meaning himself. "She couldn't take it for an hour. She'd go nuts, not being able to finish her *agenda.*" He and Joe stood up in the cold, driven sheets of rain and laughed. Then Joe put his arm around Calvin's shoulder and they walked, shivering, down over the muddy lip and across the rocky beach to the shoreline of Lake Tustumena, and knelt down. A low wispy fog clung to the water's surface, obscuring it. Calvin picked up a rock and threw it into the fog and listened to it splash. He said, "Fish probably bite good in this shit."

"You want to fish? We can."

"No." Calvin laughed again.

"We shouldn't try to move in it."

"You're right. You've been right. We'll wait it out."

Joe said, "Maybe later we'll put on the gear and do some fishing, anyway." They had Helley-Hansen rain suits, bibs and parkas; the lady in the trading post in Yakutat said they were the best money could buy. Calvin said she was charging double what you'd pay elsewhere, but Joe got sets for each of them.

Back in the tent, Joe stripped off his shirt before he grew too chilled, then crawled inside his bag to change his underwear. Through all the rented rooms and now the tent, he and Kari had maintained a strict policy of modesty between them. He had not seen her naked since that night with Rick in the Idaho motel.

From Yakutat, where the Juneau pilot had left them, Joe hired a twin-engine Otter to fly them farther up the coast to the city of Valdez, on the Prince William Sound. Joe then paid this pilot to fly a bogus package clear up to the Fairbanks airport and to check it at the held luggage counter, a trip which would take at least two days.

From Valdez their options had expanded: they could go by private boat, by ferry, by another chartered flight, or by commercial air, anywhere in the state, or even back down to Seattle. Instead, Joe did what had worked before: after buying commercial airline tickets to different cities, he stole a truck, an old Jeep Wagoneer, actually, in which the driver had left the keys (a common practice here, he noticed, when he started looking), and drove them out. And to which hidden village, to which remote mountain range were they headed? None. He drove them, as Kari had said he would, over the Thompson Pass in the Chugach Mountains and north into the night on Highway Four, running dead alongside the Trans-Alaska pipeline for 185 miles to the junction with Highway One, the Glenn Highway, which he followed west and south into Anchorage, largest city in the state, home to forty percent of its population, by first light.

While Joe and Kari waited in a room, Cal drove the Wagoneer back north to the junction of Highways One and Four, wiped it clean of prints, and hid it in brush a quarter mile off the road. This was to suggest the possibility, should the Jeep be discovered and linked to them, that they could have continued north from here. Cal then hitch-hiked back to Anchorage.

From there, it was a simple matter of splitting up and bumming rides, a common and remarkably easy mode of travel in Alaska. The only problem was that Joe's face had become rather famous in his weeks on the road. The old military photo had been published in every newspaper in the northwest, and a newer one, taken by someone at the cabinet shop only last year, had turned up, too.

Although his beard had filled out, and he wore a hat and both dark glasses and the contacts whenever he went outside, he knew he had to keep his exposure to a minimum. So, while Calvin found his own transportation, Kari—whose photo had not, to their knowledge, appeared in any newspaper yet—thumbed as Joe hid in the brush along the Turnagain Arm on the outskirts of Anchorage. She flagged down and refused four rides before she found one suitable, two half-tanked good old boys in an open pickup who would drop them off in Seward. Kari waved to Joe, and the two of them flopped into the back of the truck for one cold and crazy ride. But the guys never looked at Joe's face, and by the time they got to Seward were so drunk they wouldn't have remembered him anyway.

They had picked up supplies and gear as they went along, spreading the purchases out among as many stores as they could: the rain gear, camo-flannel shirts, wool pants and socks, and rock-gray rainproof duffles in Yakutat; camo backpacks, binoculars, waterproof boots, knives, and the cookstoves in Valdez; the tents, sleeping bags, food packets, water tablets, fishing gear, an ax and saw, two hundred feet of nylon rope, a compass, maps, cookware, and flashlights from three different places in Anchorage; and finally at two Seward stores they filled out the rest of what they'd need, including neoprene underwear, camo face paint, Gortex/Thinsulate-lined gloves and camo jackets, fuel for the stoves, a Remington Model 700 bolt-action 7-mm. Magnum rifle and scope, and five boxes of bullets.

Seward lay at the head of Resurrection Bay in the eastern half of the Kenai. To its immediate west rose the Kenai Mountains and the mammoth Harding Icefield (nearly as big as the Juneau field), the western drainage of which formed and fed Tustumena Lake. From the western tip of Tustumena, the Kasilof River ran west to the Cook Inlet. It was on one of the minor southern tributaries of the Kasilof, Burnt Creek, that Father had established the third Sanctuary of the Amonites. By air from Seward, the distance to Sanctuary was only about seventy miles. They weren't going in yet, though. Joe's game was to kill time. In Seward he chartered separately two float planes, one for Kari and Cal, one for himself alone, to confound any descriptions of the three of them which might show up in the local papers. The pilots left them, six hours and half a mile apart, on Tustumena's southern shore, still twenty miles away, through heavy brush and timber, across smaller lakes and rivers and dangerous sodden bogs, from Sanctuary, where Joe planned on delivering Kari and fifty thousand dollars worth of the remaining gold. After that, he and Calvin could disappear into the far northern interior.

The tiny single-engine plane in which Joe rode did not fly over the mountains; rather, it flew through them, never rising as high as the summits on either side. At times it passed so close to the steep, iced slopes that Joe thought he could make out the texture formed by all the individual frozen crystals. Then he watched the mountains fade down to hills, and the hills play out, dropping sharply to the low elevation of the western side of the peninsula, and open up into the vast land of lakes and forests that made up one of the prime moose preserves in the world.

Here they dove down onto Tustumena's glassy surface.

By the time Joe had unloaded and watched the plane taxi across the lake and pull itself with its buzz-saw engine back into the air, Calvin and Kari had found him. As they looked around at the black lake and the mountains to the east and the forested plateau to the west, Cal said, "Jesus Christ. They killed us and we went to heaven."

But that was before the rains came.

The rain lasted for three more days, six in all. It broke in the smallest hours of the sixth night. The silence woke Joe, who couldn't understand at first what was different. Then he heard something outside the tent, shuffling through the mud and making rapid, high-pitched grunts. It worried him enough that he put his hand on the rifle, but as he did he figured out that the noise was Calvin, laughing, and throwing mud. Joe opened the tent flap and shined a flashlight outside.

"The hell are you doing?"

"Rain stopped," Calvin said. He hopped up and down on his hands and feet.

"Things'll start to dry in the light."

"Bet yer ass," Calvin said. "Bet yer ass!"

"We'll get some real food."

"Fuckin' A," said Calvin, and flung mud up into the air. Joe zipped up the tent and lay on his back, listening. The light was still on, illuminating a circle on the tent roof.

"There's even a rhythm to the silence, if you can believe that," Kari said. "It woke me, too."

"Maybe what you people do up here isn't all crazy."

"Oh, there's something to it," she said. "What's funny is, after all this time away, eating more-or-less normally, sleeping through every night, being around you, reading real books and papers again, I'm different. I still see the truth in it, you know, the good. But I see something else, too."

"Good and evil," Joe said. "Just like everything."

"It's like a dream or something. For almost four years, Joe, I haven't spoken to anyone I used to know, seen anything I used to see, thought anything I used to think."

"Mind-control."

"But what about all the good parts?"

"What about them?" Joe rolled on his side, to face her, and tucked his head into the crook of his arm. Then he shut off the flashlight. "You've been coming back into your head, especially since Juneau. You're you, now. We still got a hundred and fifty grand. Come north with us. Or we can leave the country—"

"I can't, Joe."

"Why?"

He heard her sit up and imagined her crossing her legs in front of herself, as she did when she sat like this. He could not see her, of course, except to make out the dim outline of her hair. It reminded him of the way she sat in the Vancouver motel room, when she cautioned him about driving north. He wondered if she were going to give him another warning now. She said, "I haven't told you about when I met Father."

"No."

"I meant something to him in the beginning, after I found him. I'd gone up to the Bellevue church. But I didn't like it there. I wanted the real religion, the Master, strength and the Earth. So I asked until I found out where in Idaho Sanctuary was, and I left one night and thumbed across. I hiked in along a narrow trail. Someone had drawn me a rough map of where to look. I wandered in those mountains for two days until they found me, half-starved and frozen. The first night I was put alone in a cabin. A nice cabin, actually. I thought that's where I would live, in this beautiful cabin in the mountains." She laughed.

"No?"

"The cabin is just for the beginning. Soon you go into the dorms. But that night, the first night, he came in to me."

"Father."

"Yes. I was in bed."

She'd been lying beneath the blankets, she said, listening to the noises of the wilderness and the people in the camp, when the door moved and moonlight shone into the room. A man stood there, in the doorway. She did not panic or scream, although she remembered her heart, how hard it was beating, and that a part of her was scared. "I am God," he said to her.

She said, "It wasn't long after that we had to leave, to move up north. Luckily by then I'd already delivered."

Joe lifted his head from his arm now, and looked in the direction of her voice. What had she just said? He pushed himself up into a sitting position. "Delivered?" he asked her.

"Yes."

"Jesus," he said. "You had a baby."

He heard her breathing in the darkness. Then she said: "I had a girl. Eloise, we named her. Father has a lot of children, at least fifteen or twenty, but she's my only. She turned two and a half just before I left."

Although his eyes had begun to adjust to the dark, he still could not see the details of her face, but he imagined she looked different than he had seen her before. She sounded stronger. It was all abruptly clear now, what her run had been about—not gold, really, or Father or the Family at all, but a desperation to get back here he could not imagine, a pain that must have been pulling her apart inside, that more than justified any action, any lie, she needed to allow. A desperation probably greater than his own.

"Is she there now?"

"Yes. So, you see, I have to get back and give Father what's his, so I can get back what's mine."

"Are you worried about the phone?" She'd been unable to reach Father since Anchorage. His number had been disconnected.

"I'm sure he just thought the line was tapped."

She reached over and held his hand in hers. "Next year," she said. "When the move begins in the spring, maybe Eloise and I can leave then. He'd never allow it, but he'll be gone a lot, out there, getting things ready."

"So you do want to leave."

"I didn't. Now I do."

Whatever misgivings he'd had about her, and there were many, fell away in this light. It was as if she'd pulled up some curtain that showed him a whole new world, fresh and born again.

◇

In the hot sun the land and their gear did begin to dry. Best was to be able to eat from the land instead of from foil packets of freeze-dry. The first morning they split a three-pound lake trout Calvin caught and fried.

Always, now, they had to be careful. Low planes, which might have been surveillance flights, and which had ceased during the bad weather, appeared overhead once every couple days. It was the risk they'd taken by coming to the Kenai, near Sanctuary, and even though spotters might be using infrared detectors, Joe made sure that whenever possible they stayed out of open areas, that no one went out without wearing camo, including face paint or netting, and that whenever they heard a plane or, especially, the low flying choppers that occasionally passed over, they stopped all movement and hunkered down out of sight in the brush or trees.

Some days later, when the number of flights seemed to decrease, they broke camp and moved again, Calvin and Joe bearing loads that weighed upward of forty pounds; Kari carrying twenty, part of which was her share of the remaining gold.

Joe was surprised by the number of people they began to see, fishermen, mostly, and backpackers. It was still salmon season and this area had some of the best. Twice in two days they came upon small groups of hikers and stopped to share instant coffee and salmon jerky and to chat. The hikers warned that when Joe and the others got a little farther west, and came to some of the rivers there, they'd see so many fishermen in spots it would look possible to wade across on their shoulders.

Joe led them along the shore of Tustumena. They had to ford three rivers, all fast and cold but none deeper than their thighs. When they began to pass cabins on the lake's edge, he led them a little deeper into the wilderness, so they'd stay out of sight. Then they came upon another, smaller lake, the eastern edge of which was bordered by a mile-wide marsh criss-crossed by what appeared to be high, narrow lines of drier ground. It was a moment before Calvin realized what they were looking at.

"Beaver dams," he said. "They got this whole area sealed off. They probably made this lake." The dams were high, some up to six or seven feet, and composed primarily of small saplings.

"Can we cross on them?" Joe said.

Calvin shrugged and set out, leading the way. They were halfway across the field, the point of no return, when Calvin went through.

He yelled when he started to go. Joe, who'd been watching his own steps, looked up in time to see Calvin sink, but catch himself at the armpits.

"Get me!" Calvin said, his voice thin. "It's wet. Shit, it's cold. God, it's so cold. Get me, Joe."

But Joe didn't move to get him. He was careful, first. He set his pack down and secured it so it wouldn't slide off into the water. Then he got on his knees and worked his way toward Calvin, testing the network of branches and mud as he moved forward. Everything seemed solid enough; Calvin had just hit a hole.

"I'm freezing," Cal said. "And I felt something move. It's moving!" He thrashed, tearing his arms back and forth across the branches, ripping his shirt and cutting himself.

Joe lay down with his face near Calvin's. "Easy," he said, in the flattest, most level voice he could find. "Legs caught?"

"I can't feel them," Calvin said. "They're so cold."

"C'm'on." Joe stood and put his hands in Calvin's armpits and heaved upward. Calvin moved. Inches, but he moved.

"OK," Joe said to Kari. She helped, then. It was over an hour before Calvin was out and changed into dry clothing and they were walking again, very slowly now. This time Joe led, and tested each step with a staff he'd cut.

They didn't get across until evening, and then had to lay out the wet gear and wait the entire following day for it to dry. But Joe was happy to keep it slow. In the end, four more days passed before they covered the dozen miles to the Tustumena access, a well-traveled gravel road that led in from the Sterling Highway. Signs announced a public campground. Civilization.

"We're close," Kari said, when she stood on the road. "The mouth of the Kasilof isn't far, up that way. We hiked up here once, some of us, from Sanctuary. It didn't take a day."

They moved away from the flow of people on the road and water, now, and, working from topo maps and the compass, headed due west into the bush, hacking through brush and making plenty of noise, at Calvin's insistence, to avoid surprising any bears. When they came to a clear matted pine floor in a heavy stand of Sitka spruce, Joe dropped his pack and said, "We'll stop here."

That night, in their tent, Kari said, "Cal and I, we couldn't do this on our own, without you. You know that?"

"Cal's better than I am out here."

"Far as survival skills go. But the decisions, when, where, how. Those are yours. And the strength. Why would he even come here? He doesn't want to go to Sanctuary."

"He said he didn't care where he went."

"He didn't think this was a good idea. But he wanted to follow you. He needs you. I need you."

Joe did not answer.

"Keep me warm," she said. She turned on a flashlight and set it at the head of the tent, then unzipped the long side of her bag, and unzipped his as well. "I know you're cold, too."

He watched as she sat up on her knees and unbuttoned the long flannel shirt she wore as a nightgown.

"How I said I went with you because you were sent to save me?" she said. "I believed that. But I wanted you, too. I've wanted you. Even when I came on to you in Vancouver, to get you to unstrap me, I hated you but I wanted you, too."

She pushed his sleeping bag off him and straddled his belly. He could feel the heat of her crotch pressing down. She slid the shirt back on her shoulders, and dropped it. She wore nothing underneath but panties.

She brushed hair back off his forehead, and ran a fingertip over his eye, down his cheek, across his mouth.

He touched her soft belly.

"I know you'll have to go soon," she whispered. "But God I want you to stay."

Leaning forward and bracing herself with her left hand next to his head, she kissed him once on each of his eyes. He felt her hair on his face and her hard, dark nipples brushing his chest. Then he felt her lips move down across his cheek, tasting him, until he met them with his own.

30

IN FACT, JOE'S PLAN OF HIDING ON THE KENAI WAS SOUNDER THAN HE COULD have known because most of the feds there had been pulled away after only a few days. The reason for this, although Joe and Kari didn't know it yet, was a simple fact: Sanctuary was gone.

It had all blown apart, as it had done times before, in the middle of the night. A few of those who stayed behind, ostensibly to clean up, were veterans. One couple, a husband and wife named Terry and Jan, had been through it twice: someone shaking their shoulder, saying, "This is it. We're going now." Father moving past, touching them, giving them strength and courage, telling how it was all part of the curse and the blessing, that every great people was forced at least once from their homeland, some numerous times, that it was part of the tribulations that made it all worthwhile. Because at the end, he said, the rewards were great, and now they were almost there, to the place from which they would not move again. But bad things had happened. Evil was coming and coming fast. They had to run. And Father meant run. He handed each of them extra money and instructions on how to go about getting out to the new Sanctuary, and that very night Father left.

Over the next days vans and trucks came to take them into Seward or Soldotna or even up to Anchorage. To dissipate them, Father had said. Boats had been hired out of Ninilchik and Homer to take many of them. Some, who had extra money of their own, were instructed to wait a week or two, and then to fly to a certain lake in the Becharof National Wildlife Preserve, west of the Katmai, where they would be met by others, and led along ridges and through valleys out farther to the new Sanctuary. Some were simply left to make their own arrangements. For this was their only safety right now: to scatter on the winds, and then to come together again, in the new Sanctuary.

Jan and Terry did not remember it ever being like this. Before, they had always moved together, as a family. Now they were each on their own, banded into little groups of twos and threes and fours, some with children tagging along.

Many would not make the trip at all. It was easy, outside the insulation of the Family, to fade back into life in the city or to just move along down the road. In the first week after the crisis, the Kenai camp population dwindled to fifteen. In the second week to six, who couldn't quite bring themselves to make this next effort of traveling five hundred miles into the bush.

Terry and Jan—who had met at the famous Altamont Stones concert in 1969, lived in an Oregon commune into the midseventies, traveled for two years in India and Nepal, taught in an alternative school together in Eugene, met Father in 1988 and fallen in love with him—brought this up to each other. "We don't have to go," Jan said. "Now's the time, if there ever was one." Terry nodded. He had believed this was to be their life, now, living in the wilderness and meditating. He liked it like this, and could have gone on to his death. But the moving, the being hounded, was not what he and Jan were about anymore. They were each forty-six years old, and enough was enough.

Now they were alone with only four others, who walked through the camp wearing the dazed look of earthquake survivors, wandering in and out of the buildings. Plenty of good food had been abandoned, which they cooked and ate. They prayed with each other, and alone. But mostly they just waited—for it to sink in that this entire community had been dismantled in a matter of hours, and for the advent of the invasion Father was running from. They expected any day for men dressed in black fatigues and body armor to come pouring in from the road and from the air, carrying rifles and firing tear gas.

Instead of an invasion, though, the only thing that showed up was a single woman. She wore Levi's, a flannel shirt and denim jacket, and black leather boots, and carried a pack on her back. She had a dark complexion, a broad pleasant face and loose hair down to her shoulders. They were inside, eating lunch, when she came so they did not see her at first, and she did not see them. She had dropped her pack in the center of the dirt square and was turning around and around, taking in the abandonment.

"We're gone," Jan told her finally, from the doorway of the dorm where they were eating.

"What?"

"We're gone," she said. "My name's Jan, and I'm not here anymore."

Lunch was plain boiled noodles, salmon jerky, soda bread and water. Thin fare, but the woman seemed to actually like it. She said she wasn't really hungry, but she ate well and thanked them again and again. She said she loved dried salmon and hadn't had any in a long time.

She was from Fairbanks, she told them. She was looking for Amon Ka'atchii, to study with him. She'd heard great things, and wanted to learn.

"You a native?" one of them asked her.

"Yes," she said, refusing to elaborate any further. She didn't look quite like the full-blooded Athapaskan Indians they'd come to know from the homestead up the road. But then there were so many of mixed blood it was hard to tell who was what. They could tell from looking at her she had native blood. And, anyway, it didn't really matter.

"Where is Father?" she asked.

"Gone," Jan said. "The whole Family's moved to New Sanctuary. Far away."

"Where?"

They looked around at each other. Their instructions had been explicit—don't let any strangers see the maps, unless they were pilots or boat captains taking you out. Best would be to memorize the map and destroy it.

"Aren't you going there?" the woman asked.

They looked again at each other. Finally one young woman spoke up. "We were thinking of not going," she said. "It's been hard, this life, you know. The new place will be even harder. And there's a lot of running. People hate us."

"I want to go," the newcomer said.

"What's you're name?"

"Leanne. None of you are going?"

The young woman who'd spoken, spoke again. "I said we were thinking of not going, but I guess I'm not so sure now. I mean I am thinking of going, after all." The others looked at her with some surprise. They'd all agreed to head to Anchorage and get jobs for a while, helping each other out until they decided their next move. "I'm sorry," she said. "The thought of going back into a city, I just don't want that. I'd rather deal with this. And I at least want to see the new Sanctuary."

"You get out there," Terry said, "you'd best remember there's no way back. Too far; too expensive. Nothing passes by there."

"The boats will be there," the woman said. "We'll still go work the canneries, Father said. If I ever want, I'll cut away then, catch a flight back in. It's not like it's the end of the world."

"I'll go with you," Leanne said. "Who are you?"

"Chris," the young woman said. "But I'm not sure I'm supposed to take anyone."

"I know the wilderness," said Leanne. "The mountains. Hunting, fishing. Surviving. I'm good out there. I can help the Family. If Father Amon doesn't want me there, then I'll leave right then. I'll walk into the bush and disappear."

Chris liked the idea of company for the trip. What had held her back from going was the thought of doing it alone.

"You got any money? There's a place we could fly into, where we'd be picked up, but it'll cost over a thousand."

"How much do you have?"

"Four hundred."

"I'll take care of the rest."

"Great, then," Chris said. "Can you guys give us a lift out to the road tomorrow?" She looked at the others, who nodded.

"We'll thumb down to Homer," Chris said to Leanne. "Airport there. Lots of bush pilots. They'll go wherever you want."

Rick Agullana had lost so much blood from the bullets that the surgeon on call in Juneau's Mercy Hospital had given him a five percent chance of surviving.

Rick was lucky, though, in a couple respects. His blood type was O positive, the most common sort, so the blood bank at Mercy had fifteen type-specific units on hand to pump into him. A call went out and within forty minutes eighteen more pints were flown in from Petersburg and Sitka.

The surgeon couldn't wait to prep Rick and get him into surgery. It had been necessary to open him right there on the ER table in order to start tying off vessels and exploded sections of intestine. When the worst bleeding was stopped, and the pneumothorax where he'd been hit in the chest sealed, they moved him up to the surgical floor, and two other surgeons were called in, one of whom was from Anchorage and had had training in bowel resections at Cedars-Sinai in Los Angeles. This specialist, Rick's second stroke of luck, happened to be in Juneau for a week of consulting and teaching. The general surgeon who'd first worked on Rick in the ER commented later on the beautiful job the specialist did. In all, seven feet of small bowel, eight inches of large, the spleen, and part of the liver were removed.

Then the infection had set in. Perforated bowels are terribly dangerous for the infection they cause, and this had been not just perforated, but shredded. Rick, who was comatose from blood loss anyway, spiked a fever that at times topped a hundred and five degrees. Nurses packed him in ice, and lines carried massive doses of antibiotics into his vessels.

After three days the highest fever broke, but remained hovered around 101 for another four days. Rick stayed in his coma for several days after that. When he finally opened his eyes one morning, he saw a man in a suit reading a newspaper in the chair next to his bed. The man stood up when Rick looked at him.

"Can you hear me?" the man said. Rick watched him. Soon doctors and nurses came in and made the man leave. They worked on Rick, shining lights in his eyes and listening to his chest and abdomen until he fell asleep. When he woke up, that evening, he lay quietly in his pain and thought about things for a long time.

Several days later, when the man came back, Rick nodded at him.

"Ready to talk?" the man said. He was a little Oriental guy in a suit, and said his name was Mark Truong. He didn't call himself an agent, but Rick knew that's what he was.

"Did he get away with it?" Rick said.

"Who? With what?"

"Joe Curtis. With trying to frame me again. With the gold he stole. With the woman I love."

"He got the girl. We got the gold."

"How much?"

"One bar, a hundred ounces."

"That's not even half of it."

"No?"

"There were three seventy when he stole it."

"He stole it?"

"I watched him count it."

"In Idaho you said you were just a missionary, that you didn't know anything."

"I was just a missionary. But I lied about not knowing anything. I was trying to protect Kari. We were engaged. But after he killed those people and stole the gold, he stole her, too. They left me behind."

"We believe she's cooperating with him."

Rick nodded and turned his face away.

"You in the Family?"

"Yes."

"Joe?"

"He knew about the gold, right? And he's in Alaska, now. But I didn't know him. I just wanted to get to him to get back Kari. That's all I wanted."

"It doesn't all make sense. The agent who was on the glacier said she believed you were the Idaho murderer."

"She's wrong. What Joe Curtis did, you wouldn't believe."

"I might. What about the helicopter that was shot down. You were on that boat. Joe wasn't."

"I was just trying to stop them from shooting. I said the last thing the Family needed was to have that blood on their hands. But they panicked. They'd had the Stinger all set up."

"And you got hit."

"I guess so. I don't remember."

"You mind if I hook up a tape recorder first?"

"Not at all," Rick said. He knew the man had no reason to believe him about any of this. Maybe they knew for sure he had some complicity; maybe they didn't know exactly what, or to what extent. But they knew he was a criminal. The thing was, he knew, it didn't matter. He had a new job now, working for the feds, and as long as they liked his work, he'd be OK.

He turned to look out the window at the mountains, which had a certain beauty with their evergreeness and the way they folded shadow on top of light. But he was tired of them. He was tired of trees and rivers and fish and moose and the smell of untainted air. What he wanted was a city. A big, noisy, stinking city. When this was all over, he decided, that's where he'd head.

The *Maribel S.* had ceased to be. In her place, a newly painted ship—brick red this time instead of her old dirty white—with the common name *Wayfarer,* was set to motor north. Her bullet-pocked bow, and the additional damage that had been done to disguise her, had been patched and sealed and sanded. Eventually she'd need new wood, but this job would hold long enough to get her home. Her crew—the captain, Omaha and two deck hands—said a silent prayer as they emerged from the boathouse where they'd managed, incredibly, to stay hidden. Three times men came to the owner of the boathouse, asking questions. Once he even brought them back through on a tour, showing them there was no boat here like the one they were looking for. The *Maribel S.* by then had been dismantled, repainted and broken up to look like just another reef-wrecked boat under repair.

Now, though, it was open water clear around the rim of the Gulf of Alaska, with no place to hide. The Army or Coast Guard still had to be stopping boats, doing spot checks. Omaha and the ship's captain discussed it at length, and knew they were going to need more than righteousness and courage to get the weapons home.

It took a couple days before they'd agreed on a plan to avoid this, and another couple to build up enough nerve and stockpile enough fuel. Instead of following the coast, they'd decided now to head due west, straight out into the gulf, into open ocean, where at one point they'd be the better part of two hundred miles from nearest land. The line from the archipelago to Kodiak Island, the first land they'd see, was almost six hundred miles. If anything went wrong out there, they'd be gone. On the other hand, in all those millions of empty square miles of nothing, they'd be next to invisible.

31

THE EFFECT OF THE DISASTER ON THE PEOPLE AT JUSTICE, WHO HAD OF course, in their two and a half years in office, suffered the embarrassments of Waco and the Randy Weaver investigation, and then had to attempt to assuage the public's fury over Oklahoma City, was much the same as it had been on those at CRIDCOM and the ATF—beyond the anger and shock at the deaths, it made them hunker down and hold their breaths, waiting for an onslaught of recriminations. But the onslaught never came. News of the event had been contained; there had been press coverage of the accident, but no civilian eyewitness realized, apparently, that the chopper had been fired upon before it fell, and no reporter had uncovered the link between the celebrated pursuit of a federal fugitive named Joseph Curtis, the breaking story of theft from an army base in Washington, and this disaster. It was passed off by a Coast Guard press liaison as simply being under investigation, and now, weeks after the event, no one outside the involved government agencies and the military knew otherwise.

In any case, it had been a frightening taste of the AG's worst fear: another debacle claiming the lives of agents and innocents. It would be much worse, she said, when and if government forces invaded the camp of the Amonites.

Priorities, still, were to locate the weapons, to apprehend the men who'd shot down the chopper and to find the Idaho gunman. The people of Amon, those who were innocent of these crimes anyway, the children in particular, could be left alone then, and another disaster avoided. Amon himself would be dealt with in time. They'd watch him, and be patient, and sooner or later he'd fall.

And so far, military and Treasury investigators had heeded her guidelines. The Kenai camp had been watched until it broke up, although Father's departure had not been witnessed, or he would have been apprehended. New surveillance was being established on the Alaska Peninsula. And it had been executed so that no one in the Family could know of it, or the fact that an ATF agent had penetrated into their midst.

In the meantime, the AG said, at a breakfast meeting with her deputy and her special troubleshooter, she knew that military and Treasury and even some FBI agents, who had, after all, lost one of their own in Juneau, weren't happy with this approach. She feared someone getting trigger-happy, or getting ideas of increasing the aggressiveness of the surveillance, or of grabbing a Family member to pump for information. She wanted watch-and-wait but, with three different agencies conducting investigations, feared she couldn't entirely control what happened. So she wanted, she said, eyes and ears up there. Although she had direct and nearly instantaneous access to any information the FBI gathered, and the FBI was sending high brass up there to oversee, she wanted more than that—she wanted another sort of judgment and interpretation as well.

"What's that mean?" her deputy asked.

She put down her pecan croissant, wiped her fingers on a napkin and looked at her old friend, her special troubleshooter, the former chief U.S. Attorney in Dade Country, Florida. "How would you like to see Alaska?" she asked him.

Colonel Johnson Rozsa and General Parkins, head of INSCOM, played squash once a month or so, when one of Parkins' regular partners, who were all other generals, of course, couldn't make it. Rozsa liked the game well enough, but was happy not to play it every week. The ball didn't bounce, for one thing. He was more the racquetball sort, where you got some action off the thing so it zinged and whizzed off the walls and the glass, and you weren't constantly driving forward to dig it up out of the wood before it died there. In any case, he understood that the purpose of the game wasn't the game itself, but the time spent with one's opponent. Valuable time. Precious time.

"She doesn't want to move at all," Parkins was saying, as he sucked wind between games. The man was over sixty so Rozsa, who would be fifty in a month, laid off, let a lot of shots go, lost key points, but even so Parkins seemed bushed halfway through the session. He was talking about the Attorney General.

"They're cowed over there," Parkins said. "And I'm sympathetic. They can't be caught in another disaster, with babies getting killed on the nightly news. If word got out, it could bring them down, Rozsa, you know that? It would undoubtedly lead to the resignation of the AG herself. It could hurt the goddamned President."

Rozsa nodded his commiseration, but was thinking that that might not be such a bad thing, actually.

"Unbelievable, these situations where some lunatic fringe controls the destiny of VIPs like this," Parkins said, and shook his head. He was leaning with his butt against the back wall, hands on his knees. "But the point is, she doesn't want to move. We've suggested that, since there are earlier warrants still outstanding, they don't need to actually spot the weapons in the camp to make arrests. They've got enough circumstantial evidence from this case which, combined with the outstanding warrants, gives them more than enough justification for going in. Or for laying a trap for the man. I mean their protocol, supposedly, is that they ask him to surrender, he says no, and they grab him or shoot him. I mean, we're not saying they should go in with tanks again, although I'd like to know when federal agents suddenly started following rules of propriety."

Rozsa nodded. He was kneeling, watching the general, and smiling a little. These were all his own words, almost verbatim. It never failed to amaze him how he could plant the bug, talk from the good place inside, and let it percolate, only to come back up out of someone else's mouth, higher up the chain. This was exactly his job: thinking for these people, making them see his light, until they took it for their own. Until they spouted it back to him as if they'd sat up nights thinking it all through, and now they just wanted to bounce it off him to see what he thought.

"I know, sir," Rozsa said. "My fear, as you know, is just that if they wait too long, something more horrible than they can imagine will happen. If one of those missiles gets launched—"

"I know, I know," Parkins said, waving off the thought.

"And in any other scenario, sir," said Rozsa, "we'd just be spectators like everyone else. But talk about bringing someone down, about resignations. Can you imagine another civilian slaughter, only this time because of *our* missile, the recriminations?"

Parkins shook his head so hard that sweat flew.

Rozsa said, "For sure what's his name, the head of the base out there, would go."

"Ed Shaw," Parkins said. "I know him, the old bastard. Not such a bad guy, really."

"Be a shame," said Rozsa. "And that's not to mention what the Congress might do to our budget. We're protected now, but something like this—who knows. They're looking for any excuse to cut where they can. We might suddenly look awfully ripe."

"Goddammit, Johnson," Parkins said.

"Sir," Rozsa said. "Have you thought about the fact that this is really a different sort of war we're fighting here?"

"What?"

"I mean this is as much a war as any other, as the Gulf, say, or Nam.

Only its methods are so different that I think maybe we're not picking up on them. I mean, what's the difference, except scale, between Saddam Hussein's SCUDs and Amon Ka'atchii's Stingers? At base, I mean. Both madmen. Both terrorists. But one's on U.S. soil, and that means that although he's taken our property, and that if he uses it, we suffer directly, we can't fight him. Our hands are tied."

"They are. Yes."

"But only if we think of it in traditional terms, sir. This isn't Vietnam or the Gulf. It's America. And how does one fight wars here, sir?"

"What?"

"How do you fight wars in this country? How did Jim Wright get shot down in the House, for example?"

"Jim Wright? Well, he was—"

"Information, sir," Rozsa said. "Information."

"Information," Parkins said. He had slid down the wall now and was sitting on the wooden floor, looking at Rozsa.

"What if I were to suggest a way, in one swift action, to bring so much pressure to bear, not only on the AG, but on the Cabinet Secretaries and the President as well, that they couldn't not allow us to take out Father Amon? They couldn't say yes fast enough?"

"Go on."

"But what if I said that to do this, we'd have to expose ourselves to a little criticism up front. We'd have to expose ourselves to some small heat to bring about the larger good. It'd be risky. But definitive."

"A sort of decoy maneuver," Parkins said.

"In a sense. The heat we'd take would be justified. From what I'm sensing, we're going to take it anyway, sooner or later."

"Heat from whom?"

"From the people, sir. When they find out that these weapons were stolen from the Army."

"But how would they find out? There's some suspicion, but no one knows, yet. The press can't confirm anything."

"Yet. But what if they could? What if they knew everything, including the fact that the missiles now belong to a psycho, including our scenario of what he might do with those missiles. What if every citizen were afraid to set foot on a plane because of those missiles out there? Can you imagine the reaction?"

"What are you suggesting, Colonel?"

Rozsa smiled, and slapped the dead squash ball with his racket. The sound echoed in the little room. "Let's finish before we get cold, sir. Then maybe we can grab a drink."

32

IT BEGAN WITH DARKNESS.

Not torture, nothing cruel, but when Leanne was led into the rough tent camp the Family had scraped out in a clearing at the base of a high rocky face, she'd barely had time to glance around before she was stripped of her belongings and her clothing down to her underwear and sequestered in one of the few solid buildings there, a five-by-seven pressed-board shack with nothing but a wooden bunk, a bucket of water and an empty pail for waste. A few golden threads of sunlight leaked in here and there through pinholes in the joints of the wood, but otherwise it stayed dark inside.

There was no heat source, either, but she had blankets and hadn't been cold. Nor had she been alone. A voice began whispering to her soon after she was locked in. It sounded like jibberish at first but gradually she began to detect patterns and to hear the same sentences over and over. This whispered chanting sometimes didn't stop for hours. Two tiny meals a day were passed through a slot in the door, one in the morning consisting of a thin strip of dried salmon and a half-piece of bread, and one in the evening, of the same with a bowl of watery soup. She was given all the water she could drink.

Three days passed. She knew this from the setting and rising of the sun and also because her watch had a built-in light which showed the time and date when she pressed a button. Usually she curled up on her bed first, and hid the watch when she looked at it. On the third day, though, she forgot, and turned on the light when she was sitting upright. The voice stopped. A few minutes later the door opened. Sunlight seared through her head. Someone stepped in, lifted her arm and took the watch from her wrist, then slammed shut the door again. Soon after, the voice resumed.

She did not mind the darkness and she wouldn't have minded solitude, but that's not what this was.

On the fourth day she began to yell back at the voice. After that, a woman named Jennifer came to visit.

Jennifer was plump and happy looking. She had round red cheeks, silver-streaked hair and large, brown-stained teeth. She knelt on the floor next to the bunk in the small cabin and sponged Leanne's face with a warm, wet cloth.

"You have a fever," Jennifer said. "I told them this wasn't healthy."

"Who?"

"The Inner Council. You understand that since we just moved, and you're a stranger and all, they had to do some checking."

"What checking? What is there to check?"

"I don't know, dear. Whatever they do. They say it's all high security and you had to be kept in this disgusting jail."

"Who was talking to me?"

Jennifer gave her a funny look.

"A voice kept whispering, saying things over and over."

"What things?"

"Phrases. The earth. God will save my soul and I'll be one with the earth. That was one."

Jennifer leaned back on her heels and looked at Leanne. "Are you serious?"

"Yes," Leanne said. "Who was doing it?"

"No one was doing anything, dear. You were locked in this room and left alone. There's nothing around it, no other buildings or tents. I was the one feeding you. I'd have seen if someone was around."

"No, I heard them. They were talking. And someone saw me with my watch, and they took it—"

Jennifer gave another look and shook her head. "Your watch was taken with the rest of your belongings, Leanne. We have them all together. I checked. The watch is there. A Bulova, right?"

"Someone was watching me."

"No one was watching you, dear. Really."

"And talking."

"No one. I promise. Take off those blankets."

Leanne lay back on the cot and let Jennifer continue the sponging, down her shoulders and arms and across her belly and along her legs. Somehow, it didn't seem odd to her to let this stranger bathe her. It felt good to be wet, to get rid of some of the sweat and grime of the four days and of the plane trip and hike before that, although she'd long since stopped being bothered by her smell. She remembered that not so long ago she often took two showers a day, and was startled to realize that she'd already begun to think of her past life as a memory, as history. As if she would not be going back to it.

"You have beautiful hair," Jennifer said, stroking the top of Leanne's head. She pulled a brush from the apron she wore and said, "May I?"

Leanne sat up. Jennifer sat next to her on the cot and brushed.

"Do you know a lot about living out like this?"

"Some," said Leanne. "Why do you think so?"

"Well, you're a native and all."

"Yes," Leanne said. "I saw when I came in how bad it is here. I just got a glimpse—"

"It's not bad, dear. We're happy. And we've all just arrived, so we have a lot of work to do."

"That's what I mean. I mean, you have a lot of work to do. But winter's not far away out here. If you don't get some buildings up and lay things in in the right way, people will die."

"Really?"

"Yes."

"And you know all about that?"

"A lot. And hunting. I can help with that. You'll need full larders now. It'll be hard later, after it snows."

"I'll tell them. Thank you."

"When do I begin. You know, studying."

"Be patient, dear. Everyone's terribly busy right now. But your study begins like this, with patience. You must just wait, and hold your mind open and empty."

Jennifer leaned over and stroked Leanne's hair again and then kissed her on the cheek. "You will help us," she said. "I can feel it. I can feel that you are a strong person."

Jennifer visited later that day and again the next, staying for longer and longer periods. In between times, the voice took up its whispering, but Leanne did not mention it again. Another three days passed, by which time Jennifer was in the cabin most of the day and into the night. On the seventh day, Jennifer did not come alone. She was accompanied by two other women, and for some time after that, Leanne would only rarely be alone again.

She was led to the large white-canvas cabin-style tent where these three women lived, and where, she was told, she would live now, too. She was given a cot along one wall, and the space beneath it in which to store her possessions, which were nothing more than her boots and a few articles of clothing they'd returned to her; most of what she'd brought in her pack, including the money, she was told, was needed for the greater good of the Family.

After they showed her into the tent, Jennifer and the others sat on their own cots and watched her with looks of a kind of awe on their faces. She couldn't know it, but from the time the stories of her hearing voices began to circulate, it was rumored that she had a power of some sort. The fact that Father had still not appeared to her, that he had not come in the usual way to bring her into his fold, was another sign that she was different.

She walked to the doorway and looked out, expecting someone to order her back inside, but when no one did, she went out to look around. Then the three women got up and followed her, saying nothing, but staying no more than a few feet behind her, as she wandered through the camp they called Sanctuary.

Sanctuary, she saw, was a two or so acre clearing of low grass and bushes, bordered on three sides by rows of various colored tents, and across the center of which mud paths and cooking areas had already been worn. A layer of smoke, from open fires and cooks' stoves, hung head-high. The unbordered north side of the camp, which ended at the edge of a dense forest, was where the jail stood, and thirty or forty feet away from that, just at the edge of the woods, a small but solid-looking log cabin. Smoke curled from a stovepipe in its roof and a generator puttered off to one side. Leanne remembered hearing this sound from time to time from the jail.

The forest beyond this cabin appeared to go on for many miles, sloping upward over a series of hills, which led, in the distance, to huge, spike-topped mountains.

Hard to the west, as she'd noticed when she came in, the camp was shadowed by a towering rock cliff which she now saw was part of a several-mile-long shelf running from north to south. The camp was hemmed between this rock face, the hills to the north and, to the east, a lower, but steep, grass-covered ridge with a stream running along its base. Leanne would not have chosen this spot because the cliff would keep the camp in nearly perpetual shade after midday. She would have preferred a higher, sunlit exposure. But for defensive measures, the place was a fortress.

The fourth side of the camp, to the south, opposite the jail and the cabin, beyond the third line of tents, was different: it seemed to drop off rather than rise. And as she got closer to the tent line, Leanne could see that it was a kind of pass between the ridge and the cliff which continued down for quite a ways. The forestation was too thick for her to see where the slope led, but when she walked partway up the ridge, she glimpsed the blue of the sea, not half a mile away, she guessed.

She knew roughly where the pilot had dropped her and the girl, and knew the people who'd met them at the lake had led them southwestward. So she was somewhere on the southern coast of the Alaska Peninsula. If she could get to higher ground, from which she could see more of the ocean and the outlying mountains of Kodiak Island, she could tell more. Still, it didn't matter, she supposed. Agents would know where she was already. She had no doubt they were watching right now, ensconced on a high point somewhere with huge telescopes, maybe two or three miles away.

What Leanne didn't see among all the faces of the Family members walking around her was the face of her brother, Calvin. She had to get them to let her go out, hunting, exploring, gathering, it didn't matter. She could begin her search, then. If she knew Calvin, he wouldn't waltz right in. He'd camp out there somewhere, watching, learning something about these people first. He could be there now, she told herself, watching, seeing her. She told herself this again and again, in the hope that soon she would start to believe it.

The first time they left her alone for a few minutes, Leanne took advantage and wandered into the forest that began behind the cabin. She hadn't walked far, a hundred yards maybe, when she noticed boot prints in some soft earth at the base of a dead tree trunk. Someone had stood here for a long time, because there were many layers of prints, one over another. Then she saw triangular gouges in the trunk of the dead tree, where boot hooks had been used to climb. These were the marks of observers.

She'd been allowed to carry a small pen knife, which she used now to carve into the dead wood the message LR OK. Then she left.

A couple days later, alone again on the same walk, she saw that her message had been scratched into illegibility. As she stood, then, she heard a noise behind her and turned. A man in full gray camouflage fatigues and face paint and a knit hat with branches sewn to it, stepped out from the background brush.

"Hey," Leanne said.

"Tonnecliffe. FBI," the man said.

"Red Feather. ATF."

He nodded. "How's it going?"

"It's not, really. No sign of any military weapons. No Amon."

"You're OK?"

"Just fine."

"Your brother?"

"He's not here either."

"Curtis?"

"Nope. Sorry."

"Then we'll wait."

"Yessir," she said.

He held out a plastic bag containing a small gray device no larger than a matchbook, with a button and a red indicator light on it. She'd seen one before—it was an emitter. If she pushed the button, they'd pick up the signal and follow it to her.

She stuffed it down into a hollow in the tree.

The man took a step backward, and became invisible again.

She was kept hungry, never being allowed to eat more than what she calculated were five or six hundred calories a day. She grew weak from this, felt her muscle masses diminishing, her body fat being absorbed. She shrank within herself, too, to a hard core that she could feel deep inside, but to which she couldn't so readily gain access anymore; this was the part of her that she'd always seen as dominant, the aggressive, eager-to-please Leanne, Leanne the good student, the good hunter, Leanne the good agent; now she was just Leanne the survivor, mute, uncomplaining, watching and waiting. But she organized her mind: the surface for playing this game, for camping and praying and talking hours and hours into the night, for being kept fatigued and hungry (she knew exactly what they were doing to her; she'd learned a lot about mind control from former cult members she'd come to know), for being cajoled and informed of the Truth; but another, hidden, part of her mind for what she needed to accomplish, to keep a running log of everything she saw and to wait for an opportunity to write it down somewhere and to smuggle it out. For now all she could do was to wait and keep that part of her mind clear and ready to act.

In an unexpected sense, she felt closer to the ideal Guts had tried to instill in her than she ever had before. He used to marvel at the energy she had for chasing after game, for tracking; that was what made her happy, always moving, nose to the ground, following prints or a blood trail, no matter how old. He'd marvel but he'd shake his head; you have no patience, he would tell her. And patience is the primary virtue of a hunter. Aggressiveness and tirelessness and strength are special traits, but I'll take the patient hunter every time. She'd shake her head and lead on; he'd shake his head and follow. But now, now, to her great surprise, she found she was able to merely wait.

In her time here, she still hadn't even seen Father. She'd seen no military arms and no Calvin or Joseph Curtis and, except for occasional seconds with Tonnecliffe, had no way of making contact with the world. But she did not mind waiting for these things. She was disguised in the sanctuary of her prey. The true way of hunting. This was a state of mind she had never experienced before, and she felt the power inside her building.

The women sensed this power. Leanne was a kind of seer it was rumored; certain of the women had been told this was so. But they did not hesitate to push her hard in their teaching. They taught three times a day, sometimes for only an hour or two, sometimes in sessions that lasted six or seven hours. In some of these thrice daily tent sessions, which grew eventually to include six women besides Leanne (one of whom was Chris, the girl who'd brought Leanne out here), they sat naked on furs to have their discussions and prayer sessions. Leanne soon stopped feeling a flush of embarrassment, and then stopped thinking about it at all.

The sessions were always intense and emotional, the women growing so excited by Leanne's power and resistance and by their jealousy of her that sometimes they would pounce on her, grabbing her hair and pulling it, or scratching her or pounding her with their hands, until Jennifer would intervene, pulling them off and holding Leanne against her hot, fat body until the other women cooled off and retreated.

Sometimes they cornered her verbally, accusing her of harboring false motivations, of not seeking the Truth, but rather of seeking some worldly goal, tricking her into misstating her lessons. "But the world is what we're about," she'd say. "The *earth* is what we're about," the women would answer in chorus. "You've left the world far behind."

Then sometimes they would compliment her so profusely, so sincerely, that she wept. Her mind seemed truly to open in these moments, as if the top of her head had split and all the wisdom of all the tribes of all the ages poured in, as if she were a vessel, a conduit connecting the gods of the tribes to the earth itself. She fell over and sobbed, breathless with these plain, wrinkled women, who knew nothing of guns or bombs or illegal arms deals, who cared only for their worship and their children and the earth and for each other.

And, oddly, incredibly, she began to love them. She would come to love them as she had loved some of the women in her town on the reservation, as she loved these forests and mountains, and the wild-tasting game and fish they ate.

But she was dissatisfied, too, although again not because of anything having to do with her job or her past or even Calvin. Surrounded by this most wild of wilderness country, with slain animals being carted into the camp, and huge hook-jawed salmon dragged up from a river beyond the low ridge, she felt an intense impatience to get out into it, to press her nose against the ground and root along the game trails and riverbanks, to run in a way she had not run for nearly twenty years.

It was these, the love and contentedness, and the terrible, wonderful anticipation, that were most unexpected. Leanne did not know what to make of them, and there came a day when she did not understand anymore exactly what was happening.

◇

Time passed and the air grew consistently chilly, the nights plain cold. In the mornings, the crusty hoarfrost which coated the grass and mud lasted late into the morning. Leanne walked barefoot, savoring the burn, from her tent to the open toilet pit draped off with blankets, and squatted, and inhaled the steam that rolled up from her waste.

But she had grown concerned, too. "I'm not sure you're ready for this winter," she told the women. "I know you've lived out, but not this far out, and not without buildings. The winter here could kill you."

"Mother the Earth will protect us."

"Mother the Earth demands your respect," Leanne said. "You are not showing it to her."

So the student was beginning to teach. One of the women slipped out of the tent after Leanne said this and crossed the muddy opening to the cabin at the edge of the woods.

The next day, in the warm tent, the women were talking and laughing and then suddenly went quiet. Leanne felt a cold draft, and looked up to see a man holding open the tent's flap. He wore a crudely tanned and stitched leather coat, unbuttoned. He was tall, and thick-waisted, with uncombed black-and-white hair that stuck out from his head in hornlike points. His lips were thick, his chin broad and deeply cleft. He had heavy day-old whiskers. In all, Leanne thought, he was not an attractive man, except for the eyes, which were blue, and bright, and bore into her in a way she thought she had never felt before. Guts had had powerful eyes, too, but very different. They were black-brown and watery, and they did not bore. They spoke, and they caressed. These blue eyes she looked into now did not speak; they commanded; they compelled; and they seemed to see things that ought not be viewable.

"I am Father Amon," he said, looking at her alone.

"You're letting out our heat," she answered him. Then she slipped on her own coat and left the women and stood before Father outside.

It would not rain this day, she could tell. The sun was up in a blue diamond sky. Far, far overhead, ten miles and a million light years away, a jet on the Seattle to Tokyo route drew a white vapor trail, the only blemish on all the blueness. The air carried that autumnal bite of possibility, the sting of change that school children know so well, and adults still felt, when they allowed themselves.

"We shall walk," Amon said, and turned toward the southern edge of the camp and the canyon passage leading down to the ocean beyond. Leanne followed.

33

It was Calvin, with his quiet, steady way of working through the brush so that the noise he made didn't even disturb some animals, who, working well ahead of them, established a vantage on the top of a heavily treed ridge line from which he could see into the Kenai camp of the Amonites. By the time Kari and Joe came to within sight of him, he'd slipped back off the ridge and was waving at them to get down and keep quiet. He'd made out, he said, the figure of a man in a green coverall, up in a tree stand about a hundred yards closer to the camp. The guy was wired for sound, Cal said, with headphones and some kind of transmitter and a spotting scope with attached camera on a tripod.

"Feds," Kari said. "They've watched us here before."

"Thing is, there's nothing to watch," said Cal. "Doors are all open, shit laying around in the dirt. After your phone calls, I was afraid of this. Come on." He and Kari moved back up the ridge on their hands and knees while Joe squatted in the grass and waited.

When they came back, Kari's face was pale.

"They're cleaned out," Calvin said. "Nobody home. Must've all got busted."

"They didn't get busted," said Kari. "They've gone."

"Where?" said Joe, but he knew. Kari had told him about the new Sanctuary, in the Aleutian Mountains out along the Alaska Peninsula, hundreds of miles into nowhere.

"We best clear out of this area fast," said Cal. "These guys gotta be working through here, seeing if they can pick up on anyone from the camp who just moved out into the woods."

"We can't go back the way we came," Joe said.

"Nope. Let's head south 'til we hit another river. Then we'll follow it out. Eventually it'll cross the highway. We can go from there, grab a car, whatever."

As they walked, Joe heard Kari crying to herself. She cried most of the day.

That night in the tent Kari did not speak to him. She simply unzipped their bags and then zipped them up, together, to make a double bed, and then she kissed him, hard. Her mouth tasted like toothpaste and wild Kenai water. She methodically stripped them both and crawled on top of him, but did not let him move. She held his hands at his sides until she had satisfied herself with the kissing, what seemed like an hour's worth, before she lifted one of his hands and moved it down along her belly and between her legs. She held two of his fingers in her hand and rubbed them against herself until he felt her shudder and go weak against him.

After a moment she moved her hand from her own groin to his, and found him and squeezed him so hard it startled him. Then she began to rub him against her opening, terribly slowly at first, then more quickly, until she pressed her pelvis down against him and drove him inside of her.

She wrapped both her arms around his neck and moved on top of him, moved harder and faster, until they were slapping audibly together.

Placing her mouth over his, she blew her hot breath into his lungs, then breathed it back in, then blew it into him again, her lips sealed around his, until they were passing useless air back and forth between them in rapid, shallow pants. His head grew light, his chest heavy with the void. But from the dizziness and burning, he felt it beginning, he rose up more deeply into her and released finally with such force and for such duration that it was all he could do to stay conscious until she tore her mouth away from his and allowed the cold, rich air to rush in.

Later, when they'd caught their breath, he felt the moisture on her face, and then where the droplets had gathered in the hollow in her throat, forming a small pool.

"The danger," she said, "is that when I take you into me, I can almost forget. Almost."

With his thumb he pushed the sweat from the hollow down onto her chest and spread it out with his hand. "You have to find her," he said. "I talked to Cal about it. We'll help you. It's different now."

"Because of the baby?"

"Not only."

"What else."

"Because of us, you and me."

"Tell me."

"I just did."

"Still," she said, "I'm not so sure you should give up your chance to run."

"We might as well run out to that place as any other. We'll make a trade: gold for Eloise."

"Really?"

"Then leave."

"Joe," she said. She pressed her face into him and breathed and said, "Joe, Joe, Joseph."

"But it's a long way. I don't know how we'll do it."

"There's a man," Kari said. "I heard about him. A salmon broker named Johnny Johnson; he runs a ninety-five-foot tender boat out of Ninilchik, which is only about twenty miles from where we are right now. He did regular business with Father, buying and selling some of Father's boats' catch, carting supplies and people for the Family. I heard that when the time came, Johnny was one of the main ways Father planned on moving us out to the new Sanctuary."

"Why would he help us?"

"I don't know if he will. But he was never a Family member. Just a businessman looking for his next buck."

It was nearly mid-October. By the time they made their way out to the Sterling Highway, two days later, and found the man in Ninilchik named Johnny Johnson, and gave him 5,000 reasons to take them the 150 miles southwest to Kodiak City, where he could refuel, and another 100 northeast back across the Shelikof Strait to a certain spot on the Alaska Peninsula, and he had outfitted his boat for that rough trip, and they finally shoved off into the waters of the Cook Inlet to begin the voyage, it had been a month to the day since their escape from Juneau.

34

On that first day of walking, neither Leanne nor Father said anything until they had passed the tents and entered the woods at the top edge of the pass, not far beyond which it plunged down toward the shoreline. At this edge, although they were still surrounded by thick Alaskan spruce, there was a high, flat plateau of open rock which they climbed and from which they could see the ocean, and, on the far horizon, the mountains of Kodiak Island.

"They'll come from there," Father said, pointing at the distant peaks.

"What?"

"From Kodiak. That's where they'll launch."

"Who?"

Father put on a mildly disgusted look and shook his head. "You've been so strong; you've shown such remarkable skills and knowledge and, most important, abilities to learn and adapt. Although I suspect it's not learning so much as falling back into what you once knew. So, now, please, don't ruin it by baldly lying to me."

"About what?" Leanne said. "I came down from Fairbanks. My father worked up on the rigs. . . ."

Father shook his head and pursed his lips and stared out toward the water. "OK," he said. "Fine. Let's call it a day." He slid down off the rock to the ground.

"What do you want me to say?" she said.

"I want you to stop lying and be honest. That's what you're looking for from me—honesty—is it not? You want some information from me for your little friends. Fine, I'll give it to you. But more importantly, I suspect you want real honesty. You want to know who I really am, what it is about me that compels these good people to suffer such hardships merely because I ask them to. You believe, in your heart of hearts, that maybe I do have a little wisdom, and you want wisdom, Leanne. More than anything, you want to hear someone say something wise to you. I think it's been a long time since anyone did that."

"Stop it," she said.

"And I will. I'll tell you everything I know. I'll strip myself bare for you. I'll even give you what your friends want. But in return for that, you have to can the bullshit facade."

"What about locking me in a dark room for a week? What about the little voices I heard? I'd call that bullshit."

He nodded. "Tricks," he said. "Silly little mind-cleansing games we use sometimes when people need them. In fact, it wasn't you who needed them so much as the others who needed to see you receiving them. And the voices, well, that was courtesy of yours truly. No one else knew about it, least of all the ladies who've taken you under their wing. So when you told them about those voices, they were very impressed. They're convinced they have a real holy woman in their midst, which is why they're being so hard on you. They love you."

"I love them, too." She was shocked to hear herself admit this.

"I know you do, Leanne. We'll talk more later, when you've seen your way to being straight with me."

"I *am* straight."

He turned and walked several steps back toward camp, then stopped again, as if a thought had suddenly struck him. "You know what it is?" he said. "Faith. You don't have faith in me, yet."

"Faith about what?"

"Faith in who I am. In what I know. And you see, that's exactly where it begins. Until you have faith, you'll never learn anything, never get anywhere as far as knowledge is concerned. So that's your first lesson: have faith in Amon Ka'atchii. Do you understand?"

"No."

"It's all right. Here's my point: you're afraid I really do know who you are, but you won't admit it to me because you're not *convinced* your cover has been blown since before you came here and you don't want to give anything away. And so you won't stop lying. But if you had faith in me, then you'd believe without question that I know everything about you. Lacking faith, however, what you want is proof. You're waiting for me to give you an unequivocal sign that I really do know who you are. Remember what Christ said in Luke, chapter 11? 'This is a wicked generation; it demands a sign.' "

She stared at him, anger and confusion and hope all building up together inside her chest, and she had no idea how she felt about him, this mad gun freak, mystic. But what she did know was that how she felt was not at all as she had expected to feel. She wanted to despise him, to pity him. Whatever she was feeling, she knew it was neither of these.

"So that's your choice," he said. "Either you begin to have some faith in me, and trust that I know who you are. Or you don't have faith, and you ask for a sign from me to prove that I know who you are."

"I'm only who I say I am."

"A sign then," Father said. "Christ did that, you know. He'd chastise people for asking for proof, then give it to them anyway, curing someone's blindness or some such thing. I love that about him. He was one of the half dozen or so really top-notch prophets. Anyway, all right. Only because I'm afraid our time is short and we have lots of ground to cover, I'll humor you this once."

He faced her fully, arms crossed over his chest. She sat with her legs tucked under her up on the rock still, and felt her fingers trying to dig into the surface of the stone as she waited. She held her breath.

"Ben Regis," Father said.

Leanne felt her eyes widen. She saw him smile at her wide eyes.

"Ben's the original nice guy, upstanding husband and father. You miss him? He was up nosing around for you after that tragedy in Coeur d'Alene, while you were off chasing shadows on the coast. Ring a bell? Which do you like better, alcohol, tobacco or firearms? Me, I'm partial to firearms, as I'm sure you must have guessed. You think I'm a gun nut like those other poor misguided redneck isolationist militia assholes you have to deal with down there in Id-a-ho. Well, you're wrong. I crave weapons because people are trying to kill me. Am I a paranoid? Maybe. But I'll be no less dead if they get to me, which they might if they don't think I can defend myself."

"But that's why they're coming," she says. "Because of the weapons."

"The old catch-22, isn't it? Which came first, the defense or the offense, the threat or the paranoia? How many of my people need to be slaughtered by your people before you all start believing we have a legitimate gripe, that we are, flatly, being persecuted in the same way the Jews and the Moslems and the poor old Roman Christians were persecuted? And the pathetic misled Davidians, for that matter, Leanne? How many dead there at the hands of your comrades? And next, how many of *my* babies?"

She couldn't say anything.

"Anyway, this is enough for one day. There's your sign. Now you know that I know and I hope we can stop playing the game. You are a lovely woman, and terribly bright and driven. Your spirit is also closer to the earth than that of anyone I've met for a long time. I hope you know that; I hope you don't continue to waste it."

He walked a few steps then stopped again. "By the way, I'm giving you a present tomorrow."

With that he turned and walked into the trees.

◇

The following day, two men she did not know came to her tent and told her to get ready; they were hunting and she was to accompany them. She fairly burst with the thought of it. Jennifer helped her get dressed, and gave her back the heavy clothing she'd come in with but which she had not seen since her arrival.

She wasn't allowed to carry a gun and she had to move slowly because she was weak from lack of food, but she followed the men through the pass, past the rock plateau where she'd talked with Father, and down to the rocky shore of their ocean cove where an open whaler, a broad wooden boat maybe twenty feet long, with nothing in it but a heavy outboard and oars and some life vests, was anchored ten or fifteen yards offshore. The men shouldered a rope which had been anchored on the beach, and marched away from the water, and so pulled in the boat.

While they did this, she looked around. Farther out in the cove, a commercial fishing boat—which was the smaller of the Family's two boats, although Leanne didn't know this—was moored next to another smaller wooden boat. On shore, set in from the beach a little ways, she saw a kind of open storage shed filled with fifty gallon drums labeled *kerosene, gasoline* and *oil.* She'd wondered where they kept their fuel, having never seen any in the camp.

When they'd loaded the gear, they set out, buzzing across the water of their small inlet, and out around a high rocky point which was where the long shelf west of the camp dropped finally, abruptly into the ocean. The entire coastline of Alaska seemed to open up before them, then.

Leanne sat in the middle of the boat, faced into the wind. She could barely breathe. The wind stung her face and made her eyes flood. Bald eagles watched from their perches in barren trees. Flocks of small black-and-red ducks dotted the water's surface, rose as they passed and circled and landed again, and once one of the men patted Leanne's arm and pointed to a small creature floating on its back not far from them, watching as they passed by.

"Sea otter," he yelled, over the wind and the engine. She could see that it held something, a fish or clam, in its tiny hands against its chest.

They rode for nearly half an hour, slowly, following the shoreline. Mostly the timbered slopes dropped straight into the water, but every so often they opened up into small rocky beaches much like the one they'd left.

She did not know where they were going or what they were looking for, until the man steering dropped the engine to an idle and the other one pointed to one of these beaches some distance from them. There in the opening of the forest, on the white and black rocks, she could just make out shades of tan and brown. Deer.

"They come down to feed about this time of year. Kelp. Whole herds of them."

As they coasted closer she began to make out individual animals, and counted over twenty. When they were just off the shore, and only a hundred or so yards from the deer, the man cut the engine, and the other handed Leanne a rifle.

"Get ready. We'll be on 'em quick. Got one in the chamber."

She knelt down on the floor of the boat, shouldered the gun, and flipped off the safety. The herd of deer had stopped feeding to watch them, but made no move to escape up the steep slopes behind them. She picked out a small buck a little ways up the slope, standing broadside, and sighted through the scope. But she'd forgotten she was on water. The boat, although it had nearly stopped moving forward, rocked up and down on the swells. The trigger had been adjusted very tight, and she touched off a shot which she didn't even really hear and which hit high. She saw dirt puff a couple feet over the buck's head. He jumped, ran a few steps, but then stopped again to watch. The entire herd held its ground still, having never seen people or a boat or heard gunfire.

"Again," one of the men said.

This time, Leanne held half a breath and willed herself to relax and move with the boat, to fall into the rhythm of the swells, watched the animal move down and up in her field of view, and so timed her shot just as the boat dropped, and the crosshairs began to pass down over the deer's shoulder. The blast echoed off the rocks, and the buck collapsed and tumbled, twisting over on himself, a tangle of legs and horns, down to the rocks below. Immediately, from behind her, the other rifle sounded and another deer, this one on the beach, collapsed.

"Fire!" the men shouted at her, and she cranked a third round into the chamber and aimed and shot and missed again.

"Shit," she said. Now the herd had bolted, and moved as one body up the cliff face, following the largest buck. The engine started and they headed for shore.

"Some'll still wait," one of the men yelled. "Keep shooting."

He was right. Leanne spotted a doe this time which had circled back to watch some more, and just when the bow of the boat hit the rocks and stopped still, she held her aim and fired again, through its neck, killing it. The other man fired again, too, and made a fourth hit. By then the herd had disappeared over the top.

"Four," said the man who ran the engine. "Not bad. Could'a been six, but not bad."

Leanne trembled. Her heart pounded. She could smell everything: the salt of the sea, the fish and kelp dried on the rocks, the iron tang of fresh animal blood, the sweat of these men. She smelled on her breath the salmon and mustard she'd had for breakfast that morning, and she smelled the mountains themselves, with their glaciated caps, and the hills of dead brown grass and barren deciduous trees and patches of spruce rolling up to them.

"Ever hunted like that?" said the man behind her, the one who'd been shooting.

"No. I'm used to mountain hunting. Hard work."

"This is work, too," he said. "You got four dozen people to keep fed. So let's go."

After they climbed out and approached the deer they could see that one buck was still moving. As the men got to it, it pulled itself to its feet and tried to stagger away. The engine man grabbed it by its rack, twisted it to the ground and placed his heavy boot on its neck. He pulled a .22 pistol from his coat, held the gun down, turned his face partly away to shield his eyes, and fired into the deer's head. Then it was quiet on that open, rocky place, but for the cold wind coming down on them.

By the time Leanne had gutted one deer, the two men had the other three finished and in the boat. One of them helped her drag the last carcass across the rocks, and pile it in on top of the others.

Afterward, on their way back, she felt so exhausted she thought she'd fall asleep, but she did not want to miss any of the smells or the wind and the cold spray in her face, or the views of the brown forested mountains and the eagles and otters and ducks. Not for one instant did she want to miss any of it.

The day after the hunt, Father found her cleaning clothing in the stream. She stood up when he came by, although he did not speak to her. He stood before her and took her face between his thick hands, and looked into her eyes, into her mind and her soul.

"You're in heaven, you know," he said, finally.

"Yes," she said. "Thank you, for yesterday."

"I didn't give you anything. You helped us. We need food."

"I know. I'll get more."

He looked at her a little longer, his eyes especially bright and blue and piercing this day, before letting her face go. But before he could leave, she grabbed his sleeve and held it for a moment.

"It's good here," he said. "That's all."

She nodded and watched him walk away.

When he had gone twenty feet or so, he stopped and looked back at her. Something about his face had changed in those few seconds, but she couldn't name it until he had turned away again.

It was the eyes, she realized. When he had looked back at her, they were no longer blue, but brown-black and flat and soft, and set in wrinkles which had not been there before. She knew these eyes—they were the eyes of her old friend Guts.

Agent Tonnecliffe, Leanne's sole contact with the world outside Sanctuary, knew something had changed when she failed first to keep a meet they had scheduled, then two contingency meets. His initial thought was that she'd got into some kind of trouble with Father, and was being detained. Then maybe that she had been injured somehow; Tonnecliffe and the others were well aware of her hunting activity, and had filmed some of it.

But then a sentinel spotted her hiking alone, not far from the dead tree where they'd first met. When Tonnecliffe appeared before her, as he had the first time, he was surprised that she did not stop. She glanced at him and brushed past, headed back toward the camp.

"Leanne?" he said. She did not look at him or stop, so he followed her and caught her arm. "Hey, what's wrong?"

"Nothing," she said. "Why should anything be wrong?"

"Haven't heard from you."

"There's nothing to say, Agent Tonnecliffe. Except this—" She stood on her toes and leaned into him, so her face was next to his, and then she whispered: "Go home. All of you. There's nothing at all for you here."

"Leanne—" he started, but she had already turned into the brush. He ran after her, tried following her prints and listening for her movements. He was an expert on wilderness surveillance, which is of course why he had been assigned here. But he could not find her. She had vanished, as if she had never been there in the first place, as if she had become some kind of ghost.

Leanne continued to hunt with the men in camp, teaching them what she knew. They stalked the herds of elk and caribou which were migrating for the winter into areas near the camp. After kills, they skinned and quartered the animals and carried the quarters and hides on pack frames on their backs. It was heavy, wearing work, but she was allowed to eat more now that she had become a provider.

In the new Sanctuary, Father returned to teaching. He had neglected his people for too long, and he owed them much of himself, he told Leanne, who, in Deacon's absence, had become a confidant. The talks ran anywhere from an hour to three or four, and were held in the evenings usually, every other day or so.

While the adults listened, the children played around them, games of tag or soccer or just unorganized running.

Leanne did not know at first whether to believe that she had really seen Father's eyes change or not, whether it was a trick her mind had played. But she told the women, finally, and they assured her it had happened. They talked about the stigmata, when Father's hands would open up with nail holes and bleed as he preached. Some of them had seen this themselves.

Time passed, and soon more than a month had gone by, and things seemed as if they were just as they would always be, as if now nothing would change. They were the people of the Family, of the Earth, and they lived the life, and asked for nothing more.

35

RICK AND AGENT MARK TRUONG, WHO HAD BEEN ASSIGNED AS RICK'S handler, had been watching a small single-prop Cessna since it emerged from the mountain passes and banked toward the tiny black cinder runway near the camp they were using. The wind was stiff today and the plane's wings waggled hard a couple of times on the approach before the pilot stabilized them and touched down.

"Justice Department rep," Truong said.

"For what?"

"They want an observer in here. You know."

"What's that mean for me?"

Truong shrugged. "He knows what's going on."

Rick watched as the plane taxied back, as a man emerged and

Truong shook his hand and took his bag. Shortly a beat-up red pickup driven by a local pulled up. Truong and the JD official got in front; Rick rode in the back with the luggage, but he didn't mind. The weather hadn't really turned yet, and the air felt good.

They were staying in a set of small two-story cabins in a fishing camp not far from the mouth of the Karluk River, near the native village of Karluk, in the barely populated northwestern corner of Kodiak Island. Although these cabins were made of plywood, and contained only the simplest furnishing—a couple worn chairs, wooden beds with foam mattresses, two-burner gas stoves—they rented for $250 a night each, because in October the silver salmon and steelhead were still running, and the Karluk River was held by many to be one of the six greatest places to fish in the entire world. Every year in June when the King runs began, the proprietor told Truong, a dozen French businessmen flew in to stay for an entire month in these cabins. The total bill for room, board and transport came to something over fifty grand.

But for Truong and the other agents, this was the most strategic spot short of being on the peninsula itself, and the mandate from the top of the D of J was to stay invisible, to not put any pressure on the Family, or even let them know they were being watched. So they had three specialist surveillance men in the woods around the new camp, watching, filming and recording. One, Al Tonnecliffe, a former Navy Seal, now FBI special agent out of Anchorage, had established contact with Red Feather.

From here, the supervising agents had a direct view of the Aleutian Mountains across the Shelikof. It was a straight line from here across the strait to Sanctuary. They couldn't see anything, of course, since it was over twenty miles, but the radio and cellular fax transmissions from the observing agents were crystal clear. Besides, this was the closest they could get and still remain in some semblance of civilization.

Rick understood why they were here, but he didn't like Kodiak compared with the rest of Alaska. There were no evergreens, and as a consequence, when the summer ended, the island turned the burned-out brown of dead grass and leaves. And in this remote corner of the island, which he had never seen, where even the mountains were far away in the distance, they were surrounded by nothing but vast expanses of the matted vegetation-over-water called muskeg. It formed because the permafrost in the ground didn't allow water to drain. So the water stayed, for years, and the grass and bushes just grew up through and over it, eventually forming a layer so thick it supported weight. Usually. The thing was, you had to wear high boots to walk because you'd be going along fine and then all of a sudden your foot would break through the crust of vegetation and down into the icy, stagnant water that lay beneath it, soaking you up to your knee or even higher.

The river looked strange with no trees along it, nothing to distinguish its banks from the surrounding openness. Just a blue-brown scar sunk into the face of miles of rolling, unadulterated tundra. Hard to believe that this was one of the world's great sports destinations.

He was tired of it, he thought again. The whole outdoor thing. He was dying for hot pavement.

In the cabin of the pickup Truong briefed his visitor from Justice, none other than the AG's own special troubleshooter.

"You trust him?" the troubleshooter asked, about Rick.

"Not at all," Truong said. "I treat every word he says as a pure lie. He lied from the beginning, back in Spokane. When we debriefed Red Feather in Juneau, she was convinced it was him, not Joe Curtis, who did the shooting in Coeur d'Alene."

"You think that's true?"

"Don't know, for sure," said Truong. "No way to know yet. Maybe we don't want to know yet. He was involved, we know that. But so were the other two."

"But will this guy do what we need?"

"He's out to save his own ass, nothing more. If he thinks helping us will cut him slack, he'll do it."

"I don't know," the troubleshooter said. "These fanatics, man, you can't read what's in their heads."

"What you can't read," said Truong, "is what will happen when he's back in the presence of Amon. But right now, I believe Rick

Agullana is over Amonism. Will that change if he goes back in?" Truong shrugged and left it at that.

That evening, after an outdoor dinner of salmon steaks, octopus vinegar salad and Dungeness crab legs cooked by a Koniag woman the camp owner had hired, the men—in addition to Rick and Truong and the AG's troubleshooter, there were senior agents from both the FBI's and ATF's special response division (it was this FBI senior agent who would be the commander, the agent-in-charge, of an actual operation, if it came to moving on the Amonite's camp), and an investigator from Army CID—passed a bottle of plum brandy. They sat around a pit fire.

They also passed around a copy of yesterday's *Washington Post,* which the special troubleshooter had brought, and which had a front-page story breaking the news that Army antiaircraft missiles had been stolen from a base in Washington, and that some of these missiles had fallen into the hands of a radical religious cult which might be planning on using them against civilians in terrorist acts. A sidebar said that already airline cancellations were up dramatically. The agents had been discussing this over dinner, trying to figure where the leak had come from, and what it did to their plans.

"Has anyone talked to you about what we're thinking?" the troubleshooter asked Rick.

"Just about identifying the weapons or the boat," Rick said. His stomach hurt from the food; he was only a week out of the hospital and nowhere near fully recovered yet from the bullets he'd taken a month ago, and he had to be very careful about what he ate. Octopus vinegar salad was not at the top of the list.

"There's been a little change," said Mark Truong. "You know we have surveillance in place, but there's been no sign of the weapons or any boat. We're not doing fly-overs because we don't want to discourage them from coming in. What we want is to intercept the guns. And we want Amon, and Joe Curtis, who hasn't been spotted, either. So what we need is intelligence: where are these people? Are they expected? If so, when?"

Rick shrugged.

"You could be in a position to find out," Truong said.

"What? I don't know—"

"We think you can go back in," the troubleshooter said. "We can set you up a small transmitter in the woods somewhere."

"You're just going to turn me loose?"

"You won't run," Truong said. "But what matters is if you clue us in, if you help us avoid a gun battle and taking one of those missiles up our butts. If that happens, if they fire on us with one of those things, it'll go very badly for your deal."

"My deal? Wait a minute—"

"We're not so concerned with you running as we are with your turning back to the Family," the troubleshooter said. "Working to protect them. Feeding us crap. Let me tell you, even if that's what you feel like doing, even if Father crawls back inside your head, remember that the best protection you can give those people and yourself is to keep us straight on what's happening. Then no one gets hurt. That's my job here, believe it or not—to protect lives. No massacres and no mass suicides."

"My deal's already cut—"

"The deal's that you cooperate fully," the troubleshooter said. "If our men get fired on, then you haven't held up. And you'll pay for it. I can tell you that not as a law officer but as a lawyer for the Justice Department. If I throw the book at you, it'll be like nothing that's ever hit you before."

"What if I can't find out? I mean, they have to know I'll be wired. I can't just walk in there. They know I'm in custody."

Truong said, "We'll work out a story. And you're a pro, Rick. You'll find a way."

The troubleshooter took a hit of the brandy and stirred a stick around in the fire. "Smells good out here, you know," he said. "I'm no outdoorsman, but this is special. And that crab, I'll tell you, I've had two hundred dollar dinners in D.C. that couldn't hold a candle to that Dungie. Jesus, this is all right."

"For a visit," Truong said. "Wouldn't want to live here."

The troubleshooter said, "I was at Land's End, once, the spot the pilgrims left from, the farthest western point of England. All you can see is burned-brown hills and miles of open ocean leading all the way to the new world. It's kind of the same feel here. Only there's nothing left out there, no more new world. Just the beginning of the old one. You know what this is, what we're looking at?"

He waited. No one answered.

"It's the end, gentlemen. The true end of the world."

The next day they received faxed photographs and a brief report from Tonnecliffe. Truong read it and passed it directly to the troubleshooter, who picked up a mobile satellite phone when he was finished and called D.C. When he hung up he said, "We've got to get Rick in within a day or two. We've got nothing now but our dicks in our hands."

Then the ATF senior agent looked over the material and re-sent it to an office in D.C., the field division in Seattle and the resident agency in Boise, Idaho, where it was passed to Ed Simmons, RAC. Simmons in turn called in one of his agents, Ben Regis, and showed him the material.

The photos were of Leanne Red Feather and Father Amon. In one, they embraced alongside a river. In another, the two of them walked, alone, arm-in-arm, in the woods. In a third, shot somehow through a window of the cabin where Amon lived, Red Feather could be made out lying on what appeared to Amon's bed.

"It's her setup," Ben said, hopefully, looking up at Simmons. Simmons shook his head.

"She's cut off contact. She told the agents to leave."

"Maybe the Family was on to her. She was followed, and knew it. She had to cover herself."

"They think she's sleeping with him, Ben. She fell, that's all. She started to listen to what he was saying. You know it's hardly the first time. This is powerful shit. They may even be dosing her. We don't know."

"But Leanne?"

"She knows it better than most. That still doesn't mean she could withstand it."

Simmons didn't have to remind Ben of the agent at Waco who was pulled out of Koresh's compound just before the initial ATF assault, an agent of some years experience who'd gone in a couple months earlier undercover and ended up having to be deprogrammed and then counseled for six months afterward. His collapse led in part to the disaster.

"She's out of the loop. Even if she makes contact again, we can't rely on anything she gives us. It'll be disinformation at best. FBI's sending Agullana back in today. They think he'll at least act in his own self-interest, which means playing ball. If he hears something, he'll send word. If Curtis tries to come in alone, they'll grab him or take him out. If the boat is located before it gets to the camp, a strike force is waiting. They'll board, then maybe just smoke it, and let it sink."

"And if the weapons get into camp somehow?"

Simmons shrugged and made a face. "Who knows?"

"What about Leanne?"

"Assuming she survives, she's going to need help."

Ben looked at Simmons and raised his eyebrows to ask the question. Simmons nodded. "They're still putting together the special-response team. I got you on it, so take all your gear. It's under FBI control, but they know who you are, insofar as Leanne's concerned. I think they'll want to use you if and when they get to her. Maybe use you *to* get to her. I don't know. But for Christ's sake be careful, will you?"

Ben nodded.

"You fly up today. Get the hell home and get packed. Pick up's at three."

Ben ran.

36

EARLY THE FOLLOWING MORNING, SATELLITE PHOTOS OF THE COASTLINE extending in either direction from Sanctuary (sent courtesy of the National Security Agency to Colonel Rozsa) revealed that a tender ship which had left the city of Kodiak and been proceeding southwest down the center of the Shelikof Strait, headed, apparently, for the Aleutians, had now closed to within a mile of the coast of the Alaska Peninsula, twelve miles east of Sanctuary. Within an hour, watchers on the peninsula had picked up the ship and relayed high magnification photos and video across to the command post on Kodiak. No other working boats had been spotted in the area, and this tender did not behave as if it were transporting—rather it was skirting the coastline, stopping, then creeping forward. Looking for something, in other words.

When, by midafternoon, it had moved to less than a half mile offshore, and only three miles east of the camp, a boarding force of agents, which had been assembled at the Coast Guard base in Kodiak, was launched in two choppers. In addition, Coast Guard patrol boats closed in from out in the strait, timed to arrive simultaneously with the choppers.

Tonnecliffe and the two others had moved out from the woods around the camp that afternoon and down the coast to watch the ship before and during the assault, in case the people on board managed to launch a landing craft before the vessel was secured.

Thirteen miles of virgin terrain, mountainous and ranging from so densely overgrown as to be impassable to exposed moonlike rock formations, could have taken days to cross. But, though they'd been on the tender ship for a long time now, they were still in shape, mentally and physically, from their month in the Kenai bush, so when Joe pushed them hard, Kari and Cal responded.

They'd landed hours earlier, before four A.M., from more than a mile offshore, in a single rubber dinghy powered by a nearly silent electric motor. They were soaked from the sea, which, although it was relatively calm, had nearly capsized them any number of times. They'd changed into dry clothes, deflated the raft, and buried it, along with the motor, their wet clothing and 200 ounces of gold, all that was left from the original 370. By first light they'd already covered three moonlit miles along the shoreline.

In the end, it took them until four in the afternoon to make it to the ridge beyond which, according to the map the ship's captain had given them, lay the new Sanctuary.

Father was teaching. The fifty odd Family members who remained, who had made the pilgrimage, had gathered in the center of the clearing when he'd called them together. They did not know why, or what was wrong, but they each sensed something.

"We are about to face our final, greatest trial," Father concluded, eyes closed, arms held open and skyward. "Soon, whatever happens, we shall have to fight no longer. Soon we can rest here in the final Sanctuary. Our odyssey is at its end, my faithful. My friends. You few have had the courage and the stamina to make it this far. Now, you shall be rewarded."

Fifty faces watched him a little longer, until it was clear he had finished. Then they turned away, and went back to the pre-supper chores that needed to be done, rewards notwithstanding.

Most of the them did not see, right away, the man and woman who appeared at the edge of the ravine leading up from the ocean. One girl noticed them, though, and said, "Mama." She ran across the clearing to the woman, who was kneeling now, and opening her arms for the girl.

Five men and women with rifles were the official greeting, once Father came back into his head from his trance and saw what was what and who was who. He ordered the intruders taken to the plywood jail.

But Kari, who held Eloise in her arms, said, "We're not alone, Father. And we've hidden the gold. If you want it, let us go. It's a simple trade. Your gold for my daughter."

"She's my daughter, too," Father said as he approached her. He'd stayed back until now.

"I know," Kari said. "But that's the deal. I want to leave with her. In trade, I'll give you the money."

"You think I'd trade money for one of my children? You've come to see me as some kind of monster?"

"No," she said, and faltered, and dropped her head. "No, Father. I'm sorry. I don't mean it that way. I'm not saying you should sell her. I'm saying I want her with me, and I want to leave. She's my only child. You have so many."

"And all equally precious to me."

"I know. I *know*. But it's time now for us to go. Please, don't fight me. I did everything you asked, including this impossible task. I went down there, Father, with Rick. I let him do what he wanted to me, as you instructed. I carried the gold, and I did the things he said. Could I help it if it didn't go as planned? But I still did it. I got all the way back here with what's left of the money. I brought it home."

"But in the doing, you've lost the spirit," he said. "I can tell by your eyes."

Kari looked from Father to Joe, and back again. Then she nodded.

"Was it him?" Father pointed at Joe.

"Yes," Kari said. "He's very strong. He has his own spirit."

Father set his jaw and said, "Well, it doesn't matter anyway. Gold is worth nothing where we may all be going. The battle has found us, Kari, and we can only fight it. All the gold in the world won't help us now."

"What do you mean?"

As if in answer, a voice called out from the shadows of the forest, "Hey! Back off, people! I got you *all* covered. Lay down the guns."

The people with rifles swung around toward this voice, and a shot sounded immediately. They heard it whistle over their heads. At a sign from Father, these people set their rifles on the ground.

Calvin stepped out into the clearing with the butt of the 7-mm. Mag pressed against his shoulder. The Family watched him. "I want you to let Kari have the girl," Cal said. "So we can get out of here and leave you people be."

And it may have just happened that way if one man, who was standing a little away from the main group of the Family, hadn't knelt, pulled his .357 from the holster on his belt, and begun firing wildly at Calvin, shots which Cal heard tearing into the brush around him.

So Cal swung the rifle until he saw a flash of the man's green shirt in the scope's field of vision, and fired again, sending a bullet tearing through the man's upper arm.

The man screamed once, then fell.

Calvin said, "I definitely am not fooling around here." Then he said, "Hey, Joe."

Joe did not call out, for fear of startling the dark-haired woman who had circled out into the trees and crept back in behind Calvin. Cal only reacted when the woman drove a hard muzzle into his back, and said, "I'm sorry, Cal. But you'll have to put it down."

Joe thought it was odd, then, that this woman looked familiar. And he could see, even at a distance, from the look on Calvin's face that Calvin could not believe what he was hearing, that he thought it must be a hallucination brought on by stress and travel and bad food and weeks of living in isolation, weeks of nightmares re-witnessing a helicopter going down into the Gastineau Channel with his sister aboard because he'd led her there to her death.

Calvin smiled. "You people are good," he said.

"Down, now," the woman said.

"Real good. You got the voice right. That bitchy, pain-in-the-ass way of ordering people around." He smiled and shook his head. "You folks really got these mind games down."

He laughed out loud until the woman brought her gun butt down onto his head, brought it down lovingly, so as not to damage him too much, just enough to stun him, to disarm him and so save his life because he had no idea what these people could do with guns, how unhesitatingly they'd cut him down when they had a moment's opportunity.

Joe could only watch. When Calvin was down, Joe turned to Father, held out his hands, side by side, and said, "My name is Joseph."

Once he had Joe and Kari ensconced in the plywood jail, and Calvin under Leanne's care, Father's first act was to warm up the shortwave transmitter in his cabin and contact a certain operator in the city of Kodiak. The operator in turn left his house to find the men on a boat called *Wayfarer* which had docked a few days earlier. The message from Father was "Eagle. Three of Spades," which meant: Fly at three in the morning.

Father knew that he was being watched around the clock. He knew that if the feds didn't know it now, they'd know soon enough that Joseph Curtis, one of their most wanted, had arrived in Sanctuary. And that stepped up the likelihood of an assault one more notch. Father could only pray that the assault would wait until morning. By then, he'd have something special with which to greet the invaders.

The last surprise of this surprising but inevitable day occurred late that evening, as dusk fell, when Rick Agullana appeared at the camp's edge, looking emaciated from his ordeal, but clean and fit nonetheless. Too clean and fit. Too contrite. Too easily arrived.

Someone knocked on his cabin door and told Father the news. Father got something from one of the chests he'd brought. Saying not a word, he crossed the clearing to where Rick waited.

"Hey, Father," Rick said. "Long time, no see. You wouldn't believe, they boarded this ship and took me with 'em to ID the stuff, you know, and I grabbed this boat and rode it in, and—"

Father pulled his fist from his pocket. Rick flinched, but Father held nothing but quarter ounce gold coins, which he flung, and which struck Rick's chest and scattered on the ground.

"Thirty pieces," Father said. "It ought to be silver, but I'm afraid gold is all I have on hand."

News from the tender ship, which yielded nothing but some food supplies the captain said he was dropping off at Sanctuary on his way out to Dutch Harbor, reached Justice at 10:30 P.M. eastern time. The following afternoon they learned that Rick Agullana, whom Amon had banished into the woods rather than imprisoning, had made initial contact with Tonnecliffe and informed him that Joseph Curtis was already in the camp, but had only been there a day, and was being held in Father's jail.

"I've spoken with the Secretaries," the Attorney General said, meaning those of the Treasury and Defense. In her office sat the Deputy AG, and the Director and Assistant Director of the FBI. "Our position still holds. Curtis is strictly our interest. The military has no reason to care what happens to him."

"I don't think Curtis is the issue," the Director said, picking up the *Post* and tossing it out into the center of the table. They'd all long since read it, of course. "They're saying now the missiles may not go into the camp at all. That Amon could contact someone outside and have them deploy one elsewhere."

"Who comes up with this garbage?" said the Deputy AG.

The Assistant Director said, "The Domestic Intelligence and Threat Analysis Center. DITAC. That's what we hear, anyway. The head's a colonel named Johnson Rozsa, some kind of whiz. He's monitoring this, through CID. Advising the brass. He's pressing for an assault on the camp, to take out Amon. These are his scenarios." The Assistant Director pointed at the *Post.*

"One of those doomsday assholes with nothing to do since the wall fell," the Deputy AG said.

The AG smiled. She said, "This is U.S. soil and if they so much as wonder about acting autonomously, I'll have the President on them so fast they'll be dizzy. We can't let this new media pressure change our take. We still wait. We're conservative. We avoid a standoff at all costs, short of endangering other civilians. And we get our hands on those weapons. After that, we'll worry about Father Amon and Joseph Curtis and who shot down the chopper."

"Whatever happens," the Director said, "at least there're no goddamn TV cameras out there." Then he added, "Excuse the language, ma'am."

After the meeting, on the short walk back to their offices, the FBI Director and Assistant Director shared a few words.

"She's got the solution," the Assistant Director said. "If the army wants to take him out, I say let them. No sweat off our ass that way, and the deed is done. I've got half a dozen guys up there myself who've volunteered to go in and do it."

The Director nodded. "That place is a long way from anywhere. I meant what I said about TV cameras. It leaves open all sorts of possibilities."

The debate had now moved to the office of the Chief of Staff of the Army, General Gene Hargrave. His suite had a carefully appointed sitting area separate from the desk, over next to a wide window. General Parkins sat in a chair by the window. Colonel Rozsa was on a red-leather couch, at the other end of which sat Hargrave, above whom the idea for the press leak had not gone. That particular buck had stopped here.

"Well it's had an effect," Hargrave said, grinning a little. "The SECDEF shit his pants." The general was referring, of course, to the Secretary of Defense. "We've been on the horn together six times since last night. But his biggest concern is still where the leak came from, how this could have happened." The general laughed a little now. "Asshole. He and the White House have been deluged by reporters."

"But will it really work?" Rozsa said.

"Oh, it's working. Whether or not there's a demonstrable threat of terrorist activity is now irrelevant, Colonel. We've got a crisis of the media kind on our hands—the worst kind to have. And as we all know, it changes people. The SECDEF would do just about anything to end it, now."

Rozsa smiled.

"But it hasn't moved the AG. She's bent on maintaining observation, but no action. I spoke to her myself. I suggested again that with outstanding warrants, there's no other issue she needs to consider. She said there are plenty of other issues to consider, the least important of which is those warrants." Hargrave shrugged. "CID's up there. They're keeping us plugged in. If it does come to an assault, we'll contribute to the effort. The feds have as much as asked us for help. You're talking jungle warfare out there. No support system at all. You're going to be dropping guys in with nothing but what they can carry. I said we'd be glad to contribute."

"Have you thought, as we discussed, of putting people in up there now?" Rozsa said, cutting straight to it. "Not CID. I mean an insertion team, say six men—"

Hargrave waved his hand. "We've considered it. I even mentioned it to the SECDEF. He had to pick himself up off the floor, but I can tell you he's thinking about it. The thing is, he can't approve it, we all know that. And of course the President can't, or wouldn't. If it happens, it has to be some unilateral, unapproved action. Absolutely clandestine. The kind of operation we haven't mounted in this country for a while. I mean, you're basically talking about sending in assassins."

Rozsa nodded with approval at the Chief's bluntness. But then this was not a man who got where he was by acting precious. Parkins sat with his hands folded, listening, a distant sort of look on his face.

"The missiles wouldn't have to be brought out," Rozsa said. "They're non-reusable. All we have to do is fire them into the ocean."

General Hargrave nodded, staring all the while at his imported Persian carpeting.

"And in that isolation, sir," Rozsa said. "Who'd ever know? Who'd see it? FBI has some men in, but we can track them through CID. We can be in and out before it matters. And then they can surmise and guess all they want. But no one need ever know."

"Truth be told, Colonel," said General Parkins, speaking up for the first time, "I'd bet the FBI would help us."

Hargrave looked from Rozsa to Parkins, and back. "Well, gentlemen, we're not to that point yet. But it won't hurt to have a blueprint, will it?"

"I think it would be prudent, sir," Rozsa said.

"Then why don't we base it out of Fort Lewis? First Special Forces is there. We can shoot a few men right up the coast. And there's a certain symmetry to using Lewis, since that's where it started, no?"

Rozsa and Parkins both nodded.

"I'll call General Shaw out there myself," Hargrave said. "This is absolutely classified. No one outside this room gets briefed unless and until I give an explicit OK. And make sure you understand this is all contingency right now, nothing more."

"Yessir," Rozsa said. Parkins was mute.

"We've got detailed satellite photos of the area. This office will hand pick a strategist to lay out the assault. I want you, Colonel, to act as my personal liaison. No couriers on this, and no written orders. Strictly word of mouth." Hargrave stood up. "That's all for now. Good day, gentlemen."

Rozsa and Parkins saluted.

37

INSIDE FATHER'S LITTLE CABIN, IT WAS WARM AND WOODEN, AND SMELLED human and wild all at once. The cabin was a single room, with a lower-ceilinged sleeping alcove built off the back. Father gave Leanne a drink of something warm and slightly alcoholic she'd never tasted, and some bread and meat. She was hungry. Father sat at the rough wooden table with her and watched as she ate.

It was late, nearly midnight, and Leanne had walked over from her tent where, until a few minutes ago, she'd been with Calvin, at first tending the cut on his head, then explaining to him how she was alive and how she'd come to be here, and finally arguing with him again, when she'd started to talk about Father and the Family in a way he did not like, when he saw how she'd so obviously adapted to life here, and when he remembered that it was her who'd whacked him in the head.

Finally Cal had slept, so Leanne left him there. Father had shown no concern about Cal and no desire to avenge the man Cal had wounded; it was Joe and Kari, along with Kari's daughter, who were locked in the jail.

On her way to Father's cabin, Leanne was aware of people working. She'd heard bodies shuffling, the squeaks and scrapes of tools and materials, thumps from heavy things being lifted and set down. But she couldn't see much of it. They worked without lights. Even the moonlight at this time was largely blocked by the wall to the west.

Nearer to Father's cabin, the sounds of work were drowned out by the kerosene-powered generator, which had always been used sparingly, but which she realized now had been running incessantly since Cal and the others had arrived.

Father laid his hands on the table between them when she was finished.

"They won't come in here just to get him, you know," she said.

Father raised his eyebrows, pretending he didn't understand her meaning.

"Joseph Curtis," she said, not wanting to play. "They wouldn't take that kind of risk just for him."

"Why mention it?"

"You're obviously getting ready for something."

He shrugged.

"Something I don't know about?"

He shrugged again.

"Fine," she said.

"Let me tell you something, Leanne," Father said. "An admonition, of sorts. I was just thinking of it. I want you to hear me. I want you to remember what I say." He waited.

She nodded.

"You're just discovering who you really are. My admonition is this: don't ever underestimate the power of being needed." And that was it; that was all he said. They sat looking at each other for another moment, Leanne sort of half smiling at another of the vague quasi-profundities she'd come to expect from him.

"I won't say I know what that means, exactly."

"I told you to remember, not interpret."

A man opened the door of the cabin. Seeing Father and Leanne at the table, the man mumbled an apology and turned to leave.

"No," Father said. "Come on. We don't have time for proprieties." So the man came inside and went to a corner of the cabin, to a stack of three shallow wooden boxes next to the radio, and lifted one.

"We're out," the man said. Father nodded and stood up. "You'll excuse me?" he said to Leanne, and followed the man outside.

She sat for a little while and waited, and when Father did not return, stood up herself and went to look at the remaining two crates, which it seemed to her had been here before, but covered with something maybe. Also, she thought the stack had been much higher—maybe five or six crates instead of these two.

So she looked inside one—the wooden top simply slid out of its grooves. Inside were rows of flat, hard plastic bars, olive drab and slightly curved so as to be concave on one side, convex on the other. The concave side, she noticed then, was made of a softer plastic. She lifted one, which was heavy, and saw the metal tabs at one end where wires or clips were meant to fasten. She knew what these were. In the crates, too, were small, hand-held plungers and connecting wires.

She'd seen before, hung on nails on the wall of the cabin outside which the generator hummed, the same wall where the boxes were stacked, four simple brass electrical switches, numbered consecutively and attached to wires which led up and out through a chink between the logs of the wall. She'd noticed them, but hadn't thought about their purpose since the generator rarely ran.

Now, though, she found a flashlight by the table and went outside. Around the side of the cabin, by the generator, she saw that the wires connected into a crude electrical box, which in turn was connected to the generator, and also had running from it a number of variously colored, insulated wires, including an inch-thick bundle which snaked around to the front of the cabin.

Leanne was surprised at so much wire. She couldn't imagine, at first, what it could be for. She followed the bundle around front, where it was anchored at the base of the cabin, then fanned in all directions out into the camp. Leanne saw that many of the strands, which seemed to run in pairs, had been buried so as to be undetectable more than a few feet away from the cabin.

She still saw no sign of Father, so she pulled a pair of wires from the dirt and followed them out into the camp, until she came to their end, in front of one of the tents. Under tufts of brown bear grass which had been piled as camouflage, the wires connected to two of the curved plastic bars she'd seen in the cabin, which stood up now on short wooden legs, and were fastened back to back, with their concave sides pointing in opposite directions, one toward the tents, one out into the center of the camp. In what little ambient light there was, she saw another pile of grass tufts farther up, and out in the center of the clearing, yet another.

Just then, with the physical sensation of waking from a long and marvelous dream, she understood everything.

Joe knew events were spinning more and more quickly out there in the night, heading toward the brink of chaos. But here inside this dark shack they called a jail, Kari and her daughter sleeping together on the cot, he felt, beyond his own usual facade of calm and rationality, a peacefulness enveloping them, a kind of stasis.

Sometime after midnight, he listened as someone undid the padlock on the door and opened it. He could see little in the dark. Then someone said, "Hey, pardner."

"Cal?"

"And Leanne," said Cal. "Come to break you out. She knew where Hitler kept the key."

"Shh," Leanne said. "Both of you, sit down."

"Leanne's in a panic, all of a sudden," Cal said. "It finally hit her this is a nut-case she's been with all this time."

"Shut up, Cal," Leanne said.

Joe squatted and balanced himself with one hand on the wooden floor between his legs. "Lots to talk about," he said, then.

"Yes," Leanne said, kneeling next to him. "I found—"

"Wait a minute," Calvin said. "Joe Curtis, Leanne Red Feather. I don't think you two've actually been introduced."

They sat cross-legged on the floor while Kari and Eloise slept.

"Something's going to happen soon," Leanne said. "He knows what it is. He's getting ready right now, this night. But that's not the problem. He's got Claymore mines. Boxes of them, maybe fifty or sixty altogether." She described what she'd seen, how the wires ran, and where.

"He hard wired them to the generator," Joe said. "Maybe all on one switch."

"Four," Leanne said.

"What's that mean?" Cal asked.

"Usually they're fired with a hand-detonator," Leanne said. "Maybe you can set off two or three at once. But wired in like this, assuming they got the voltages and amperages right, they could set them all off at once."

"Take out a lot of people," said Joe.

Leanne said, "In case there's an invasion. Federal agents come in looking for big hardware, machine guns and missiles, and instead Father's planning on ambushing them all with some old Claymores. Like a big joke. Only what will happen when he kills a team of agents? And what will happen to any of the people who're in the tents?"

"That's what I don't get," Joe said. "Is this some suicide thing?"

"He'll have some of the people out in the bush," Leanne said. "But some, including the children, will be in here. And either way, whether they die from the mines or in the aftermath of retribution, they'll still be dead." She dropped her head. "Goddamn him; he could have negotiated his way out again. He could have turned a few men over. Even if he went down, he could protect . . . us." Her voice trailed off.

"Listen," Joe said, and he started to talk. He described for Calvin a Claymore mine, which is nothing more than a heap of steel ball bearings embedded in C-40 and sealed in a plastic shell which, when detonated, shreds any flesh within about a sixty or seventy foot arc. He asked Leanne to describe everything she remembered about the things

Father had brought out here, gear, weapons, clothing, anything she'd seen in the cabin or elsewhere.

Then a roaring rose and rent the night's fabric. Kari awoke, and the four of them rushed outside, as did all the Family members, to watch as a series of floodlights along the ground, in the center of the camp, exploded into life.

When nothing of interest was discovered on the tender ship, Agent Tonnecliffe slept in preparation for his solo night watch.

He liked doing the night here in the bush, where, because of the lack of any artificial light pollution, even a match could be visible for hundreds of yards. He liked the sounds of the night wilderness, the prey birds who sounded occasionally, the cracking of underbrush when something large and nocturnal moved past, aware of his presence, no doubt. He liked it, too, because he could move in much closer to the camp, to within a couple hundred yards, as long as he was careful to avoid the night patrols Father sent out.

These past days the moonlight had been particularly bright, so that early in the night he could see some distance. He was positioned east of the camp, up on the ridge line, from which vantage, although these people worked without artificial light, he could tell the activity level had picked up. He heard it, first, then caught movements, at first over on the north side, by Father's cabin, then more toward the center of the camp. Still, even with the moonlight and later, after the moon had set and he broke out the infrared scope, he wasn't able to make out much of what they were doing.

By two-thirty, in any case, the night had grown velvety black and the movements in the camp had ceased. Tonnecliffe had settled in and allowed himself to doze a little. He awoke when he realized that noise and movement had picked up again in the camp, dramatically so this time. He heard the unmistakable clang of steel hitting steel, and set up the infrared scope on its pod again to watch.

They were building something flat, and they were in a hurry.

He watched for another minute before it struck him, almost at the same moment he heard the engine of a small plane approaching from out over the straight. Then he knew.

On his radio, he raised Kodiak command in time to say, "They just put together a portable runway. It's coming in now. Right now!" And the men on Kodiak, over the radio, in the background, could hear the noise of a small plane coming in low and fast and very close. Tonnecliffe saw lights over the trees, before he was blinded by the floodlights which were suddenly switched on alongside the portable runway.

The plane circled once and then dropped startlingly fast between the north and south tree lines toward a slick metal band no wider than a pickup truck and stuck down on top of the lumpy matted grass and dirt. Tonnecliffe watched as the plane set down on this ribbon and skidded to a stop. He had never understood how these guys could land on something like that, and at night? But he knew Alaska bush pilots who had done things nobody would believe.

By now the other two agents were on the ridge next to him.

"What the fuck?"

"I picked it up too late," Tonnecliffe said. "I blew it. By the time I realized it was a runway, they were here." He checked his watch. It was after three.

The agents watched as a man got out and received hugs from those around them, watched as Father greeted him with an embrace and a kiss on the forehead. Watched as other men in the Family began unloading heavy crates from the back of the plane.

"They did it," Tonnecliffe said into his radio. "Kodiak, I repeat, the arms are in Sanctuary. The weapons are in."

"Roger," was the only response that came over.

So they understood now why Father was so busy this night, what he was getting ready for. After Kari went back to bed with Eloise, Joe and Cal snuck with Leanne to her tent where she told them, "Agents could be here as early as morning. We may only have that long."

Joe described a kind of blueprint that had been forming in his head, a scenario to be played out if each of them could hold up. Then he said, "Something else. What about my case?"

"Rick's working for them," Leanne said. "I don't know what kind of deal he's made, but I'll do what I can do. I mean, when the time comes, when and if they get here, which I believe they will, I can tell them what I believe. I don't know if that carries much weight, anymore, but I can try."

"The problem is," Joe said, "maybe I'll get off, maybe not. But if I do, what about Kari?"

"I've thought about that," Leanne said.

"What?" says Cal.

"If Joe's exonerated, what does that mean?"

Joe had come to realize long ago what it would mean—that Kari was by definition guilty. In the end only one of them, at best, could go free. If Joe had been framed by Rick, then he'd been framed by Kari, too; there's no other way all that paraphernalia could have ended up in the room in Seattle.

"I want to write two things," Joe said. "One is a letter to my brother, giving him my car and all my stuff, which I'll ask you to mail when you can. The second, I'll need your help with, to make it right."

Later, when they were finished with the documents, Leanne said, "The most important thing: at the end, if it's up to you guys to do it, tell all the people, make sure they know, that the key is to not resist. If anyone resists, especially if anyone fires, it'll be very bad. Lie to them, tell them Father sent the message, do whatever you have to. Just, if it falls to you to do it, make sure they know that."

Cal snuck with Joe back to the jail shack. Before they got there, though, Joe stopped Cal and said, "Just between us."

"Yeah?"

"You look around out here. And then you think of going back in, getting locked up."

"Hey, I've been there," said Cal. "But I knew I was gettin' out soon. If I hadn't, I guess it would'a been worse than dying, if that's what you're asking. And going from this place to one of their stinking holes—I couldn't."

Joe nodded.

Cal said, "Know how I imagine death? White and silent. Like it'll be around here in about a month."

They looked at each other, running a thousand thoughts a second between them.

"Hey, brother," Cal said, grabbing Joe's arm and squeezing it hard. "It was one mother of a run, wasn't it? And I'm here for the duration. We'll play it however you want."

"I've got an idea how to work it."

"I thought maybe you did," said Cal.

38

IN LATE OCTOBER IN SOUTHERN ALASKA, THE DAYS ARE STILL NOT TERRIBLY different in their hours from those other parts of the country experience. They're beginning to shorten some, so that daylight doesn't come until after eight o'clock, but nothing like the four-hour, 11 A.M.-3 P.M. days December will bring. In any case, when Leanne found Father in his cabin, with Omaha, at seven, it was still night-dark outside. The inside was lighted by a kerosene lantern hanging from the ceiling.

Father introduced Omaha as his second-in-command, now that Deacon was gone.

Leanne nodded, then said to Father, "What can I do to help?" She hadn't seen him since he left her in the middle of the night.

He was sitting at the same table. He watched her for a few moments, judging, deciding, then said, "What do you want to do? You want to shoot ATF agents?"

"Is that what you need?"

"Would you do it?"

"Would you ask me to?"

Omaha laughed. He did not know this woman, and was surprised to hear her talking to Father like this, and more surprised to hear Father responding.

"I could negotiate—"

"We're not negotiating," Father said.

"Where do you have people?"

"Around," Father said. "All over. Two up on the cliff, one with a big gun, one with an automatic rifle. Behind us, on the hills, they're spaced every fifty yards with rifles. Up on the ridge, the same. And along the south perimeter. We also have people out farther, with hand radios. So we know."

"There's a place I know of, from when I got here, I think you should see. I've never told you about it."

"Why now?"

She raised her eyebrows. "Well we're down to it, aren't we? This is it."

"Yes," he said. "This is it. You think they'll be here today."

"Oh, I think they're probably here somewhere already, Father. I think when that plane touched down, they launched. They're just waiting for light."

He nodded.

"Which is why I want you to see what I know is there. A monitoring station. We should take it out now."

"Go with her," Amon said to Omaha.

"I want you to go. I want your opinion. I think you should see it."

Father looked at her and scratched his whiskery chin.

He knew, she thought. He had to know what she was up to. He was too smart not to.

"How far?" Father said.

"Not far. You'll be surprised. It's right here behind the cabin, not much more than three hundred feet in."

"What?"

She nodded.

"And you didn't think before this I should know?"

"I was trying to maintain a certain facade. Besides, they stopped using it for a time. They've started again. I was out there yesterday. I checked."

Father watched her. His face was blank; even the blue eyes seemed muted, less sharp than usual. She felt uncomfortable, his judging her, making up his mind about something, deciding about her, maybe about what to do with her. He saw through her, she knew. She was transparent to him, and everything she'd said to Joe and Rick was written on her skin for him to read.

But he said, "Hurry up, then. Omaha, stay inside here. Don't let anyone in. Don't answer any questions."

Father put on his hide coat and walked out into the night, leaving Leanne to follow, pretending that he'd been shocked by her story, that he hadn't known about the tree and the observers all along.

Joe waited a while in the jail shack with Kari and Eloise.

"What's going to happen?" Kari said.

Joe shook his head. "You two just stay in here."

She put her arms around his neck and pressed her face against him.

"Mama?" came a small voice from under the blankets. "Don' go."

"I'm not, baby."

"Never, never go."

"No, honey, I won't."

They waited. The girl grew quiet again. Not long after that Cal slipped in again.

"She got him out," Cal said. "We best hurry."

Joe stood. Kari held his hand for a moment, then let him go.

In a command room at the Army's Fort Richardson Reservation, on the Glenn Highway just north of Anchorage, Johnson Rozsa sat alone with a Major named Garfield. Garfield, who was based at Fort Lewis in Washington, was a Special Forces commander, a veteran of Nam and Grenada and the Gulf. He'd been around and he'd fought. He hadn't been one of these rump riders, even after he'd moved up the chain of command. Always wanted to be on the ground, moving, he said. Mixing it up. Garfield had personally killed sixty-four men. That wasn't counting what the people under his orders had done.

Rozsa had just got off the phone with Lieutenant Bliss in the Pentagon who, although he didn't know where the Colonel was, exactly, still served as Rozsa's direct link with CID. After talking to Bliss, Rozsa called Hargrave on a highly secure line and exchanged a few coded lines of dialogue. When he hung up, he said to Garfield, "They got the missiles into that camp out there. Imagine that? With all those federal officers watching."

Garfield laughed.

"Get to Egegik now, and into position. There's still a chance Justice will decide to move, in which case we'll make our presence known to them and coordinate with their efforts. If they decide to sit much longer—well, let's say that one way or another, the sun won't set again on Stingers in that camp."

Garfield saluted and left.

The town of Egegik was on the Bering Sea side of the Alaska Peninsula, roughly across from the Amonites' camp. The pilot ferrying Garfield's squad would use that as the coordinating point from which to travel across toward the Amonites' camp, where, at the first sign of light, a mile north of the camp, the men would parachute into the bush, rendezvous, and make their way in by foot, which they felt they could do with little risk of detection since the federal forces were still largely located on the tender ship they'd taken yesterday, or across the strait on Kodiak.

Rozsa would monitor from the little room on the army base, which, aside from himself and Garfield, only the reservation commander, General Shaw down at Fort Lewis, and Generals Parkins and Hargrave in the Pentagon, knew was being used at all.

Father carried the flashlight. He followed Leanne to the old dead tree, the spot where she first saw Tonnecliffe. At the tree, she stopped, placed a hand against its barkless surface and said, "Explain something to me, first. Why come all the way out here, through all the expense and hardship, losing half your family, just to commit suicide."

"Is that what this is about?" Amon said. "A lecture? I'm too busy, Leanne. I'm leaving."

"Wait," Leanne said. She had her hand inside a hole in the tree. Father shined his light into her eyes, blinding her. "Talk to me," she said.

"About suicide? None of us wants to die."

"Then you're a fool, one thing I never took you for. Because if those agents come and you do what I think you're planning on doing—you know as well as I do what will happen."

"We came here to find a home, Leanne. Not to die, although not one of us is afraid to. I had hoped wildly that the forces behind you would have left us alone here."

"I've tried to make them," she said. "Why did you have to bring in the big guns. You guaranteed their coming here now."

"They were coming anyway. One way or another."

"You're wrong."

"Then you've lost your worldly edge, my dear. Your savvy. Because they've been coming."

"They only want the goddamn weapons, and Joe Curtis."

"They want me, Leanne. They want you. They want Omaha. And poor Rick and Kari. And then, when they've got us, they'll decide they want the rest of the Family. They'll kill us or lock us away and that will be that. Another little mess cleaned up. You really think if I just call them and hand over the guns and your friend Joe they'll all go away? You really have gone soft."

"I'm telling you they will."

"They won't. But they won't take us, either. Not one of us. We'll be set free, one way or the other."

"Father—"

"And what's better, when they come for us, they'll be set free, too."

"Amon—"

"You can go if you like, Leanne." He was still holding the light in her eyes, so she couldn't see him. "Just walk out to the ocean. They'll see you on the beach; they're watching. They'll take you back, put you in a treatment program somewhere, whitewash your brain again. In a year or so, you'll be good as new."

"I won't let you kill all these people."

"But it's you who are killing them. You and your friends. You've been trying to kill them for years."

She pulled her hand from the hole in the tree, revealing not a gun, which he'd expected, but a Ziploc bag containing a small device with a single button on it and a light which glowed red, especially so when Father's flashlight went out, leaving Leanne seeing brilliant swirling colors in the darkness.

Cal led Joe to Leanne's tent, where she'd stashed their rifle and from which they had a view of Father's cabin. Light shined from the single front window. While they watched, no one came and no one left. Men and women passed nearby, but the door didn't open. When the way seemed clear, when no one was passing or working near the cabin, Cal nodded to Joe. They ducked and ran.

At the door, Joe pounded. Inside someone said, "What?"

"Hurry up," Joe said.

"What? Can't open it."

"Father," Joe said. "He's in trouble."

He heard a bar lift and watched the door open a crack, then drove his weight hard against it. He lost his balance and tumbled inside, and found himself on top of another man, a black man who was beating him on the head and the back. Joe closed his eyes and just hung on until Cal stuck the muzzle of his rifle against the black man's head and said, "Calm down."

The man did.

Cal had shut and barred the door, leaving the three of them alone. "What's your name?" Cal said.

"Omaha."

"Well, Omaha. We're gonna do a little business here. I strongly urge you to help, because if you don't I'll kill you. Promise. I been dying to blow somebody's fucking head off around here. Are we together?"

"Oh, yeah," Omaha said. He still lay on his back on the floor. Joe had stood up and brushed himself off, and was already at the switches on the wall, looking them over. "Don't fuck with that," Omaha said. "You don't know nothin' about that."

"He will soon enough," Cal said. "You must have guys out in the woods with the guns, right?"

Omaha shrugged.

"It's your head," Cal said. "I mean it. I'm just looking for an excuse."

"Yeah."

"With the M-60s?"

"Some."

"How many."

"Mm. Six 60s. Ten, twelve others, with 16s."

"Can you reach them?"

Omaha didn't answer but glanced at a desk, on which sat two different radio sets.

"Which?" Cal said.

"The top one," said Joe. "CB. Wouldn't use short-wave in this close. It's probably already set to the right channel. Listen, I have to go outside and look at this wiring." He found a flashlight and opened the door a crack, to make sure no one was waiting, then left.

"How about the missiles?" Cal said.

"They're here. Jus' outside, in crates."

"Three of them?"

"Yeah."

The generator stopped running, then. Omaha glanced up at the lantern hanging from the ceiling, but did not move. A moment later the generator started up again, and Joe came back in.

"OK," he said.

"You're sure?" Calvin asked.

Joe nodded. "It looks like they're still connected, but they're not."

"What?" Omaha said. "What'd you do?"

"Then that's it," Cal said. "Omaha, buddy. You have a very important part to play right now. You'll probably win some prize if you do it right. If you don't—" Cal lifted the rifle. "I want you to get on the radio and call in all your friends with the guns out there."

"What?"

"I want you to tell them to bring their weapons in. That Father said everyone is to wait in their tents until they hear different. Got it? And under no circumstance is anyone to fire any shots. Period."

Omaha laughed. "Makes you think they listen to me?"

"I think you'll convince them. Say Father's out doing something important, and this is what he said."

"But he told 'em to stay out."

"So make it convincing."

"Where is he, anyway?"

Cal shrugged. "But he won't be back, I can tell you that."

"Jesus." Omaha shook his head. "You feds or something?"

"Nope," said Cal. "I'm a parole violator from Idaho. And this man here is the famous Joe Curtis, hot off the FBI's most wanted list."

"No shit."

"How about you?" said Joe. "After you make your radio calls, why don't you tell us who you are, what you've done, who did it with you. That kind of biz."

"You serious?"

"Yes."

"Why you need to know that?"

"Information," said Cal. "Might have to trade it."

When Leanne's eyes began to adjust to the dark again, she could see Father, still standing a few yards away from her. She thought he would have left.

"Don't push it yet," he said.

"It's been pushed."

"How long?"

"Minutes," she said. "Why haven't you run?" But she knew why. She knew well that he'd known all along what she planned on doing out here, which was turning him over because she believed this would save the lives of the people who would otherwise die in a firefight. So why had he come? she asked herself. So easily, just like that, walked with her out into the dark woods where she could betray him. Maybe it was because he couldn't, in the end, watch his people die—even if he believed they'd die no matter what happened. Or maybe it was because he'd decided, after all, that Leanne was right.

"I prayed," he said to her then, in response to her unspoken thoughts. "After I saw you earlier."

"And what did you learn?" she said. He did not answer.

"Run now," she said. "While you still can. Go away. Hide—"

"I wouldn't," said a voice from somewhere out in the blackness. Leanne recognized it as Tonnecliffe. "We've got night scopes and automatics. So let me see hands."

"Do me," Father said.

"No!" Leanne shouted. "Don't!"

"What do you mean, 'don't,' " he said. "You've already done, my dear. You decided what needed to be done, and you executed it. As you have always done, and always will do. But I'm sorry for you, for what you'll go through. Myself, I'm going home."

She saw Father step back away from her, in the direction of the camp.

"Don't move another step," Tonnecliffe shouted.

Father said, "You should come with me, Leanne." She watched him pull something from inside his coat and point it at her.

"No!" she screamed. And then, believing she'd been shot, that Father had killed her as his last act, because she'd seen the muzzle flash from his gun, Leanne felt herself falling, her legs knocked from beneath her, the earth pulling her down until she met it hard with her face, sparkles and lights going off inside her head, her brain turning with the impact, the sound of the blast only now registering.

She heard a second shot then, after she had fallen, this one sounding from the woods, ten or fifteen yards away she judged. She sat up in time to see Father crumple.

She waited for the pain, but when none came, other than an ache in her jaw and cheek, she knew that she had not been hit after all. Someone had tackled her, pulling her from the bullet's path. And she knew, from the smell and the way this someone was holding her still, with his arms around her arms, keeping her down, so she could not crawl to Father, trying to cover her head as terrible white lights flashed on all around them, just who it was.

In the light, she saw Amon lying stone still, his head red with blood. She looked away. She looked behind her, at the face of the man who had tackled her, at Ben. With their eyes, for one moment, they met, and language passed between them, a thousand words of sorrow and regret and gratitude and love.

"I get all the way to Kodiak," Ben said. "Then they weren't going to let me come in after you. Like they could have stopped me."

"I would have died," said Leanne. She touched Ben's face. "But then, you knew that."

A hand clamped over Leanne's mouth. She couldn't breathe. She felt her arms pinned behind her, then handcuffed, and she was dragged swiftly, roughly away through the night. Still, even during the harsh handling, which she knew was just fed boys carrying out protocol, she felt Ben's presence, buoying her, watching out, making sure nothing too bad was going to happen from here on out.

39

OMAHA HAD JUST GOT ON THE CB AND CONTACTED THE FIRST SENTRY when the sound of gunfire reached them.

"What was that?" asked the woman on the other end of the radio, who happened to be manning an M-60 up on the cliff.

"That was Father. Don't worry about it," Cal whispered, and Omaha repeated it into the radio.

"What're we supposed to do?" the woman said.

"Come down. Get in the tents," said Omaha. "Stay real quiet. No movement. No sound. No firing. All right?"

"But—"

"Look, don't argue," Omaha said. "Jus' tell who's with you, and do it."

"Good," Cal said. "One of the lives you save may be your own."

Joe was rifling the three storage chests Father had brought along from the Kenai. He was looking for anything they might need, and was amazed at what he was finding.

On Kodiak, the agents were getting a transmission from Tonnecliffe that changed everything: "We have Red Feather; Amon is dead."

After the special troubleshooter called the AG directly with this news, the FBI Special Agent in Charge put it through to the special response team, still out in the Shelikof on board the tender ship, which they'd commandeered as a sort of floating launch site, just offshore and around a point in the coastline from Sanctuary.

The AG had ordered the men to stand by until further surveillance information was available: was the Family still preparing a defense; were the military weapons locatable; was there any indication of mass suicide?

Then a second transmission from Tonnecliffe came over: they'd just heard a plane come in fairly close and low. It sounded as if the plane had slowed significantly for a minute before picking up again and leaving. Were FBI or ATF pulling some maneuver without informing him? Could the Amonites have another craft trying to come in? Also, all the Family members who'd been out in the forest, waiting, with guns, seemed to be abandoning their posts and going back in.

"What the hell's this all about?" the special troubleshooter said to no one. He called Justice again, then said to the other commanding agents, "We'd better get out on that ship, now."

Minutes later the Coast Guard bore them across the choppy waters of the Shelikof Strait.

As the sky grew light, Cal and Joe gathered Kari and Eloise from the jail and locked Omaha inside. They could hear Family members, men and women, coming in from the woods, reporting back to their tents as they'd been ordered.

"What's happening?" Kari said.

"Shh," said Joe. "We've got to hide."

"What then?" she said to Joe. "Are you leaving? Are you going north?"

Joe shook his head.

"What? We still want to go with you."

He looked at her, then said, "C'mon."

Rozsa, who had been fed, via Army CID and Lieutenant Bliss, the gist of the Justice Department orders—to stand ready but not to move—made a unilateral decision, then. It was against his orders, since federal agents were standing offshore, ready if ordered to enter the camp, and since the operation could have been accomplished more or less legitimately and aboveboard, especially since Amon was dead, but Rozsa smelled a swifter and more satisfying end to it: with Amon gone, the culties would be confused. The Stingers would be there for the taking. All he had to do was take them. He informed Garfield, who was on the ground now not a half-mile north of the Amonites' camp, of recent developments, and ordered him to proceed unilaterally.

Calvin led Joe, Kari and Eloise to an indentation in the base of the face of the cliff, a shallow cavelike spot Leanne had told him of which was cut-off from view of the camp by large boulders.

Cal and Joe looked at each other for a moment. This would be the last time until it was finished, one way or the other. But as Cal turned to make his way back into the camp, someone stepped into the opening of the alcove and said, "What's going on, kids?"

Rick grinned at them. He looked bad; he'd been sleeping in the woods, with only a few blankets someone had given him. His hair was snarled, his skin greasy, his eyes dark and sunken. He needed a shave and he smelled. He grimaced at Joe and Kari. "Long time, no see. Payback time. And I got a lot coming."

"Hey," Cal said. "I been looking for you."

"Who're you?" Rick said.

"Got a message," Cal said, and dove into Rick, dragging him to the ground. They scrambled around, but it wasn't long before Cal had an arm around Rick's neck and was squeezing hard.

"Now listen. We've got about a minute left before we're into a major fuck-up zone. You want to mess with these people, you're screwing yourself. They're your ticket out."

"What?"

"You gonna come with me and listen? Leave them alone?" Cal squeezed a little harder.

"OK," Rick said. Cal let him up. He looked once again at Joe and Kari, then turned and left. Cal followed.

As they hurried back into camp, Cal said, "Joe confessed to everything. The shootings in Coeur d'Alene, helping to arrange for the arms being shipped up here, kidnapping Kari, stealing the gold. Everything, all on paper and with an agent of the ATF."

"Bullshit."

"Not bullshit, moron. That's how he's playing it. You got any brains, you'll let him."

"Why would he?"

"You wouldn't understand. Just believe me. And don't be stupid. Get in a tent and keep your damn mouth shut."

Later, as the sun cracked the ocean horizon to the southeast, the Special Agent in Charge, now on the tender ship, received a radio call from Tonnecliffe.

"Yeah, who the hell else you got in here?"

"No one's in yet," the SAC said.

"I told you all the Amonites came back in. We counted heads. But we've picked up new movement north of the camp, we're getting something else on one of the mikes. No visual yet, but it sounds like a group."

The troubleshooter put this through to Justice, then, as he strapped on a Kevlar vest, said, "Get us the hell in there."

40

FROM THEIR PLACE AT THE BASE OF THE CLIFF, THROUGH A FISSURE BETWEEN two rocks, Joe found that he could watch some of what happened.

What he saw, not long after it was fully light, was five men who seemed to simply materialize from the woods behind the jail and Father's cabin. They did not step out, or even move, but were just there, painted the grays and blacks and greens of the surrounding forest, carting rifles and belts loaded with other munitions, wearing helmets fitted with headsets and microphones which rested on tiny arms in front of their mouths.

The thing was, the camp was dead. Nothing moved. No sound. Direct sunlight had just hit the tops of the white canvas tents, and the five men looked back and forth at each other, waiting for something to happen. They looked in Joe's direction, but above him. He heard a noise then, up on the cliff, and knew another man was up there, watching, lying with a rifle, no doubt.

The five men moved farther into the camp, stopping to check out the cabins, the smaller one with a padlocked door, the other open and apparently empty (two men glanced inside), then out into the clearing bordered by tents. The men stood up from their wary crouches and looked at one another again.

And then they saw movement at the other end of the camp, the southern end, at the head of the pass which led down to the ocean, as a different set of men materialized, these too dressed in camouflage and carrying rifles.

The five who'd come in first hit the ground and aimed their rifles.

The new men, Joe could count six or so, knelt and aimed back.

Then a voice from up on the cliff, the man Joe had heard, said, through a megaphone, "Freeze where you are. Drop your weapons."

Another voice, through another megaphone, from the trees at the head of the pass, said, "We are U.S. federal agents. Identify yourselves immediately."

The five men lying in the center of camp looked at each other. No one spoke, for all but one of them was on standing orders to do anything but identify themselves. Then one of them said, "Shit," and stood up and lowered his rifle so it pointed toward the ground. The other four followed suit.

Now the agents approached the men in the camp, each group regarding the other, and keeping their rifles ready.

From the command room at Fort Richardson Rozsa was yelling into his microphone, "What's happening? Come back, Grizzly."

"Uh, sir," Garfield's static-laced voice answered. "We're having a little tête-à-tête here with half-a-dozen federal agents, who came into the camp a little, uh, unexpectedly."

Rozsa let go the transmit button, stood up, then sat back down. "Oh, Lord," he said. "Oh, shit."

◇

At Justice, later that day, when the AG heard what the agents had found, she did not hesitate or say anything. She picked up a special blue phone in her office, which connected without her having to dial.

When a man answered by simply saying, "Yes," the AG said, "I need to talk to him immediately."

"One moment, ma'am," the man said. The AG was put on hold while the man summoned his boss, the President, who was still out of breath, since he'd just come in from a jog.

Major Garfield now said, "We were told you weren't coming in. What the fuck? You guys just change your minds like that?"

"Who the *hell* are you?" said one of the agents.

"Major G.T. Garfield, U.S. Army. We were sent in as backups, in case you moved and needed some support."

"What support? You just said you didn't think we were going to be here."

"Well, we thought we heard something. We came in to check."

The FBI agent, who was Tonnecliffe, looked toward the woods he'd come out of, and waved. More agents materialized, along with several men not dressed in camouflage, but in regular outdoor wear.

With them was a woman wearing the clothing of the Amonites, a gray tunic and leggings under a deerskin coat. She was handcuffed and led by a single agent whom she spoke to from time to time. He seemed to speak back to her in a familiar way. This was, of course, Ben Regis and his old partner, Leanne Red Feather.

"Well," said Garfield, the army man. "Where the fuck are they?"

"You check the tents?" Tonnecliffe said. Garfield looked at him, then pulled his rifle up quickly again, as did his men.

But before they could check anything, another voice sang out, this one from the doorway of Father's cabin.

"Hey, guys," it said.

A dozen automatic rifles swung around toward Calvin. Leanne screamed out, "No!" But Cal had his hands in the air. The men could see he wasn't armed.

"Let me say right off," Cal said. "We'll give you everything you came for. In return, we want some consideration. Before you ask who am I to negotiate with you, let me point something out. Take a look in the dirt around where you're all standing. Go ahead, check out those little suckers you see there."

One of Garfield's men had already examined one. "Claymore, sir," he said.

"Oh, Jesus H. Christ," Garfield said. The irony, that these special forces soldiers and special FBI and ATF agents had, in the search for some very high-tech contraband, walked into a potential ambush by something as crude and old-fashioned as Claymore mines, which were really nothing more than simple bombs with steel shot attached to them—a weapon any kid could make in his garage—was lost on none of them. Garfield, in fact, remembered the days when VC sappers, the Vietcong saboteurs, would slip at night into U.S. encampments surrounded by a circle of Claymores aimed outward, and turn the mines around to point in, so that when the VC attacked the next morning and the U.S. soldiers triggered the mines, they shredded themselves. Garfield felt about that stupid right now.

Cal said, "There's maybe fifty of those puppies hard-wired all around you geniuses. And there's someone out there, somewhere, watching us, with a switch in his hand. Anything happens, say one of the snipers you have up there on the cliff or in the trees takes a shot, my man makes the connection. Or you suddenly bolt for the woods. You're all instant bear food.

"But that's not all. We also have a video camera mounted. There's a small transceiver, and a little relay tower out in the woods. We're feeding live across the strait to Kodiak. If we want, gentlemen, this is all gonna be on the goddamn national news tonight."

It was this last lie, which had come to Calvin just moments before, that he knew would stop them all. What weapon did he really have to use against such forces? The Claymores, which would have killed them all, himself included, had been disarmed by Joe anyway. The M-60s were stashed behind him under blankets in the cabin. But this—exposure—he knew that'd drive them nuts.

Now he saw men in both groups frantically talking into their mouthpieces or radios. Then they begin to step backward.

"Ah, ah," he said. "Please don't leave. You'll never make it to the woods."

They all stopped. They watched him. No one moved.

"So at least point the guns away."

They lowered their barrels.

"Next," Cal said. "Who's in charge of this circus?"

One of the men in civilian clothes stepped forward. He said, "I represent the Attorney General of the United States." It was the special troubleshooter himself.

"Well, good," Calvin said. "Here's what it is: we'll give you back the big weapons, the Stinger missiles, the M-60s and as many of the M-16s as we can round up, which won't be all of them. Any other weapons here, we keep. Also, I'll turn over the man who committed the murders in Idaho. Agent Red Feather has already got a full and signed confession from him."

"Joseph Curtis?"

"Yep."

The troubleshooter looked around at Leanne and Ben Regis and nodded. Ben undid her cuffs, and she pulled a piece of paper from her jeans. Someone carried it over. The troubleshooter read it.

"He also helped with the arms?"

"Yes."

"What about the others?"

"One died in Juneau. One's locked in that shack over there. You can take him when you leave. The others were just hired hands."

"And Curtis kidnapped the girl."

"Yes."

"Why'd he kidnap her?"

"I don't know. You'll have to ask him."

"Where is he?"

"Hid. He'll turn himself over when you're all offshore and everyone else is safe. He wants to make sure this is the end of it."

"How will he do that if we're offshore?"

"Boat?" Cal said. "We must have one around here somewhere."

◇

From their spot, Kari could make out enough of what Cal said. She held Joe by his shirtfront and said, "What did I hear? What?"

He looked down into those eyes, but did not speak. He waited, and watched her as the necessity of it struck her, as she thought it all through and understood how it would happen, as she came to realize that he had bought her and Eloise freedom, but at the cost of himself.

"Why would you do this?" she said.

He just looked at her still, at her eyes, especially, which he wanted to be able to remember for however much time he had left.

"But I want you," she said. "I have to have you, too."

"No," he told her. "You have to have her." Who was still sleeping there inside one of the down bags Joe and Kari had bought.

"And what about Kari Downs?" the troubleshooter said.

"She's here. She and her daughter will go back with you. You want to take a statement from her then, fine."

"Maybe she knows why he kidnapped her. I know they got to be pretty friendly later."

Cal said, "I think he was good to her. Sometimes that matters."

The troubleshooter nodded and said, "I guess." He didn't ask any more questions because he suddenly didn't want to find any chinks in the logic of what he was being told, no weak spots in the story. He wanted very much to believe it, to take this deal and be done. It was a good deal. He looked around him at all the armed men, and at the Amonites who had begun to come out of their tents. He nodded, as if something had gone right for him, for them all. He said, "The body of Amon is here, behind me, in the trees. Shall we leave it for you to bury here?"

The people of the Family nodded.

The FBI Special Agent in Charge stepped forward and said, "We'll need the weapons that came in, and we'll need Rick Agullana."

"Oh, he's skankin' around somewhere," Cal said. "You want him now or later?"

The man shrugged. The troubleshooter said something to him.

"Send him out with Curtis," the SAC said.

Cal smiled. "If that's the way you want it."

People piled the guns, M-16s and M-60s, in the center of the clearing between the tents. Soldiers carried the Stinger missiles in their crates from beside the cabin.

"We can't leave, finally, without Curtis," said the special troubleshooter.

Cal said, "He'll be out. 'Cause the last damn thing we want is you back in here."

"It's the last damn place I want to be," the troubleshooter said.

Joe watched as Kari and Eloise walked hand-in-hand out from the hiding place into the camp. Leanne was allowed to come out and meet them, to help Kari gather some belongings in one of the backpacks. Then the two women walked arm in arm from the camp, Kari crying, and Eloise still holding her hand. Joe craned and watched them for as long as he could.

Then he saw the agents and soldiers, some bearing the confiscated weapons, fall in behind. One of them led Omaha, who was now in cuffs.

Joe didn't come out until he was plenty sure they were gone and then not until he was finished saying good-bye in his mind.

Cal was waiting. He said, "Hurry up, bud. We still got a lot to do."

41

A NUMBER OF THE FAMILY MEMBERS HIKED WITH CAL DOWN TO THE seashore to watch as the open wooden boat carried Joe and Rick toward the tender and Coast Guard ships which were moored three or four hundred yards out to sea. The wooden boat moved slowly, as if it were reluctant to make this run.

Calvin waved with his hand high over his head.

Rick sat up in the bow, where he shouldn't have been because his weight that far up caused too much drag. But it didn't matter to anyone, now.

The two of them, with Joe back at the motor, steering, passed from the cove on which Sanctuary lay, past the wall of rock tumbling frozen into the sea, into wider waters where the ships waited.

So now it was time. Joe took a lighter from his pocket and leaned forward. Rick didn't understand what he could be doing.

It turned into a dream as Rick watched Joe pull a kind of black hood up over his head. He could see Joe smiling at him in some insane way. Again, Rick regretted not killing Joe when he'd had the chance. And then Joe was waving good-bye.

Joe lifted a tarp which covered some equipment in the center of the boat, and threw it overboard. It was not equipment, after all, Rick saw, but gasoline cans.

He looked at Joe again, who seemed to be receding backward, moving away.

Then smoke poured up from the bottom of the boat, the dense, acrid obfuscating sulphur smoke of a riot bomb, the sole purpose of which is only to blind and confuse. But Rick could still see because the smoke blew backward, away from the motion of the boat, away from him, back over Joe, who was lost in it.

In this smoke, the world seemed to grow hazy around its edges, this ocean, that land, those mountains, all part of a dreamscape Rick had never before experienced. He looked again at the two five-gallon gas cans, each of which had taped to it two Claymore mines. He saw the wires feeding out from the mines, and looked up again to Joe, but could not find him, could not see where the wires led. And this seemed terribly important to him in that moment.

He imagined himself driving back into Joe, tearing the wires loose, diving overboard. But, from the moment Joe had lit the fuse of the sulphur bomb, everything happened so quickly, there wasn't time to react.

Rick looked over at the cold, cold water. He was so tired of cold.

He thought: this is what it's like to know you are killed. Because in that tiny piece of a second, he knew. But, as if the hand of God itself were swinging down to smack him in the face, all he could do was close his eyes.

From the deck of the tender, Kari and Eloise, Leanne and Ben, Mark Truong and the SAC and the troubleshooter, were all watching when, as the boat reached the midway point from the shore to where they stood, yellowish smoke started pouring from within it.

"What is it?" someone shouted, but no answer came.

They watched, then, as the boat erupted in a thirty foot high, gasoline fueled mushroom cloud of bright orange-yellow. They all stopped any movement; they did not breathe or look at each other or comment or cry out at this rolling, rising burst. It seemed so distant, just a momentary blinding flash of light.

It was not until another second passed, and the concussion of the blast rolled over the water and hit them, both with its sound and with its moderate force—a wave of movement in the air, perhaps a puff of warmth—and then a blacker, oilier, deadlier smoke appeared, that they began to react, with "ohs," with grunts, with whispers of "God."

The explosion was not a profound one. It did not rock them backward or shake them. And after the initial blast, there wasn't really much to see: the burning fragments of a wooden boat, some brightly colored pieces of plastic and nylon floating on the ocean's surface.

Rick and Joe were gone.

Kari cried out and collapsed to her knees. Eloise watched her, then began to cry herself.

Leanne stood mutely leaning against Ben, her knuckles pressed to her mouth. He held her with his arm around her shoulder. Leanne remembered, then, that in her pocket she carried a letter from Joe addressed to Terry Curtis, and she knew now that Joe had known all along it would end in this way, that he had written this letter as his last statement, his farewell.

The agents whispered among themselves. But there was really nothing at all left to say.

42

At justice, after the special troubleshooter finished delivering his brief of all the details, his audience, the AG, the Deputy AG, and the head of the FBI, sat shaking their heads, imagining how much worse it could have been.

For daring to go ashore when he first heard of the strange movements in the woods, for confronting the army's unethical strike force, which, of course, he had not planned on doing but which happened nonetheless, the troubleshooter earned the deep gratitude not only of the AG, who told him so several times, but of the President as well. In time he would reap great political benefits from this, not so much in the broad, national sense, but in more important ways, the politics of the quiet corridor, of a name mentioned in a certain tone over a certain sort of lunch, of a nod of affirmation.

The body of Rick Agullana had been recovered from the ocean, where it was found burned and floating shortly after the explosion. That of Joseph Curtis was not spotted immediately, and the decision came quickly not to extend the search. So the Justice Department closed the file on this case, except for the prosecution and sentencing of DeMore Knight, aka "Omaha," who, after talking for days about what he had done and witnessed, agreed to a plea bargain, as a result of which he would serve at least three years of a fifteen-year sentence for receiving stolen government property and trafficking in illegal weapons.

It was found that Father Amon Ka'atchii's will and trust, which had been filed with an Anchorage attorney, in fact deeded all the land of Sanctuary, as well as the fishing boats and rights, collectively to his children, none of whom were mentioned by name.

Colonel Johnson Rozsa retired in another six months, after twenty-nine years of service. He'd have preferred to stay longer, to move up the chain a few more steps but, though he was never to be told point blank, his over-reaction to the threat of the Stinger missiles, and then his ordering in of Garfield's squad when Amon was known to be dead, their confrontation with the agents, their walking into a crude ambush setup of Claymore mines, their having to be ferried out to the Coast Guard boats, all of this caused the wrong heads to shake, the wrong mouths to purse. Rozsa had to be ascribed some of the responsibility for the embarrassment, for the reaction, the dressing down delivered by the President himself, the surprise resignation of the Chief of Staff of the Army. So, Colonel Rozsa was nudged out of the fold.

Terry Curtis got a job as a route driver for the Krustee Bakery in Detroit, and managed to keep up the rent payments on his brother's apartment until a time, a few years later, when he'd be able to make the down payment on a small house of his own. He would marry and have one child, a son, and his relationship with his parents would grow stronger with each passing year.

He and his parents never for a moment believed any of the FBI or press accounts of what Joe had allegedly done in Idaho and afterward. Joe's father blamed it at first, alternately, on cults, Communists or crazies, but would, in the years to come, develop an elaborate theory of how the government itself had used his son to cover up a military scandal. He became a vocal member of an antigovernment activist group in Dearborn, and attended meetings and training exercises of the famed Michigan militia.

Kari and Eloise Downs stayed for several months in Leanne Red Feather's empty apartment in Boise. They never returned to live with Kari's family in Sacramento, although they visited for several days a few months after their return from Alaska, and again at odd times after that.

Kari would settle eventually in Durham, North Carolina, after meeting and marrying a divorced pilot for Delta Airlines. She joined a church there, an upper middle-class Presbyterian church, and became a pillar of the congregation. She had two more children, both daughters, and, when they were a little older, she began spending more and more of her time traveling, flying the world, staying now in one of the cradles of history, now in some exotic nowhere, taking all three girls with her whenever she could. They would grow up to be true women of the world, educated and experienced in magnificent ways.

Kari never returned to Alaska, however.

Leanne would, in years to come, go back north to see her brother, from time to time, in Kodiak or Anchorage. But at first she was placed immediately into a residential psychiatric program to help her deal with her experiences. She had never felt "programmed" so the notion of "deprogramming," which wasn't much used anymore anyway, never bothered or frightened her. She had a nice young psychiatrist named Dorothy Fender who seemed mostly interested in just listening to the stories Leanne had to tell. Dorothy often just shook her head and smiled and said things like, "Amazing" or "Incredible." Leanne was released after three months, whereupon she had dinner with Ben Regis and told him good-bye. The next day she submitted her resignation to Ed Simmons, who tried to stand up and shake her hand but had trouble getting out from behind his desk.

Leanne floated back into Montana, where she spent time up on the Flathead Reservation north of Missoula, near the town of Arlee, mostly listening to the children, some of whom still knew a few Salish words, and who seemed to like to talk to her.

She would never stop chasing after people, though. It wasn't long before someone who'd learned who she was approached and asked for her help in finding a daughter who'd disappeared down Helena way. Then it would be someone's husband who'd wandered off. Then an insurance company which needed an experienced investigator to look into some questionable claims. And so on.

In her work, she crossed paths once in San Francisco with a private investigator named Roy Jameson. It took them each a moment to place the other. When they did, Jameson bought her a nice dinner, in return for her telling the story again.

On the afternoon of the day on which the boat exploded, the people who had been watching with Calvin looked at him when the fireball rose, to see how he reacted. But all he did was smile a little, and check his watch.

Now, hours later, he was back on the beach, squatting and looking out to sea. Again some of the Family members had gone down with him. He seemed to want to wait there, but for what they did not know. The people came and went, sitting with Calvin awhile, then hiking back to camp while others came down to sit. He was never alone.

It was not until three o'clock, four hours since the explosion, that Cal stood and rushed knee-deep into the water. And then the people with him saw it, something black on the surface, now rising up before them.

A man. As he waded toward the beach, he pulled his black hood back, revealing a head of blond hair over pale silver eyes.

"I was hiding in the rocks out there," he said when he'd come ashore. "Until the ships left." The people looked at him as if they didn't believe he was real. No one said anything.

"It's me, Joe—" he said, but Calvin pressed a hand to his mouth, then hugged him hard around the neck. During the embrace Cal whispered in his ear: "Joseph Curtis is dead. Don't ever forget that."

The idea had been inspired by what they'd seen, or thought they'd seen, happen to Leanne in the helicopter. Go down in the ocean, you're dead forever, if you want to be.

In one of Father's chests they'd found an old wetsuit, used but, as it turned out, still sound, which sealed the plan. It was enough to protect Joe from the frigidity of the ocean when he slipped over the side of the boat before pressing the plunger which set off the Claymores. Still, although he had allowed fifteen feet of lead wire from the plunger, he had only sunk six or seven feet beneath the surface when he pressed it. It was enough distance to save his life, but not to escape all consequences. The concussion knocked him out for a moment, although he came to near the surface and had the presence of mind to stick his head up and breathe. But now Calvin noticed that one of Joe's ears was leaking blood.

"You all right?"

"I can't hear. It hurts like hell." Joe didn't know it yet, but the ear was dead, its drum irreparably exploded.

Calvin turned to the people with him and said, "This is who saved your lives."

In the camp, by a huge bonfire in the center of the clearing, cut and bruised from the ocean, but wrapped in an elk skin, dry and warm now, full of food, he sat, remarkably whole except for the ear which still leaked blood, and a faint crackling inside his head which he recognized as the precursor of one of his headaches—an affliction which would not ever leave him.

But only one thing came into his mind as relevant: "It'll snow soon," he said. People around him stopped to listen. He hadn't said much since his return, and they were curious. He seemed to live inside himself, much like another man they had admired.

"We work hard, we could raise a couple more rough cabins in a month. Then next year—" He shrugged. A few more tools, some better equipment, get the fishing boats working again, bringing in money and supplies, there wasn't much he figured they couldn't do out here. He even knew where there was some gold they could use to start paying for it.

He looked around at the women and men, at the children playing in the dirt nearby, at the fire and the tents, the forest and the dusky sky, and marveled at the fact that this was how people once lived forever. He saw that it could be a long life, learning new skills of survival, but also teaching these people how to build this place up—to construct by hand rock-solid buildings that would last for generations in spite of the hard winters, to maintain perpetually the tools and machinery they relied upon—how to make it all work even in ways he guessed they had not yet imagined.

Acknowledgments

I thank, first, Roger and Marcia Rom of Kodiak, Alaska, gracious hosts, sippers of Cuervo and cookers of fine fish, without whose invitation this story would have headed south before it began. Roy Jones, proprietor of the Amook Lodge, Larsen Bay, Alaska, gave us a glimpse at one of the last untouched lands in the world, as did Brice Crowell, who shepherded us over the Karluk River portage and revealed some of the wonders of the muskeg tundra. I thank both of them as well.

Thanks, too, to John Boening and the University of Toledo English Department, who arranged for me full library privileges and unfettered access through their gateway to the incredible Internet, and to Tom Barden and his wife, Rayna Zacharias, who have been friends, editors and insight providers for a long time. They pitched in again with this book and their touch is apparent throughout.

I discovered the Richard Hugo stanza used in the epigraph in William Matthews' introduction to Hugo's collection of autobiographical essays, *The Real West Marginal Way* (Norton, copyright Ripley S. Hugo, 1986). The last sentence of this stanza, Matthews points out, appears on Hugo's gravestone in St. Mary's Cemetery, Missoula.

Special thanks again to my front-line triad of reader-critics, my wife, Lisa, my editor, Leslie Schnur and my agent, Gail Hochman, and also to my brother, Scott Holden, Navy vet, itinerant researcher and world-class fact checker, who put in many hours on this book, especially while digging out background and stats on the military and its weaponry.

I ended up calling on several technical experts and professionals and must express my gratitude to each of them who, with their collective knowledge and their generosity in sharing it, helped this story along greatly toward whatever veracity it now possesses. They are: Margaret Noē, former assistant prosecuting attorney, Lenawee County, Michigan; Brett Holden, poet, arms expert and near-Ph.D.; Bill Swonger and his Cessna Skylane; and finally, though there must be many things about this story he will find impossible, Gary Clifton, private investigator, former agent of the Bureau of Alcohol, Tobacco and Firearms, incurable storyteller, and a pretty fine novelist in his own right.